PAST CRIMES

A Compendium of Historical Mysteries

ASHLEY GARDNER

JENNIFER ASHLEY

JA/AG Publishing

CONTENTS

INTRODUCTION

In *Past Crimes*, I present three complete novellas in the mystery series I write as Jennifer Ashley and those I write as Ashley Gardner.

I love a good mystery, and I thoroughly enjoy writing in the worlds of the past, when fingerprinting, DNA, and much of the forensics of the modern world did not yet exist. The sleuths were forced to rely on observation, witness statements, and their own persistence to find the true culprits and bring them to justice. It is also fascinating to learn about the legal systems, policing (or lack of it), and trial procedures (if any) of days long past. On the other hand, each of these periods I present here (Ancient Rome, Regency and Victorian Britain), carry the seeds and ideas of what our modern legal systems became.

In this anthology, I introduce **Leonidas the Gladiator** — a freed gladiator of Nero's Rome. He survived the games, but can he survive life on the streets of Rome? Gladiators were nurtured, fed, and doctored to keep them in top fighting shape for the inevitable day they'd enter the amphitheater and live or die. Leonidas finds himself at a bit of a loss now that he's a free man, with Cassia, the capable scribe-slave sent to look after him, as his only guide.

Blood Debts introduces Leonidas, Cassia, and other characters and Rome of AD 63 as Leonidas tries to clear himself of a murder, with Cassia's able assistance.

Kat Holloway, a highly sought after Victorian cook at twenty-nine years of age, appears in *A Soupçon of Poison*, where she too must clear herself of a murder, with the help of the mysterious Daniel McAdam. *Soupçon* introduces Kat, who continues in **The Below Stairs Mysteries** published by Berkley (which I am writing as Jennifer Ashley). I also include an excerpt of what is officially Book 1, *Death Below Stairs*. (Regard *Soupçon* as a prequel.)

Finally, we have *The Necklace Affair,* a novella that occurs in the middle of the long-running, and probably my most popular series, the **Captain Lacey Regency Mysteries**. **Captain Gabriel Lacey** is a former calvary officer in the British Army who returns to London after the Napoleonic wars with no prospects and no money. Always one to help the downtrodden, Lacey is nonplussed when a society matron in tears begs him to find her stolen necklace and prevent her maid from being convicted of the crime. Lacey can't say no to a lady in distress—no matter how unprepossessing she is—and recruits his friends to help him. He uncovers layers of unhappiness and corruption in upper-class London and once again is at loggerheads with James Denis, a crime lord who wants Lacey under his thumb.

While *The Necklace Affair* occurs in the middle of the series (fits after Book 4), I actually wrote the draft of it right after Book 1. The cast is small, and I indicate enough of who is who for a new reader to understand and follow the story and become acquainted with the characters.

I hope you enjoy this sample of my historical mysteries! For more about all series, visit my mysteries website:

http://www.gardnermysteries.com

A SOUPÇON OF POISON

Kat Holloway Victorian Mysteries by
Jennifer Ashley

CHAPTER 1

LONDON, 1880

I AM A COOK, AND BETTER THAN MOST, EVEN AT MY young age of nine and twenty, and the gentry and aristocracy pay highly to have me.

Sir Lionel Leigh-Bradbury of Portman Square gave me less than I might have had elsewhere, but when the agency told me he'd agreed to the large number of days out a month I'd requested, I leapt at the position.

I had never actually met Sir Lionel—the housekeeper and the agency made all the negotiations with me—until I'd been in his employ nearly two months. Then, one evening, he abruptly summoned me.

Copley, the thin, sour-faced butler with a walleye, delivered the news to the kitchen. "'Is royal 'ighness demands your presence. In 'is library."

I stilled my knife on the carcass of an onion spread before me. *"Now?"* I asked crossly.

I had much work to prepare for supper, having no assistant. Sir Lionel employed only one footman and a scullery maid in addition to housekeeper, butler, and cook. He kept the housekeeper and butler only because he'd inherited them with the house and title.

Copley banged down his salver and threw himself into a chair by the fire. "No," he snarled. "'E must 'ave meant in a fortnight."

Copley despised all women in general and me in particular. He was pinch-faced, bad-tempered and usually half drunk with gin.

I began chopping again, with more vigor this time. "He stays above stairs, and I stay below," I said. "It is the proper way of things."

"Am I to blame for 'is upbringing? You'd best get to it, woman."

I sighed, finished the onion, and carefully washed my knife before putting it away. Onion juice left to dry can be disastrous to cutlery. I put the onions in a bowl, wiped my hands, and went to face my employer for the first time.

Sir Lionel sat alone in the library on the second floor. The high-ceilinged, dark-beamed room was cold, musty, and dimly lit. Tall bookcases lined the room, each packed so tightly with books I doubted that any could be pried out and actually read.

My employer reposed at a writing table with about a dozen photographs on it. As I came as close as I dared, I saw that the photos were of older Leigh-Bradburys, of Sir Lionel in formal dress, and one of a young woman, pretty, whom I did not recognize. That photo looked old, but the frame was new, so perhaps it was a beloved sister or beau who had passed away.

Sir Lionel had limp brown hair that hung from a bald place on top of his head, a white face, and a long nose. His limbs were almost as thin as Copley's, and his long coat hung on his bony shoulders. He was middle-aged and had recently inherited this house, all its contents, and his baronetcy from his uncle.

I stopped a foot or so from the desk and folded my hands on my plump abdomen. "You asked to see me, sir?"

Sir Lionel looked me up and down, his prominent Adam's apple moving. "*You* are my cook?"

I inclined my head. "I am Mrs. Holloway, sir."

"*Mrs*. Holloway." He leaned forward a little as he said the name. "You are married?"

My matrimonial state was none of his business. "All cooks are called missus, sir," I said stiffly.

Sir Lionel continued to stare at me, his blue eyes so wide they protruded. The good Lord had blessed me with a comely face—so I'd been told—a mass of curling dark hair, and a figure that was curved and not angular, but I saw no reason for such amazement.

"You sent for me, sir," I prompted as Sir Lionel continued to stare at me.

"Oh. Yes. I wanted to … I wanted …" He trailed off and assumed a fretful frown. "I am feeling unwell. The dish you prepared for my supper last night is to blame."

"The cassoulet?" I said in surprise. "Of course it was not to blame. Everyone in this house partook of that dish, and no one has any ill effects. It was perfectly fine."

"It tasted off."

"Nonsense. The chicken was freshly killed and the vegetables fine and crisp. I was lucky to get them and at a fair price."

Sir Lionel tapped the arms of his chair. "I have eaten only your cassoulet since last night, and I am ill. What else could it be?"

I eyed him critically. "If you've eaten naught else, it's no wonder you're ill. I'll make you a cup of beef tea, sir, and send you up some seedcake."

He looked indignant. "I do not want—"

"Certainly you do," I interrupted. "Your humors are out of balance and need some easing. I ate a good portion of that cassoulet, and as you can see, I am fit and hale. You want a bit of grub in your belly, that is all."

Sir Lionel gave me a dazed look, as though not used to being told what to do, even if it was for his own good. "Er, yes, quite. Yes, yes, send it up, whatever you like."

I gave him a little bow and turned away, feeling his gaze on my back all the way to the door.

Downstairs, I cut up seedcake and fixed a thick broth of beef with black pepper. I set this all on a tray, which was carried upstairs by the footman, because Copley was snoring and unlikely to rouse himself the rest of the night.

My cakes seemed to have done the trick, as did my supper of thick slices of pork, hearty bread, and onion soup, for I heard no more complaints about illness and no more words against my cooking. I did not see Sir Lionel again for another three weeks.

Late one night, after the other staff had gone to bed, I sat in the kitchen at the wide wooden table, sharpening my knives.

A cook's knives are her greatest asset, and if they go dull, they are no use at all and should be replaced. As decent knives are hideously expensive, I kept mine in good repair.

I did not trust anyone with the task of sharpening but myself, so I sat on my stool, alone, and drew a blade across the damped stone. The only sound in the silent room was the scrape of stone on steel and the hiss of the oil lamp beside me.

The solitude comforted me. I'd had a trying day.

Copley's bunions had played him up, making him more sour than usual, and he'd gone so far as to throw a bowl of porridge at me. John the footman had dropped and shattered a crock full of sugar. The scullery maid had taken sick, so I'd had to do all the washing up myself.

Because of that, by the time I'd gotten to the market, all the best produce was gone. My bread had over-risen and deflated upon itself while I was out because John had been too stupid to follow the simplest instructions.

I'd made my disapprobation known, and the others had retired somewhat earlier than usual, leaving me alone with my knives.

Where Sir Lionel found me.

"Mrs. Holloway?"

I peered through the kitchen's gloom, my comfort evaporating. The master of the house stood at the door to the stairway, his breathing loud and hoarse. He moved across the flagstones to the table where I sat, and gazed at me with eyes that were sunken and petulant.

I jumped to my feet, annoyed. The kitchen was my demesne. The master might own the house, but a good employer understood that not interfering in the kitchen made for a tranquil domestic situation. Sir Lionel had his rooms above stairs where I did not trespass, and he had no reason to trespass on *me*.

"Might I help you with something, sir?" I asked, striving to remain polite.

"Good heavens, Mrs. Holloway." Sir Lionel, his voice breathy, looked past me at the table. "What is it you're doing?"

Dancing naked upon Hampstead Heath. "Just giving my knives a bit of attention, sir. I like them nice and sharp."

"Yes, I am certain you do."

Before I could decipher this comment, Sir Lionel had moved abruptly to my side and pinned me against the table. He was stronger than his size let on, and he held me fast with his spindly arms.

"Mrs. Holloway, I can think of nothing but you. Of your eyes, your hair ..." He pulled a lock free from my cap. "Your bosom, so comely. Do you have children?"

"One," I gasped, the truth I kept hidden bursting out in my amazement.

He did not seem to hear me. "My nursery maid had a bosom as large as yours. She let me feast upon her."

I scarcely wanted to think about *that*. I desperately craned my head away from his port-laden breath and blood-shot eyes.

"Let me feast upon you, Katharine."

Oh, this would never do. I groped behind me across the smooth boards of the table and closed my fingers around the handle of a knife.

It was my carver. I pulled it around and brought it up right under Sir Lionel's chin.

Sir Lionel squeaked in alarm. His gaze shot to the knife then back to me, spots of red burning on his cheeks. He must have seen something in my blue eyes he so admired, because he released me and took a hasty step backward.

"Sir," I said in a hard voice. "You employ me and pay my wages. I cook. That line should *never* be crossed."

Sir Lionel's mouth opened and closed a few times. "It should not?"

"No, sir. It should not."

His petulant look returned. "But you are so beautiful."

I held the knife point steady, though I was shaking all the way through. "You flatter me, sir. I am a cook, is all. You go along upstairs and to bed. You will feel better in the morning."

"No, no ...er. I am going out."

"Right, then, sir. Off you go."

Sir Lionel eyed the glinting knife blade, stared at my bosom with stark regret, turned on his heel, and marched out of the room.

Not until I'd heard him tramp all the way up the stairs and slam the door above did I let out an explosive breath and drop to the stool, the strength gone out of me.

"Fool," came a voice.

I smothered a yelp as Copley materialized from the shadows. My knife clattered to the table. "What the devil do you mean, skulking about like that?" I cried.

Copley gave me a sickly grin, his walleye gleaming. "Ye could 'ave gained some favors with 'im, woman. You give 'im a bit, and 'e gives you a rise in wages. Any sensible woman would think it a bit of luck."

"I *am* a sensible woman," I said firmly. "Which is why I told him to be gone."

"Maybe 'e'd even marry you." Copley sniggered, a dry sound.

"Oh, most like. The gentry don't marry cooks." Thank heavens. On the other hand, I might have just lost myself my post.

Copley scooted close enough to me that I could smell the gin on his breath. "I'll keep this atween you and me. Can't let it get about that you cast your eyes upon the master, can it?"

He'd turn it about and spread that story, simply because he could. "You are a little swine," I said. "I did nothing of the sort."

"But none know it but me, you, and 'is nibs, do they? And I seed 'ow quick you was to shove a knife at 'is throat."

"I only meant to frighten him." I let my tone grow chilly. "I thought it most effective. Didn't you?"

Copley's gaze slid to the knife that rested near my hand, and he faded back from me. "I'll remember it. I will." And thankfully, he shuffled away, heading upstairs to his bed.

I went back to sharpening the blades that had done me so much good tonight, but it was a long time before I could stop shaking. Longer still before I could make myself retire to my tiny bedchamber tucked behind the kitchen and sleep.

THE NEXT DAY, DANIEL MCADAM CAME WHISTLING DOWN the kitchen steps to deliver a bushel of apples.

Daniel McAdam had, as we ladies put it, a way with him. I'd known him for about a year, ever since the day he'd stepped into old Mrs. Pauling's kitchens, where'd I'd formerly worked, to get out of the rain. Daniel ever after paused to flirt with me, harmless like, whenever he made a delivery to Mrs. Pauling's house, and now to Sir Lionel's.

I knew little about Daniel, even after a year. He was a man of all work and a jack of all trades. He delivered goods, carried messages, and ran far and wide about London — once I'd seen him driving a hired carriage, competently maneuvering it through the crowds.

I did not know where he lodged or where he disappeared to for weeks at a time. He'd only wink and answer evasively whenever I brought up these subjects.

I knew Daniel wasn't married because I'd asked him that, point blank. When a man flirts with a woman, she ought to know where things stand.

Daniel had dark hair and dark blue eyes and a tall, attractive body. He could read and write and was quite clever, though he never admitted to any schooling.

I concluded that he must be the son of a middle-class gentleman, possibly illegitimate, but he never spoke of his family. He turned his hand to a good many menial tasks, things even a destitute gentleman might shun, which was why I thought him a bastard son. Father genteel, mother a tavern maid or something of the sort, and now Daniel had to grub for a living.

No matter who he was, Daniel seemed to be happy puttering about London, making friends with everyone he met and doing any odd job he could.

It was a daft way to live, and I told him so. He only laughed and said: *Some of us were born to work and others to keep the devil amused.*

He always said something nonsensical when he did not want to give an answer.

This morning, Daniel set down the apples and waited with good humor while I wiped my hands of puff pastry dough and poured him a cup of steaming tea.

Daniel swallowed a long drink and grinned at Copley, who leaned against the wall, barely able to stand. "You'll kill yourself with gin, Copley." Daniel took a flask from his pocket and dropped a dollop of whiskey into his own cup.

Copley gave him a sour look. He'd woken with a raging headache and had been sick in the basin twice already. "I were up late. Woke by the master and Mrs. Holloway a'carrying on, weren't I?"

Daniel raised dark brows. I dumped a large ball of butter onto my dough and vigorously attacked the mess with my rolling pin.

"Why don't you tell 'im, Mrs. H?" Copley rasped.

"About 'ow the master tried it on with you, and ye almost slit 'is throat?"

CHAPTER 2

Daniel did not change expression, but his blue gaze focused on me. "What happened, Kat?" he asked, his tone gentle.

Daniel was the only person I allowed to call me *Kat*. Not that I'd given him permission. He'd simply taken it up, and I'd not prevented him.

I rolled the pastry dough flat and used my scraper to fold each third in on itself before going at it again. Puff pastry was difficult to get right, and a kitchen full of curious people was not assisting me to concentrate.

"Nothing as interesting as Copley makes out," I said crisply.

"Even so, tell me."

When Daniel McAdam spoke in that voice—quiet and friendly, yet full of steel, people tended to obey him. I stopped pounding at the dough, which needed to rest and cool anyway, and gave him an abbreviated account of the incident. Copley snorted a few times and inserted foolish comments at intervals.

13

Daniel helped himself to another cup of tea, minus the whiskey this time, and sipped it as I talked. When I finished, Daniel rose from the stool where he'd been sitting and set the cup on the draining board by the sink. "Copley," he said in that steely voice. "A word, if you please."

Copley looked surprised, but as I said, people tended to obey Daniel without quite knowing why.

Copley followed Daniel across the kitchen and out the scullery door. The scullery maid, sniffling with her cold, let dirty water drip all over the flagstone floor while she watched Daniel with lovesick eyes.

I have no idea to this day what Daniel said to Copley, but when Copley returned he was subdued. He skulked across the kitchen without looking at me and stomped up the stairs.

THE VERY NEXT MORNING SIR LIONEL STARTED TAKING his vengeance on me for not only rejecting his advances but putting my knife to his throat. He did nothing so direct as sack me—oh, no. He went about it by more subtler means, trying to vanquish me, if you like.

Now, you may wonder why I did not simply pack up my knives and march out, but while good cooks are in demand, good places aren't all that thick on the ground. As horrible as Sir Lionel was, he lived in London, where I needed to stay, the wage was decent, and I had my many days out a month, which was the most important thing to me. So I stayed and put up with him.

Sir Lionel did not come to the kitchen again—he'd learned that lesson. He sent his demands through Mrs. Watkins, the housekeeper. Sometimes Copley delivered the messages, but even Sir Lionel realized that Copley couldn't be trusted when he was befuddled with drink, so Mrs. Watkins brought down most of his orders.

Mrs. Watkins had worked in this house for many years, previously for Sir Lionel's uncle, and she didn't think much of the current master. She was straight-backed and pinch-nosed and set in her ways, and didn't hold with all this cooking nonsense—a bit of boiled mutton was all a body needed, and any simpleton could buy that in a shop. For all her decided opinions, Mrs. Watkins wasn't a bad sort, although she didn't approve of cooks being as young as I was.

I couldn't help my age—I'd been assistant to one of the best cooks in London at fifteen, and had proved to have a talent for the job. That cook had passed on when I'd been twenty, word had spread that her apprentice could replicate her meals, and agencies fought to have me on their books.

However, I had to be choosy where I worked, and my situation with Sir Lionel, unfortunately, was ideal. Except for Sir Lionel, of course. Mrs. Watkins made it plain that Sir Lionel was a disappointment after his uncle, who'd been a true gentleman, she said, but Mrs. Watkins, like me, needed the position.

Sir Lionel began his game of revenge by sending down odd and impossible requests for his dinners—wild birds that wouldn't be in season for another few months, tender vegetables that had gone out of season months before, and dishes even I had never heard of. I had to read through my treasured tomes to find recipes for what he wanted, and some I simply had to invent. Even the exhaustive Mrs. Beeton failed me from time to time.

Some days I'd nearly make myself ill getting the meal finished to his order—I had my pride, after all—and he'd send word at the last minute that he would dine at his club and wouldn't be back until morning.

The delicate meal wouldn't keep for a day, so I and the household staff ate it. I had to watch John the footman bolt my coq a vin like it was mutton stew and listen to Mrs. Watkins complain that food should be simple without all this fuss. Copley would eat steadily, then follow the meal with a mug of gin and belch loudly.

The morning after, Sir Lionel would send down a sternly worded note that I'd spent far too much money on food-stuffs and threaten to take it out of my wages.

A lesser cook would have fled. But it built up my pride that I was mostly able to fulfill his bizarre requests and build a meal around them, no matter how much Sir Lionel made clear he did not appreciate it. I rose to the challenge, wanting to prove he could not best me.

Where he came up with his ideas for what he wanted me to cook I had no idea. Sir Lionel did not strike me as a refined gentleman with cultivated tastes. Likely he found descriptions of dishes in books, or he had a friend who made up the meals for him, laughing about the good trick they were playing on a cook who needed to learn her place.

Then came the day I nearly threw down my apron and ran out the door to never come back. Mrs. Watkins, at seven o'clock in the evening, brought me down a note telling me he wanted truffles a l'Italienne with beef in pepper sauce that night.

"Truffles?" I bellowed. "Where does he think I will find a handful of black truffles at this time of day?"

"I couldn't say." It was obvious Mrs. Watkins had no idea what a truffle was. "But he is adamant."

It was impossible. I knew all the good markets and who

might have decent exotic fungi, but I had no time to get to them before they shut up for the night.

As luck would have it, an urchin I'd seen helping Daniel unload his goods a time or two was hanging around the scullery door. He'd been hoping for scraps or a chat with the scullery maid, but I stormed out to him, seized him by the ear, and told him to find Daniel for me.

"Scour the town if you must," I said. "Tell him Mrs. Holloway desperately needs his help. There's tuppence in it for you if you hurry."

The urchin jerked himself from me and rubbed his ear, but he didn't look angry. "Don't worry, missus. I'll find 'im."

The lad was true to his word. Daniel came knocking within the hour, and the lad happily jingled the coins I dropped into his hand.

Daniel listened to me rant, his warm smile nearly enough to calm my troubles. Nearly. When I finished, Daniel held out his hand.

"Give me your list, and I'll find the things for you," he said.

"How can you?" My voice rose, tinged with hysteria. "In half an hour?"

Daniel only regarded me calmly as he took the paper upon which I'd written ingredients. "The sooner I am gone, the sooner I can return."

I let out my breath, my heart in my words. "Thank you. I don't know who you are, Daniel McAdam, but you are a godsend."

Something flickered in his dark blue eyes, but his crooked smile returned. "I've been called much worse, Kat, believe me. Back in a tick."

He did return very quickly with a bundle of all I needed, including the finest truffles I'd ever seen and a small bottle of champagne, which Sir Lionel never stocked in his cellar. I did not like to ask how Daniel had come by the rarer things, and he did not volunteer the information.

Daniel tried to refuse money for the foodstuffs. He held his up his hands, spreading his fingers wide. "It was a challenge, Kat. I never knew the intricacies of food purchasing or how many markets we have in London. Keep your money for the next meal he demands."

"Don't talk nonsense. I'll not take them as gifts. Stand there while I get you some coin."

I hurried down to the housekeeper's parlor where we kept a locked tin of cash on hand for extra expenses. Only I and Mrs. Watkins had the key to it—Copley couldn't be trusted not to spend the money on drink.

Daniel hadn't given me a tally, but I counted out what I thought would be the cost of the goods and rushed back out, to find Daniel nowhere in sight.

"Where is Mr. McAdam?" I asked the urchin, who'd remained to make sheep's eyes at the scullery maid.

"'E's off," the urchin answered. "Said 'e couldn't wait."

"Blast the man," I said fervently.

I put the money back into the tin but vowed I'd force it upon him somehow one day. A woman couldn't afford to have a man do her expensive favors, especially a man as beguiling as Daniel McAdam. I'd learned all about the dangers of pretty men at a very young age, and I'd had enough of *that*.

SIR LIONEL'S NEXT UNREASONABLE DINNER DEMAND came the very next day. He decided, at five o'clock, if you please, that he'd entertain friends at his dinner table at seven. Mrs. Watkins brought down the order and stepped back as I read it.

Leek and cream soup, whitefish in a velouté sauce, green salad, squab stuffed with peppercorns, beef in a wine sauce, asparagus with egg, fricassee of wild mushrooms, soft rolls, a chocolate soup and a berry tart for pudding.

"Has he gone mad?" I screeched. "I haven't a scrap of chocolate in the house, no hope of fresh fish or game birds today." I flung the paper to the table. "That is the last straw, Mrs. Watkins. Either we come to an understanding or I give my notice. I ought to simply give it now and leave, let him and his guests do with salt pork and potatoes."

Copley, lounging in his chair near the fire, cackled. "Mrs. H. can't do it. All I hear is what a grand cook she is, how everyone wants her, how she's wasted in this 'ouse. She's asked to cook a few bits of fish, and she 'as hysterics. If you're so sought after, my girl, why ain't ye cooking for dukes, or for one of the royals?"

I dragged in a breath, trying to ignore Copley. "I agree that if I can pull this meal together it would make my reputation. But . . . oh—"

"Would it?" Mrs. Watkins picked up the list again, which she'd written in her careful hand at Sir Lionel's dictation. "I confess, I've never heard of velouté or eaten chocolate soup."

"Well, you shall eat it tonight. You, Mr. Copley, can cease laughing at me and help. I shall need a good bottle of sweet white wine and a robust red for the beef sauce and the chocolate. A claret for the table. *Asparagus*—I ask you. Any I can find will be woody and tasteless. But perhaps . . ." I trailed off, my inventive mind taking over.

"Ye can't be wanting *three* bottles," Copley said, sitting

up. "The master comes over snarling if I open more than one a day."

"If he wants this food and wants it done well, he'll not quibble."

Copley scowled, unhappy, but he stomped away to fetch what I needed. I always thought it a mercy Copley found wine sour and without a good kick or Sir Lionel's wine collection, a fine one built up by his uncle, would be long gone.

"How many at table?" I asked Mrs. Watkins.

"Three," she said, folding her hands. Her long string of keys hung from her belt like a jailer's. "The master and two guests, a Mr. and Mrs. Fuller."

"At least he didn't invite twenty," I said. "Small blessings, I suppose." I scanned the kitchen, and sure enough, found Daniel's lad and the scullery maid outside together on the steps.

"*You,*" I called to the youth from the back door—I really ought to learn his name. "If you find Mr. McAdam for me in half an hour, this time I'll give you a shilling."

The boy grinned, saluted me, and off he went.

CHAPTER 3

DANIEL CAME IN TWENTY MINUTES. I EXPLAINED MY predicament, and again, he showed no qualms about searching the city for all I needed.

"How can you?" I asked, handing him the list I'd written out. "I *could* find all this, if I had a day or two."

Daniel shrugged. His dark hair was spotted with rain, which had begun to fall hard. Perhaps we'd have a flood, and Sir Lionel's guests wouldn't be able to come.

"My deliveries take me all over London," Daniel said. "I know who has what, who can get what."

He spoke easily, as though producing expensive food-stuffs out of the air was nothing. "What on earth do you deliver?" I asked.

Another shrug. "This and that." Daniel winked, actually tweaked my nose, and then disappeared up the stairs, whistling.

"That man is trouble," Mrs. Watkins said darkly, folding her arms as she watched him go.

"Daniel? I mean, Mr. McAdam?" I quickly turned to

start scrubbing down my work table. "He's a kind soul, is all."

"Hmph." Mrs. Watkins made a motion of dusting off her hands. "I say trouble. Well, I must get on making sure the house is to rights. Sally!" she shouted at the scullery maid. "Get in here and wash up those dishes, girl, or I'll take a strap to you."

DANIEL RETURNED MORE QUICKLY THAN I'D THOUGHT HE could. I was in the butler's pantry, arguing with Copley about the wine, when Daniel arrived, dumped several boxes next to my work table, and disappeared again.

Copley did know a surprising amount about wine, which explained why he kept his post as butler, plus he could put on a toffy accent for the guests when he chose. I finally came away with a decent German Riesling and a deep red Côtes du Rhône, with his promise to decant the best of the claret.

By the time I emerged, Daniel had come and gone. I was disappointed not to speak to him, but I was soon too busy to think more about it.

Daniel had brought me everything I needed, even fresh fish. They were perfectly fine, firm, slick, with no fishy smell to clog up the kitchen.

Now to prepare all these dishes in no time at all, including a white sauce that needed to simmer, and make feather-light rolls to go with everything.

If I'd been in a larger household, with several assistants, I could do this meal in a trice. As it was, I was soon in despair. The fish had to be cleaned, the fowls plucked and readied, the vegetables scrubbed and chopped. The velouté had to be constantly stirred so the delicate thickened stock didn't burn, the tart shells formed, chilled, and baked. I gave vent to my feelings, which only sent everyone else running away, leaving me on my own.

Almost. As I was up to my arms in fish entrails, the urchin came tripping into the kitchen without so much as a by-your-leave.

"I don't have any more errands for you," I said to him in irritation.

The lad, not cowed, didn't leave. "Mr. McAdam sent me. He says whatever you need help with, I was to do, even if it were cooking."

I stared at him in surprise. He was a sturdy young man, about fifteen, I'd say, with strong-looking hands. He was also filthy.

"John!" I bellowed. The footman popped his head around the corner from the servants' hall, where he was frantically polishing silver. I pointed my bloody fillet knife at the urchin. "Get him cleaned up and lend him some clothes. You can't come near this kitchen, lad, until all that dirt is off you. No one wants fleas in their dinner. Make sure he scrubs his hair, John. With soap."

John nodded solemnly, the urchin sent me a grin, and both youths were off.

When the urchin returned, he was urchin no longer. Now that his hair was clean, I saw it gleam dark red. His face was freckled, a fact I hadn't been able to detect under the grime, and his eyes were clear and brown. He had even teeth and good breath, and he'd trimmed his nails and scrubbed under them. John had lent him some trousers, shirt, and coat, all of which were a bit tight, but he'd do.

"What's your name?" I asked him.

The lad shrugged, an imitation of Daniel's. "You can call me James."

Which meant that might or might not be his name, but I had no time to quibble. "Very well, James, I need you to prepare this fowl for me. Here's how you do it . . ."

James proved quite competent. I could tell he'd never done any cookery before, but he was a quick learner, and worked steadily, without idle chatter or asking useless questions. Between the two of us, I prepared a meal a duchess would swoon over.

Perhaps I *would* seek out a duchess, one who stayed in town much of the time, and show her what fine dishes I could contrive.

But the main reason I did not seek out a society hostess was because working in smaller houses for bachelors like Sir Lionel meant I had much time to myself. Not today, obviously, but most of the time. A cook working for a duchess who had dinner parties every day would be laboring from dawn to midnight, never mind how many underlings she had. I had reason to want to come and go as often as I could, and so I stayed in houses like this one.

The finished meal did me proud. I thanked James profusely, asked him to sup with the rest of us, and happily gave him a few more shillings. The dishes went up to the dining room via the lift in the corner, and Mrs. Watkins saw that all was served.

Why not Copley? Because he'd fled the house while I had been ordering everyone about in the kitchen, got roaring drunk, and collapsed when he finally came back in. John and James carried him off to bed, which left Mrs. Watkins and John to see to the dining room. Mrs. Watkins was angry at this turn of events, but I knew she'd manage.

Every plate came back scraped clean. My pride puffed up. They'd loved it.

I was, as far as I was concerned that night, the greatest cook in the land.

❀

IT WAS LATE BEFORE I CRAWLED OFF, EXHAUSTED, TO SEEK my bed. My bedroom was a cubby-hole of a chamber, but I liked it because it lay right behind the kitchen fireplace, which kept it warm and dry.

I was deep in the slumber of the just when the scullery maid, Sally, shook me awake into darkness. "Oh, Mrs. Holloway," she said breathlessly. "There's someone above stairs."

I screwed my eyes shut against the flickering flame of her candle. "Of course there's someone above stairs. Likely his royal highness stumbling to bed after drinking himself into a stupor."

"No, ma'am. It ain't Sir Lionel." Sally regarded me in terror. "The guests left hours ago, and the master dragged 'imself off to bed already. It ain't John or Copley neither. I 'eard 'em snoring when I passed their rooms. And Mrs. Watkins went off to visit her sister."

I levered myself to a sitting position. I did not ask why Sally hadn't woken the men instead of trotting all the way downstairs to me. Copley and John would be useless and we both knew it.

"Get the poker then, girl. If it's burglars, we'll set about them."

Sally's eyes grew even more round. I threw back the covers and swung my feet to the floor, pressing them into my slippers. Sally scuttled into the kitchen and wrested the poker from its place with so much clanking I was sure the thieves would hear and run away directly.

I didn't bother with my knives. They were suited to hacking chickens, chopping onions, and frightening overly amorous masters. For fending off marauders, a poker or a stout stick works much better. To use a knife, you must get close, and those you're fighting might have something just as nasty to hand.

I took the poker from Sally, bade her bring her candle, gathered my dressing gown about me, and led the way up into the darkened house.

Sir Lionel's house, on the north side of Portman Square, was typical of those in London at the time. We climbed the back stairs to the ground floor, emerging into a hall that ran the length of the house. A staircase with polished banisters and carved newel posts rose along one side of the hall, leading to the floors above us. Rooms opened from the opposite wall of this staircase—reception room and formal dining room on the ground floor, drawing rooms on the next floor, private chambers, including the library, above that.

I went into the dining room after checking that the front door was still bolted. The walls in there were dark wood panels hung with paintings I suspected were not very good. No expensive artwork for Sir Lionel.

The room was empty. The dining table had been cleared, a cloth cover draped over it to keep it clean between meals. The chairs were straight, the curtains drawn. Nothing to be seen.

The reception room was likewise empty, nothing disturbed, no open windows anywhere.

I was beginning to believe Sally had dreamed it all, but one never knew. A thief could have forced open a back window and be merrily burgling the house above us.

I led Sally on up the stairs. We checked the front and rear drawing rooms and found nothing amiss.

I'd check one more floor and then retire to bed. If Sir Lionel wasn't stirring, then Sally had heard John or Copley moving about for whatever their reasons.

On the next floor, I saw that the door to Sir Lionel's library stood ajar. It was dark inside the room, no glow of a fire, lamp, or candle.

While I did not truly believe thieves would grope around in absolute darkness for valuables in Sir Lionel's library, the open door made me uneasy. I heard no sound within, not a rustle or thump of books as burglars searched for hidden caches of jewels.

I noiselessly pushed the door open and went inside.

Whatever fire had burned that day in the grate had smoldered to ashes. Sally kept bumping into the back of me, because she held the candle and stared into the flame until she was night-blind. But I could see a bit by the streetlight that glittered through the front windows, the curtains wide open.

What I saw was Sir Lionel. He was slumped forward over his desk, his head turned to the side, his mouth open, eyes staring sightlessly. My carving knife was buried to the hilt in his back.

Sally screeched and dropped the candle. I snatched the candle from the floor before a spark could catch the rug on fire, and raised the light high.

My entire body went numb, no feeling anywhere. "May God have mercy," I croaked, my throat tight and dry. "What a waste of a carver. And them so dear."

CHAPTER 4

I WOKE JOHN IN HIS ATTIC CHAMBER—COPLEY HEARD Sally's scream and came down on his own. I sent John for the constable but ordered Copley to stay with the body while I went downstairs and dressed myself.

By time I returned to the library, the constable, a lad I'd seen walking his beat on the square, had arrived with an older sergeant. They'd lit up the room with every lamp and candle they could find and stoked the fire high. I imagined Sir Lionel's ghost cringing at the expense.

The sergeant, a squat, fat man with one string of hair across his bald pate and a wide, thick-lipped mouth, turned to me.

"It's *your* knife, eh?"

Copley looked innocently at the ceiling, but I knew he must have been filling the constable's ears with tales of my adventures with Sir Lionel.

"Of course it is mine," I snapped. "It came from the kitchens."

"'E made a grab for ye tonight, did 'e?" the sergeant asked. "And so you stuck your knife into 'im?"

I stared in astonishment. "Of course not. I've been in bed asleep these past hours. Why would I have come to the library in the middle of the night, in any case? My bedchamber is next to the kitchen, and I have no need to be above stairs at all."

The sergeant did not look impressed. "'E made a grab for you afore this, didn't 'e? And you stuck your knife to 'is throat?"

I switched my glare to Copley. He wouldn't meet my eye, but a smile hovered around his thin mouth. I said tartly, "That was weeks ago, and it was only to frighten him. I certainly would *not* have plunged my knife into a side of beef like Sir Lionel Leigh-Bradbury. It would ruin the knife. Carvers are expensive."

The constable's eyes glittered a way I didn't like. "But it was *your* knife. It would be 'andy."

"Absolute nonsense. Why would I carry my kitchen knife upstairs to the master's rooms?"

"Because 'e sent for you, and you were frightened. You brought your knife to make you feel safe-like."

"Don't be ridiculous. If I'd feared to answer his summons, I'd have stayed securely in my kitchen, or asked John to come with me. He's quite a strong lad."

The sergeant pointed a broad finger at me. "You 'ad a go at 'im before, Mr. Copley says. This time, you went too far, and did 'im."

My mouth went dry, but I kept up my bravado. "I did not kill him, you ignorant lout. Why should I?"

"Who did then? With your sticker?"

I clenched my hands. "Anyone could have taken the knife from the kitchen."

"Mr. Copley says you keep 'em put away special. No one else would know where."

"Copley does," I pointed out.

Copley sneered at me. "Bitch. She stabbed 'im. She must 'ave."

I put my closed fists on my hips. "Who says so? Did you see me, Mr. Copley?"

"Yes."

My mouth popped open. He was a liar, but Copley's look was so certain that the sergeant believed him.

"I 'eard a noise and came down," Copley said. "And there was you, a-bending over the master's body, holding the knife."

Bloody man. "Of course I looked him over when I found him here," I said, trying not to sound desperate. "He was already dead. And *you* saw nothing at all, Mr. Copley. You only came charging in because Sally was screaming, *after* we found him."

Copley scowled. "I saw ye, I tell ye."

"You saw me discovering the knife, not plunging it in," I countered, but my blood was cold. "Ask Sally." But when I looked about for the scullery maid, I did not see her or hear her anywhere.

The sergeant was obviously on Copley's side, the young constable and John confused. All men against one woman.

"No more o' this," the sergeant said severely. "You'll promenade down to the magistrate with me, missus, and he can hear your story."

My body went colder still. If I could not convince the magistrate of my innocence, I would be thrown to the wolves—or at least, to an Old Bailey trial and a jury. A long bench of men would gaze at me disapprovingly and pronounce that cooks should not stick their carving knives into their masters. And that would be the end of me.

At twenty-nine summers, I found life sweet, and I had more to live for than just myself.

I wanted to bolt. To run, run, run, snatch up my daughter from where I'd hidden her and flee. To the coun-tryside—no, not far enough. The Continent, or farther, to Asia, perhaps, where I could cook for some colonial nabob who wouldn't care too much what I ran from as long as I could give him his familiar English fare.

I closed my eyes, and I prayed. I hadn't gone to church in about half a dozen years, but praying and church are two different things. I begged God to have mercy on me, and I opened my eyes again.

"Very well, then," I said, straightening my shoulders. "But no cuffs, if you please. I am a respectable woman."

I lifted my chin and marched before them out of the room, down the stairs, and straight out of the house.

THE MAGISTRATE WHO EXAMINED ME AT BOW STREET WAS a jovial man whose rotund body betrayed that he liked his meals and missed few. I had to stand up before him while those also awaiting examination filled the room behind me— I was a nobody, and warranted no special treatment.

Most of the people at the house had been arrested in the night for theft, drunkenness, fighting, being loud and disor-derly, and for prostitution. A few well-dressed solicitors wandered the crowd, looking for clients to take to barris-ters, but they didn't bother approaching me. I had a bit of money put by, but I doubted I'd be able to afford an eloquent, wigged barrister to argue in my defense.

The magistrate's chair creaked as he leaned over his bench and peered at me nearsightedly. "Name?"

"Katharine Holloway, sir," I said, though it was sure to be on the paper his clerk had handed him.

"And you were the mistress of Sir Lionel Leigh-Bradbury of Portman Square?"

I gave him a look of shock. "Indeed not, sir. I was his cook."

The magistrate stared at me with unblinking, light blue eyes. "His cook? Well, madam ... you certainly cooked his goose."

The stuffy room rang with laughter.

"I did not murder him, sir," I declared over the noise.

"You claim to be innocent of this crime, do you?" the magistrate asked. "Even though the butler saw you chopping his onions?" More laughter.

"Mr. Copley saw nothing," I said indignantly. "He is a drunken fool and a liar. Besides, it was a carving knife, not a chopper."

The magistrate lost his smile. "It makes no difference whether it were for skewering or filleting. The butler saw you with your sticker, and he stands by that. Do you have any witnesses as to your character? Someone who might argue for you?"

I thought quickly. Daniel leapt to mind, but I had no way of knowing where to find him. Besides, why should he speak for me, when we were only friends in passing? This magistrate, with his obnoxious sense of humor, might accuse me of being Daniel's mistress as well.

"No, sir," I said stiffly. "My family is gone. I am on my own."

"You sound proud of that fact. No woman should be pleased she has no one to take care of her."

I raised my chin. "I take care of myself."

The magistrate studied me over his bench, and I read the assessment in his face: *No better than she ought to be.*

"You take care of yourself by giving your master supper and then stabbing him through the heart?" the magistrate demanded. "I suppose you thought him ... *well served.*"

His clerks and constables as well as many of London's unwashed, roared again. I suppose this magistrate spent all his quiet time inventing quips to bring out when the opportunity arose, for the entertainment of the court.

The magistrate gave me a wide smile, betraying that his back teeth were going rotten. "Katherine Holloway, I am binding you over for the willful murder of Sir Lionel Leigh-Bradbury of Portman Square. You will be taken to Newgate to await your trial. That will give you time to *simmer in your own sauce.*"

The room went positively riotous.

I was icy with fear but refused to bow my head. I stood there, staring at the magistrate until he signaled to his bailiff. The bailiff, a tall man with wiry hair, seized my arm and pulled me from the room.

THE JAILER WHO LED ME TO A CELL IN NEWGATE HAD legs far longer than mine, and I had to scuttle swiftly to keep up with him.

He took me down a flight of stairs to a chilly room already filled with people. The jailer shoved me roughly inside then retreated and locked the door. I stumbled and collided with a stone wall, pins falling from my hair, the dark mass of it tumbling down. I clung to that wall, unwilling to turn and face the crowd behind me.

What on earth was I to do? Who could help me? I needed a solicitor, but as I said, I doubted I could secure even the cheapest brief to stand up for me. I might appeal to Daniel, because he'd been kind to me, but even if he would be willing to help, I had no idea how to find him or where to send him word.

Daniel might not be in London at all. He disappeared from the metropolis now and again for weeks at a time, I supposed to work other odd jobs. I could send someone to search for him or for James, but still I had no way of knowing where to start looking—except at posh houses where he *might* make deliveries—nor anyone to send.

I turned around and slid down the wall to sit with my knees against my chest. I could not remain here. It was not only my own well-being I thought of—I took care of my daughter with my wages, and what would become of her if no more money went to the family she lived with? They were kind people, but not wealthy enough to care for a child not their own. No, I had to get out.

But perhaps Daniel would hear of my arrest. He'd go to Portman Square on his usual rounds and find me gone. The newspapers, not to mention the neighbors' servants, would be full of the tale of Sir Lionel's murder.

Then again, Daniel might believe with everyone else that I'd killed Sir Lionel. He'd go about his business, thinking himself well rid of me. I'd be convicted by a jury and hanged, my feet twisting in the breeze. Copley would come to the hanging and laugh at me.

Anger at Copley nudged away despair. If I survived this, so help me, I would exact my revenge on the man. I had only a vague idea how I'd go about doing so, but I would have plenty of time to think.

The window high in the wall darkened, and I grew

hungry. My fellow inmates slumped around me, grumbling quietly among themselves. The stink of urine, sweat, and human confinement blanketed the room.

"Eat this, luv. You'll feel better."

I looked up. The woman who stood over me had snarled red hair and smelled of gin and sweat, but the look in her blue eyes was kindly. Her red satin dress was almost clean and well-mended, as though she kept it carefully, but it hung on her thin frame without stays.

Her costume made me guess her profession. Yesterday, I would have swept by such a woman, perhaps thinking on the evils of the world that drove women to lowly things — where I might be myself had I not been lucky enough to learn cookery. Today, as the woman smiled at me and held out a bit of pasty, I wanted to embrace her as a sister.

She placed the cold pie into my hands and sat down next to me as I took a hungry bite. The pie was soggy and laden with salt, nothing like the light-crusted savory concoctions I baked myself. But at the moment, it tasted like the finest cake.

"Me name's Anne," the woman said. "You're wrong about me, you know, luv. I'm an actress."

I studied her with renewed interest but could not remember seeing her on a stage at Drury Lane or Haymarket. However, the fact that she was an actress did not necessarily mean she was a principal — one could be buried in the chorus, quietly anonymous.

"I was unjustly accused," I said, brushing a tear from my cheek.

"Ain't we all, luv? But me old lad will come for me."

Alas, I did not have an old lad, but I did have a lass who needed to be taken care of. If perhaps I *did* get word to Daniel, I would at least ask him to see that she got the stash of money I had managed to put by. Daniel could be trusted with that, I felt certain.

But now that I had time to think, what did I know about Daniel, really? Next to nothing. He'd been a bolstering help to me these last few weeks, and he flirted with me, but in a friendly, harmless way. He never tried anything improper, though he must know by now that I might not say no to improper advances from Daniel McAdam.

I knew nothing of Daniel beyond that. Not where he dwelled or who his family was nor what he did when I did not see him. I only knew that I wanted to lean my head against his strong shoulder, feel him stoke my hair, and hear him say, "There now, Kat. Never you worry. I'll see to everything."

I chewed on the pasty and remained miserable.

THE NEXT MORNING, ANNE WAS RELEASED. I CLUNG TO her hand when she said good-bye, knowing hers might be the last kind face I ever saw. I begged her to look for a man called Daniel McAdam and tell him what had become of me. She promised to do her best.

Anne went out, and I cried. I wept hard into my skirt and huddled like everyone else. I was thirsty, exhausted, and worried for my fate.

Later that day, the door to the common room opened, and the bailiff bellowed, "Mrs. Holloway!"

I scrambled to my feet, my heart beating wildly, my limbs cramped from sitting on the cold stone floor. I had no idea what was happening—was it time for my trial already? Or perhaps the magistrate simply wanted me back so he could make a few more jokes at my expense.

I found, to my astonishment, that the person the bailiff took me to in the jailer's room was James, the lad who worked for Daniel. Still more astonished when James said, "I'm to take you home, Mrs. Holloway. You won't stay here another minute."

I had no words, not to thank James, not to ask questions. As I stood like a mute fool, James took my hand and pulled me from the jailer's room, through the courtyard, and out the formidable gate into the light of day. Or at least a rainy afternoon.

The area around Newgate was a busy one. James had to walk me through the bustle a long way before he pushed me into a hansom cab in Ludgate Hill.

I finally found my tongue to ask questions, but James did not enter the cab with me. He only slammed the door and signaled the cabby to go. I craned my head to call out to him as the cab jerked forward, but James gave me a cheerful wave and faded into the crowd.

Had Daniel rescued me? I wondered. If so, where was he? And why wasn't James coming with me?

James had said he'd been sent to take me home. What did he mean by *home?* Sir Lionel's house would go to whoever inherited the baronetcy—a younger brother, nephew, cousin. If his heir did not want a cook who'd been arrested for murdering the previous master, then I had no home to go to.

The cab took me, however, directly to Portman Square, and Sir Lionel's house.

CHAPTER 5

DANIEL WAITED FOR ME ON THE STAIRS THAT LED DOWN to the scullery. He ran up them with his usual verve to assist me from the hansom, then he paid the cabby and took me down into the kitchens.

I was shaking with hunger, worry, and exhaustion. I was grimy and dirty, my clothes filthy. A long bath, a hearty meal, and a good sleep would help me considerably, but I had not the patience for any of those.

I broke from Daniel and faced him, hands on hips. "Explain yourself, Mr. McAdam."

In spite of my bravado, my voice shook, my weakened knees bent, and I swayed dangerously.

Daniel caught me and steered me to the stool where I'd sat sharpening my knives the night Sir Lionel had come down. As I caught my breath, Daniel found the kettle, filled it with water, and set it on the stove, which had already been lit.

"Nothing to explain." Daniel moved smoothly about, collecting cups and plates from the cupboards, and rummaged in the pantry for leftover seed cake and a crock of butter. He knew his way around a kitchen, that was certain. "James told me you were in trouble, and I went along to see what I could do."

"But I was released," I said, trying to understand. "No one is released from Newgate. No one like me, anyway."

"Ah, well, the magistrates were made to see that they had no reason to keep you. The fellow who examined you is a fool, and the charge of murder has been dismissed."

I stared at him in astonishment. Daniel poured water, now boiling, into a teapot. He brought the pot to the table, and when the tea had steeped a few minutes, poured out a cup and shoved it and a plate of buttered seed cake at me.

"Get that inside you. You'll feel better."

Indeed, yes. I fell upon the feast and made short work of it. Soon I was no longer hungry and thirsty, but I remained half-asleep and filthy.

"What did you do?" I asked. "I sent Anne to find you, but I thought perhaps you'd do no more than see I had a solicitor, if that."

Daniel finished off his tea and poured himself another cup. "If you mean Anne the actress, yes, she did find James —James is a friend of her son's. But James had already seen you being arrested from here. He followed you to Bow Street and realized you were being taken off to Newgate. After that, he legged it to me and told me all. I regret you had to stay the night in that place, but I could not put things in motion sooner. I am sorry."

I listened in amazement. "You mystify me more and more. Why should you apologize, let alone rush to my rescue? *How* did you rush to my rescue? I'm only a cook, not a duchess, with no one to speak for me."

Daniel lifted his dark brows. "Are you saying a cook

should be tried and condemned for a murder she did not commit, because she is *only* a cook?"

I was too tired to argue with him or even to understand what he was saying. "How do you know I didn't murder Sir Lionel? It was my knife in his back."

"Which someone other than you took from this kitchen and used. Someone evil enough to push the blame onto to you." Daniel sat down, comfortably pouring himself a cup of tea. He pulled a flask from his pocket, tipped a drop of whiskey into it, then a drop into mine, if you please.

He went on. "If you *had* killed Sir Lionel, why would you leave the knife in him instead of cleaning it up or getting rid of it? Why would you go happily back to bed to wait for the constables to arrive instead of running away? It was you who raised the alarm and sent for the police, wasn't it?"

"Yes." I had done all that. It seemed so long ago now.

Daniel sipped his tea, and I took another drink of mine. Whatever spirits he'd poured into the tea danced on my tongue and warmed my gullet.

Daniel watched me over his cup. "Tell me about these people who came to dinner with Sir Lionel last evening."

I could barely remember. "Mrs. Watkins would know better than I about his guests. She served at table, because Copley was a mess."

"Mrs. Watkins doesn't seem to be here. In fact, the staff have deserted the house. Does Mrs. Watkins have another address?"

I clattered my teacup to its saucer, my hands shaking. "Mrs. Watkins has a sister in Pimlico—Sally, the scullery maid, told me she'd gone there, if I remember aright. However, if you imagine I can give you the particulars of all the people who worked here and where they might be, along with the names and address of the friends who visited Sir

Lionel last night ..." I broke off, no longer certain where the sentence had been taking me. "You clearly have never been up before a magistrate and thrown into a common cell at Newgate for a night. It clouds the memory."

"Oh, haven't I?" Daniel's dark eyes twinkled. "But that's a tale for another day. Come along, Kat. You have a good rest, and we'll talk when you wake."

I found myself on my feet, again supported by Daniel. "I'm wretched dirty. I need a wash."

"I have plenty of hot water going on the stove. Off we go."

He steered me to my little bedroom and then went back out to carry in steaming water and pour it into my basin. Daniel left me to it, saying a cheerful good-night.

I was so exhausted I simply stripped off every layer of clothing I wore and dumped them on the floor. I washed the best I could, then crawled into bed, still damp, in my skin.

Some believe it is very wicked to sleep without clothes, but I'd already been a sinner, and I couldn't see that God would care very much whether or not I pulled on a nightgown. I was asleep as soon as my head touched my pillow, in any case.

When I woke, it was bright daylight. I spent some time trying to convince myself that everything that had happened to me had been a bad dream, and that I'd rise as usual and go out into my kitchen to cook. I had an idea for tea cakes with caraway and rosemary that I wanted to try.

I threw back the covers to find myself unclothed, which reminded me of my quick bath, after which I'd been too tired to don a nightdress. This told me my adventures had been real enough—I was usually quite modest and would never risk being caught without any sort of clothing on my body.

The events of the night before notwithstanding, I rose and did my toilette, put on a clean frock and apron, pinned up my unruly hair, and set my cook's cap on my head. The familiar routine comforted me, and besides, I had no idea what else to do.

When I opened the door, the sharp smell of frying bacon came to me. I moved out to the kitchen to find Daniel at the stove, cooking. The urchin, James, a bit cleaner than he usually was, sat at the kitchen table.

When I looked at James this morning, I noticed something I had been too distracted to note in the past—he and Daniel had the same eyes. But then, I hadn't seen the two together when James's face hadn't been covered with dirt. Now I saw that the shape of James's jaw, the jut of chin, the manner in which he sat sipping a mug of tea, mirrored Daniel's almost exactly.

"You're his son," I exclaimed to James. I had no idea whether this fact was a secret, but I was too bewildered and tired to guard my tongue.

James gave me his good-natured look, and Daniel glanced over his shoulder at me. "Ah, Kat," Daniel said. "Awake at last. You slept the day away, and a night."

I rocked on my feet, disoriented. "Did I?"

"Indeed. I didn't have the heart to wake you yesterday, but I knew you'd be hungry this morning. Sit down—these eggs are almost finished."

"You have changed the subject," I said. "As usual when you do not wish to answer. Why did you not tell me James was your son? Why did *you* not tell me?" I shot at James.

James shrugged. "Embarrassing, innit? For me, I mean. T' have to admit *he* sired me?"

"I don't see why," I said. "You could do much worse than Mr. McAdam."

James grinned. "Suppose."

Daniel shot him a weary look, which made James more amused. I realized they must banter like this all the time. It reminded me of the jokes I shared with my daughter, and my heart squeezed.

By habit, I brought out my bin of flour and the sponge starter I kept on a shelf beside the icebox. I stopped after lugging the flour bin to the middle of the table. Who was I baking for? Did I still even have employment? And why were Daniel and James here, when no one else seemed to be?

"Where is everyone?" I asked. "Did Mrs. Watkins return? Copley? Sally?"

James answered, Daniel still at the stove. "The house be empty. Dangerous, that. Anyone could come in and make off with the silver."

"Have they?" I asked. "Was Sir Lionel robbed? And that's why he was killed?"

My hands measured the flour and bubbly starter into a bowl, and I took up a wooden spoon to mix it all together. The familiar feel of my muscles working as the dough grew stiffer calmed me somewhat. If there'd only be three of us today, I wouldn't need more than one loaf.

I stirred in the flour along with a dash of water and a smidgen of salt, then scraped the dough onto my table and began to knead. Neither Daniel nor James admonished me to stop. I'd refuse anyway—the vigorous kneading helped my agitation. I dumped the ball of dough into a clean bowl, covered it with a plate, and set it aside to rise.

As I wiped my floury hands, Daniel shoved a large helping of bacon and eggs at me. "Eat all that. Then we'll talk."

"Talk." I picked up the fork he'd laid beside the plate, suddenly hungry. James, likewise, was digging into the repast. "I think I never want to talk again. Perhaps I'll retire to the country. Grow runner beans and pumpkins, and bake pies the rest of my life."

"I'd eat 'em," James said. "She's a bloody fine cook, Dad."

"Watch your language around a lady, lad." Daniel scraped back a chair, sat down, and watched us both eat. He wasn't partaking and didn't say why, but I was beyond curiosity at this point.

Once I was scooping the last rom my plate and finishing off my second cup of tea, Daniel said, "Kat, I want you to tell me about the meal you served to Sir Lionel. Every detail. Leave nothing out."

"Why?" I came alert, able to now that I had a bit more inside me.

Daniel laid his hands on the table, giving me a kindly look, but I saw something watchful behind the compassion. "Just tell me."

It was the same gaze I often found myself giving him. Wanting to trust him, but knowing so little about him I was not certain I could.

"There was nothing wrong with my meal," I said firmly. "Was there?"

James frowned across at his father. "What are you getting at, Dad? You're upsetting her."

"Sir Lionel didn't die from the knife thrust," Daniel said, far too calm for the dire words he spoke. "That wound was inflicted post mortem. Sir Lionel had already been dead, though not for long, of arsenical poisoning. His guests, Mr. and Mrs. Fuller, also suffered from poisoning. Mr. Fuller died in the night. Mrs. Fuller, her doctor says, has a chance at recovery, but he can't say for certain whether she will live."

CHAPTER 6

I SAT STARING FOR A FULL MINUTE, PERHAPS TWO, MY mouth hanging open. James looked no less astonished than I did. James had helped me with that meal, not only cleaning the fish and fowl but laying out ingredients for me, learning to chop mushrooms, and stirring up dough.

"No arsenic could have been in *my* supper," I said, when my tongue worked again. "They must have come by the poison elsewhere."

Daniel shook his head. "The coroner who examined the body said that the poison had entered the stomach at the same time as your meal. I'm sorry, Kat. You must take me through every dish. Please."

"Well, it could not have been in my food, could it?" I said in rising worry. "You brought me most of the ingredients that night, and I taste everything. If arsenic had been slipped into the sauces in my kitchen, it would have killed me too. And all the staff. I always hold a portion back to serve with our supper."

"Tell me," Daniel said gently.

I heaved a sigh. I could barely remember my name let alone everything I'd made that fatal evening, but I closed my eyes in recall.

"A cream of leek soup. Whitefish with a velouté—a thickened broth and wine sauce. A salad of greens with a lime dressing and tart apples, asparagus with boiled eggs, roasted squab stuffed with peppercorns with a red wine sauce. A fricassee of mushrooms. There wasn't time for rolls with all this, so I made savory scones instead. For pudding, a thin chocolate soup to start, then custard tart with whatever berries I could find and a burnt sugar sauce. Copley chose the wine for me—perhaps *he* put poison in the wine, for whatever twisted reason he had. He's a villain; I've always said so."

Daniel shook his head. "There was nothing in the glasses, or the bottles. The coroner worked all night, testing everything he could."

"How do you know all this? Was there an inquest?"

Daniel shrugged. "He told me. He's a friend of mine."

Daniel McAdam, friends with a coroner. Why was I not surprised? "But how did he find the wine glasses?" I asked. "And the wine? Sally scrubbed everything and put it away."

"Not the wine glasses. She'd left them. The wine was still open in the butler's pantry. The police took all this away while you were ... detained."

The prison came back to me with a rush. I pinched my fingers to my nose, willing it away. When I opened my eyes, I found Daniel looking at me with such sympathy mixed with self-chastisement that it made me a bit dizzy.

I drew a breath, continuing the argument to stop the wild thoughts in my head. "The poison could *not* have been in the food," I said. "I told you, I taste everything before I allow it to go up, and every person downstairs had a helping of what every person upstairs ate. And we're all hale—well, I am, and James here appears to be."

"We're looking for the other staff," Daniel said. "We'll know soon enough."

I fixed him with a stern look. "If the coroner believes the cook poisoned the entire dinner party then why am I not still in Newgate?"

"Because of James," Daniel said, unworried. "If you had poured a box of arsenic into any of your dishes, James would have seen. You could, I suppose, have built yourself an immunity to arsenic so it wouldn't hurt you, but I know James did not. And he's not sick at all."

No, James was very healthy indeed, and listening with interest. He asked the question that was next in my mouth. "Why do you want to know all about the food, then, Dad? If you already know she didn't do it?"

Daniel opened his hands on the table. "To decide which dish might best conceal it, and how it was served. The wine and peppercorn sauce, the mushrooms, and the burned sugar on the pudding interest me most. They could have disguised the taste."

I only watched him, bewildered. "But who would have introduced this poison? I place the dishes in the lift myself. Are you saying you believe someone very small was hiding in the dumbwaiter with a vial of poison? Or something as nonsensical? Or do you believe Mrs. Watkins did it, or John, as they served the meal? Sally went nowhere near the food at all—she was busy washing up all my pots and pans."

"I can rule out none of them," Daniel said.

I blew out my breath. "I cannot imagine why on earth Mrs. Watkins, John, or Sally would do such a thing. None of them are mad, I don't think."

"They are not here either," Daniel pointed out. "Once

you were taken away, John disappeared, as did your scullery maid, as well as your butler and several choice bottles of wine."

"Of course," I said in exasperation. "Copley took the wine to sell, no doubt—he refuses to drink the stuff himself. I imagine the others didn't return because they thought they had no place here anymore. Sally was terrified and fled before I was even arrested."

"Perhaps," was all Daniel would say. "Would it be too much for you, Kat, to cook the same meal, as you did that night? So I can see exactly how it was prepared?"

At the moment, I never wanted to cook anything again. But I heaved a sigh, climbed to my feet, and went through the larder to see what foodstuffs I'd need.

I had everything but the mushrooms, berries, fresh fish, and birds. James was dispatched to procure those. The left-over greens were a bit wilted, but edible, apples drying, but again, usable.

I set everything out as I remembered. A bit difficult because I never cooked to an exact recipe—I knew what went into each dish from experience, then I threw in a bit of this or that I had on hand or left out things I did not, so each meal was unique. A long time ago, when I'd first been a cook's assistant, I'd doggedly learned every step of a recipe and followed it religiously, until a famous chef I met told me to trust my own instincts. After that, my skills rose quickly.

I tried to remember what I'd done as I worked. I set Daniel to helping me chop leeks and greens, core the apples, stir the roux for the velouté, and cream the butter for the scones.

Daniel proved to be quite skilled at cookery, though it was clear he'd never handled a chef's knife before. I had to show him, with my hand over his, how to chop the leeks. His skin was warm, his breath on my cheek, warmer.

I might have stayed in the circle of his arm for a while longer had not James come banging back in. I nearly cut myself scrambling away from Daniel, who moved the knife safely aside, his eyes alight with amusement.

I set Daniel to washing and chopping the mushrooms, and James competently cleaned the fish in the scullery.

We created the meal again, which took the rest of the day, and then partook of it, enjoying the lightness of leek soup, the savory fish, the tenderness of the game birds with peppercorns, the sweet and tart tastes in the salad. The scones came out light and crumbly, the custard creamy with the bright bite of berries to finish.

When we ended the meal, Daniel pushed back his plate, clattered his fork to it, and let out a sigh. "You are an artist, Kat."

"It's only a bit of cookery," I said modestly, but I was pleased.

James wiped his mouth with the napkin I'd given him. "'Tis bloody hard work. All that, and you eat it in ten minutes."

"*You* eat it in ten minutes," Daniel said with fatherly fondness. He took a sip of the wine I'd brought out of the butler's pantry for the peppercorn sauce.

Daniel seemed to know about wine—he didn't quaff it but savored it, pronouncing the vintage excellent. He was a paradox, was Daniel, though I had long since discarded the belief that he was a simple delivery man.

"You do well in the kitchen," I told James. "You learn quickly and have a feel for the food. Perhaps you could study a bit and become a chef."

"A chef?" James snorted. "Cooking for pampered

gentlemen who complain when their dinner hasn't been boiled long enough? No, thank you."

"Well." Daniel leaned back in his chair. "There was nothing wrong with that meal. Plenty of opportunities for you to slip in the poison, and you too, James—and me—but if everyone in the kitchen ate of the dishes, and you and James are well, I cannot see how the poison came from the meal as you cooked it."

"Thank you very much," I said. "You might have taken my word for it before we did all that work." Not that I'd eaten so well in a long time. I suspected part of Daniel's motive had been to partake in an expertly cooked elegant meal, which I doubted came along for him very often. I'd rather liked cooking with Daniel—and James, of course.

Daniel and James obligingly helped me clean up. I expected them, as men often did, to abandon me once the enjoyment was over, but James scrubbed plates and Daniel dried them with good cheer.

I told them to leave me after that. I had nowhere to go and would make do with my bed here tonight, but tomorrow, I'd look for other digs and a new place.

James departed, his pockets full of leftover scones. Daniel lingered on the doorstep. "Are you certain you'll be all right, Kat?"

"Not entirely." The kitchen was echoing without Daniel and James in it, the rooms above me, too silent. However, the street was busy and noisy, and the neighbors and their servants were near to hand. "I don't have much choice do I? But I am made of strong stuff, do not worry."

"Hmm." Daniel glanced at the ceiling, as though he could see the entire house above us. "Lock this door behind me then. I've already bolted the front door but keep the door at the top of the back stairs locked. And don't go out until morning."

His caution unnerved me. I felt the weight of the house above us, empty and waiting. I drew a breath and repeated that I'd be all right, and at last, Daniel departed.

I locked the kitchen door then scurried up the back stairs to the door at the top, its green baize tight and unblemished, as though nothing untoward had occurred beyond it. I opened the door and peered out into the cold darkness of the house.

I was too sensible to believe in spirits, but the shadows seemed to press at me. Sir Lionel had died here, alone and unpitied.

I quickly closed that door, locked it, and descended again to the kitchen, where I rechecked the back door and made certain none of the high windows were open. The kitchen was stuffy with the windows closed, but I'd put up with it.

I retired to bed, but I could not sleep for a good long time, as tired as I was. I kept picturing the rooms upstairs, dark, deserted, silent.

At last I did drift off, only to be woken by a loud *thump*. Then came a creak of floorboard above me. Someone was in the house.

I had a moment of panic, wanting to put the bedcovers over my head and pretend it hadn't happened. But I hardened my resolve and sat up.

Burglars must have broken in—empty houses were good targets, especially those belonging to rich men. Sir Lionel's heir would no doubt arrive to take possession soon, but until then, a house full of silver, wine, and other valuables was a sitting duck waiting to be plucked.

I wasn't having it. I sprang quietly out of bed, pulled on

a blouse and skirt over my nightclothes and found my good, stout boots. I'd run for the constable who patrolled the street—never mind he'd had a hand in my arrest—and bring him in to the take the thieves.

As I left my tiny bedchamber and made my way through the short hall to the kitchen, I heard the burglar start down the back stairs.

Damn and blast. The entire expanse of the kitchen lay between me and the back door. I knew why they'd come down here—the master's collection of wine and much of the silver lay in the butler's pantry beyond the kitchen.

I'd have to risk it. Taking a deep breath, I scurried across the flagstone floor toward the scullery and the back door.

A dark figure leapt down the last part of the stairs and grabbed me before I could reach for the door latch—the door was already unlocked, I saw belatedly. I let out a scream. A hand clamped over my mouth and dragged me back into the kitchen. I fought like mad, kicking and flailing with my fists.

"For God's sake, Kat, *stop*!"

Daniel's voice was a hiss in my ear, and a second later, I realized it was he who held me. I broke away. "What the devil are you doing, frightening me out of my wits?" I asked in a fierce whisper.

"Shh." He put a finger to my lips.

I understood. Though it had been Daniel creeping down to the kitchen, someone was still upstairs, robbing the place.

"It's Copley," Daniel said into my ear.

I started in indignation. "That rat. We should run for the constable. Catch him at it."

"The police are already waiting outside. When he runs

out with the goods, they'll nab him. He won't have any excuse or chance to hide."

I went quiet as the floorboards creaked again. I might have known. "What if he comes down here?" I asked.

"Then I'll lay him out and deliver him to the Peelers."

I liked the idea, but I had to wonder. "Why are you hand in glove with the police?"

Daniel's vague shrug was maddening, but I fell silent. We traced Copley's path across the ground floor above us until he disappeared into the rear of the house.

"The garden door," Daniel said in a low voice, no more whispering. "That's how he came in. He'll find plenty of the Old Bill waiting for him as he goes out."

The nearness of Daniel was warming. "How did you know he was here at all?"

"I was watching the house, saw him pass a few times. Then he nipped around the corner to the mews behind it. I told the constable to bring some stout fellows, and I followed Copley inside."

"You were watching the house?" I was befuddled from being jerked from a sound sleep and having Daniel so close to me.

Daniel gave me a nod. "I wanted to make sure all was well. I worry about you, Kat."

He looked at me for a long moment, then touched my chin with his forefinger, leaned down, and brushed a kiss across my lips.

I was too astonished to do anything but let him. Daniel straightened, gave me a wry smile, and moved around me to let himself out the kitchen door.

A blast of cold air poured over me, but my body was warm where he'd held me. I touched my fingertips to my lips, still feeling the pressure of his soft kiss.

CHAPTER 7

DANIEL RETURNED IN THE MORNING, KNOCKING ON THE kitchen door, which I'd re-locked.

He'd brought James with him again, to help me with the morning chores necessary to any house, no matter I was its only resident. James whipped around, carrying in coal and helping stir up the fire, while I mixed up dough for flat muffins and fried the last of the bacon.

I kept glancing sideways at Daniel as we ate at the table, though he did not seem to notice. He said nothing about the adventure of the night before—not to mention the kiss—as if none of it were of any moment.

I was no stranger to the relations between men and women—I had a daughter, after all—but what I'd had with my husband had been sometimes painful and always far from affectionate. The gentle heat of Daniel's mouth had opened possibilities to me, thoughts I'd never explored. I'd had no idea a man could be so tender.

Daniel seemed to have forgotten all about the kiss,

however. That stung, but I made myself feel better by pretending he was being discreet in front of his son.

After breakfast, I mentioned I needed to tidy myself and return to the agency to find another post, but Daniel forestalled me. "First we are visiting Mrs. Fuller."

I blinked as I set the plates on the draining board. "The woman who shared the fatal meal? She has recovered?"

"She has, and was lucky to. The coroner tells me there was a large quantity of poison in the two men, enough to kill a person several times over. Mrs. Fuller is rather stout, so perhaps the arsenic did not penetrate her system as thoroughly. Her doctors purged her well."

"Poor thing," I said. "Do you think Copley somehow added the poison to the meal? To clear Sir Lionel out of the way so he might help himself to the goods?" I contemplated this a moment, rinsing plates under the taps. "Perhaps he only pretended to be too drunk to serve that night, so the food wouldn't be connected with him."

Daniel shook his head. "I think Copley is more an opportunist than a schemer. Though he might have seen an opportunity to administer the poison and taken it."

"I still don't see how. Copley is limber and thin, but I can't imagine him crouching in the dumbwaiter shaft with a bottle of poison."

Daniel gave me his warm laugh. "Nor can I. Ready yourself, and we'll go."

James finished the washing up so I could change. I put on my second-best dress, the one I kept clean for visiting agencies or my acquaintances on my day out, or my occasional jaunt to the theatre. For church and visiting my daughter, I always wore my best dress.

This gown was a modest dark brown, with black piping on cuffs, bodice, and neckline. I flattered myself that it went with my glossy brown hair and dark blue eyes. The hat that matched it—coffee-brown straw with a subdued collection of feathers and a black ribbon—set it off to perfection.

Daniel gave me a glance of approval when I emerged, which warmed me. Ridiculous. I was behaving like a smitten girl.

But then, he'd never seen me in anything but my gray work dress and apron. James grinned at me, told me I was lovely, and offered me his arm. Sweet boy.

Mrs. Fuller lived on Wilton Crescent, near Belgrave Square. A fine address, and the mansion that went with it took my breath away. Daniel and I were let in by a side door, though James remained outside with the hired coach.

The ceilings of the house above stairs were enormously high, the back and front parlors divided by pointed arches. Plants were everywhere—we had stepped into a tropical rainforest it seemed. Rubber trees, elephant's ears, potted palms, and other exotic species I couldn't identify filled the rooms. The furniture surrounding these plants was elegantly carved, heavy, and upholstered in velvet.

The butler led us through the front and back parlors and into a bedchamber that looked out to the gardens in back of the house.

This room was as elegant as the others, the ceiling criss-crossed with beams carved like those in an Indian mogul's palace. Mosaics covered blank spaces in the ceiling, and outside in the garden, a fountain containing tiles with more mosaics burbled.

Mrs. Fuller lay on a thick mattress in an enormous mahogany bedstead with curved sides. Mrs. Fuller was indeed stout, about twice my girth, and I am not a thin woman. Her face, however, was pretty in a girlish way, the hair under her cap brown without a touch of gray.

I curtsied when the butler announced us, and Daniel made a polite bow. "I apologize for disturbing you, madam," Daniel began. "The police inspector thought Mrs. Holloway might be of assistance, as he discussed with you."

"Yes, indeed." Mrs. Fuller lifted a damp handkerchief from the bedcovers and wiped her red-rimmed eyes. "I am anxious to find out what happened. Forgive me, my dear, if I am not myself. It is still incredible to me that my dear husband is gone, and yet, here I am. You are the cook?"

"I am." I gave her another polite curtsy. "My condolences, ma'am. Yes, I cooked the meal, but I promise you, I never would have dreamed of tainting it in any way."

Mrs. Fuller dabbed her eyes again. "They told me you were innocent of the crime. I suppose you are suffering from this in your own way as well. Your reputation ... you are an excellent cook, my dear. If it is any consolation, I so enjoyed the meal." Her smile was weary, that of a woman trying to make sense of a bizarre circumstance.

Daniel broke in, his voice quiet. "I've asked Mrs. Holloway about what she served and how she prepared it. It would help if you described the meal in your own words, Mrs. Fuller, and tell us if any dishes tasted odd."

Mrs. Fuller looked thoughtful. I pitied her, ill and abruptly widowed. She could have doctored the food herself to kill her rich husband, of course, but her husband dying did not mean she inherited all the money. That would go to her oldest son, if she had sons, or to nephews or other male kin if she did not. She'd receive only what was apportioned to her in the will or in the marriage agreement, though the heir could be generous and give her an allowance and place to live. However, the heir did not have to, not legally.

One reason not to marry in haste was that a widowed woman might find herself destitute. Careful planning was best, as were contracts signed by solicitors, as I'd learned to my regret.

"Let me see," Mrs. Fuller began. She then listed all the dishes I had prepared, forgetting about the mushrooms at first, but she said, "oh, yes," and came back to them. No, all tasted as they should, Mrs. Fuller thought, and she heaped more praise on my cooking.

"The custard at the end was very nice," she finished, sounding tired. "With the berries, all sweetened with sugar."

She had described what I did. Nothing added or missing. She and Sir Lionel had taken coffee, while her husband had been served tea, so if the poison had been in the coffee, she would have still have been ill but her husband alive.

Daniel seemed neither disappointed nor enlightened at the end of this interview. He thanked Mrs. Fuller, who looked tired, and we began to take our leave.

As her maid ushered us out of the bedchamber, a thought struck me. "A moment," I said, turning back to Mrs. Fuller. "You said the custard and berries were sweet with sugar. I put a burnt sugar sauce on the custard, yes, but did not sprinkle more sugar on top. Is that what you meant?"

Mrs. Fuller frowned. "I meant that there was sugar in a caster that came with the tarts on the tray. We all made use of it."

"Ah," I said.

Mrs. Fuller drooped against her pillows, the handkerchief coming up to her eyes again. The maid gave us a severe look, protective of her mistress, and Daniel led me firmly from the room.

I tried to walk decorously out of the house, but I moved faster and faster until I was nearly running as we reached the carriage.

"What the devil is it, Kat?" Daniel asked as he helped me in and climbed up beside me. "What did she say that's got you agitated?"

"The caster." I beamed as James slammed the door. "*There* is your incongruity."

Daniel only peered at me. "Why?"

"Because, my dear Daniel, I never sprinkle extra sugar on my custards, especially with the berries. Ruins the contrast—the custard is plenty sweet with the burnt sugar sauce, and the slight tartness of the berries sets it off perfectly. Extra sugar only drowns the flavor. I would never have sent up a caster full of it on a tray to ruin my dessert. I didn't, in fact. That means the poison must have been in the sugar."

Daniel's eyes lit, a wonderful sight in a handsome man. "I see. The murk begins to clear."

"Does it?" I deflated a bit. "Now all we need to know is where the caster came from, who put the poison into it, and how it got on the table that night."

Daniel gave me a wise nod. "I'm sure you'll discover that soon enough."

"Don't tease. I am not a policeman, Mr. McAdam."

"I know, but perhaps you ought to be." His amusement evaporated. "I must ask the inspector how he and his men missed a container full of poison when they searched the house."

He had a point. "The poisoner obviously took it away before the police arrived," I said.

"Oh, yes, of course. Why didn't I think of that?"

The wretch. My gaze dropped to his smiling mouth, and the memory of his brief kiss stole over me. If Daniel noticed my sudden flush, he said nothing, and we arrived at Sir Lionel's house again.

Nothing for it, but we began to search the place, top to bottom, for the sugar caster. I had to first explain to James what one was.

"A small carved silver jug-like shape, with a top," I said. "Like a salt shaker, but wider and fatter."

James nodded, understanding, but try as we might, we could not find it. We searched through the dining room, opening all the doors in the sideboard and the breakfront, then I led them downstairs to the butler's pantry.

The walls were lined with shelves that housed much of Sir Lionel's collection of silver, some of it handed down for generations through the Leigh-Bradbury family. Silver kept its value where coins, stocks, banknotes, and even paintings might become worthless. Heavy silver could at least be sold for its metal content if nothing else. Sir Lionel's plate had the hallmark of a silversmith from two centuries ago and was probably worth a fortune.

I discovered that at least a third of this valuable silver was missing.

"Copley," I said, hands on hips.

Daniel, next to me, agreed. "Meanwhile—no sugar caster?"

"If it's in this house, it wasn't put back into its usual place. Did Copley rush out of here with it in his bag of stolen silver?"

"Very possibly," Daniel said. "I will question the inspector who arrested him."

I became lost in thought. How likely was it that the poisoner had tamely returned the caster to the butler's pantry, ready for Copley to steal it? Unless Copley had poisoned Sir Lionel for the express purpose of making off with the silver. Why, then, had Copley waited until Sir Lionel had been found? Why not put the things into a bag and be far away when I'd stumbled across the body? The answer was that Copley most likely hadn't known that Sir Lionel would be killed. He was an opportunist, as Daniel said.

Daniel's shoulder next to mine was warm. I did not know what to make of him. Would I ever know who he truly was?

Well, I would not let him kiss me again and then disappear, leaving me in the dark. I was a grown woman, no longer the young fool I was to let a handsome man turn my head.

I voiced the thought that we should look for the caster in *un*usual places, and we went back to the dining room. After a long search, I spotted the sugar caster tucked into a pot containing a rubber tree plant.

The plant and its large pot stood just outside the dining room door, a nuisance I'd thought it, with its fat leaves slapping me across the back if I didn't enter the doorway straight on. As I impatiently pushed the leaves aside, I spied a glint of silver among the black earth.

I called to Daniel, and put a hand in to fish it out. He forestalled me, shook out a handkerchief, and carefully lifted it.

He carried the caster into the dining room, both of us breathless, as though the thing would explode. James fetched a napkin from the sideboard, and Daniel set the caster into the middle of it. With the handkerchief, he delicately unscrewed the top, then dumped the contents of the caster onto another napkin.

It looked like sugar—fine white sugar used to put a final taste on pastries, berries, cakes.

James put out a finger to touch the crystals, but Daniel snapped, "No!"

James curled his finger back, unoffended. "What is it?" he asked.

"Who knows?" Daniel said. "Arsenic, perhaps? Or some other foul chemical. I'm not a scientist or doctor."

"Or chemist," I said. "They sell poisons."

"True." Daniel wrapped the caster's contents in one napkin, the caster in the other, and put them all into the bag he carried.

"What will you do with those?" I asked.

"Take them to a chemist I know. Very clever, Mrs. Holloway."

"Common sense, I would have thought."

The teasing glint entered Daniel's eyes again. "Well, I have a distinct lack of common sense when I'm near you, Kat."

James rolled his eyes, and I frowned at Daniel—I refused to let him beguile me. "Be off with you, Mr. McAdam. I must put my things in order and find a place to stay. Another night in this house would not be good for my health, I think."

"I agree." Daniel gave me an unreadable look. "Where will you go?"

I had no idea. "I suppose I'll look for a boardinghouse that will take a cook whose master died after eating one of her meals. I'm certain I'll be welcomed with open arms."

Daniel didn't smile. "Go nowhere without sending me word, agreed?"

"Send word to where?" I looked him straight in the eye. "Your address, sir?"

Daniel returned my look, unblinking. "Leave a note here. I'll find it."

We continued our duel with gazes until finally Daniel gave me the ghost of a smile and turned away.

When James started to follow Daniel downstairs, I stopped him. "Where *does* he live, James?" I asked in a low voice.

James stuck his hands in his pockets. "Tell ya the truth, missus, I don't know. He finds me. He always seems to know where I am."

"And your mum?"

James shrugged, hands still in his pockets. "Never knew her. I was raised by a lady who chars for houses until he found me. But I've never stayed with him. I board with some people—respectable. He pays for it."

I was more mystified than ever. James behaved as though this were the normal course of things, though I saw a tiny flicker of hurt in his eyes that his father didn't want him rooming with him for whatever his reasons.

Daniel had banged out the front door. James rushed to catch up with him, and I closed and bolted the door behind them.

The house became eerier once they'd gone. I hastened down to my rooms, packed my things in my box, then left the box and went out again in hat and coat. I dutifully left a note for Daniel about where I was going on the kitchen table, which I'd cleaned and scrubbed after this morning's meal.

The first person I looked up was Mrs. Watkins, the housekeeper. She might have heard of a house looking for a cook, or might know where I could rest my head tonight.

Mrs. Watkins's sister lived in Pimlico. I found out exactly where by letting myself into the housekeeper's room and going through her small writing desk. Mrs. Watkins would have left all the paperwork and keys for the house for the next housekeeper, even if she'd gone in haste. I discovered everything neatly organized, as I'd thought I would.

I took an omnibus to Pimlico and found the house, a respectable address in an area of middle-class Londoners. Mrs. Watkins's sister, it turned out, ran a boardinghouse herself—for genteel, unmarried women, and Mrs. Watkins had just taken the last room.

"Mrs. Holloway!" Mrs. Watkins exclaimed in surprise when she entered the parlor to find me there. I'd asked the maid to send up word that Mrs. Watkins had a visitor, but I had not given my name.

"Good evening, Mrs. Watkins," I said.

"I heard ... I thought ..." She opened and closed her mouth, at a loss for words.

"Yes, I was taken before a magistrate, but then released." I made a dismissive gesture, as though I survived ordeals like being locked in Newgate every day.

Mrs. Watkins remained standing with hands clenched as she adjusted to this turn of events. "Well, I have to say I never thought you could have done such a thing. You have a temper on you, Mrs. Holloway, but plunging a knife into a man takes a cruelty I don't think you possess."

"The knife didn't kill him," I said. "He was poisoned. As were the others at the table. Now then, Mrs. Watkins, why did you set a sugar caster on the table when I didn't send it up with the meal?"

Mrs. Watkins gave me a perplexed frown. "What sugar caster?"

"The one Sir Lionel and his guests used to liberally sprinkle sugar all over my tart. Which they should not have —the flavor was just fine. If they'd known anything about food, those two men would be alive today."

Mrs. Watkins continued to blink at me. "You are making no sense. There was no sugar caster on the table."

"Then why did Mrs. Fuller say there was?"

"Gracious, I have no idea."

We eyed each other, two respectable-looking women standing in the middle of a carpet in a sitting room, the carved furniture and draped tables hemming us in. A lamp, already lit against gathering gloom, hissed as its wick drew up more kerosene.

The two of us were dressed similarly, our bodices tightly buttoned to our chins. I wore a jacket of dark gray wool, while Mrs. Watkins was dressed in a simple ensemble for an evening indoors. She was tall and bony, I plump and shorter of stature.

No one could have mistaken us for anything but two ladies who'd had to grub for our living, except that we had a bit more responsibility and wisdom, and had left behind the lower levels of the serving class.

And yet, was that all we were—respectable women in the upper echelon of the servant class? Who really knew anything about us? I had a daughter but no sign of a husband. Mrs. Watkins—what had she been in life? Behind the layers we showed the world, what secrets did we keep?

"Are you certain there was no sugar caster?" I asked after a silence.

"Positive."

There it was. Either Mrs. Watkins lied, or Mrs. Fuller did. Was the liar the poisoner? Or did each of them lie for some reason I could not comprehend?

I needed an independent party to tip the balance. John the footman, Sally, or even Copley. John certainly would have seen what had happened at the table that night. He wasn't the brightest of lads, but he was worth speaking to— unless he'd done the poisoning, of course. And then there was Sally. She'd discovered Sir Lionel. Her fright and shock had seemed real enough, but I had been too stunned myself to pay much attention.

I thanked Mrs. Watkins, wished her the best, and left the house, pondering over what she'd told me. If she lied about not placing or seeing the caster on the table, why had she? I had no idea. What a muddle.

John proved to be elusive. According to Mrs. Watkins's notes, which I read back at Sir Lionel's house, he'd been a cousin of Sir Lionel's coachman, but that coachman had been dismissed before I'd been employed there. The coachman now drove for a banker with a house in Dorset. John had no other relation, it seemed, and I had no idea how to go about looking for him. John might even now be in Dorset in search of a new position. Sally had a family in Southwark, the notes said, and I wondered if she'd retreated there.

I wrote a brief letter to the coachman who was John's cousin, addressed it in care of the banker in Dorset, and took it out to post.

Night had fallen. Streetlamps outside Sir Lionel's had been lit, and Portman Square teemed with people. London never really slept.

It was too late for the errand I truly wanted to run, so I began a brisk walk to a boardinghouse I'd lodged in before. Not the best, and the cook was deplorable, but needs must.

I had reached Oxford Street when I saw him.

Traffic blocked me from crossing, so I turned aside to buy a bun from a vendor. A little way behind me, a few well-dressed ladies and gentlemen were coming out of a large house and ascending into a coach.

One of the gentlemen was Daniel.

CHAPTER 8

I WAS SO ASTONISHED, I FROZE, THE WARM BUN HALFWAY
to my lips.

Gone was the rather shabbily dressed man with heavy
gloves and mud-splotched boots who argued in a good-
natured way with his son. This gentleman wore a dark, well-
tailored suit, which was clean and whole—in fact, it looked
costly.

Creased trousers covered shining boots, and his overcoat
against the evening chill fit him perfectly, made for him. A
neatly tied cravat and a gold watch chain in his waistcoat
completed the gentleman's ensemble.

Daniel's hair, instead of being its usual unruly mop, was
slicked to flow behind his ears. He paused on the doorstep
to set a tall silk hat on his head.

This couldn't be Daniel McAdam, could it? *My* Daniel?

My first inclination was to dart forward and look this
person in the face. And if it were Daniel, ask him what the
devil he meant by it.

I almost did. I hastily checked my steps, however, when I saw a woman emerge from the house and take his arm.

She was obviously a highborn lady. Her gown spoke of elegance and refinement, silk and lace, with a glitter of diamonds at her throat. Not a courtesan, I thought. While courtesans could dress as finely as any lady, this gown was demure while also being highly fashionable.

A sister, I reassured myself quickly. Or a cousin. Something innocent. But the way Daniel handed the woman into the coach told me differently. He held her hand longer than was polite, helped her inside with a touch on her waist that lingered.

A sister might laugh at his care. This lady turned and gave Daniel such a warm smile that I nearly dropped my hunk of bread.

Daniel glanced around him, scanning the street in a surreptitious manner, as I'd often seen him do—assessing the lay of the land.

That glance clinched the matter. He was Daniel, and not simply a man who resembled him. His clothes were different, but his mannerisms, the look, the way he moved —Daniel.

As his gaze roved the street, I ducked back from the streetlight, earning me a growl from a passerby I nearly trod on. I begged his pardon and pushed myself into the shadows of a house, where the gaslight didn't reach.

I could scarcely breathe. Daniel finished scrutinizing the street and climbed up into the coach with the lady. The other lady and gentleman who'd come out of the house had entered the carriage as I'd watched Daniel. A footman from the house shut the door and signaled the coachman to go.

My heart was like stone as the carriage creaked away. I

handed the uneaten bun to a beggar, drew my jacket about me, and walked on.

❦

THE LANDLADY AT MY OLD BOARDINGHOUSE LET ME HAVE a small room at the top of the house. It was cramped and cold, and I grew nostalgic for my cubbyhole behind the kitchen fireplace at Sir Lionel's.

It was not only the cold that kept me awake. I saw Daniel over and over in my mind, setting his fashionable hat on his head and touching the lady's back as he handed her into the carriage.

He'd been comfortable in those clothes, as comfortable as he was in his rough trousers and worn knee boots. He knew how to wear a gentleman's suit without awkwardness, and the lady with him seemed to find nothing amiss

Which was the real Daniel?

Or had I been mistaken? Daylight had been waning, gas lamps throwing a harsh glare on the street. Perhaps I had spied a man who had greatly resembled Daniel ... down to the turn of his head, the flick of his eyes, his way of looking about as though memorizing everything in sight.

The logical way to resolve the issue was to return to the house at Oxford Street, knock on the door, and demand to know if Daniel had been there last night. I had a good excuse to go to the house—I was a cook looking for a new position. Cooks didn't generally walk the streets knocking on doors, but it could happen. I would ask the domestics there about the household, perhaps make friends with their current cook, and discover what was what.

Another logical course was to ask Daniel point blank.

That is, if I ever saw the man again and could strike up the courage to question him. I might not like the answers.

Or I could forget about Daniel altogether, visit my agency, find another place, and resolve to speak to him no more.

None of the scenarios satisfied me. I rose in the morning, cross and sandy-eyed, nibbled at the breakfast of under-cooked bacon, overdone eggs, half-burned toast, and ice-hard butter, and went out. I wended my way back to Portman Square and Sir Lionel's, where all was quiet, to fetch my box.

I made certain that the kitchen and my room had been put to rights—when Sir Lionel's heir took possession of the house I didn't want him blaming the previous staff for anything untoward. I'd need help shoving my trunk up the stairs outside, so I put on my hat with the feathers and black ribbon, and went out to ask the neighbor's boot boy to assist me.

I found James sitting on the scullery stairs. "Morning, Mrs. Holloway," he sang out.

I jumped. "James," I said, hand on my heart. "Good heavens, you should not do that."

"Sorry, missus."

I felt awkward speaking to him now. Did James know? Were James and his father deceiving me together, or did Daniel keep his own son in the dark as to whoever he truly was?

"No matter," I said. "You're just the lad. Can you help me with my box? I have a cart on the way ..."

A cart pulled up in the street at that moment, and Daniel climbed down from it, his feet in scuffed boots landing outside the railings above me. I gulped and hastened back into the kitchen, not ready to encounter him just yet.

Daniel came ruthlessly inside. James darted past him to begin shoving my large, square trunk across the flagstones, but Daniel stood in the middle of the kitchen, his soft cap crumpled in his hand. His hair was its usual rumpled mess, his boots muddy, his loose neck cloth letting me glimpse a sliver of chest.

This was Daniel McAdam. The worker, unashamed of doing manual labor for a living. I had to have been mistaken about the other.

Daniel's good-natured expression was in place, as though he'd spent the night doing nothing more than drinking ale with his fellow delivery men in a public house.

"I thought you'd be agog to know what I learned from my chemist," he was saying.

I'd forgotten about the blasted chemist, and I *was* curious, drat him. "Did he discover what was in the sugar caster?"

"He did," Daniel said readily. "Nothing but sugar."

"Oh." I blinked, my thoughts rearranging themselves. "Then what was it doing in the plant pot? And why did Mrs. Watkins swear up and down that the caster hadn't been on the table at all?"

Daniel's gaze sharpened. "Mrs. Watkins, the housekeeper? When did she say this?"

"Yesterday afternoon, when I went to call on her. She's staying with her sister, Mrs. Herbert, who runs a boardinghouse. I believe I told you about the sister in Pimlico."

"And you went there to confront her alone?" Daniel's look was narrow and so angry that I blinked. "Without a word to me?"

"I left you a note." I pointed to the table, where the note had lain, though I'd put it on the fire this morning, no longer needed.

"You should not have gone alone," Daniel said sternly, his tone unforgiving. "You should have told me and had me come with you."

"To a ladies' boardinghouse?" I asked, my eyes widening. "They wouldn't have let you in. Besides, you had business of your own last night, did you not?"

Was it my imagination, or did he start? "I could have put any business off. This is important."

I had been avoiding looking straight at him, but now I lifted my chin and met his gaze.

"What *was* your business last evening?" I asked. "Did it take you to Oxford Street?"

Daniel focused hard on me as he went more still than I thought a human being could become. Everything affable about him fell away, and I was left looking at a man I did not know.

James and the neighbor's boot boy were pushing my box up the outside stairs—*thump, bump*—bantering with each other, laughing. Inside the kitchen, all was silence.

Daniel studied me with a gaze I could not read. No more warmth and helpful friendliness in his eyes, no more clever delivery man trying to find out who'd killed Sir Lionel. He was not even the cool gentleman I'd spied last night in Oxford Street. Daniel stood upright like a blade and looked as deadly.

"Then I *did* see you," I said softly.

His one, short nod lanced my heart. A rich gentleman did not pretend to be a poor one without ulterior reason— nor the other way around. Not very good reasons, either.

"The lady," I said, wanting to know the worst. "She is your wife?"

A shake of the head, as perfunctory as the nod. "No."

"Affianced?"

Daniel waited a bit before the next shake of head.

"Lover? I must admit, Mr. McAdam, I am quite curious."

"I know you are." His words were quiet, as were his eyes. "Mrs. Holloway, I have done you a great disservice."

He hadn't answered my last question. The knife in my heart twisted. "How so?" I asked. "By lying about who you truly are? I have known others who have done the same thing." The father of my daughter, for instance.

"I know."

It took a moment for me to comprehend those two simple words. *I know*. My beloved hat felt too tight on my head.

"What on earth do you mean by that?" I snapped. "You know what?"

Daniel's expression didn't change. "I know that the man who married you already had a living wife. That he abandoned you and left you to face the world alone, with a child. That you fought hard to gain the position you have. That you're a bloody good cook." The corners of his lips twitched as he said this last, but I'd never warm to his smile again.

"And yet," I said. "I know nothing about you."

"That is something I cannot remedy. Not yet. I regret that, Mrs. Holloway, believe me."

I noted that he no longer addressed me as *Kat*. "Well, I *don't* believe you. I was a fool ever to believe in you." I stopped the tears in my voice and cleared my throat. "Thank you for releasing me from prison, Mr. McAdam—or whatever your name is. Now, I must get on. I have to find another place so I may earn my keep, and my daughter's. Good day to you."

"I have already found another place for you."

I stopped in the act of pulling on a glove. "I beg your pardon?"

Daniel took a step toward me, cool and efficient. "The Earl of Clarendon, in Berkeley Square, needs a cook, one with excellent skills. You may start there anytime you wish."

Anger boiled through me, stronger than I'd felt in a very long time. How dare he? Daniel had caused me to make an idiot of myself, and now he sought to repair the damage by sending me off to the home of ... who? One of his dear friends? His relations?

"No, thank you," I said coldly. "I will go to my agency and see what is on their books. As is proper. Good *day*, Mr. McAdam."

"Kat, you need to take the position," Daniel said, his voice unyielding. "That and no other."

I thunked my small handbag onto the table. "Why? You tell me right now, Daniel. Why should I believe a word you say?"

His eyes flickered. "Because you will be safe there."

"*Safe?* From whom?"

"From those who wish you harm because of me." Every word was as hard as stones. "Sir Lionel died because of me. I did not kill him, but I caused his death. That is why I knew you never killed him—stabbed, poisoned, or otherwise, no matter what he'd done. When I learned he'd made advances to you, I warned him off and ensured that James or I watched you at all times. That is another reason I know you did not kill him—James or I would have seen."

I struggled for breath. "What are you talking about? *You* warned him off? What have you to do with Sir Lionel Leigh-Blasted-Bradbury?"

"Kat, believe me, I wish I could unburden myself to you, but I cannot. Not because I do not trust you, but because it wouldn't be safe for you. Or your daughter. Suffice it to say Sir Lionel mixed with people he should not have. In exchange for him continuing to live a free man, he was to tell me of all interactions he had with these people and the information they imparted to him. I believe that somehow, they got wind of what he was doing, and killed him."

"By poisoning my dinner?"

"By poisoning him *somehow*. I thought Mrs. Fuller had done so, making herself sick as a blind. But she was genuinely distressed and confused and grieving for her husband. I don't believe now she knew what dealings her husband had. The sugar caster ... I admit I have no idea how that fits in."

"I see." I said the words, but I saw nothing. I only knew that I had been made to think one way, when events had been something else entirely.

I could blame Daniel for deceiving me, but I mostly blamed myself. I'd been flattered by his attentions and preened myself because the handsome Daniel had interest in me.

"I thank you for explaining," I said, finishing drawing on my gloves. "I shall be boarding at Handley House in King Street, Covent Garden, if I can help you further in the matter of Sir Lionel. Good morning."

Daniel stepped in front of me. "I wish you to take the post in Berkeley Square."

His tone was firm, but I was tired of being told what to do. "No, thank you," I said. "I will find another position soon. I will send you word—somehow—of where if it will make you feel better."

I marched around him, straightening my hat as I went, and this time Daniel did not try to prevent me.

I went up the stairs without looking back, and to the

street. I told James where I needed the trunk to be sent, and made my way to catch a hansom cab to take me to my boardinghouse.

After settling myself in there, I paid a visit to my daughter.

CHAPTER 9

ONCE MY SO-CALLED HUSBAND HAD VANISHED INTO THE mists, and it became clear that I had never been legally married, I knew I'd have to work hard or my child would starve. Because I was unlikely to find a post as a disgraced woman with an illegitimate offspring in tow, I called myself by my maiden name—appending "Mrs." to it—and found a family who would foster my daughter.

The woman who took her in had been a friend to me since childhood. She'd been a kindly girl and was now a kindly woman. Her husband was good-natured and liked children, so my Grace lived with them and their four offspring in their tiny house and seemed to be happy.

Grace was never formal with me and unashamedly ran to throw her arms around me when I arrived. At ten years old, she was a beauty and possessed an understanding beyond her years. Grace did not resent the fact that I could not have her living with me where I cooked. She understood that we had to make our way in the world the best we could. One day, she said, she'd do the work and look after *me*.

I took her to walk with me in Hyde Park—our treat, after ices from a vendor. "Is everything all right, Mama?" she asked, slipping her hand in mine. Grace was always able to sense my moods.

I had not told my daughter about the horror of being arrested and imprisoned. I'd told my friend who looked after Grace but she'd agreed it wise not to mention it to the children, bless her.

"I am sad and confused, Grace," I said. "That is all."

"Because of the murder in Sir Lionel's house?"

So, she at least knew about that. Well, it is difficult to keep sensational news from a child, no matter how sheltered.

I admitted as much. "I will have to find another place. I'm not sure where it will be."

"I know *you* didn't poison anyone with your cooking, Mama," Grace said. "It must have been someone else."

"Yes, indeed. The puzzling thing is how." I pondered, forgetting to be cautious. "The arsenic was in no dish of mine. Mrs. Fuller said there was sugar; Mrs. Watkins says there was none. The sugar in the caster was tested—it was only sugar."

"Perhaps the caster was replaced with another," Grace said. "Afterward."

"An intriguing idea." I tapped my lower lip. "But why put the one with only sugar in the plant pot?"

"They meant to retrieve it later?" Grace, with her pointed face and fine hair, looked nothing more than a sweet-tempered child, but I knew what a quick mind her young face hid. "They meant to switch it for the clean one, but were interrupted. They didn't have time to fetch it out of the plant."

"Hm. A line I will have to investigate, I think."

"Will you tell me? If I'm right, will you tell me what happens?"

I squeezed her hand. "Of course I will."

We walked back to the omnibus and returned to my friend's home. My visit to Grace had lightened my heart. I never mentioned Daniel during this visit, and as I left my daughter, I realized he didn't matter. As long as I had Grace in my life, the attentions of deceitful gentlemen were of no moment to me.

I could not keep my thoughts entirely from Daniel, unfortunately, try as I might. As I made my way back to the boardinghouse, I wondered anew who was the lady in Oxford Street, the one he'd claimed was not his wife. Was she another person Daniel was deceiving? Or was he watching her, as he'd done with Sir Lionel?

He'd said Sir Lionel had been meeting with certain people and reporting what they told him to Daniel, in exchange for Daniel ... doing what? Not telling the police Sir Lionel was spying, or plotting crimes, or whatever it was? Who were these bad people Daniel feared would hurt me? Or was *Daniel* the bad person, and whoever Sir Lionel had been in league with were on the side of good?

No, I couldn't believe that last. Sir Lionel had been mean-spirited, rather stupid, and cunning at the same time. He could not be up to any good no matter what he did.

Grace's idea about the sugar caster interested me, though. I could imagine someone at the table stealthily pocketing the caster full of poison, meaning to replace it on the table with one without poison. But they hadn't managed it and had to stash the clean caster in the plant. Because the people at the table had started feeling ill and rushed away? Or had the person trying to replace the caster been interrupted by John or Sally coming to clear the table?

But then, why had Mrs. Watkins claimed there was no sugar caster at all? Copley had been too drunk to wait at table that night ... or had he been? Had he crept upstairs and set the poison on the table, removing it again when Mrs. Watkins's back was turned?

There was nothing for it. I had to speak with Copley.

This entailed finding out where he was being kept, now that he'd been arrested for stealing Sir Lionel's wine and silver. I regretted hastening away from Daniel so abruptly, because Daniel would know.

I knew I'd never find Daniel if I wanted to—even if I waited outside the house in Oxford Street, there was nothing to say he'd return there—so I hunted for James. Sure enough, James was lurking around Sir Lionel's house with the excuse of doing odd jobs in the neighborhood. Daniel had told him to continue watching the place, he said.

When I told him I needed to speak to his father, James nodded and told me to wait inside Sir Lionel's house. He handed me the key, said he'd send Daniel to me, and ran off with the energy of youth.

I entered through the back door and went to the only place in that house I was comfortable, the kitchen. The familiarity of it wrapped around me, wanting to draw me back.

Too bad Sir Lionel had been such a terrible master. Perhaps when his heir moved in, he'd need a cook. The heir would be of sunnier disposition, appreciate my food, and not make strange demands on me or disgust me with amorous advances. Miracles could happen.

To pass the time, I went into the butler's pantry and looked through the silver in the glass wall cabinets. All was as it should be, except of course for the missing pieces that

Copley had stolen. The settings all matched—the Leigh-Bradburys had used the same silversmith for years.

I frowned. I went to the housekeeper's room, fetched her keys, and returned to the pantry to open the cases. I studied the silver plates, candlesticks, and serving pieces like the chafing pan, a footed dish in the shape of a shell, the cruet stand, and a wine bucket. These pieces were larger, difficult to carry off without being noticed, which was no doubt why Copley had left them. Copley had taken smaller pieces—salt cellar, cups, spoons, finger bowls.

In a drawer below the glass-fronted shelves I found pots of silver polish and rags, as well as the velvet-lined boxes for the place settings. There were two unopened store-bought pots of polish with pink labels. A third pink-labeled pot had been opened, as had a pot of homemade polish—washing soda and salt, which the polisher would wet with lemon juice or vinegar before rubbing on the silver.

I took a delicate sniff of the homemade polish then closed the lid and slipped it into my pocket.

"Kat?" An alarmed voice was calling with Daniel's deep timbre. "Are you here? Where are you?"

I locked the cabinets, not hurrying, returned the keys to the housekeeper's room, and made my way to the kitchen.

Daniel breathed out when he saw me. "Damn it all, Kat ..."

"Please do not swear at me," I said calmly. "And I am *Mrs. Holloway*."

"Why did you have James find me?" The irritation and anger did not leave his voice.

"To take me to see Copley. I assume you know where they've put him?"

Daniel gave me a nod, his look hard. "At the moment, in hospital. He's seriously ill."

My brows lifted, my heart beating faster. "Oh, dear. In that case, I must speak to him at once."

❀

COPLEY HAD BEEN JAILED AT NEWGATE, BUT HAD BEEN taken to the infirmary. He lay in a bed in a long, mostly empty ward. The ward was gray and unfriendly, windowless and gloomy, but it was a step better than the common cells. Just.

Copley looked terrible. His face was as gray as the walls and had a yellow cast to it. His entire body trembled, and when we approached, he turned over in his bed and vomited into the bucket at his bedside.

The air around him stank. I took a handkerchief from my bag and pressed it to my nose.

"Copley," Daniel said. "Sorry to see you so wretched, old chap."

Daniel was in his scruffy clothes again, holding his cloth cap. He looked like a carter or furniture mover, come to help the neat and tidy woman at his side. When we'd entered the jail, however, we'd been treated deferentially and led to Copley without question.

"What d'ye want?" Copley rasped. "Let me die in peace. Why'd ye bring *her* here?"

"You might not die," I said cheerfully. "Mrs. Fuller managed to recover. I imagine because someone politely replenished the sugar on her tart for her instead of making her shake it on herself. *You* probably only held the caster long enough to hide it in the plant pot, and luckily, you wore gloves."

Daniel glanced at me, perplexed, and Copley blinked. "What th' devil are ye going on about, woman?"

"It is simple," I said. "*You* took the sugar caster from the table." I pointed a gloved finger at Copley. "You did so when you thought no one was looking. Maybe when you and John were clearing up? Or John was clearing up while you helped yourself to any leftover food and drink." Those plates had been *very* clean when they'd returned to the kitchen. "You didn't have time to do anything with the caster — perhaps someone nearly caught you with it. Or you hid it when I sent John for the police and was downstairs dressing, fearing it would be found on you or in your room if there was a search. You stole many of the smaller pieces that night and stashed them to fetch later. Why not the sugar caster too?"

"Yes, all right," Copley growled. "I plucked the bloody thing off the table when I saw it, but Mrs. Watkins and John were right on top of me, so I hid it in the plant."

"Why not take it back downstairs with the other pieces?" I asked. I thought I knew the answer, but I wanted Copley to say it in front of Daniel.

"Because it weren't ours," Copley said angrily. "Not Sir Lionel's. I thought maybe them Fullers brought their own caster with them and forgot and left it behind. John would return it to our cabinet, not knowing the difference, then Mrs. Interfering Watkins would find it and send it back to Mrs. Fuller."

Daniel listened with a sparkle in his eyes. "You're saying the caster didn't belong in the house?"

Copley wet his lips, but he was losing strength, so I spoke for him. Copley really was a pitiful wretch.

"The sugar caster was made by a different silversmith," I explained. "If you check its hallmark, you'll see. Sir Lionel's family has used the same silversmith down the generations. All the pieces match. But I advise you, Mr. McAdam, that if you do handle the caster again, or your chemist does, please wear gloves. And ask your chemist to check the contents of *this*."

I brought out the small pot of homemade silver polish, which was still wrapped in my handkerchief. I set pot and handkerchief into Daniel's outstretched hands—which were covered with thick workman's gloves. He handled the pot with respect, but looked at me in bewilderment.

I turned back to Copley. "Did you or John ever use homemade silver polish?"

"No." Copley's voice was weak. "I used the stuff from Finch's. Much better for keeping off the tarnish."

"That's what I thought. Thank you, Copley. I do hope you mend soon."

"Would if the buggers in this place would give me a decent drop to drink."

I gave Copley a nod, pleased with him, and excited by what he'd told me. "That is possibly true." I said. "Shall we depart, Mr. McAdam?"

DANIEL INSISTED ON HIRING A HANSOM CAB TO TAKE US back through London. I didn't like to sit so close to him in the small vehicle, but rain had begun to pelt down, and I would have to endure the annoyance for a dry ride to King Street.

Daniel began speaking as though we had no tension between us. "You believe the poison was *on* the caster itself?" he asked. "Coating it?"

I nodded. "Test the homemade silver polish I gave you. If it were rubbed into a paste onto the caster, anyone lifting it would get it on their fingers. Then if they ate bits of food

—eventually, they would ingest enough of whatever it is to make them ill. Or the poison could sink in through the skin. I'm not certain about that. Perhaps it would work by both means."

"Mrs. Watkins didn't take ill," Daniel pointed out. "If she handled the caster ... though she insists it wasn't there. What about poor John? We need to find him."

"John always wore gloves when waiting at table. Mrs. Watkins did not, but she was right as rain when I saw her yesterday, obviously not ill from poison. It is bad manners for ladies and gentlemen to wear gloves at table, and so the diners had no protection."

"But Copley?" Daniel frowned as he puzzled things out. "Why did it take him some time to become ill? Butlers wear gloves while they're setting up or serving at table, as footmen do."

He knew a lot about butlers, did he? "True, but I've watched how Copley sometimes takes his gloves off."

I demonstrated, delicately tugging at the fingers of one glove with my teeth, loosening it before drawing it off. "This is why I do not believe Copley poisoned Sir Lionel and the Fullers. If he'd coated the caster with poison, he'd have been more careful."

Daniel made a sound of agreement. "So, Copley is a thief, not a murderer."

This wouldn't help Copley much—he'd stolen items of high value and might be hanged for it, or perhaps transported if someone spoke up for him. Poor drunken fool.

"I will visit Mrs. Fuller again," Daniel said briskly. "And see if the caster came from her household. It is still possible *she* did the poisoning—or someone employed by her at her instruction."

I didn't think so, but I said nothing. Mrs. Fuller would

have been certain to take the caster away and dispose of it, I would think, even if she'd deliberately made herself ill. The caster would not have been there for Copley to try to steal.

When the hansom stopped in front of my boarding-house, I began to descend, but Daniel caught my hand and drew me back.

"I want you to take the post I spoke about," he said. "I will tell Clarendon's housekeeper to expect you for an interview."

I'd had enough. I jerked from his grasp but remained in the hansom. "Let me speak plainly, Mr. McAdam. You have deceived me at every turn. Believe me, I am vexed with myself for letting you. However, I have made my way in this world on my own for a number of years now, and I will continue to do so. I am grateful for what you have done for me—I sincerely thank you for saving me from the magistrates—but I have my life to get on with. I am not a silly woman; I will take every precaution for my own safety."

How this speech affected Daniel, I could not tell. He only regarded me with calm eyes—the eyes I'd once thought so handsome—and did not change expression.

"Very well," he said, his voice cool. "Then I will bid you good night."

I made a noise of exasperation. The least he could do was look contrite. He'd withdrawn, the affable Daniel gone, a cool shell in his place.

So be it.

My heart ached as I scrambled down from the hansom and made for my lodgings. I'd fallen for Daniel McAdam, whoever he was, but that Daniel did not exist. This was the painful truth I had to accept, and continue with my life.

CHAPTER 10

I SAW NOTHING OF DANIEL OR JAMES FOR THE NEXT FEW days. I unpacked my box at the boardinghouse and visited my agency to find another post.

Difficult this time of year. Families of the big Mayfair houses were mostly gone to the country, and those who hadn't left already were packing to head out for the hunting and shooting seasons.

After that would be Christmas and New Years', the majority of society families not returning until spring. So many already had cooks installed in their London houses, cooks who went on preparing meals for the skeleton staff in the winter or for renters.

The minor gentry also went to the country or else they wanted a woman who'd plunk a joint of beef and watery potatoes in front of the family every evening and naught else. At least when Sir Lionel had been baiting me, he'd stretched my abilities and let me create meals worthy of a master chef.

I came away from the agency the days I visited it

depressed and disgruntled. I might have to swallow my pride, hunt up Daniel, and take the post at Berkeley Square.

I did make a journey south of the river to see Sally, who had indeed returned home. She flew at me and hugged me, having believed me already convicted and hanged even in this short time. She was not much help, though. She knew nothing of the sugar caster or of the extra box of polish. She wasn't allowed to polish the silver, only to wash plates and crockery. The sugar caster never came near her sink, and she never went to the dining room or Sir Lionel's library.

She had nothing but honest innocence and confusion in her eyes, and I came away, unenlightened. She was about to start a new post in another kitchen, she said, thankfully. Her family needed her wages.

James arrived at the boardinghouse to visit me about a week after that. He did not actually come to the back door and request to speak with me; he simply skulked about in the street until I went out.

He told me with his usual cheerfulness that Daniel had found the footman, John, who was in Dorset, as I'd suspected. John was in raring good health, thank the Lord. Daniel had asked John to give him the gloves he'd used when serving that last meal and taken them away.

Daniel's chemist had tested the caster and found it coated with arsenic. That sort of thing could seep through the fingers or be eaten, with the same result—horrible illness and probable death. It could happen quickly, or take time—there must have been much of the stuff on the caster. Mrs. Fuller had indeed been very lucky.

When James finished giving me this news, I decided to ask him what I had been wondering about him point blank. "James, does it bother you that your father is not what he seems?"

The lad considered my question, his father's brown eyes in his smudged young face regarding me calmly. "I lived with the charwoman, as I said. She had a man also boarding in her house who wanted to use me as his fancy boy and beat me regular when I refused. One day, me dad—Mr. McAdam, as ye know him—came along, had the man arrested, and took me away."

James rubbed under his lower lip. "At the time, I thought me dad were the same—a man what liked boys, only he had a few more coins to rub together. But he got angry when I accused him of that. He told me he was my pa and would take care of me now. He showed me how we looked alike, and he knew all about my ma—may she rest in peace—and eventually, I believed him."

He shrugged. "Dad comes and goes all the time. I never asked where. If he has a posh house and family besides me —well some gents do, don't they? A house for the wife and one for the mistress? A house for his legitimate family, and one for his by-blows?"

I listened with mixed emotions. Daniel had been good to rescue James and make sure he was well looked after. On the other hand, James made a true point about gentlemen leading double lives.

"Thank you for telling me," was all I could think to say.

James grinned. "Don't look so primmed up, missus. I've always known I weren't the Prince of Wales. I'm a gent's bastard, Dad's kind to me, and I get by."

Would that I could take such a casual attitude. Daniel indeed led a double life—a triple one, perhaps.

However, I'd had my fill of men who did whatever they pleased, never mind who they trampled over or cast aside along their way, uncaring of how many women bore their children and were left to raise them on their own.

"Thank you, James, for telling me the news. I know you had no need to keep me informed."

"Thought you'd like to know. Dad said you'd be interested but didn't think you'd want to see him."

"He thought right." I dug into my pocket and pulled out a coin, but James lifted his hands and stepped away.

"Don't insult me now," he said. "I did ya a favor." He renewed his grin, tipped his cap, and jogged away into the busy London street.

WHEN NEXT I HAD THE TIME, I MADE MY WAY TO PIMLICO to visit Mrs. Watkins. Daniel might be questioning Mrs. Fuller and her staff up and down, but I wanted to quiz Mrs. Watkins again about that bloody sugar caster.

I met her in the sitting room of her sister's boardinghouse. She was having the same difficulty as I in landing a new post, but I imagined she'd find one before I did. More Londoners needed housekeepers while they were away than wanted to bother with cooks, especially cooks of my calibre.

"Perhaps I should open a restaurant," I said. "Though where I'd find the funds for such an endeavor, I have no idea."

"You'd soon tire of it," Mrs. Watkins said with conviction. "Instead of cooking for one table that complains, there'd be many tables complaining all night. My sister ran a restaurant for a time, but gave it up for a boardinghouse. An easier task, she says."

The maid brought tea, Mrs. Watkins poured, and we drank.

"Are you certain about that sugar caster?" I asked after we'd sipped.

Mrs. Watkins coughed, set down her teacup, and wiped her mouth with a napkin. "The one you asked me about before? Of course I am certain, Mrs. Holloway. I would have noticed it."

I took another sip of tea. The service was elegant, delicate porcelain with sprays of pink roses on it. No silver in sight, except for the small teaspoons. "You see, Mrs. Watkins, John says he saw the caster there. So did Mrs. Fuller. And Copley stole it, the wretch, hiding it to take away later. So you must have either been extremely unobservant, or are telling me an untruth."

"Well, you may believe what you like." Mrs. Watkins's indignation made her cup tremble as she picked it up again. "John is not bright, Copley only saw a silver piece he could steal, and Mrs. Fuller is obviously lying. *She* must have poisoned the meal, perhaps in the wine. They poured that themselves."

I sipped tea again and gave a little shrug. "It may be as you say."

"I will tell you what I think." Mrs. Watkins leaned forward, the cameo at her throat moving. "That delivery man, Daniel McAdam, as was always hanging about the house. He must have had something to do with it. There's something not quite pukka about him."

I nodded, saying nothing.

I had, in fact, considered Daniel as a suspect. He certainly was good at misleading. If he'd been watching Sir Lionel as he'd said, having Sir Lionel report to him, perhaps he'd begun to see the man as a danger.

Sir Lionel could report to these bad people that Daniel was requiring Sir Lionel to give him information. To shut Sir Lionel's mouth, Daniel poisoned the caster and got it to the table somehow—perhaps through Copley. When I was arrested for his deed, he felt remorse and decided to help me.

I had not pursued this line of thought, because my emotions about Daniel were jumbled, and I refused to trust my own judgment where he was concerned, at least not for the moment.

The maid brought in a stack of clean plates and began to lay them on the long table on the other side room. Tea would be served to the other tenants soon, and I ought to go.

I rose, but instead of leaving, I walked to the table. The maid was setting at one end a silver cream pot, sugar bowl with lumps of sugar in it, and sugar caster for the finer sugar that would be sprinkled on tea cakes.

I took up the caster, turned it over, and examined the hallmark, finding it identical to the one on the caster we'd found at Sir Lionel's.

The maid, ignoring me, moved to the other end of the table and laid out a twin of the cream pot and sugar bowl — two sets for a large number of diners.

I moved to her, lifting the second sugar bowl as though admiring it. "Do you have two of everything?"

"We do," the maid said, continuing to lay out forks and spoons. "It's not posh silver, but it's nice looking, I think. Except for the second sugar caster. That's gone missing."

I turned around to Mrs. Watkins, the caster and sugar bowl in my hand. Her face had become a peculiar shade of green.

"So the caster *didn't* come from Mrs. Fuller," I said to Mrs. Watkins. "It came from here."

A number of things happened at once. The maid looked up in surprise, her expression holding nothing but bewilderment. The door to the parlor opened and Mrs. Watkins's sister rushed inside. Mrs. Watkins left the sofa and came at me in a run.

Certain Mrs. Watkins meant to attack me, I held up my hands protectively, the silver pieces still in them. Her sister, Mrs. Herbert, came after her.

At the last minute, Mrs. Watkins swung around, putting herself across me like a shield. "Leave her be," she said swiftly. "Mrs. Holloway knows nothing. She'll say nothing."

I stared in surprise at Mrs. Herbert, the sister, and then realized that I'd seen her before—in a photo in Sir Lionel Leigh-Bradbury's library. She was older now—that photo had been of a fresh-faced young woman. I recognized the straight nose and regular features, the happy eyes of that girl. Now cynicism and age lined her face.

"Who are you?" I blurted out.

"I was his affianced," Mrs. Herbert snapped. "I broke the engagement when I realized what a parsimonious, evil little man he was. I married a better man. And then Sir Lionel ruined him. My Charles died in disgrace and penury, because of *him*."

Thoughts rearranged themselves rapidly in my head. Mrs. Watkins swearing the sugar caster hadn't been there, John swearing it had, and Copley plucking it from the table after supper and hiding it.

"You gave Copley the poisoned polish and told him he must use it, didn't you?" I asked Mrs. Herbert. "Paying him a nice sum for his services? I have no idea if he knew what it was—he might have been more careful if he did. Then you told Copley to carry the caster to the table. I shouldn't wonder if you promised him he could have it. If his greed made him ill or killed him, so much the better."

Mrs. Watkins, whom I'd never seen less than dignified, shook with tears. "Oh, Letty. How could you?"

"I have no remorse," Mrs. Herbert said, her head high. "Sir Lionel held a minor government post, and he filled enough ears with lies to have my Charles investigated for treason. The case dragged on and on until Charles sickened and died. He was proved innocent in the end, but too late for him. Sir Lionel killed my husband, as good as stabbing him through the heart."

"Is that why you stuck my carving knife into him?" I asked. "To make a point?"

Mrs. Herbert looked momentarily puzzled. "I never went into the house. Or near it."

Of course she hadn't. That way, nothing would connect her to the crime. The damning sugar caster would be taken away by Copley, cleaned and sold. No one would know it came from Mrs. Herbert's house.

But Copley had bungled it, lost his nerve, possibly when John had come to clear the table, and stuffed the caster into the rubber tree's pot to be retrieved later. He'd been caught going back into the house to find it and the other pieces he'd stashed, while the poison was working inside him to make him sick.

I could picture Copley creeping up to Sir Lionel's library, where the man sat, dead already, to stick my carving knife into his back to both ensure the man was dead and throw blame upon me. The scullery maid had heard him moving about and came to fetch me, so Copley had to flee back upstairs and pretend to be just waking up, no time to pick up the caster.

And then the house had been full of police, rambling all over it for the next day or so, and Copley had made himself scarce to wait until the house was empty again. He couldn't have known that I'd be released from prison and Daniel would be watching to catch him.

"How could you?" Mrs. Watkins repeated. "A second man died, and his wife was taken ill."

"Copley is ill as well," I put in.

Mrs. Watkins went on, ignoring me. "Any of us in that house could have touched that piece or used the polish, Letty. John, the scullery maid, Mrs. Holloway, even me."

Mrs. Herbert scowled. "Would serve you right for working for that monster, taking his money."

"I did it for *you.*" Mrs. Watkins began to sob. "I was trying to discover how to ruin him. For you!"

Mrs. Herbert paused at that, then her expression hardened. "I am not sorry that Sir Lionel is dead. My Charles has been avenged."

With that, she came at me in a rage. Mrs. Watkins caught her sister before she could reach me. I was about to spring forward and give Mrs. Herbert a good thump, when the woman's heel caught on the carpet, and she collapsed to the sofa.

The strength went out of her, her face growing pale, her pupils narrowing to pinpricks. Her breath came in gasps, full-blown hysteria on its way.

Mrs. Watkins sank down beside her sister, crying as well, the two of them becoming a wailing mess. The maid looked on in shock.

I put down the silver pieces, opened my bag, removed my smelling salts, and went to the two ladies, waving the little bottle under their noses.

Mrs. Watkins sat up abruptly, but Mrs. Herbert remained slumped against the sofa's back, breathing hard. I could see the innocent beauty she'd been before she'd been trapped by Sir Lionel. Sir Lionel had been an odious man, and I couldn't help believe he'd been justly punished.

On the other hand, there was nothing to say Mrs.

Herbert wouldn't simply become a crazed poisoner. She'd not worried a bit about the rest of us being sickened as well, from the Fullers—people she'd never met—to her own sister. In addition, I'd almost been tried for the crime, my fate, certain hanging.

I took from my bag the vial of laudanum I'd brought for the purpose of subduing Mrs. Watkins—because I'd thought it she who'd poisoned Sir Lionel and the Fullers. While Mrs. Herbert lay gasping like a fish, I held her nose and poured the laudanum into her mouth, forcing her to swallow.

Mrs. Watkins was still crying, but she made no move to stop me. Perhaps she too worried that her sister had gone a bit mad.

After that, I strode out of the room and out of the house, in search of a constable. I nearly ran into James, who was hovering near the railings that separated the house from the street.

"Gracious, what are you doing here?" I asked him.

"Following you," James said. "Dad told me to. You all right?"

"No. Fetch a constable, will you? I've found the poisoner of Sir Lionel Leigh-Bradbury."

I had the satisfaction of seeing young James gape at me before his face cleared, and he beamed.

"I knew you could do it!" he shouted, then was away in a flash, running to find the nearest constable.

CHAPTER 11

I WAS NEVER CERTAIN WHAT HAPPENED TO MRS. HERBERT. She was arrested, likely shut in to the same kind of cell I had been, her trial scheduled.

I walked away from Mrs. Watkins, her house, Sir Lionel's, and all the rest of it. I visited my daughter again, holding her close until I could breathe once more.

I knew, though, that I'd never be free of it in my heart. I'd lived in a house where a man had been poisoned and died, and I'd condemned a woman to death for it. She'd go to the crowded cell in Newgate where I had waited in fear, only she would not be set free.

I'd met Daniel, half fallen in love with him and had been sorely deceived by him. After Grace's father deserted me, I'd vowed I'd never let a man trick me again, and yet the first fine pair of eyes I saw, I was off. I badly needed to curb these tendencies.

My agency did at last find me a post a few weeks later, in a large house in Richmond. The lady of the house had heard of my cooking from my previous employer, Mrs. Pauling, and was happy to have me.

Richmond was a bit far from my daughter for my taste, but the pay was good, I had an ample number of days out, and it was only a short train ride to the heart of London. Perhaps I could bring Grace out to Richmond to visit me, and we could walk along the river and see the sights. She'd like that.

The house was a good place, with the kitchen run efficiently—even more so once I'd taken command.

One cold winter day, as I went over a list of what I needed to prepare supper, a gentleman walked, unannounced, into the kitchen.

This house had a large servants' hall across the passage from the big kitchen, its own laundry rooms, housekeeper's parlor, a butler's pantry far larger than the closet-sized one at Sir Lionel's, and a fairly cozy bedroom down the corridor for me. The corridor and rooms were always teeming with the servants needed to tend a large household.

The gentleman could only have entered the servants' area by coming down the stairs that led to the main house, or in through the scullery door from outside. Either way, he'd have been noticed and politely questioned by the three strapping footman, the butler—who was a proper butler and not a wastrel like Copley—and the housekeeper, long before he reached the kitchen.

However, no one seemed to have stopped him, and the entire staff, when I looked around, was startlingly absent.

The gentleman was Daniel. He was dressed in what I would say were middle-class clothes—not so posh as the ones I'd seen him wear in Oxford Street, but not so scruffy as his work trousers and boots. His hair was tamed but not pomaded, a bit rumpled, but combed flat. He set a hat and pair of leather gloves on my kitchen table and rested one hip on the tabletop as though perfectly at home.

"It is good to see you, Kat."

I waited a few heartbeats until I was certain my voice would not crack. "Good day, Mr. McAdam. How is James?"

"He is well. Working." A wry look entered his eyes. "That is, when he's not off doing what he bloody well pleases."

"Ah." I knew Daniel wanted me to smile, so I did not. "What brings you to Richmond?"

"Hope." Daniel's gaze fixed on me. "I want us to be friends again, Kat. Like before."

"Oh, do you now?" I laid down the list of foodstuffs and clicked the pencil next to it. "Well, I'm certain *you* would feel much better if I agreed. If I forgive you, you will be much relieved."

Daniel lost his forced, polite look. "Damn it, Kat."

He came to me and pulled me around to face him, holding my arms with his hard hands. I felt the solid lip of the table behind me as I looked up into his angry face. Daniel's eyes had a dangerous glint in them. I had no idea what he was about to do, but I lifted my chin.

"Threatening me will not help your cause," I said crisply. "Remember, I'm a dab hand with a knife."

Rage turned to frustrated amusement. Daniel cupped my face with a firm hand, leaned down, and kissed my mouth. "I could fall in love with you, Kat Holloway," he said, his voice low.

My heart fluttered like a dove's wings. However, I refused to let him know that I could fall stupidly in love with him in return.

"The lady in Oxford Street might be a bit put out," I

said. "Mr. McAdam dallying with a cook? Not the done thing."

Daniel made an impatient noise. "The lady in Oxford Street is—was—an assignment. Like Sir Lionel. Both of those are finished."

"Are they?" My heart beat thickly, and I could barely think. The kiss had been a rather fine one, Daniel stood close, and my coherence was running away. "You should be on to the next thing then."

"I am. Unfortunately. But I had to ..." Daniel trailed off, his fingers on my face softening. "I wanted to make sure you were well, Kat."

"I am," I said, surprised my voice was so steady. "As you can see. This is a fine kitchen."

"It is." Daniel drew a breath, lowered his hand, and deliberately stepped away from me. "What is it you prepare tonight, Mrs. Holloway?"

I had to consult my list, because my menu had just gone clean out of my head. "Beef bourguignon. Sorrel soup, fish in white wine, and lemon tart to finish."

"Ah, Kat, you make my mouth water." Daniel kissed his fingers to me, slanting me his wicked look. "If I happen to be passing in my delivery wagon after supper, might I beg a scrap or two to sustain me?"

He wanted to transform back to the Daniel I knew best, did he? "What about this?" I asked, waving my hand at his suit. "This ... banker's clerk, or whatever you are? Where will he be?"

"Gone after this evening, I'm afraid."

"I see. Will I ever, perchance, meet the real Daniel McAdam?"

Daniel lost his smile. "Perhaps one day. Yes, definitely one day, I'll bare my soul to you, Kat. I promise."

My voice went quiet. "Will I like what I see when you do?"

"I don't know." The words rang true. "But I believe I am willing to risk it."

I had no idea what to say to that, or what I ought to do. Forgive him? Turn my back on him forever? Do neither, and go on with him as though nothing had happened?

One thing was certain—there was far more to Daniel than met the eye. I was curious enough, blast it, to want to learn everything I could about the man.

"In that case," I said, taking up my pencil again. "If you are not too late, I might save back a bit of lemon tart for you."

Daniel's smile returned. "I would enjoy that very much."

We shared a look. Daniel took up his hat and gloves, giving me a bow.

"You have more skills than cooking," he said. "Perhaps you will help me on another hunt someday."

I shivered. "Indeed no. Once was enough for me."

"Was it?" Daniel carefully pulled on his gloves. "We'll see. Good afternoon, Mrs. Holloway. I look forward to speaking with you again."

And I, you, I wanted to say, but held my tongue. "Good afternoon, Mr. McAdam."

He shot me a grin, came back to me, kissed me on the lips, and strode out, whistling.

AUTHOR'S NOTE

Thank you for reading! *A Soupçon of Poison* was one of the first historical mysteries I wrote—or at least started to write. I found the opening chapter for this novella stuck in a file in a box when cleaning out my flooded house. I enjoyed the chapters and remembered my plans for the characters of Kat and Daniel, so I dusted off the story (literally), wrote the rest of it, and published it.

Because of the great response from readers to Kat Holloway and Daniel McAdam, I decided to continue her series as I'd planned to do before my writing career went in a different direction.

While *Soupçon of Poison* is a novella, the remaining books in the series will be full-length novels, published under my Jennifer Ashley name.

Kat's adventures continue in *Death Below Stairs*, Book 1 of the Kat Holloway Below Stairs mysteries. An excerpt follows—plus see the Also by Ashley Gardner and Jennifer Ashley page at the end of this anthology for links to more information. Kat has her own website as well:

www.katholloway.com.

I hope you enjoy this heroine and series!

All my best,

Jennifer Ashley

(aka Ashley Gardner)

EXCERPT: DEATH BELOW STAIRS

KAT HOLLOWAY BELOW-STAIRS MYSTERIES, BOOK 1

Chapter One

LONDON, MARCH 1881

I had not been long at my post in Mayfair, on Mount Street, when my employer's sister came to some calamity.

I must say I was not shocked that such a thing happened, because when a woman takes on the dress and bad habits of a man, she cannot be surprised at the disapprobation of others when she is found out. Lady Cynthia's problems, however, turned out to be only the beginning of a vast tangle and a long, dangerous business.

But I am ahead of myself. I am a cook, one of the finest in London if I do say it, and also one of the youngest to be made head cook in a lavish household. I'd worked some time in the winter at a house in Richmond, and it was a good position, but the family desired to sell up and move to the Lake District, and I was loath to leave the environs of London for my own, rather private, reasons.

Back went my name on the books, and the agency at last wrote to my new lodgings at Tottenham Court Road to say they had found a place that might suit. Taking their letter with me, I went along to the house of one Lord Rankin in Mount Street, descending from the omnibus at South Audley Street and walking the rest of the way on foot.

I expected to speak to the housekeeper, but upon arrival, the butler, a tall, handsome specimen who rather preened himself, took me up the stairs to meet the lady of the house in her small study.

She was Lady Rankin, wife of the prodigiously wealthy baron who owned this abode. The baron's wealth came not from the fact that he was an aristocrat, the butler, Mr. Davis, had already confided in me—the estate had been nearly bankrupt when Lord Rankin had inherited it. Rather, Lord Rankin was a deft dabbler in the City and had earned money by wise investment long before the cousin who'd held the title had died, conveniently childless.

When I first beheld Lady Rankin, I was surprised she'd asked for me, because she seemed too frail to hold up her head, let alone conduct an interview with a new cook.

"Mrs. Holloway, ma'am," Davis said. He ushered me in, bowed, and withdrew.

The study in which I found myself was small and overtly feminine. The walls were covered in yellow moiré, the curtains at the windows, white lace. Framed mirrors along with paintings of gardens and picturesque country lanes adorned the walls. A delicate, gilt-legged table from the last century reposed in the middle of the room, with an equally graceful chair behind it. A scroll-backed chaise, covered with shawls, sat near the desk.

Lady Rankin was in the act of rising from the chaise as we entered, as though she had grown weary waiting for me and retired to it. She moved listlessly to the chair behind her desk, sat upon it, and pulled a paper in front of her with a languid hand.

"Mrs. Holloway?" she asked.

Davis had just announced me, so there was no doubt who I was, but I nodded. Lady Rankin looked me over. I remained standing in the exact center of the carpet in my second-best frock, a brown wool jacket buttoned to my throat, and my second-best hat of light brown straw perching on my thick coil of dark hair.

Lady Rankin's garment was white, filmy, and high necked, its bodice lined with pearls. Her hair was pale gold, her cheeks thin and bloodless. She could hardly be thirty summers, but rather than being childlike, she was ethereal, as though a gust of wind could puff her away.

She glanced at whatever paper was in front of her—presumably a letter from my agency—and then over the desk at me. Her eyes were a very light blue and, in contrast to her angel-like appearance, were rather hard.

"You are very young," she observed. Her voice was light, as thin as her bones.

"I am nearly thirty," I answered stiffly.

When a person thought of a cook, they pictured an older woman who was either a shrew in the kitchen or kind-hearted and a bit slow. The truth was that cooks came in all ages, shapes, and temperaments. I happened to be nine and twenty, plump and brown haired, and kind enough, I hoped, but I brooked no nonsense.

"I meant for a cook," Lady Rankin said. "Our last cook was nearly eighty. She is . . . gone. Living with her daughter." She added the last quickly, as though fearing I'd take *gone* to mean to heaven.

I had no idea how Lady Rankin wished me to answer

this information, so I only said, "I assure you, my lady, I have been quite well trained."

"Yes." Lady Rankin lifted the letter. The single page seemed too heavy for her, so she let it fall. "The agency sings your praises, as do your references. Well, you will find this an easy place. Charles—Lord Rankin—wishes his supper on the table when he arrives home from the City at eight. Davis will tell you his lordship's favorite dishes. There will be three at table this evening, Lord Rankin, myself, and my . . . sister."

Her thin lip curled the slightest bit as she pronounced this last. I thought nothing of it at the time and only gave her another nod.

Lady Rankin slumped back into her chair as though the speech had taken the last of her strength. She waved a limp hand at me. "Go on, then. Davis and Mrs. Bowen will explain things to you."

I curtsied politely and took my leave. I wondered if I shouldn't summon Lady Rankin's maid to assist her to bed but left the room before I did anything so presumptuous.

The kitchen below was to my liking. It was nowhere near as modern and large as the one I'd left in Richmond, but I found it what I was used to and comfortable.

This house was what I called a double town house—that is, instead of having a staircase hall on one side and all the rooms on the other, it had rooms on both sides of a middle hall. Possibly two houses had been purchased and knocked into one at some time and the second staircase walled off for use by the staff.

Below stairs, we had a large servants' hall across a passage from the kitchen. Past the kitchen on the same passage was a scullery—which also connected to the kitchen and had a door that led out and up the outside stairs. On the other side of the kitchen was a larder, and beyond that a laundry room, a room for folding clean linens, the house-keeper's parlor, and the butler's pantry, which included the wine cellar. Mr. Davis showed me over each, as proud as though he owned the house himself.

The kitchen was a wide, square room with windows that gave onto the street above. Two dressers full of dishes lined the white-painted walls, and a hanging rack of gleaming copper pans dangled above the stove. A thick-legged table squatted in the middle of the floor, one long enough on which to prepare several dishes at once, with space at the end for someone to sit and shell peas or whatever I needed them to do.

The kitchen's range had been neatly fitted into what had been a fireplace, and this fireplace was large, the stove high enough that I wouldn't have to stoop or kneel to cook. I'd had to kneel down on hard stones at one house—where I hadn't stayed long—and it had taken some time for my knees and back to recover.

Here I could stand and use the hot plates that were able to accommodate five pots at once, with the fire below behind a thick metal door. The fire could be stoked without disturbing the ovens to either side of it—one oven had racks that could be moved so several things could be baked at the same time, and the other spacious oven could have air pumped though it to aid roasting.

I was pleased with the stove, which was quite new, likely requested by the wealthy lordship who liked his meal served precisely when he arrived home. I could bake bread in one oven while roasting a large joint of meat in the other, with all my pots going above at once. The greatest challenge to a cook is to have every dish ready and hot at the same time so none come to the table colder than any other. To aid this, a shelf above the stove that ran the length of it could keep finished food in warmth while the rest of the meal was finished.

The sink was in the scullery so that dirty water and entrails from fish and fowl could be kept well away from the rest of my food. The larder, a long room lined with shelves and with a flagstone floor, looked well stocked, though I'd be the judge of that. From a cursory glance, I saw bags of flour, jars of barley and other grains, dried herbs hanging from the beams, spices in tinned copper jars with labels on the front, and crates of vegetables and fruit pushed back against the coolest walls.

The kitchen itself was fairly dark, as most kitchens were, despite the high windows, so we would have to burn lamps or gaslight all the time, but otherwise, I was satisfied.

The staff to run this lofty house in Mayfair wasn't as large as I'd expect, but they seemed a diligent lot. I had an assistant, a rather pretty girl of about seventeen who seemed genial enough—she reminded me of myself at that age. Whether her assistance would be useful remained to be seen. Four footmen appeared and disappeared from the servants' hall, as did half a dozen maids.

Mrs. Bowen, the housekeeper, was thin and birdlike, and I did not know her. This surprised me, because when you are in service in London, you come to know those in the great houses, or at least *of* them. However, I'd never heard of Mrs. Bowen, which either meant she'd not been in London long or hadn't long been a housekeeper.

I was disturbed a bit by her very thin figure, because I preferred to work with those who enjoyed eating. Mrs. Bowen looked as though she took no more than a biscuit every day, and then only a digestive. On the other hand, I'd known a spindly man who could eat an entire platter of pork and potatoes followed by a hearty dose of steak and kidney pie and never had to loosen his clothing.

Mr. Davis, whom I soon put down as a friendly old gossip, gave me a book with notes from the last cook of what the master preferred for his dinners. I was pleased to find the dishes uncomplicated but not so dull that any chop-house could have provided the meals. I could do well here.

I carefully unpacked my knives, including a brand-new, sharp carver, took my apron from my valise, and started right in.

The young assistant, a bit unhappy that I wanted her help immediately, was soon chatting freely with me while she measured out flour and butter for my brioche. She gave her name as Sinead.

She pronounced it *Shin-aide* and gave me a hopeful look. I thought it a beautiful name, conjuring mists over the green Irish land—a place I'd never been—but this was London, and a cook's kitchen was no place for an Irish nymph.

"It's quite lovely," I said as I cut butter into the flour. "But I'm sorry, my girl, we can't be having Sinead. People get wrong ideas. You must have a plain English name. What did the last cook call you?"

Sinead let out a sigh, her dreams of romance dashed. "Ellen," she said, resigned. I saw by her expression that she disliked the name immensely.

I studied her dark brown hair, blue eyes, and pale skin in some sympathy. Again, she reminded me of myself— poised on the edge of life and believing wonderful things would happen to her. Alas, I'd found out only too soon the bitter truth. Sinead's prettiness would bring her only trouble, well I knew, and life was apt to dash her hopes again and again.

"Ellen," I repeated, trying to sound cheerful. "A nice,

solid name, but not too dull. Now, then, Ellen, I'll need eggs. Large and whole, nothing cracked."

Sinead gave me a long-suffering curtsy and scuttled for the larder.

"She puts on airs," Mrs. Bowen said as she passed by the kitchen's door. "Last cook took a strap to her." She sounded vastly disapproving of the last cook, which made me begin to warm to Mrs. Bowen.

"Is that why the last cook was dismissed?" I already didn't think much of this elderly cook, free with a strap, whoever she was. Sinead's only crime, I could see so far, was having dreams.

"No." Mrs. Bowen's answer was short, clipped. She ducked away before she could tell me anything more interesting.

I continued with my bread. Brioche was a favorite of mine — a bread dough made rich with eggs and butter, subtly sweet. It was a fine accompaniment to any meal but also could be served as pudding in a pinch. A little cinnamon and stiff cream or a berry sauce poured over it was as grand as anything served in a posh hotel.

It was as I began beating flour and the eggs into the milk and sugar that I met Lady Rankin's sister. I heard a loud banging and scrambling noise from the scullery, as though someone had fallen into it down the stairs. Pans clattered to the floor, and then a personage in a black suit burst through the scullery door into the kitchen, boot heels scraping on the flagstones, and collapsed onto a chair at the kitchen table, flinging out arms and legs.

I caught up my bowl of dough before it could be upset, looked at the intruder, and then looked again.

The person wore black trousers, a waistcoat of watered silk in a dark shade of green, with a shining watch fob dangling from its pocket, a smooth frock coat and loose cravat, a long and rather dusty greatcoat, a pair of thick leather gloves, and boots that poked muddy toes from under the trousers. The low-crowned hat that went with the ensemble had been tossed to the table.

Above this male attire was the head and face of a woman, a rather pretty woman at that. She'd done her fair hair in a low bun at the back of her neck, slicking it straight from a fine-boned face. The light color of her hair, her high cheekbones, and light blue, almost colorless eyes were so like Lady Rankin's, that for a moment, I stared, dumbfounded, believing I was seeing my mistress transformed. This lady was a bit older though, with the beginnings of lines about her eyes, and a manner far more robust than Lady Rankin's.

"Oh Lord," the woman announced, throwing her body back in the chair and letting her arms dangle to the floor. "I think I've killed someone."

Chapter Two

As I stared at the woman in alarm, she looked up at me, fixed me with a gaze that was as surprised as mine, and demanded, "Who the devil are *you*?"

"I am Mrs. Holloway." I curtsied as best I could with my hands around my dough bowl. "The new cook."

"New? What happened to the last one? Nasty old Mrs. Cowles. Why did they give her the boot?"

Since I had no idea, I could not answer. "Has something happened?"

The lady shoved the chair from the table and banged to

her feet, her color rising. "Good God, yes. Where the devil is everyone? What if I've killed him?"

"Killed who?" I asked, holding on to my patience. I'd already decided that the ladies of this family were prone to drama—one played the delicate creature, the other something from a music hall stage.

"Chap outside. I was driving a rig, a new one, and he jumped out in front of me. Come and see."

I looked at my dough, which could become lumpy if I left it at this stage, but the young lady was genuinely agitated, and the entirety of the staff seemed to have disappeared. I shook out my hands, wiped them with a thick towel, laid the towel over the dough bowl, and nodded at her to lead me to the scene of the problem.

Fog shrouded the street onto which we emerged from the scullery stairs, Lady Cynthia—for that was Lady Rankin's sister's name—insisting we exit the house through the servants' entrance, the way she'd come in.

The fog did nothing to slow the carriages, carts, delivery wagons, small conveyances, and people who scurried about on whatever business took them through Mount Street, which was situated between Grosvenor Square and Berkeley Square. London was always a town on the move. Mud flew as carriage wheels and horses churned it up, droplets becoming dark rain to meld with the fog.

Lady Cynthia led me rapidly through the traffic, ducking and dodging, moving easily in her trousers while I held my skirts out of the dirt and dung on the cobbles and hastened after her. People stared at Lady Cynthia in her odd attire, but no one pointed or said a word—those in the neighborhood were probably used to her.

"There." Lady Cynthia halted at the corner of Park

Street, a respectable enough place, one where a cook should not be lurking, and pointed.

A leather-topped, four-wheeled phaeton had been halted against the railings of a house on the corner. A burly man held the two horses hitched to the phaeton, while a lad patted them, trying to keep them calm. Inside the vehicle, a man slumped against the seat—whether dead or alive, I could not tell.

"Him," Lady Cynthia said, jabbing her finger at the figure inside the phaeton. "He popped out of nowhere and ran in front of me. Didn't see the bloody man until he was right under the horses' hooves."

I was already moving toward the phaeton, Lady Cynthia behind me, pressing myself out of the way of carts and carriages rumbling through, lest I end up as the man inside. "Did you summon a doctor?" I asked her, raising my voice to be heard over the clatter of hooves and wheels.

"Why?" Lady Cynthia gave me a blank stare with her pale eyes. "He's dead."

I reached the phaeton and opened the door to study the man slumped in the seat. I let out a breath of relief—he was quite alive. I'd unfortunately been witness to those brutally and suddenly killed, but the one thing I'd mainly observed about the dead was that they did not raise their heads or open eyes to stare at me in bewilderment and pain.

The burly man holding the horses called to Lady Cynthia. "Not dead, m'lady. Just a bit bashed about."

"You, lad," I said to the boy with him. "Run for a doctor. Perhaps, my lady, we should get him into the house."

Lady Cynthia might wear the clothes of a man, but she hesitated in the fluttery way young ladies are taught to adopt these days. Cooks, I am pleased to say, are expected to be a bit more formidable. While the boy raced away at

ASHLEY GARDNER & JENNIFER ASHLEY

my command to summon a physician, I had no compunction about climbing into the phaeton and looking the fellow over myself.

He was an ordinary person, the sort one would find driving a cart and making deliveries to Mayfair households, though I saw no van nearby, nothing to say who his employer was. He wore a plain but thick coat and linen shirt, working trousers, and stout boots. The lack of rents or stains in his clothing told me he was well looked after, either by a wife, or perhaps he could afford to hire out his mending. Or perhaps he even took up a needle himself—but the point was he had enough self-respect to present a clean and neat appearance. That meant he had work and was no ruffian of the street.

I touched his hand, finding it warm, and he groaned piteously.

Lady Cynthia, hearing him, looked much relieved and regained some of her vigor. "Yes, inside. Excellent idea Mrs. . . . Mrs. . . ."

"Holloway," I reminded her.

"Holloway. *You.*" She pointed a long, aristocratic finger at another sturdy youth who'd paused to take in the drama. "Help us carry him into the house. Where have *you* been?" She snapped at a gangly man in knee breeches and heavy boots who came running around the corner. "Take the rig to the mews. *Wait* until we heave this man out of it."

The thin man, who appeared to be a groom—indeed, he would prove to be the head groomsman for Lord Rankin's town stables—climbed onto the box and took the reins, sending Lady Cynthia a dark look. His back quivered as he waited for the burly man who'd been holding the horses and the youth to help me pry the hurt man out of the phaeton.

I looked into the youth's face and nearly hit my head on the phaeton's leather top. "Good heavens," I said. "James!"

James, a lad of about fifteen or so years with dark eyes, a round, rather handsome and freckled face, and red-brown hair sticking out from under his cap, shot a grin at me. I hadn't seen him for weeks, and only a few times since I'd taken the post in Richmond. James didn't move much beyond the middle of London, as he made his living doing odd jobs here and there around the metropolis. I'd seen him only when I'd had cause to come into London and our paths happened to cross.

James, with his father, Daniel, had helped me avoid much trouble at the place I'd been before Richmond, and I'd come to count the lad as a friend.

As for his father . . .

I could not decide these days how I regarded his father. Daniel McAdam, a jack-of-all-trades if ever there was one, had been my friend since the day he'd begun deliveries in a household I'd worked in a year or so ago. He was charming, flirtatious, ever ready with a joke or an encouraging word. He'd helped me in a time of great need last autumn, but then I'd learned more about Daniel than perhaps I'd wanted to. I was still hurt about it, and uncertain.

After James and the burly man worked the injured man from the carriage, I pulled myself upright on the phaeton's step and scanned the street. I have sharp eyes, and I did not have to look far until I saw Daniel.

He was just ducking around a corner up Park Street, glancing behind him as though expecting me to be seeking him. He wore the brown homespun suit he donned when making deliveries to kitchens all over Mayfair and north of Oxford Street and the shapeless gloves that hid his strong hands. I recognized his sharp face, the blue eyes over a well-formed nose, the dark hair he never could tame under his cloth cap.

He saw me. Did he look abashed? No, indeed. Mr. McAdam only sent me a merry look, touched his cap in salute, and disappeared.

I did not know all Daniel McAdam's secrets, and I knew he had many. He'd helped me when none other would, it was true, but at the same time he'd angered and confused me. I was grateful and could admire his resolve, but I refused to let myself fall under his spell. I had even allowed him to kiss me on the lips once or twice, but that had been as far as *that* went.

"Drat the man," I said.

"Ma'am?" the groom asked over his shoulder.

"Never mind." I hopped to the ground, the cobbles hard under my shoes. "When you're done in the stables, come 'round to the kitchen for a strong cup of tea. I have the inkling we will all need one."

A doctor came and looked over the man Lady Cynthia had run down. He'd been put into one of the rooms in the large attic and pronounced to have a broken arm and many bruises. The doctor, who was not at all happy to be called out to look at a mere laborer, sent for a surgeon to set the arm. The surgeon departed when he was finished, after dosing the man with laudanum and giving Mrs. Bowen instructions to not let him move for at least a day.

The man, now able to speak, or at least to mumble, said his name was Timmons and begged us to send word to his wife in their rooms near Euston Station.

At least, this is what Mr. Davis, the butler, related to me. I had scrubbed my hands and returned to my brioche when the hurt man had been carried upstairs, as I needed to carry on with my duties if I was to have a meal on the table when the master came home. Lady Rankin had said he returned on the dot of eight and expected to dine right away, and it was after six now. Ellen-Sinead, though curious, obediently resumed her kitchen duties.

As Sinead and I worked, Mr. Davis told us all about the doctor's arrival and his sour expression when he'd learned he'd come to see to a working-class man; the surgeon, who was much more cheerful; and the fact that this Timmons would have to spend the night. One of the footmen had gone in search of his wife.

By that time, I had shaped my rich bread and was letting it rise in its round fluted pan while I turned to sort out the vegetables I'd chosen from the larder—plump mushrooms that were fresh smelling, asparagus nice and green, a firm onion, bright tomatoes.

"Lady Cynthia is beside herself," Mr. Davis said. He sat down at the kitchen table, propping his elbows on it, doing nothing useful. My chopping board was near him, and I thumped the blade menacingly as I cut through the onions Sinead had peeled for me. Mr. Davis took notice. "She's a flibbertigibbet but has a kind heart, does our Lady Cynthia," he went on. "She promised Timmons a sum of money for his trouble—which Lord Rankin will have to furnish, of course. *She* hasn't got any money. That's why she lives here. Sort of a poor relation, but never say so."

"I would not dream of it, Mr. Davis." I held a hothouse tomato to my nose, rewarded by a bright scent, the tomato an excellent color. I longed to bite into it and taste its juices, but I returned it to the board with its fellows and picked over the asparagus. Whoever had chosen the produce had a good eye.

Mr. Davis chuckled. I'd already seen, when he'd led me through the house, that he could be haughty as anything above stairs, but down here in the kitchens, he loosened his coat and his tongue. Mr. Davis's hair was dark, though gray at the temples, parted severely in the middle and held in place with pomade. He had a pleasant sort of face, blue eyes, and a thin line of mouth that was usually moving in speech.

"Lady Cynthia and Lady Emily are the Earl of Clifford's daughters," Mr. Davis said, sending me a significant look.

Interesting. I left the vegetables and uncovered the fowl I was to roast. I'd cook potatoes and onions in its juices and throw in the mushrooms at the end, along with the tomatoes for tang. For fish, I had skate waiting to be poached in milk, which I'd finish with parsley and walnuts. Early March could be a difficult time—the winter fruits and vegetables were fading, and spring's bounty barely beginning. I enjoyed cooking in spring the most, when everything was fresh and new. Biting into early greens tasted of bright skies and the end of winter's grip.

I had heard of the Earl of Clifford, who was famous for being a bankrupt. The title was an old one, from what I understood, one of those that kings had been bestowing for centuries—reverting to the crown when the particular family line died out but given to another family when that family pleased royalty enough to be so rewarded.

I did not have my finger on every title in Britain, but I had heard that Clifford was the eighth of this earldom, given to a family called Shires. The present Lord Clifford had, in his youth, been renowned for bravery—deeds done in Crimea and that sort of thing. He'd come home to England to race horses, tangle himself in scandals, and have notorious affairs with famous beauties. He'd finally married one of these beauties, proceeded to sire two daughters and a son, and then gambled himself into ruinous debt.

His son and heir, as wild as the father, had died tragically at the young age of twenty, going slightly mad and shooting himself. Lady Clifford, devastated by the death of her favorite child, had gone into a decline. She was still alive, I believe, but living in poor health, shutting herself away on her husband's estate in Hertfordshire.

The daughters, Ladies Cynthia and Emily, had debuted and caught the eyes of many a gentlemen, but they'd not fared well, as their father's debts were common knowledge, as were their mother's nerves and their brother's suicide. Lady Emily, the younger, had married Lord Rankin before he was Lord Rankin, when he was but a wealthy gentleman who'd made much in the City. Lord and Lady Clifford must have breathed a sigh of relief when he'd put the ring on her finger.

I had known some of the Clifford story from gossip and newspapers. Now Mr. Davis kindly filled in the gaps as I plunged a tomato into hot water, showing Sinead how this loosened the skin so it could be easily peeled.

"Lady Cynthia was not so fortunate." Mr. Davis stretched out his long legs, making himself as comfortable as possible in the hard wooden chair. "She is the older sister, and so it is a scandal that the younger married and she did not. And of course, Lady Cynthia has no fortune. She is agreeable enough, but when she found herself in danger of being on the shelf, she chose to become an eccentric."

While I left Sinead to finish peeling, seeding, and chopping the tomatoes, I warmed butter and basted the hen, which was a plump, well-juiced specimen. Lord Rankin, it seemed, spared no expense on his victuals. Happily for me, as a cook's job is made ten times easier with decent ingredients.

"Poor thing," I said, shoving the fowl into the roasting

oven and licking melted butter from my thumb. I closed the door and fastened it, and snapped my fingers at the lad whose task it was to keep the stove stoked. He leapt from playing with pebbles in the corner and grabbed a few pieces of wood from the box under the window. He opened the grate and tossed in the wood quickly, but I was alarmed how close his little hands came to the flames. I warned him to be more careful. I'd have to make up the balm I liked of chamomile, lavender, and goose fat for burned fingers if he wasn't.

The boy returned to his game, and I wiped my hands and looked over Sinead's shoulder as she moved on to tearing lettuce for the salads. I liked to have my greens washed, dried, and kept chilled well before serving the meal.

"Lady Cynthia took at first to riding horses in breakneck races," Mr. Davis continued. "Amateur ones of course, on the estates, racing young men fool enough to take her on. She has a light touch with a horse, does Lady Cynthia. She rode in breeches and won most of her gallops, along with the wagers. When our master married Lady Emily, he put a stop to Lady Cynthia's riding, but I suppose she enjoyed wearing the breeches so much she didn't want to give them up. Our lordship don't like it, but he's said that as long as Lady Cynthia stays quiet and behaves herself she can wear trousers if she likes."

Mrs. Bowen chose that moment to walk into the kitchen. She sniffed. "Speaking of your betters again, Mr. Davis?" She studied me getting on with the meal, then with head held high, departed for the servants' hall, disapproval oozing from her.

Mr. Davis chuckled. "Mrs. Bowen puts on airs, but most of what I know about the family I learned from her. She worked for Lady Clifford before she came here."

I pretended to absorb myself in my cooking, but I was curious. I have a healthy interest in my fellow beings, unfortunately.

As Davis went momentarily silent, my thoughts strayed again to Daniel. He popped up here and there throughout London, always where something interesting was happening, and I wondered why he'd chosen the moment when Lady Cynthia had run down a cart driver.

"If Lady Cynthia hurt this man for life with her recklessness," I observed, "it could go badly for her."

Davis shook his head. "Not for the daughter of an earl decorated for bravery and the sister-in-law of one of the wealthiest men in London. Lord Rankin will pay to keep our Lady Cynthia out of the newspapers and out of the courts, you mark my words."

I believed him. Wealthy men could hide an embarrassment to the family, and Lady Cynthia viewed herself as an embarrassment—I had noted that in her eyes. I myself saw no shame in her running about in gentlemen's attire—didn't we enjoy the courageous heroines who dressed as men in plays of the Bard? Cheer for them in the Christmas pantomimes?

I saw no more of Lady Cynthia that evening, or indeed of anyone, as I turned to the business of getting the supper done. Once I gave my attention solely to cooking, 'ware any who stepped in my way.

Sinead proved to be capable if not as well trained as I liked, but we got on, and she burst into tears only once. She ceased her sobbing after she cleaned up the salt she had spilled all over the lettuce and helped me pull the roasted fowl out of the oven, bubbling and sizzling, the aroma splendid. I cut off a tiny piece of meat and a speared a square of potato and shared them with her.

Sinead's face changed to rapture. "Oh, ma'am, it's the best I ever tasted."

She exaggerated, I knew, although I suppose her comment was a testament to the previous cook's abilities. I thought the fowl's taste could have been richer, but I would not be ashamed to serve this dish.

Mr. Davis and the footmen were already in the dining room above. I rounded up the maids to help me load a tureen of steaming asparagus soup into the lift, followed by the lightly poached skate, and then when it was time, the covered plate of the carved fowl with roasted vegetables and the greens. I hadn't had time to fix more than the brioche for pudding, and so I sent up fruit with a bite of cheese alongside the rich bread.

It was my habit never to rest until I heard from the dining room that all was well. Tonight, I heard nothing, not a word of praise—but not a word of complaint either. The plates returned scraped clean, although one of the three in each course was always lightly touched.

Such a shame to waste good food. I shook my head over it and told the kitchen maids to pack away the uneaten portions to give to beggars.

I'd learned long ago that not every person on earth appreciates good food—some don't even know how to taste it. Instead of growing incensed as I had done when I began, I now felt sorry for that person and distributed the food to the cold and hungry who better deserved it.

"Who is the faint appetite?" I asked Mr. Davis when he and I and Mrs. Bowen at last took our supper in the housekeeper's parlor, with Sinead to wait on us.

"Tonight, Lady Cynthia," Mr. Davis said between shoveling in bites of the pieces of roasted hen and potatoes I'd held back for us. "She is still most upset about the accident. She even wore a frock to dinner."

Apparently, this was significant. Mrs. Bowen and Sinead gave Mr. Davis amazed looks.

One of the footmen—I thought his name was Paul—tapped hesitantly on the door of Mrs. Bowen's parlor and entered when invited.

"I beg your pardon, ma'am," he said nervously. "But his lordship is asking for his evening cup of coffee." He swallowed, his young face rather spotty, his Adam's apple prominent. He darted Mrs. Bowen a worried look. "He's asking for Sinead—I mean Ellen—to deliver it."

An awful hush descended over the room. I was struck by the paling faces of Mrs. Bowen and Davis and the unhappiness in the footman's eyes, but mostly by the look of dread that came over Sinead.

She set down the teapot she'd lifted to refill Mrs. Bowen's cup and turned to that lady pleadingly, distress in every line of her.

Mrs. Bowen gave her a sorrowful nod. "You'd best be going on up, girl."

Sinead's eyes filled with tears, every bit of cheerfulness dying. She wiped her hands on her apron, curtsied, and said, "Yes, ma'am," before she made for the door.

She found me in the doorway, blocking her way out. "Why?" I asked the room, not excluding the footman. "What is the matter with Ellen taking the master his coffee? Mrs. Bowen, Mr. Davis, you tell me this minute."

Mr. Davis and Mrs. Bowen exchanged a long glance. Sinead would not look at me, her cheeks stark white and blotched with red.

It was Mrs. Bowen who answered. "I am afraid that his

lordship occasionally believes in the idea of . . . I suppose we could call it droit du seigneur. Not often, fortunately."

"Fortunately?" The word snapped out of me, my anger, which had touched me when I'd seen Daniel in the street, finally finding a vent.

I was well aware that a hazard for young women in service, no matter how grand the household, was that the master, and sometimes his guests, saw no reason not to help themselves to a maid, or a cook's assistant, or, indeed, even a cook, when they fancied her. The young woman in question was powerless—all she could do was either give in or find herself another place. If she fled the house without reference, gaining new employment could be difficult. If she gave in to the master's lusts, she risked being cast out with a stain on her character. If her own family would not let her come home, or she had no family, she had no choice but to take to the streets.

I had learned as a very young cook's assistant to keep myself buried in the kitchen and rarely cross the paths of the gentlemen of the household. As cooks seldom went above stairs, this had worked well for me. My ruin had been entirely my own fault and nothing to do with any house in which I'd worked.

"It does not happen often, does it?" I asked testily.

I was pleased that at least Mr. Davis and Mrs. Bowen looked ashamed, Mrs. Bowen bordering on wretched. "Only when his lordship has been made unhappy," Mr. Davis said.

And he'd been made unhappy today by Lady Cynthia running down a man in the street, a story everyone in Mayfair likely knew by now. "Good heavens—why on earth do you stay here?" I demanded of all present. "There are masters respectable enough in other houses, and wives who will not put up with that sort of thing."

Mr. Davis regarded me in some surprise. "We stay because it's a good place—you'll see. His lordship is generous to the staff. Always has been."

"I see. And sending a young woman as sacrifice every once in a while is a small price to pay?" My mounting anger made my blood fire in my veins. "Well, I will not have it. Not in my kitchen."

"Mrs. Holloway, I understand your unhappiness," Mrs. Bowen said. "I share it. But what can we do? I try to keep the maids occupied away from his lordship, but it is not *my* house. Her ladyship ought to keep him under her eye, but she cannot."

I full well knew Mrs. Bowen was right. Some gentlemen are high-handed enough to believe *everything* they do is justified. Those who have power and wealth behind them are only encouraged in their prideful thinking. The frail Lady Rankin likely knew what was going on but hadn't the strength to confront him about it.

My heart sank at the thought of having to look for another place when I'd only just found this one. The kitchen was well stocked, the house efficiently run, and the street near to an omnibus that would take me easily to the place in London where my heart was. Why, oh why, did the master and his base needs have to ruin a perfectly good situation?

My fury made me reckless. "I won't have it," I repeated. "Ellen, sit down and calm yourself. *I* will take Lord Rankin his coffee."

BLOOD DEBTS

Leonidas the Gladiator Mysteries by Ashley
Gardner

CHAPTER 1

ROME, AD 63

"THE BAKER OWES US MONEY."

I crawled out of sleep when a slim stick tapped my side and a woman's voice slid through my dreams. Cassia had learned to use the stick to poke at me, because I usually came roaring awake, ready to murder all within reach.

When she'd first come to live with me, Cassia had shaken me from a dream in which I'd been surrounded by swords, the ghosts of men I'd slain rising up to drag me down. I'd been naked and without weapons, only my balled fists for defense.

I'd grabbed the arm that had come at me and torn open my eyes to find Cassia in terror, her slender wrist in my deadly grip. I'd nearly broken her arm before I'd let go.

Hence, the stick.

I was too exhausted this morning for roaring, so I mumbled, "Wha'?"

"The baker." Cassia returned the polished branch of walnut to the corner and picked up the wax tablet on which she did the household accounts, such as they were. "Quintus Publius. You guarded his shipments from Ostia three weeks ago, and he has yet to pay a thing. He owes us ten sestertii."

"Mmph." I scrubbed my face, hoping to sink back into darkness. "Send him a notice." I settled my head on my hard pillow. "You like to send notices."

"I have sent him seventeen," Cassia said crisply. "He ignores them. You ought to go yourself. He will not be able to ignore *you*."

I opened my eyes all the way. Cassia sat in her usual place, a stool on the other side of our one-roomed apartment, near the door. She wore a modest sheath of a dress, sandals I'd bought her, and held her stylus poised over her tablet. I always thought of her like that, eyes on the hinged wooden and wax tablet in her hand, stylus at the ready to add a notation.

Her black hair, pulled up out of her face, curled wildly about her forehead and cascaded down her back in one tail. No hairdresser had styled those curls—Cassia was a slave, bestowed upon me by my unknown benefactor, a man who'd apparently followed my career in the arena more ardently than I had.

This man, whoever he was, had decided I needed looking after, and sent Cassia to be my caretaker when I'd gained my freedom six months ago. Cassia had grown up the daughter of a slave, who'd been a scribe to a very wealthy patrician family in Campania. She was here now because, after her father's death, the master of the house had decided to notice that Cassia had become a woman, and Cassia's mistress had made certain she was quickly sold.

Cassia didn't know who our benefactor was either. Everything went through another scribe, a dried stick of a slave called Hesiodos, who steadfastly refused to tell us.

Cassia dressed her hair simply, because she wasn't good at hair, she'd told me, or clothes, or cooking, or really much of anything else, which was why no one had known what to do with her once her father had gone to the gods. Her master had known what he wanted, and so Cassia's mistress had ejected her.

What Cassia excelled at was accounts. And noticing things, important things. And driving a man spare so he couldn't sleep.

These days, I liked sleep. There was no reason to pull myself out of bed—no training, no meals of barley and vegetables, or grand feasts in my honor the night before the games. These feasts had always been wasted on me because I could never swallow a bite.

"Tomorrow." I closed my eyes, seeking the comfort of oblivion.

Often the dreams broke through to haunt me, but sometimes there was nothing. Sweet peace. I must not have slept at all in the seven years I was a gladiator because now I could not get enough of it.

"Leonidas." Cassia's firm voice broke that peace.

This time I came up with a hint of a snarl. *"Wha'?"*

"If the baker pays us, we can remain in our palatial surroundings. Otherwise, we'll be out on the street. And hungry. We can prevent this by prying what we are owed out of Quintus."

The interesting thing about our so-called benefactor is that he didn't pay our rent or provide us food. He'd found me this apartment, bestowed upon me a slave no one else wanted, and then left the rest of our living up to us. What this man would demand in return for this uneven generosity remained to be seen.

Cassia trailed off, watching to gauge the effect of her

words on me, every one of them reasonable, every one unarguable.

The trouble with Cassia was that she was nearly always right. A man needed money to live. A gladiator in a ludus did not, but I was no longer kept at others' expense. The animal, freed from its cage, didn't know how to hunt.

My hint of a snarl turned into a real one as I hauled myself up and off the slab of wood our landlord called a bed. The blanket Cassia must have laid over me in the night slid from my bare body as I rose to my feet. Cassia averted her gaze, her cheeks burning red.

I'd never met a woman shy with men before, one who didn't openly size up the goods, especially when they took up half the apartment. But then, my experience with women had been in brothels and with those eager to sneak themselves into a gladiator's cell. Cassia had lived with modest women who'd covered themselves at all times and required her to as well.

Cassia's head remained bent, her eyes fixed resolutely on her tablet. Maybe she'd caught sight of a mistake in her calculations. No, Cassia didn't make mistakes. She was simply uncomfortable with so much naked flesh in such a small space.

I'd never noticed my own body much until Cassia's arrival. I'd thought of male bodies in terms of places to stab —chest for heart and lungs, abdomen for guts, throat for a rapid kill. Women's bodies were somewhat different—their parts fit with mine for a short time of mind-numbing pleasure to chase away the demons.

Cassia, on the other hand, saw *me*, Leonidas, the whole person. No one else ever had. Instead of being flattered, I always felt the immediate need to cover myself.

I reached for a tunic and pulled it on. Cassia flicked me a glance, and she breathed out, no mistaking her relief.

I pretended to ignore her while I sluiced clean water from the ewer over my face and looked around for my sandals. There they were, my one pair, in a neat line by the door. Cassia tidied every night after I went to bed—if collapsing onto my mat of reeds on a wooden block could be given such a formal term.

"Not that tunic," Cassia said behind me. I felt her critical eyes on my back. "A clean one."

I halted. No wonder Jupiter constantly fled Juno. She was probably always going on at him about wearing clean tunics and combing his hair.

I'd forgotten—clean tunic on the peg, dirty one on the floor for Cassia to take to the laundry.

As I put my hand on the fabric at the back of my neck, ready to pull off the offending garment, Cassia said, "No, no, on second thought, you ought to wear that. The wine stain from last night's meal is the exact color of blood. It makes you look as though you wrestled someone into submission. He'll pay up like a lamb."

No gladiator, no matter how much in fear of his life, had ever been as ruthless as Cassia when someone owed her money. Owed *me* money, I should say. I did the jobs, she kept note of them, and then sent me to bully those who didn't pay.

Cassia wasn't wrong, though. We needed the cash or we wouldn't eat or have anywhere to sleep. I was bad at the basics of life, Cassia was good at it, and so we went along.

I settled the tunic without a word, smoothed my hand over my close-cropped hair, and ducked out into the morning sun.

I'd managed to block out the noise and brightness of the Roman morning while I'd slept, but now they both hit me full force.

Cassia and I lived one floor above the shop of a wine merchant at the base of the Quirinal. It might have been cheaper for us to live in an insula, but I had a horror of those huge blocks of buildings made to house so many living beings. They fell down on occasion, burying all within them. Our apartment had been built for the wine-seller's mother-in-law, standing empty after she'd passed. We had one rectangular room and a balcony that was nothing more than the flat roof of the wine shop below.

The street flowed with activity. The current of men in tunics—a few with togas—swept past the wine shop with its amphorae resting in rows neat enough for Cassia's approval, drawing me with them into the pulsing heat of Rome.

My route today took me past the forum of Augustus, the emperor and god, whom even I'd heard of. Elderly men in the baths would reminisce about how wonderful Rome had been in the golden age of Augustus, and how we'd never see its like again.

From what Cassia told me, we now had more bath houses, a greater abundance of clean water, wares from every corner of the empire, and more relative peace than in the time of Augustus, but I'd noticed that the more gray hair a man had, the more nostalgic he became. Cassia also pointed out that these men could only have been tiny children when Augustus died, and would hardly remember life under his rule.

My steps turned me toward the Subura, an area that ran along the base of the Quirinal and Viminal hills. Smoke coated the air because of the fires perpetually burning to heat the baths for the day. The aqueducts that provided water for baths and every fountain in the city stalked along the tops of the hills above me.

I heard my name on occasion as I walked under the colonnade that shaded the street. This was usual as I moved about Rome—my fights in the amphitheatres had been celebrated. But if I turned aside to speak to every person who hailed me, I'd never reach my destination. I wouldn't mind, but if I didn't return soon with the money, Cassia would give me her sorrowful look and make another note on her tablet.

"It's him," I heard a man exclaim. "Leonidas!"

"Where?" another responded. "No, it isn't. You're daft."

"Yes, it is. That was him. I saw the scar."

The scar in question cut along the base of my throat and down into my tunic. If the cut had landed with the force intended, my blood would have spilled in a swift torrent, and I would have died on the arena sand. My own strike had lessened the blow, and the other man had died instead.

I am called Leonidas because my lanista, a man who bought and trained gladiators, said I fought with the intensity of Leonidas the Spartan king and his men at Thermopylae. Thus, Leonidas the Gladiator was born. Since I'd been eager to shuck my old name, which had only brought me trouble, I didn't object. Leonidas I became at age eighteen, and so I remained.

"Leonidas!" The last voice was very young, very eager, and fearing disappointment. "Look!"

I turned my head. A grubby boy stood in the shadow of an archway, holding up a terra cotta cup for me to see. The side of the cup bore a crude sketch of a man who could have been anyone, except for the scratched letters that spelled out, *Leonidas*. I recognized the word, because it was the only one I knew how to read.

At this man's feet was sprawled a second gladiator, his fallen trident beside him. The one Greek letter I knew, theta, was scratched beneath him, meaning the man on the ground was dead.

Hot wind swept down the street. With it came the scent of sand, blood, sweat, and the metallic tang of the inside of my helmet. I couldn't see the thousands surrounding me in the amphitheatre, but I could hear them. The roar of voices, the chant of my name. *Le-o-ni-das*. The press of air and heat sent sweat trickling down my bare back and legs.

A rush of fear, rage, and desperation came at me, swirling away the packed streets of Rome. I seemed to look through the grill of my eye pieces, the helmet a cage, and saw the trident come at my midsection. A shout left my mouth as I barreled it aside with my elbow, the trident's point glancing off my helmet. In another second, the man was down, the crowd screaming for his death. *Iugula! Kill him!*

Sweat poured down my body as air raked my lungs. Someone brushed past me, and my vision swam back. A lower-class woman surrounded by her friends on their way to the market parted to flow around me. The gaggle of them laughed together, the soft fabric of a fluttering skirt brushing my ankles.

As the fog began to clear, I crouched down in front of the boy. He was somewhere between five and maybe eight summers, skinny with poverty, teeth half gone, hair brittle and lank. His tunic was threadbare, sandals held on with twine.

Somehow he'd found the money to buy the piece of junk

he held, showing one of my forgotten bouts from years ago. I'd forgotten none of them.

I wanted to dash the cup to the ground, tell him to spend his money on better things, but the boy held the cup as though it were precious gold.

Cassia's voice buzzed like a fly at the back of my skull. *Whatever did you do that for, Leonidas? You could at least have given him the price for it, poor lad.*

I touched the cup. "It was hot that day," I said. "The amphitheatre in that town was gravelly, and we had to wear sandals. I had grit in my shoes."

The boy's eyes widened in fascination.

"He fought well," I went on, tracing the fallen body of the man who'd called himself Dionysius. "I was lucky to win. Was almost skewered by the trident a couple of times."

The boy listened, open-mouthed, dark eyes round with wonder. To him, the fight was a legend. To me, it had been just another day at the games.

I fished a copper coin from the pouch at my waist and dropped it into the cup. "Go tell the fruit seller to give you his best for that—tell him I sent you."

The boy nodded, his eyes and mouth no less round. I rose and shooed him off. He scampered away, his head high, joy in his step.

I was that boy once—the memory tapped me out of nowhere. Had nothing and no one, only a few precious things to keep me from complete despair. I watched him bob along until he was lost among the crowd, swallowed by Rome's million inhabitants.

The baker's shop was around the next corner, built a little way from the end of a row of shops, an open counter in front where the baker did business. Ovens fired in the back, the wall above them pocked with round holes where the bread taken from the ovens would cool.

I'd come at a lull in the baker's day. His morning bread would have been finished and fetched by the women or household slaves of this area, giving him time to bake other things to sell, or perhaps doze under the counter.

Quintus was awake, however, puttering about, a small, bald man in a tunic and sandals. He was wiry, every muscle tight from shoveling bread into and out of ovens all day, his back a bit hunched from the same.

I said nothing as I approached the concrete slab of the counter, noting that the mosaic on the top depicted sea creatures, nothing to do with bread or baking.

I leaned my hands on the counter and waited. Quintus shoved himself halfway into a roaring oven and came back out with an empty paddle and not so much as a burn or singed hair.

"Yes?" he asked impatiently as he turned around. "You'll have to—"

He halted in mid-word, his parted lips showing me brownish teeth in blackening gums. He snapped this mouth shut and swallowed. "Leonidas."

I could not have been a welcome sight. I stood two feet taller than the baker and was twice as broad. The famous scar that trailed down my neck symbolized my defeat of death. My hands, now fists, were as big as the stones he used for grinding seeds to paste.

Quintus looked so terrified I feared he'd drop dead on the spot. Cassia would be most put out if I let him die—we'd likely never get paid.

"It's Cassia," I said, making my tone apologetic. "She likes her accounts to balance."

Quintus gulped. "She is Greek," he said, as though that explained it.

Desperate, I could have told him. Cassia had a horror of being on the street, wretched and homeless, a dangerous situation that could end quickly in defilement and death.

I tried to feel the same fear and could not. I hadn't felt anything in a long, long while.

For Cassia's sake, I was here, badgering a man who thought he'd gotten away with not paying his debt to the second most dangerous man in Rome. That was what I'd heard people call me. I assumed they believed the princeps, Nero, to be the first.

"I'll take half," I said. "That should keep her quiet for a while." I sent Quintus a look that suggested we had to do what was necessary to keep the women who ran our lives happy.

He wet his lips. "I don't have it." His face was bright red, whether because he lied or told the truth and was afraid of it, I could not say. "I swear to you, I don't have it. I don't even have half. But ..."

Quintus trailed off, his flush fading as something like relief took over. "Gaius Selenius owes me money. Quite a bit of it. Part of the shipment you guarded from Ostia was his—I moved it at my own expense. If you go along and pry the money out of *him,* I can pay you. And a few coins extra for your trouble."

I smothered a sigh. A disadvantage to being one of the most famous gladiators of the day, even as a *veteres,* was that other men expected me to do their dirty deeds for them. *Rough up a man who insulted me. Find a man who owes me money, and we'll all get paid.*

The fact that Quintus hadn't gone after the money owed himself meant that Selenius frightened him. Selenius might be surrounded by bodyguards or have a vicious disposition, more inclined to have a small man beaten than pay his debt to him. What luck that I'd come along this morning.

But there was nothing for it. Unless I turned the baker upside down and shook him, I would not return with money today. The thought of facing Cassia empty-handed was not a happy one.

"Where is this Gaius Selenius?" I asked, resigned.

Quintus brightened. "On the Clivus Suburanus, in a *macellum* near the Porticus Liviae. His shop is in the middle of the market, by the atrium. He's a money-changer."

Better and better. Money-changers were a despised class of men, lumped with usurers and tax collectors. Even gladiators, though we were *infamis*, at the very bottom of society, had higher reputations.

I abruptly turned from Quintus without a farewell or another word, joining the crowds in the increasing heat of the day. Once the sun hit its zenith, in the sixth hour, shops would close, business would halt, and men and women alike would wander to the baths, to meals, to lounge in the shade and wait for evening. I'd go back to sleep.

Once in the street, I turned down a winding lane toward the Clivus Suburanus. The twisting sway was so narrow I could lift my arms and touch walls on either side, and still my elbows would be bent. Despite the stink of refuse that curled in my nose, the tall, crammed-together buildings in this passageway shaded me from the blazing sun.

At the end of this lane, I turned into a wider, airy street of shops that were doing a brisk business. A tavern served food and drink to plenty of people who'd found time to stop and ingest barley and beans, soup and pork.

All manner of things were sold on this street—silk cloth from the east, spices and peppers, clay lamps and pots, fruits and vegetables, fresh flowers, sandals, and the baskets to carry it all in. A person could clothe himself, get his dinner, light his house and decorate it, buy his bedding, and purchase a pot for his slops, without ever having to turn a corner.

I'd lived most of my life in this city, first snatching survival in the streets, then in prison, then in the ludus. The lanista didn't lock us in; we were free to move about and take odd jobs in the city, as long as we were back in our cells at dusk.

But I hadn't really seen the place until I'd emerged from the ludus a free man. The city had gained a new tint, the stones a golden glow, the hills a grandeur. Even the fires that constantly burned gave it a scent that I'd come to associate with my home.

I turned at last to the Clivus Suburanus and found the passage leading to the *macellum*—an indoor marketplace housed within a large building. I ducked in, following the baker's directions.

This *macellum* was owned by a patrician who probably lived in a villa in the hills. He'd turned his property into rental spaces for sellers of food and other goods. The main building had shops around all of the outer walls and a few in the middle near the atrium. I had been here before—thick walls and the arched roof kept out the heat, which made it a popular place.

A niche in a wall inside the main door held a terra cotta carving of an erect phallus, a symbol of fertility—five times the size of any man's prick and correct in every detail. It was customary to give such statues around the city a rub for good fortune. I gave this one a pat in passing, both for luck and in hopes of sympathetic magic. My phallic instrument had been sleeping as much as I had lately.

The *macellum* was quieter than usual, only a few slaves in tunics buying wares for whatever household they worked for. Two were Gauls, with very pale hair and blue eyes, wooden baskets on their arms to hold what they purchased for their master or mistress. They were big men, muscular and tall. I was taller than most Roman men, which made people question my ancestry, but these two both topped me by an inch.

They stopped and stared at me as I went by. They might have recognized me from the games or they thought me as unusual as I thought them.

The two slaves finished their transaction across the counter of the stall nearest the main entrance, a vendor of *garum*, the smelly fermented fish sauce that made Cassia blench.

As I reached the inner shops near the atrium, all was quiet. It was nearly midday, and most of the vendors in here had already shut down, slipping away home for a nap or to the baths to relax.

Selenius had one of the innermost shops, a square room with a door on one side, and a counter on another, which could be closed off by a series of vertical wooden boards stuck into slots in the counter and locked in place with iron bars. Other shops had already put in their boards, guarding whatever was inside from casual thieves until they opened the next day.

I was relieved to see Selenius's shop still open. The sooner I made him give over Quintus's money, the sooner I could drop our earnings in front of Cassia and resume my sleep.

The mosaic tiles on his counter spelled out words, possibly that this was the place of Selenius. I glanced about for bodyguards but saw none. I didn't like that. A man who dealt in coins, counting out Roman ones in exchange for whatever people in the far-flung corners of the world used for money, had to be cautious. Coins ran the Roman Empire, and everyone wanted them.

Selenius didn't appear to be here either. I wondered if someone had run ahead and warned him I was coming. If so, he'd left his shop open to all who might traipse through at this quiet hour.

There wasn't much light inside the shop. The only illumination came through the square hole in the exact center of the building, which lit the atrium, much like it would in a rich man's private house.

I could see nothing in the shadows over the counter, so I walked to the open door that would let Selenius in and out, and peered inside.

The shop was about ten feet wide on a side, perhaps ten feet high, a perfect cube. There was another door, I saw from this point, a shorter one that presumably led to the shop next door.

I noted a long bench, which Selenius would set outside when he was open for business—the inside of the shop was for storage and safeguarding his stockpiles of coin. I saw no coin, however, but it likely had been taken away and locked up for the day.

As I ran my gaze over the space, it came to rest on a man lying in an unmoving huddle under the counter. His face, head, hands, legs, and long tunic were soaked with blood, and blood had spread in a puddle that stopped shy of the doorway where I stood. A black line ran across his throat, and his eyes were fixed in frozen terror.

I stood in silence, looking down at the man, trying to feel horror, dismay, fear ... but there was nothing. I remained unmoving, as though the entire world had come to a halt, until a small noise made me jerk my head up.

The door across the shop had opened. A boy stood on the threshold, a small lad clutching a cup with my name etched on it. He gaped over the blood at me, eyes wide, and then he dropped the cup, which shattered into the crimson pool at his feet.

CHAPTER 2

"Stay there," I said in a hard voice.

The boy remained frozen in place, his chest moving with his sharp intake of breath.

I backed out of the doorway I stood in and strode rapidly to the next shop. I reasoned it must be unlocked if the boy had come through it, but it was not. The boards had been fixed in place above the counter, the iron bars firmly run through rings in the boards and into the stone walls. No opening under the counter or around the side of the wall held any crevice that would admit a small boy. Then how had he gotten in?

I returned to Selenius's stall, the boy obediently waiting. Terrified, he still followed the orders of Leonidas, champion of the games.

I stepped carefully around the pool of blood, the stink of it making my vision blur. I sucked in deep breaths through my mouth, willing my thoughts to remain in the present, and skirted the blood to reach the boy.

"How did you get here?" I demanded.

He pointed to the black opening of the door behind him. I couldn't see where it went but a noisome smell leeched from the shadows.

I glanced at the man on the floor—I assumed he was Selenius, though I'd never met him. The blood came not from many injuries but from the large one across his throat. The vessels in his neck had been severed, and blood had poured forth to kill him quickly.

Whoever had done this had known exactly where to cut. It was the sort of execution a soldier would know how to perform—or a gladiator.

Very little frightened me anymore, but the thought of being tried for another murder, found guilty, and tossed back into the arena filled me with slow dread. Quintus the baker had sent me here—had he known Selenius lay dead and hoped I'd be taken for the crime?

I thought of Quintus's polished face and ingenuous dark eyes, which I swore had no guile in them, apart from avoiding payment of my fee. He might be as ignorant of this death as I'd been.

No matter what, we couldn't linger. The boy had stooped to the fragments of his precious cup. I pushed his hands away, not wanting him to cut himself on the shards, but I gathered every single one of them. Put together, they had my name on them, and I wanted no connection in anyone's mind between dead Selenius and Leonidas the Gladiator.

I shoved the fragments into the pouch at my belt and leaned down to lift the boy. Before I could, he grabbed one more piece from the floor, and then I hefted him into my arms.

He weighed next to nothing, bones in a threadbare tunic.

I decided not to ask where he lived. If I carried him home, people would remember — I could not move a step in this city without it being remarked upon.

It would be the talk of every supper for days to come if I were seen walking about the city with a small boy under my arm. I couldn't hide him under a convenient toga, because ex-gladiators, freedmen who were barely human, didn't wear them.

"Where does that lead?" I pointed through the doorway behind him.

"Down," was the helpful reply.

He'd come in here, so he must be able to get out. I ducked with him through the doorway to find a brick-lined passage that soon grew very dark. I smelled waste, human and animal, which meant this tunnel probably went to a maintenance hatch to the sewers. Rome was pockmarked with shafts that led to the considerable network of tunnels and sewers that crawled to every corner of Rome.

The boy was much smaller than I was — I hoped he didn't expect me to slither through tiny orifices in the bowels of Rome. It would be a stupid death for me to get stuck in an opening with the city's waste flushing through it to drown me.

I set the lad on his feet but kept hold of his hand. "Show me," I said as I closed the door behind us.

He started off at a rapid pace, dragging me down low-ceilinged tunnels, my skin scraping on the walls as I staggered along.

We twisted and eventually plunged downward, the stone floor sloping inward from the walls, but not to the sewers as

I'd feared. The last passage ended in a rough set of steps that led down to a wooden door.

I carefully opened this door and peered out.

It took me a moment to gain my bearings. We were at the base of the Esquiline Hill, near the area called the Figlinae, where potters had their factories. The street before me was lined with shops, this obscure narrow door obviously for maintenance purposes. People thronged here as they did everywhere, barely noticing us as we emerged from a battered door in a wall of shops and warehouses to blend in with them.

A short walk took us to the fountain of Orpheus at a broad crossroads, where a marble Orpheus tried to tame stone animals with his lyre. We turned here and journeyed back through the Subura to the Forum Augusti, where I lost hold of the boy's hand in the crush of people.

In three steps I caught up to him and lifted him into my arms. The boy never struggled or cried out, didn't protest or question. He simply rode against my chest, sanguine that his hero Leonidas held him.

I hefted him around the corner toward the wine shop, and then took the wooden stairs two at a time, to burst through the door into our apartment.

Cassia looked up from the tablets and scrolls that surrounded her, her pen falling from her fingers in surprise. She leapt to her feet, one scroll rolling up on itself and spattering ink, as I lowered the boy to his feet and shut the door.

"This is Cassia," I said to the boy. "She'll take care of you."

I had the pleasure of seeing Cassia, who always knew what to say at every occasion, at a loss for words. She opened her mouth, switched her stare to the lad, closed her mouth, and looked back at me.

"Who—?"

"I don't know," I cut her off. "I found him. Or, he found me. The money-changer is dead—Quintus sent me to collect a debt from him, but he's dead. Someone killed him."

I spit out the explanation as swiftly as possible, my entire body willing me to walk across the room and collapse upon my bed. I'd sleep and let Cassia sort it all out. When she'd finished, she'd wake me and tell me what to do.

Her mouth hung open again, showing even white teeth against her red tongue. She moved her gaze to the boy, who had put his fingers to his lower lip and watched her apprehensively.

"Killed?" she repeated in a faint voice.

"Murdered, butchered, his throat sliced. Professional." I moved my arm as though I cut across a man's throat. "I came here. I told no one."

As I spoke, I untied my pouch from my belt and shook the fragments of terra cotta onto the table. Cassia touched them, mystified.

"Give me the piece you picked up," I said to the boy. "Cassia can stick this together for you again."

Cassia turned over the shard that had *Leonidas* scratched on it, and her lips formed an *O*.

The boy opened his fist and dropped what he held onto the table. It wasn't a fragment, or even pottery, but a small roll of papyrus.

Cassia snatched it up and smoothed it out, her eyes widening as she studied the spidery writing within. She sat down, her interest caught, her entire body growing animated as it did when something intrigued her.

"Where did he find this?" she asked without looking up.

"At Selenius's shop," I said. "I thought he'd picked up another piece of the cup."

"No." Cassia turned the paper around and held it up to me as though I'd be astonished by it. Then she seemed to remember I couldn't read a word and laid it back down. "It's a voucher. For a traveling patron to change for Roman coin."

I didn't respond. When Cassia began speaking like a scribe I gave up following her. I crouched down by the boy who was torn between bewilderment and fascination.

"What's your name, lad?"

The boy took his fingers out of his mouth. "Sergius."

I waited, but he said nothing more. I didn't know if that was his praenomen or his family or clan name. He might have had no other if he was a boy from the streets. What if he was from a brothel?

My chest burned. I'd gone to brothels ever since I'd figured out what my wick was for, and as a gladiator I'd been a welcome guest—my lanista paid for the best. I favored women only, fully grown ones, that is, but there were plenty of Romans who indulged in young men; for some, the younger the better.

Lads and girls Sergius's age would have no choice but to fulfill the indulgence. They weren't old enough to seek a living elsewhere, and likely their parents had sold them to the brothels when they couldn't afford to feed them.

The children in these places were hollow-eyed and broken, knowing they could not protest or stop anything the customers wanted to do to them. I'd noticed the relief on their faces whenever I walked past them for the women who actually had breasts and hips.

I'd not been able to do a damn thing to help them. I had been owned myself at the time, and now I barely had enough to keep me and Cassia fed. I hadn't been back to the brothels in a long time.

But I'd sacrifice to any god willing to listen to keep this little lad away from them—a boy whose only delight was a cheap cup with my name on it.

"Do you have a family?" I asked him.

Sergius considered this and then shook his head.

"Where do you live then?"

"With Alba."

Since any number of women in the empire could be called Alba, this didn't help much.

"Is she your mother?"

A shake of his head, a faint distaste that I'd even think so.

"Mistress of a brothel?" I asked.

A nod. That clinched the matter. He'd not be returning to Alba.

"Did she send you on an errand today?" I continued.

Another nod.

"And what was this errand?"

"Fish sauce. Then I saw you."

Cassia had lifted her head to listen, her elbows on the table as she held the small piece of papyrus between her fingers.

"And you followed me," I said. "After I left the baker's."

Sergius gave me a single nod. "Took a shortcut."

Interesting. "How did you know where I was going?"

"I heard Quintus tell you to go to Selenius. I ran to get there first."

"And what did you see?"

Horror crept into his eyes. "Saw him dead."

"That was Selenius, was it?"

Sergius nodded vigorously. "Didn't like him. Mean. Ugly. Stank."

He hadn't smelled that good dead either. "You knew him?"

"Saw him about when I went to the market for Alba. He had his slave kick me if I came too close to his bench. Once he knocked me down."

My anger at Selenius bloomed, no matter the man was dead.

The small slip of papyrus fluttered between Cassia's fingers, distracting me. I eyed it in irritation. "What is that? Explain in words I will understand."

Cassia laid down the paper and smoothed it out, taking on the patient look she did whenever she had to teach me something.

"When a man from the outreaches of the empire decides to travel to the city of Rome, he will need money. But it is dangerous to walk the roads with a box full of coins if one does not have armed bodyguards every step of the way. Therefore, a man can go to a merchant or shipping agent who is part of a business in Rome, pay a certain amount of money, and obtain a voucher. When he reaches Rome, he takes the voucher to a shipping agent of the same company, who will then give him the amount he paid in. A small fee is involved, of course, but this way, a man can travel and not risk being robbed of all he has in the world."

A clever arrangement—*if* the man didn't lose his voucher and if he could be reasonably certain he'd get his money back at the other end.

"Selenius wasn't a shipping agent," I pointed out.

"Some money-changers honor the vouchers," Cassia said. "If they have an arrangement with the shipping company. Money-changers have plenty of coins, don't they?"

"All right then, this Selenius was a man travelers visited

to collect on their vouchers," I said, making certain I'd followed her explanation. "What of it?"

Even ordinary transactions excited Cassia's heart, but this did not explain her elation over the slip of paper.

"This voucher is a bit different." Cassia held it up again, smiling hugely. "This one is a forgery."

CHAPTER 3

I STARED AT THE PAPER SHE WAVED BUT WAS NO MORE enlightened than before.

"How do you know that?"

Cassia laid the sheet neatly on the table next to the broken cup. "When I was in the household of Glaucia Rufina, I traveled extensively with her. It was my task to go to the shipping agents and money-changers and pay in and take out. I kept track of all the finances." She trailed off.

She meant before Glaucia Rufina's husband had laid his hands on Cassia, and Cassia, once a trusted slave with many privileges, found herself banished.

Now she kept accounts for me. My finances were a fly to the elephant of those of a lady like Glaucia Rufina, but Cassia kept them with the same efficiency. She never complained about the difference in amount except when there wasn't enough to feed us or pay the rent. I'd realized that Cassia liked figures, any figures, didn't matter how large or small. As long as she had numbers to play with, she was content.

"I've handled many of these, some from this very man Gaius Selenius," Cassia said. "This is neatly done. Selenius decorates his with a symbol derived from his mark, so that all will know it's his. There has been an attempt to copy the mark, but it's not quite right. As I say, though, very neatly done. Most people would be fooled." She sounded admiring.

"Why kill him for it?"

Cassia shrugged. "It might have nothing to do with his death. What did you do when you found him? Did you tell anyone?"

"No." I glanced at Sergius, who had lost interest in the conversation and was looking about the apartment in curiosity.

Cassia's eyes widened as she followed my gaze. "You don't think …?" She swallowed, turning back to me in consternation. "You said you thought it was professional."

"I don't know." I balled my fists. "Might have been professional. Or luck."

A frightened person could slice a knife across another's neck and kill him without much effort. The human body was a fragile thing. Trainers, as well as the physicians who'd patched us up, had showed us every single vulnerable point on a man's body and how to stab them to bring about his swift end.

Cassia's dark eyes began to sparkle as they did when she was interested in a thing. I watched her run through scenarios and calculate their likelihood with lightning rapidity. I could do such a thing when it came to a fight, although it was best to let my training take over and not think very hard. Cassia could evaluate a dozen problems from what to eat for breakfast to who might have murdered a money-changer in the time most people could think to wonder what the weather was like.

"You must report it," Cassia said abruptly. "The baker knows you went to Selenius. He sent you. Did others see you near Selenius's shop?"

I told her about the few people who'd been left in the *macellum*, including the two Gauls who'd been finishing their business with the *garum* vendor.

"When someone finds Selenius dead, they will remember Leonidas the Gladiator walking in and then vanishing." Cassia's cheeks lost color, and she twisted her fingers together as she did when she was particularly worried.

"Leonidas, who knows how to kill," I finished for her. This was not the first time someone had connected me, a professional murderer, with a death. "The baker could have known Selenius was dead—he sent me to discover him and to be taken for the murder, so he wouldn't have to pay our be-damned fee." I paused. "I'm sorry I didn't get your money, Cassia. I should have shaken it out of him."

"Never mind about the money." Cassia sprang up and came to my side. She didn't touch me but she stood close enough that I felt the warmth of her stola. "You cannot be accused of this crime. You did not commit it."

I was stunned by two things: First, Cassia saying the words *Never mind about the money.* The second was her stout belief that I had not killed the man. She could not possibly know whether I had gone into the deserted shop of Gaius Selenius, taken all his money, and slit his throat. She hadn't been there, couldn't have seen.

But she believed in me, had from the day she'd met me.

That is, from the moment she'd realized I wouldn't set upon her, ravish her, beat her, and throw her into a corner as she'd fully expected. I'd only asked her what she wanted for dinner.

"If they come for me," I said slowly. "How do I prove I did not kill him?"

Cassia took a step back and surveyed me with calm assessment. "You haven't a drop of blood on you. *That* is a wine stain." She pointed at the purplish splash on the side of my tunic. "You don't even have blood on your shoes—you must have stepped carefully."

I nodded. I had, not wanting to touch what had poured from Selenius's throat.

"Was the blood liquid?" Cassia asked. "Still flowing? Or dried?"

I had a good memory for details, which Cassia had once told me she admired. This surprised me, as I hadn't thought it any sort of special trick. She'd responded that she wrote everything down because she *didn't* have a good memory. I'd had to think on that for a while.

I brought to mind Selenius's wide-open eyes, the blackening gash on his pale neck, the red pool of blood. "Somewhere in between. No longer flowing. Patches shining here and there. Selenius's face was gray."

"Which means he died some time before you arrived. Not a long time, or the blood would be completely dried. It would have helped if you'd touched his body and could tell me whether it was cold or not, but no matter. How long did it take you to reach the shop from the baker's?"

I had little idea of time other than morning, noon, and evening. I could barely make out a sundial, and there hadn't been one conveniently along my route.

"I walked to the baker's from here," I said. "I stopped when Sergius showed me his cup, and then I reached Quintus. Spoke to him for only a few moments. Walked straight from there to Selenius's shop on the Clivus Suburanus, not long before the fountain of Orpheus."

Cassia nodded as she no doubt calculated exactly how many strides I'd taken and how soon that had put me at the *macellum*. She was very good at such reckonings. I'd come to believe she could tell the legions exactly how far they could march every day on the supplies they had and still have energy for battle.

Cassia moved to the table and lifted one of her many wax tablets. "You left here at the beginning of the fifth hour," she said. "I'd say it took you about a quarter of an hour from the baker's to Selenius's." She marked a note. "From the state of his blood, Selenius might have been killed a half hour to an hour before you arrived. That can save you, if a competent physician examines the body and Quintus will agree you were talking to him at the time we say. As you had no notion who Selenius was before Quintus mentioned him, there was no reason for you to kill him before you visited the baker." She sank to her stool as she made her notes, then she tapped the stylus to her lips. "This would clear Quintus as well. He was putting bread in the oven as you arrived, you say, and that's a tricky business. The dough has to rise to a certain point but no further or it's ruined. He'd have to be there to shovel it into the oven at the crucial moment."

Cassia could not cook—she knew the theory of cooking, baking, beer brewing, wine making, and many other crafts of food, but she could not execute any of these herself. We bought all our meals from the tavern down the street.

"That means the boy didn't do it either," I said in a low voice. Sergius had wandered to the corner where my bed was, and now pulled back the shutter to look down into the street. "He followed me to the baker's."

"Unless he did it before you saw him the first time," Cassia pointed out. "Though that's unlikely. I see no blood on him either. Dirt, yes. Whoever cares for him doesn't bathe him." She shook her head in disapproval.

Cassia was always clean, from the toes that peeped from her sandals to the curls on top of her head. She bathed every afternoon and came home smelling of scented oil. I believe one reason she didn't complain about being a slave to a gladiator is that I did not hinder her leaving for the baths at the eighth hour of every day precisely.

"I'm not taking him back to the brothel."

"I agree. Poor lad." Cassia set her stylus on the table. "Where *will* you take him?"

We both knew he could not stay here. We barely had the coin to feed ourselves, in spite of our "benefactor." Cassia tirelessly worked to uncover his identity, but she'd so far not been successful.

I thought in silence then said, "Marcella."

Cassia's brows rose. "Widow of your friend, who has five children of her own?"

"She is kind and always needs help on the farm."

Marcella had been the wife of a gladiator who'd called himself Xerxes. I never learned his real name—I don't think he remembered it. He'd been *secundus palus* at our gladiator school, the second-best fighter. The *primus palus*, the top fighter, had been me. Many commented on the irony of our names—Xerxes the Persian and beaten down Leonidas the Spartan at the Battle of Thermopylae—but we only stared at those who mentioned it until they quietly slunk away.

Xerxes, probably the closest friend I'd had in life, had married and produced five children, even though he'd returned to the ludus every day for training and to the arenas for the games. He'd never been paired with me, and that fact had eventually gotten him killed. If I'd been his opponent that fatal day, I'd have let him win. I'd had nothing to lose—he'd had everything.

Marcella had been grateful to me for returning his body, along with his meager belongings. I'd contributed some of my winnings to help her set up a monument to him with a long inscription she'd told me said what a good husband and father he'd been. Xerxes, dead at age twenty-six.

Cassia watched me a moment and then simply went back to studying the false voucher, which told me she approved of what I wanted to do.

"Can you mend this?" I asked, stirring the shards of the cup with my finger.

Cassia switched her gaze to it, considering. "I believe so. I'll go to the potters' yard and find some paste."

She'd likely have it fixed better than new, or talk the potters into doing it for her. I held out my hand to Sergius. "Come with me."

Sergius looked around from where he held the shutter open, letting in a chunk of hot sunlight. His eyes filled with fear. "To Alba?"

"No. To my friend. She has a farm."

Sergius's face screwed up as though he had to think hard about this. I began to wonder if there was something wrong with him. He'd been streetwise enough to find his way through Rome but had not enough wit to tell me all of his name or who this woman called Alba was until I'd pried it from him.

If Alba owned the boy and I stole him away, I'd be taken to court. If I returned him, he'd go back to being a body to fulfill some senator's lustful fantasy. One of those fantasies could get Sergius killed.

I prayed Mars was looking out for me today, and made my decision. I'd take the boy to Marcella, and if this Alba fussed about it, I'd ask Cassia to come up with the money somehow to pay her off.

"Never seen a farm," Sergius said doubtfully.

Cassia stood and went to him, leaning down to speak in a bright tone I'd never heard her use. "Well, today you will, my lad. I'll mend your cup, and Leonidas will bring it to you later." She straightened up, reached to him as though to pat his head, then withdrew her hand before it touched his greasy hair.

Marcella would bathe him. She had a spring on her farm, which she diverted to her own makeshift baths, and her children spent every summer day in them. She laughed and said they were half fish.

I held out my hand. Sergius, at last making up his mind, came and took it.

Cassia sent me a look I could not interpret. I ignored her and led Sergius out.

I saw Cassia dart back to her table to make a mark on her tablet as we left, likely the time I departed and where I was going. I felt relief more than annoyance. Her record-keeping had saved my life more than once.

I TOOK SERGIUS THROUGH STREETS THAT HAD EMPTIED for the heat of the afternoon. The sixth hour had passed — work was finished, time to sleep out of the sunshine or head for the baths to while away the bright hours of the day.

We walked toward the Forum Augusti. From there we'd make our way to the Porta Capena as Marcella lived a few miles west of the city along the Via Latina.

If Selenius's body had been discovered, there was no sign of it in the people who wandered around the end of the

Forum Augusti's walls and down to the district called the Carinae. No one pointed at me and cried *murderer*! At least not today.

Even so, they noticed me. As they had this morning, people pointed, whispered, noted my passing. They'd wonder about the boy now too.

I halted at the corner of a lane that led to a small piazza. A narrow fountain spouted from the side of a tall tower that connected to the aqueducts, the overflow from the fountain's stone basin sliding down the street until it found the nearest drain in the concrete curb. Most fountains did this, rendering Rome's streets damp streambeds. Water flowed constantly into and out of Rome without a break.

I crouched down next to Sergius. "Do you know a faster way to the Porta Capena?"

The lad nodded readily, as though he'd been waiting for me to ask.

I rose and took his hand, letting him pull me along through the packed houses and apartments between the Oppian and Palatine hills. If we continued on this road, we'd skirt the Palatine and turn near the Circus Maximus to reach the gate, a route that would take us through some of the most populated streets in Rome.

As I'd hoped, Sergius knew a way around. He moved unerringly down a side passage to a scarred door much like the one he'd brought me through earlier.

This door was locked, but Sergius lifted an iron sliver that had been tucked under a rock, picked it open, and returned the iron sliver to its place. No one paid any attention to him, I noted. They looked at *me*, but they took no heed of what the small boy a few feet from me was doing.

Sergius opened the door a few inches and slid through. If I hadn't been watching him, he'd have disappeared before

I'd been aware. I waited until the street cleared a bit then caught the door before it closed and slipped inside after him.

I found myself in a dark, narrow passageway that smelled of urine and decay. For a moment, I imagined myself in the outbuildings of an amphitheater, waiting with both beasts and men to go to what might be our last fight. Darkness crept over my mind, wanting to suck me into it, but I shook it off and hurried after the boy, the sound of his footsteps guiding me.

The passageway led downward, and the floor grew wet as I descended. Soon my large sandaled feet sloshed in water and who knew what else, the walls now damp to my touch. I came to a branch in the passageway, emptiness to the right and to the left. I could no longer hear Sergius.

"Hey!" I shouted.

My words echoed back to me, but no reply from Sergius.

The darkness was complete, the light that had streamed through the cracks of the outer door far behind. I felt a rush of air to my left, and the soft grunt of a man striking out.

My instincts, honed from years of training for the deadliest games in the world, had me grabbing the wrist of the hand that came at me, turning it back and breaking the bone, even as a knife slashed through my tunic, biting into my flesh.

CHAPTER 4

THE MAN WAILED. I HEARD A THUMP AS HE FELL BACK against the wall, and another cry of pain. A knife clattered to the damp floor, and I picked it up. It had cut me, but only a glancing blow.

"Don't kill me," the man wheezed. "Please …"

I groped until I found him then hauled him up by the back of his neck. He continued to plead and beg, and he smelled like filth.

"Who are you?" I demanded.

"No one." His whisper was hoarse. "No one."

"Tell me, *No One*, do you know the way from here to the Porta Campena?"

His groan cut off. "What?"

I squeezed his neck a bit harder. "Do you know where this tunnel leads?"

"Yes, yes. Don't hurt me anymore. Sir."

I wasn't a patrician or an equestrian and never would be, but I didn't correct his use of the honorific. Down here in the dark, I could be anyone.

"Show me," I said.

The man trembled all over. I loosened my grip but not enough to let him run away. He shuffled forward, me half supporting him with one hand on his neck, the other under his unhurt arm.

We moved a long way through the barrel vault of the tunnel, the stench of the damp floor nauseating.

I didn't usually mind closed-in spaces, feeling safest in my life when I'd been holed up in my tiny bedchamber in the ludus. The cell at the ludus had been my sanctuary, a place where no one expected me to do anything but lie on my back and wait for the next day. Perhaps that's why I slept so much now—bed was the only place in which I felt protected.

But this noisome corridor was not the same as my dry little room at the ludus where Xerxes had scratched erotic pictures onto the walls for me. It was wet and stank, and we kept going down, down into blacker darkness. I expected to find raw sewage at any moment, and the rush of water from under every latrine and domus in the city, carrying away leavings of its citizens. Romans considered gladiators excrement, but I had no wish to become it in truth.

The tunnel began to slope upward again, and at long last, I no longer waded through liquid. After the tunnel dried out, a slit of light cut through the wall and made me blink.

I'd learned how to keep flashes of light from blinding me —an opponent could move his shield to catch the sunlight and beam it into the small eyeholes of my helmet. If I let such a thing distract me, it would be for the last time.

The man I propelled along obviously hadn't had arena training. He screwed up his eyes and tripped, and would have fallen had not my firm grip kept him on his feet.

The chink of light belonged to a wooden door whose vertical slats had warped as they dried in the sun. The door was locked, but the latch that held it was easily broken with one shove. We emerged into a narrow street that looked like all other narrow streets in Rome. The smoke from a tavern mixed with the stench of slops and a waft of spice from a nearby warehouse.

"Where are we?" I asked.

The man peered about, barely able to open his eyes in the bright sunshine—he must have been in the tunnel a long time. "Bottom of the Caelian Hill," he said breathlessly. "Near the old wall."

The Caelian was a smaller hill across from the Palatine, the base of it filled with tiny lanes and too many houses. Finer houses spread out as the hill rose, and an aqueduct marched across the top, its arches raised against the sky.

I studied the man I held. He was grimy, his smell unfortunate, his face black with muck, his skin dark from both the sun and whatever were his origins. I'd thought he would be older, but a fairly young face turned up to me, his dark eyes above unshaven cheeks filled with pain. I'd cut his skin when I'd broken his wrist, and the blood had stained his tunic and the pathetic remains of his sandals. He might have been twenty at most, which was a man by Roman standards, but his look was that of a youth.

He was also a slave, I realized by the tattered remains of his garments. A runaway one probably. Not that I would immediately haul him back to his master—if the master had been good to him, he wouldn't have run.

He gaped as he took me in, finally seeing what sort of man had hold of him. "I didn't mean ... I didn't mean ..."

"To try to rob me in the dark?" I finished for him. "An easy mistake."

"I thought—" He broke off, his gaze going to the scar that ran down my neck. "Who *are* you?"

"You'll have to get that wrist seen to," I said, ignoring the question. "The best *medicus* for setting bones is Nonus Marcianus. He lives at the bottom of the Aventine, near the fountain of the three fish. Tell him Leonidas sent you and that he should go to Cassia for his payment. Can you remember that?"

The man stared at me in shock. "Leonidas?"

"Yes, *that* Leonidas," I said impatiently.

He shook his head in confusion. "Never heard of you. I meant that the name is unusual. Greek—Spartan. But you don't look Greek."

The fact that he didn't know of Leonidas the Gladiator surprised me. I had been the most famous fighting man in all of Rome until the last year, and everyone in Rome went to the games. I'd traveled with my lanista for exhibitions outside Rome many a time, so people the length of the empire had seen me. Either this man was from a very remote outpost, or he'd been living in the sewers a long, long time.

"Go to Marcianus," I said firmly. "Remember, fountain of the three fishes. Ask there for him."

The man nodded, his greasy hair falling into his eyes. Nonus Marcianus would not thank me for sending him this squalid specimen, but I knew he'd see to him without hesitation.

As the man finally shuffled away, I heard light footsteps. Sergius came running down the street to me, having popped through another door.

"I lost you!" he said breathlessly, panic in his voice.

I held out my hand, hiding my relief. "Now I am found again."

The relief startled me. I had fully prepared to walk through the tunnels in search of the boy if I had to, and the thought of not finding him had made me cold.

I put my speculations about these feelings aside as I led Sergius onward. Both of us were dirty and smelly from the tunnels, but the people we passed as we walked under the aqueduct and out through the gate were just as stained from travel, tired and ready for journey's end.

I wondered if any of the travelers had the slips of papyrus they'd take to a shipping agent or money-changer to redeem the equivalent of the funds they'd paid into an account in their own cities. They'd be unlucky if they'd been told to go to Selenius to collect. If it was discovered the slips were forged, they would be worth nothing.

It set me to thinking. Had a traveler approached Selenius with a forged chit, and Selenius indignantly refused to honor it? Had the man with the forged paper grown enraged and murdered him?

Or was Selenius the forger? He could give the false slips to confederates who'd take them to the far corners of Rome, where agents might not realize the forgery and give out the coins. A nice scheme, if true. Selenius and his friends could divide the money without it costing them a single *as*.

Perhaps someone in the provinces had caught on to the fact that he was being robbed. That man might have come to Rome to confront Selenius, even to kill him.

I had little doubt that Cassia had already considered these speculations. While I traveled to the country, she'd be finding out who Selenius's confederates or angry customers might be. How Cassia would discover these things, I didn't entirely understand, but she knew every slave and every scribe in every house from the Palatine to the top of the Esquiline and every villa beyond that.

We weren't going far, but I tagged along behind a merchants' caravan, holding tight to Sergius's hand, carrying him when grew he tired. Even this close to Rome, even in these peaceful times, even in the middle of the afternoon, robbers could hide and strike a lone, exhausted traveler. I didn't worry for myself, but having to look after a child would hamper me if I had to fight.

The merchant didn't mind me joining them—he welcomed the muscle against robbers. Carrying Sergius must have made me look trustworthy, because the merchant didn't seem to worry about *me* trying to rob him.

I strode in silence, and Sergius offered no conversation. I realized as we went that I didn't know how to talk to children. I didn't much know how to talk to grown men either, so that wasn't such a surprise. But I hadn't given up the vague idea I'd have children of my own one day. It would be a quiet upbringing if I couldn't think of anything to say to them.

Sergius eventually settled into the crook of my arm and fell asleep against my shoulder. It puzzled me he was so trusting of me, if men at his brothel had used him as I suspected they had. But then I was Leonidas, the hero on his cup come to life. Perhaps he saw me as his champion, or maybe he was too simple to understand I could be as dangerous to him as any drunkard in a brothel.

Marcella's farm lay five miles outside the city. I left the Via Latina at a crossroads, saying farewell to the merchant and suggesting a safe house along the way to spend the night. We parted, and I made my way over a hill and into a green valley.

I'd always marveled that Xerxes had come out here most evenings to look after the farm and his wife, and then hastened back to the ludus the next morning for training.

He'd been a slave, sold to the ludus by his former master when it was clear he'd do well as a fighter, but he'd been allowed to marry and move into Marcella's farm. Our lanista believed in giving us rope, but only so much. Xerxes wouldn't have gotten far if he'd tried to run.

But Xerxes had always returned, right on time for training—he was a stickler for duty and his honor. He'd died for that honor, leaving Marcella alone with five children to raise.

On the other hand, if Xerxes had tried to run away and been caught, he'd have been sent to the mines or quarries, which would also be death, only slower. At least in the amphitheater, he'd gone out a hero.

Marcella didn't see it that way. She'd loved Xerxes and deeply grieved his passing. Still did.

Her farmhouse was a square building presenting a blank face to the world, with its doors and few windows overlooking a protected courtyard. At night, she brought in the animals and her equally wild children, and locked the place tighter than the best fortress on a hostile border.

Marcella was in the courtyard with one of her daughters, a mite with long black hair and Xerxes's merry eyes. She and Marcella were milking a goat that wasn't happy with the process. Sergius, who'd woken, looked about with interest.

Marcella rose from the ground, her mouth open as she saw me walk into the courtyard. Her daughter caught the goat before it could dart away, holding it with her arms around its neck.

"Who in the name of all the gods is *this?*" Marcella planted her stare on Sergius.

I set the boy gently on his feet but he looked as skittish as the goat. "This is Sergius. I ... found him."

Marcella only raised her brows, waiting for an explanation.

I would never have called Marcella pretty—her dark hair was too thin, her body fleshy rather than curved, her face too flat. But she had a vitality that made a person forget she was plain. I'd met courtesans praised for their astonishing beauty who'd be invisible next to Marcella. I understood why Xerxes would have done anything for her.

There were five little Xerxes on this farm, three boys and two girls. Marcella ruled them with a firm but kind hand.

"And you decided to bring him to me?" Marcella demanded as she ran her dark gaze over the thin boy.

I shrugged. "Xerxes always told me he needed more hands in the fields."

Her lips firmed. "This lad couldn't lift a rake. He'll need a lot of feeding up before he's any use on a farm."

Sergius stared up at her, his mouth open, a mixture of fear and interest in his eyes. Marcella joined us and crouched down next to him. "I've just made a stew, child. Would you like some?"

Sergius glanced at me for confirmation, and when I nodded, he turned back to Marcella. "Yes."

"Oh, he can speak," Marcella said. "That's a mercy. Fabricia, turn her loose and take Sergius inside. If your brothers and sister remember to come in for dinner, we'll eat."

Small Fabricia unwrapped herself from the goat, who tottered two steps and then halted to graze on stray bits of grass. The little girl, who hadn't lost her smile since I'd walked in, waved at me and took Sergius by the hand. She towed him off, Sergius looking back at me uncertainly, but I saw his curiosity about not only his surroundings but Fabricia as well.

I held out one of the few coins I carried. "I'll send more money for him when I can. And visit him."

Marcella straightened up, pulled pieces of straw from her hair, and accepted the coin. She'd need it, and she knew it. "I suppose you'll tell me the story someday. How is your other stray—I mean Cassia?"

Marcella had the idea that I let Cassia live with me out of kindness. I shrugged. "Cassia is Cassia."

"Good. I like her."

She studied me with her lively dark eyes, as though she expected me to say more about Cassia. I kept silent, not wanting to blurt out anything about murders and forgeries, not until I made sure I wouldn't be arrested for the crime. I didn't want my ill fortune coming back to haunt Marcella and her brood.

"You are well?" I asked Marcella when the silence had stretched to awkwardness.

For a moment, Marcella's animation deserted her, and I saw a blankness that I sensed many times in myself.

"Well in body," Marcella said. She put a hand on my wrist. "You are kind to ask."

Her touch meant nothing more than gratitude. I knew that. Marcella had only ever loved Xerxes, and he her.

I had no intention of offering bodily comfort to Marcella, if I could even perform on command, and she had no intention of accepting it. I'd once suggested she find another husband to help her, and she'd laughed at me, telling me she'd pushed out enough children, thank you very much.

Marcella withdrew her hand. "I might have enough stew to tempt even your appetite. If not, I'll round up something."

"No need. I'll eat when I reach home."

Marcella gave me a doubtful look. "It's growing late. You won't reach Rome before dark."

"I walk quickly," I said with a faint smile. "I don't want to leave Cassia alone."

Marcella regarded me without speaking for a moment. "I see. Greet her for me. And don't worry—I'll look after your boy. That is, if you promise to return and tell me how you found him, and why you decided you should be responsible for him."

I nodded solemnly. "I promise."

She burst out laughing, something Marcella could do spontaneously. I didn't always know what she found funny, but she had a comforting laugh.

"Go on with you, Leonidas. May the gods look favorably upon you."

"And you," I returned. We exchanged another look, she still finding something very amusing, and I went.

I HAD TAKEN A LONG TIME TO WALK FIVE MILES TO Marcella's, as the merchants had moved slowly to conserve the strength of their donkeys and their own feet. Traveling back took less time, as I moved at my own pace in the falling darkness.

It was dangerous to walk alone at night, even for a large and terrifying man like me. I'd easily take on any lone attacker, but a dozen men could have me on the ground before I positioned myself to fight. Bandits weren't known for following the rules of one-on-one combat. Gladiators fought plenty dirty, but we were nothing compared to desperate brigands.

I relied on the fact that I looked like a man who didn't have two coins on me to keep the robbers away. I wore a simple tunic belted at the waist and sandals, the dress of a freedman. No one would mistake me for anyone of high birth and fortune. In Rome, a man's clothing denoted what he was—slave, patrician, senator, a retired gladiator. The penalty for pretending to be in a different class could be dire.

I rarely had the chance to walk alone under the stars, and I found myself enjoying it. The air was cool, the sky open above me, the space of the gods filled with thousands of lights, some brighter than others.

As I drew closer to the city, the tombs of prominent Romans surrounded me, cold monuments to what once had been living, breathing people. I was tired of death, but these marble and concrete tombs did not bring me melancholy— they were monuments to honor memories, not bloody bodies strewn in my path as I walked from the amphitheatre, surviving once more.

I did not worry about gaining entrance to the city. Wagons and carts were only allowed in to make deliveries or take wares out again in the middle of the night. The edict made sense, as any other time of day, the heavy vehicles would block the streets, and we'd be bottled in.

Citizens paid for the convenience of moving about more easily during the day by nights filled with noise. Warehouses backed onto apartments, and a single domus might have storage houses all around it, with wares delivered after dark.

I was never bothered by the noise—I slept through it all —but it drove Cassia mad. She'd been raised on a villa in Campania where her father had been a slave, and where all had been, she said, blissful quietude.

One day, perhaps we'd have enough money to live in a

small house in the hills—a modest home if not a grand villa. Of course, I'd have to find a way to buy Cassia or free her from our benefactor. She didn't belong to me; she'd been lent.

I caught up with another merchant a half mile from the gate, and earned a ride on the back of his cart filled with unknown metal objects in exchange for my protection. I dangled my feet from the back of the cart, whatever was in his bags poking me in the thighs.

We went through the gate without hindrance, and I slid off the cart near the Circus Maximus. The merchant headed for a warehouse on the Aventine, and I continued around the Circus and up to the Subura, after a farewell and a thanks. I still didn't know what was in the wagon—bowls, urns, statues of gods?

I walked up the stairs to our small apartment, and inside.

Cassia launched herself up from the table and at me, her dark eyes wide, worry in every line of her. I felt her slim arms around my body, her many-curled head land on my shoulder.

"Leonidas," she said brokenly, in a very un-Cassia-like way. "They found Selenius. The vigiles said they'd scour the city for you, and you didn't come home. I thought … I thought …"

To my astonishment, she burrowed her face into my tunic, trembling and holding on hard.

CHAPTER 5

"They can't be searching for me very diligently." I rested my hand on Cassia's back, finding it supple and warm under her linen gown. "I walked from the Circus without seeing a one of them."

The vigiles were night watchmen whose main job was to keep public order and look for fires—if a fire broke out, they hastened to pull down houses to prevent the spread of flames. A mob of them might track down a killer, but if their commander thought they had better things to do, they'd let others find and drag the criminal to the magistrates.

"I traveled with a merchant and his family on the way," I went on, feeling the need to explain. "It took more time to reach Marcella's."

Cassia unwound herself from me, and I let my touch slide from her. She wiped the back of her hand across her eyes, which were red-rimmed and wet.

"Of course," she said. "I knew it would be something like that. Or that you'd decided to stay the night at the farm.

You ought to have." Cassia took a step back. "Why didn't you? It was dark …"

I shrugged. Then yawned. I was exhausted and my bed beckoned. I should be as worried as Cassia that Selenius had been found and men were searching for me, but …

"Why are they looking for me?" I asked abruptly. "Was I accused?"

Cassia wiped her eyes again, tucking back a lock of hair that had tumbled down. "Not yet. But another shopkeeper near Selenius's stall said he saw you. Others observed you visit Quintus the baker before that, and Quintus volunteered that he'd sent you to Selenius to collect a debt. The shopkeeper in the *macellum* can't be sure when he last saw Selenius alive. Before you went in search of him, anyway."

I silently called down every curse I could think of on Quintus the baker and observant shopkeepers.

I should have felt more fear, anger, or indignation at the very least that I'd be taken in for killing a man I hadn't. I had been worried about just this thing earlier.

But after visiting Marcella, remembering Xerxes, I was numb—nothing penetrated the fog in my head.

I was tired, I told myself. Cassia had awakened me from sleep too abruptly this morning, and I'd spent the day running around tunnels in the city followed by walking the five miles to Marcella's farm and back.

I turned away from Cassia and sought my bedchamber, stumbling in my haze of fatigue.

Cassia stepped in front of me. "You can't go to sleep now —we must clear you of this murder."

I gently brushed past her. Cassia would have to find a way to help me on her own, and I trusted that she would.

As I more or less fell onto the bed, I thought about the tunnels Sergius had showed me, and realized that anyone who knew of them could have crept undetected into Selenius's shop. The man who'd attacked me showed that desperate people might lurk in the tunnels, looking for a victim to rob.

I'd tell Cassia about them. Show them to her. She'd no doubt figure out exactly how much time it would take for a man to slip through the tunnels from every part of the city and out again in any other part, drawing little maps and diagrams to explain it to those who could not understand.

I was already half asleep by the time my reed bed crackled beneath my body. I heard Cassia let out a long sigh, then felt my sandals loosen and slide from my feet. A light blanket found its way across my legs, cutting the cool breeze that curled through the open window. Cassia hummed quietly, as she often did, but then the sound cut off.

"Oh, Leonidas," Cassia whispered. "Whatever will become of me if I lose you?"

A good question. She could not return to her former mistress, and our current benefactor might find a less salubrious man to lend her to, one who might beat her or force her.

I needed to stay alive, and free, to keep her safe. I would clear my name, and Cassia would help me.

It was my last thought before oblivion. Tonight, I hoped, I would be able to rest without dreams.

THE DREAMS LEFT ME ALONE UNTIL DAWN, AND THEN they came swooping.

In them, I saw Selenius, standing upright and regarding me calmly while blood flooded from his sliced throat. He didn't seem to be aware that he was already dead—he only held out a slip of paper, demanding a huge amount of money for it. I couldn't pay, but he offered to take the boy Sergius in lieu.

I shouted at Sergius to run, but the lad was frozen in place, staring at me in terror across the blood-drenched floor.

It's all right, Marcella whispered from far away. *Sergius is safe. You took him to the farm, remember?*

The voice changed from Marcella's to Cassia's, but my worry only rose. Cassia should not be here. Selenius's smile when he saw her exactly matched the shape of the cut in his neck.

I'll take Cassia instead, Selenius seemed to say. *Beautiful morsel. Proud bitch. Better on her hands and knees, I think.*

Another man had said those very words to me at one time. I'd nearly killed him. I lunged at Selenius, and his blood showered me as he fell, warm and stinking.

"Leonidas!" A blow fell on my stomach, a strangely light one.

The thump didn't fit with my dream, and I swam toward light, blinking open my eyes to see Cassia standing at arm's length, her stick tapping me just above my navel. The blanket was around my hips, tangling my legs.

"Leonidas," Cassia repeated, sounding relieved. "Marcianus is here."

MORNING HAD BROKEN SOMETIME WHEN I'D BEEN asleep. Rome was washed with golden light, the cool of the night lingering in the streets to temporarily drive out the acrid scents of smoke, food, and humanity.

A man sat at our table, hunched in conversation with

Cassia. He had a fringe of graying hair, a thin but well-muscled body, a bulbous nose, and brown eyes that in turn could be kind or stern. Kind when he was feeding me a tincture and telling me that setting my bone would hurt but he'd be swift, stern when admonishing me to rest and on no account fight for at least forty days.

His name was Nonus Marcianus, and he was a physician, a *medicus*, for Rome's most lucrative ludus. He'd been healing beaten-down gladiators for years, becoming an authority on broken bones, lacerations, wounds deep and shallow, and the chances a man had of living or not. His balms and potions, which he'd learned to mix in the East, had lowered the incidences of festering wounds and rotting limbs in our school. The gladiators, even the most brutish of them, had only good words for Nonus Marcianus.

He was a learned man of a Roman equestrian family, though born in the Greek isles, migrating to Rome after he trained as a physician in Greece. He'd taken to Cassia right away, as though pleased he'd found an equal in understanding.

They spoke Greek, Cassia relaxed and smiling as she chatted with him, Marcianus looking content as he answered her questions—or whatever he was saying. I couldn't understand a word.

Both broke off as I entered, and Marcianus rose. He wore a tunic that hung below his knees, and he'd laid his toga, the garment of a respectable citizen, across the back of his chair.

"Greetings of the gods to you, Leonidas."

"And you," I answered, trying to clear the sleep from my head.

I'd put on a clean tunic without Cassia saying a word. I'd had enough of the stained one I'd worn all day yesterday, which had been further ripened by my walk to the farm and back. I'd be visiting the baths today—the smell of unwashed gladiator was not my favorite.

"Your lanista rues the day he lost you," Marcianus said as we both sat down.

Cassia brought Marcianus a cup of wine, apologizing that it wasn't the best. Marcianus politely accepted. A bowl of nuts had found its way to the table as well. We never had much food in the apartment, but Cassia always managed to find refreshments for special guests.

"Does he?" I asked without much interest. I took up a handful of almonds and popped them into my mouth, enjoying their smoky flavor. Cassia bought them roasted with a touch of salt.

"Aemilianus has taken a contract with a patrician putting on games in Ostia, I hear. The prices Aemil can ask have gone a long way down without you at the school. He toys with asking you to return to perform in special bouts."

I was already shaking my head. No more games, no more amphitheatres. It wasn't fear that kept me from fighting—I continued to practice and train, even dropping in for sessions with Aemil on occasion, but I refused to take another life. Ever. For any reason.

"I told him you wouldn't," Marcianus said, looking satisfied. "I will convey your answer."

I said nothing, only scooped up another handful of almonds.

Cassia seated herself at the table again, opening her tablet and taking up a stylus. She made a note—I wondered if she'd marked down the exact day and time I'd turned down my old trainer's offer to return and make him some money.

I knew why Marcianus had come. I'd told the man in the

tunnels to seek him, and that Cassia would pay the fee, if we had any money to give Marcianus, that is. What I did not know was why Marcianus wanted to speak to *me*. He hadn't come to convey the message that my lanista wanted me to fight for him again—he wouldn't have bothered to trudge all the way across Rome for that.

"Who was the man you sent to me?' Marcianus asked. "It was a straightforward fracture—you twisted his wrist to block a knife thrust. Why did he try to kill you?"

Cassia's eyes widened, and she sucked in a breath. I'd fallen asleep before I could tell her about the man with the knife, and obviously this was the first Marcianus had mentioned it. "He attacked me in the tunnels," I said. "They are part of the sewers, I think. It was very dark, and he must have been hungry."

"Hungry and terrified," Marcianus said. "I set his wrist and gave him something to eat. He wouldn't say his name, and he ran off as soon as I let him go. But he was impressed with you."

I shrugged. "I hurt him pretty badly. I didn't want him to die."

Marcianus acknowledged this. "The wound didn't bleed much. As I say, it was clean. Very professional."

I shrugged again. I didn't admit how much the blood on the man's tunic, put there by me, had unnerved me.

Marcianus gave me a keen eye, as though he knew what was going on in my head. "I heard the vigiles were looking for you last night. They must have given up."

"They sleep during the day," Cassia said sourly. "I have no doubt they or the urban cohorts will try again later."

"I didn't kill Selenius." I spoke in a firm voice. I didn't think Marcianus would be sitting here so calmly if he thought I'd murdered a man, but I wanted to make certain he knew the truth. "I don't know who did."

"Tell me about his body," Marcianus said, interested. "I'll look at it if I can—who is his family?"

"I only heard of him yesterday," I began with a growl, but Cassia pulled another wax tablet to her and opened it.

"Gaius Selenius was unmarried," she said as she consulted her notes. "His house is on the Esquiline, where he lived with his sister, Selenia, and his nephew, who is also called Gaius Selenius—he adopted this nephew. The sister collected Selenius for burial, so I imagine his body is still at the house. Selenia and her son will inherit the business. I believe young Gaius is already having the shop cleaned."

Marcianus snorted. "He wastes no time."

Cassia did not look as disapproving. "Selenius's rivals will waste no time taking his customers. If the Selenia and Gaius need the business to live, they will have to make sure they don't lose too many punters to the taint of Selenius getting murdered in his own shop. You know how superstitious Romans are."

Marcianus's smooth face split into a smile. "So are Greeks, dear lady. But in a different way, I grant you. The sister and nephew will have to appease Selenius's spirit, yes, and any other spirits who took the opportunity of the violent death to flock in. And you are right. Such a thing should not be delayed. However ..." Marcianus returned his attention to me. "If I cannot convince the poor woman to let me have a look at her brother's body, we have only you, Leonidas, who can tell me of him. So please describe what you saw. Leave nothing out."

I didn't want to revisit the room awash with blood, even in my mind, but did want to hear what Marcianus made of the death.

I closed my eyes.

If I concentrated on a thing I could remember it in its entirety. I don't know whether this came from my training to always know where an enemy stood, or simply something in my humors, but I could picture a scene vividly for some time if I tried. Probably why I had so many nightmares. A curse from the gods, I thought it. Maybe one day I'd assuage whatever god I'd offended and be granted the blissful ability to forget.

"Selenius's shop," I said. "Ten feet on a side, and in height. Light came through the open wall above his counter, from the atrium in the center of the *macellum*. He was lying under the counter, head bent against the wall, feet spread. His right sandal had one thong broken. His tunic must have been recently laundered, or it would not have been so white. That made the blood on it so much more vivid."

I broke off, bile rising. If I hadn't been so worried about Sergius as I'd stood at the edge of the pool of blood, I'd have been out in a back lane, vomiting until there was nothing left.

Marcianus's tone gentled. "Can you describe the patterns the blood made? Think of it as paint—where had it been stroked?"

I swallowed. Paint and blood might look similar, but paint smelled clean in comparison.

"A line around his neck," I said. "A stream down his throat, though some had dried and was caked. His tunic soaked with it, like it had caught a wave from the sea." I swallowed again. "It spread from under his body, past his feet, to collect in a pool. It lapped almost all the way to the walls to either side of him. Only a small patch was left bare." I'd used that patch to step around the room to Sergius.

"Hmm." I heard Marcianus's interest but didn't open my eyes. "What else?"

I didn't want to mention Sergius. I trusted Marcianus with my life, but he was a conscientious man. If he decided Sergius had killed Selenius, or at least had witnessed the death, he'd hunt the child down and take him to a magistrate.

I wiped Sergius from the picture in my head. "There was a door on the other side of the room. I thought it led to the shop next to Selenius's, but it didn't. It went to tunnels that came out on a street not far from the fountain of Orpheus."

"Hmm," Marcianus said again.

"Hmm, what?" Cassia asked. "Your *hmms* have me most intrigued."

"It was a warm day," Marcianus said. "And yet you say the cut on his neck was black, the blood there dried. I can't be certain until I see this man myself, but I would guess he died somewhere in the fourth hour. Possibly close to the fifth, but no later."

Cassia gave a little victory hop in her chair. "Ha! Leonidas was asleep—sleeping quite soundly—until nearly the fifth hour yesterday. It took me the longest time to wake him. He left at a few minutes past the fifth hour—I made a note of it." She pulled out a tablet filled with scratches to show Marcianus.

Marcianus had seen Cassia's records before, but he still looked awed upon viewing them. By habit, every day, Cassia noted every single time I came and went from the house, and every time she did, every place we walked, every coin we spent, and on what. She claimed she did this to keep us from running out of money, but I suspected she simply enjoyed it. A person can make a note of an expense without writing a lengthy record of every moment of the day.

"If your notes can convince a magistrate, then Leonidas has nothing to worry about," Marcianus concluded. "A witness to Leonidas's sleep or Selenius's death would be better though." He meant a witness to my sleep other than Cassia. A slave's testimony was not always regarded as relevant.

"Our neighbors," Cassia said in perfect seriousness. "They likely heard Leonidas snoring."

Marcianus chuckled. "You will have to ask, my dear. Leonidas, let me see your hands."

I frowned a bewildered moment, and then held them out, palm-up. Salt from the almonds sparkled on my skin. I hadn't had time to bathe, so I carried the dirt from walking through the tunnels, my journey to Marcella's farm, my ride on the merchants' wagon, and whatever I'd touched between the Porta Capena and home last night.

Marcianus clasped my wrists and dragged my hands to him, bending close to examine them.

His strength always surprised me. Marcianus was a small man, but he could yank a reluctant gladiator around with ease. I didn't like others touching me—I'd been pushed, shoved, and manhandled since I was a boy—but I'd learned to put up with Marcianus.

He leaned over my right palm until his nose nearly touched it, and then ran a fingernail over the crease between my forefinger and wrist. "No blood there. Even if you wash carefully, blood can linger in the tiniest grooves in the skin. If you'd killed Selenius, you'd have had it all over you."

Marcianus released me with satisfaction. He rose with his usual vigor, lifted his bunched toga, and looped it around his arms. He'd need more help to position it correctly, but Cassia remained seated. Draping togas, she'd told me, was no more one of her talents than dressing hair.

Marcianus drained his cup of wine, dabbed his mouth with the back of his hand, and headed for the door.

"I will visit the man's sister and try to examine the body," he said, pausing on the threshold. "Don't worry, lad. I'll make sure you aren't taken for it."

I'd stood up to see him out, though Marcianus was already halfway down the stairs before I reached the door. He waved up at me, turned the corner of the landing, and was gone.

Cassia remained on her stool. She studied her tablet, her smiles gone, her expression troubled.

I sat down on the stool Marcianus had vacated. "What?"

Cassia let out a sigh. "Nonus Marcianus will do his best, but the only thing that will clear you for certain, Leonidas, is finding out who truly did this."

I agreed with her, but there was no use restating it. "Why didn't you mention the forged vouchers?" I asked. When she hadn't, I didn't bring them up either, because I knew she'd have a reason why not.

"They may have nothing to do with the murder, and Marcianus might have asked why I hadn't alerted a magistrate about them right away. He is a stickler for the rules."

I reached into the bowl of almonds and closed my large hand around its remaining contents. "So are you."

Cassia gave me a prim look. "Only when it's expedient. Ah, well, I suppose we'd better make a start."

I dumped the handful almonds into my mouth and chewed. "You make a start," I said. "I'm for the baths."

CHAPTER 6

I HEARD CASSIA'S LIGHT STEPS BEHIND ME AS I WALKED out the door.

"Why on earth are you going to the baths when you're a wanted man?" she asked, quieting her voice so the patrons of the wine shop wouldn't hear. "You'll be dragged to prison."

I looked back at her. Cassia's dark eyes held fear, a lock of her hair escaping to brush her cheek.

"No one has come to fetch me is because they know I won't run," I said. "If I'm arrested at the baths, at least I'll be clean."

I turned away before she could argue. Strangely, she did not. When her voice came to me as I reached the landing, it was hushed.

"I'll prove it wasn't you, Leonidas," she said. "Marcianus and I will prove it."

I believed her. I'd never met a person with as much clarity of thought as Cassia. She'd explained, when I'd remarked upon this once upon a time, that if I considered her intelligent, it was because her father had been a brilliant teacher and writer, and he'd taught Cassia how to think. *She* didn't believe herself to be unusually clever—she thought she'd never live up to her father's greatness.

No matter. I had faith in Cassia. She, a Greek woman and a slave, had more honor and loyalty in her than most Roman men who'd been raised to such concepts. She'd not thank me for the comparison, but it was true.

Instead of heading for the small bath complex I usually frequented, I walked to the Campus Martius and the Baths of Agrippa.

I preferred my friendly bathhouse near the old wall under the shadow of an aqueduct, where slaves and freedmen, along with plebs from the Aventine and the lower slopes of every hill, mingled without inhibition.

The more ostentatious baths, like the ones built by Agrippa seventy and more years ago, also welcomed slaves and freedmen. But it was understood, if not ruled, that we'd keep to ourselves and not interfere with the enjoyment of our betters. The patricians and equestrians also saw no reason not to order any slave they saw to do their bidding, even if it was said slave's afternoon off.

I sought the Baths of Agrippa today because large bath complexes were founts of all gossip. If anyone knew anything about Selenius and his murder, it would be discussed in the *caldarium*.

I made for the Campus Martius via the Pallacinae neighborhood and its lines of shops shaded by colonnades. I welcomed the coolness under the arches, fading into the crush of shoppers and merchants on this fine summer morning.

Rome would celebrate the festival of Fortuna soon, and Cassia and I would join the festivities, which would involve the death of unfortunate animals, a feast, and plenty of wine. I'd eat a morsel of meat to honor the gods, but I didn't have much taste for cooked flesh. The wine I'd drink until I couldn't stand.

I skirted the enormous portico of the Saepta Julia, which had seen gladiatorial games in its vast center. A building crane rose somewhere behind it, men on a high rooftop manipulating a stone block into place on some new edifice, while the crane's great wheel slowly turned.

I walked past the Pantheon of Agrippa, funded by the man who'd dedicated many public buildings to the honor of the great Augustus. Cassia told me Agrippa was to have been Augustus's heir and the next princeps, but he'd died too soon. Perhaps the uncertainty of these times could have been mitigated, she liked to say, if he had lived.

I paid little attention to politics except to avoid the intrigues that swept the city from time to time, resulting in entire families dead or exiled. I preferred to be a nobody not doing anything in particular, rather than a patrician in a hilltop villa wondering when the Praetorian Guard would come for *him*.

The bath complex I entered on the other side of the Pantheon was grand. Columns soared to a lofty ceiling held up by caryatids, paintings of lavish landscapes and villas covered the walls, and a mosaic of Neptune in his chariot pulled by sea serpents flowed across the main floor.

I stripped down in the *apodyterium*—the changing room —and found an eager attendant who helped me rub oil into every inch of my grimy skin. I even poured oil over my head, my hair kept shaved close enough that I could clean it that way. The attendant, who asked me incessant questions about what it had been like in the amphitheatres smacking my sword into my friends' guts, finally turned away to the next bather. I left for the gymnasium, which was under the open air.

I'd been to these baths only once before, but one of the trainers there, a former gladiator himself, long retired, welcomed me. He had wooden practice swords in a rack, and he and I hacked at posts set up at intervals around the room while the sun poured down on us.

The routine of the thrusts and steps returned to me, so familiar I could go through them while my mind floated.

The exercise shook off my fog. As it did, I realized something that others might not—a gladiator doesn't slice with his sword—he stabs. We'd been taught that a hard thrust was more effective than a swipe. I would have stuck my sword straight into Selenius's throat, not tried to cut him open.

The killer, I reasoned, must have come and gone through the tunnels. The shopkeeper and the two Gauls in the *macellum* had seen me enter, but they'd seen no one else, according to Cassia. That meant the murderer had either been a person they saw in the market every day and so didn't notice, or he'd come in and gone out through the tunnels, as I had. An avenue I would explore this afternoon, when the shops were quiet again.

The trainer admired my patterns and asked me to show him a few moves. We sparred in slow motion, attracting much attention from the other bath-goers. I kept my movements slow and deliberate, knowing that if my body felt the moves of true combat, I might instinctively go for the kill, no matter that our swords were carved from wood.

I ended the bout first, saying I needed to get on with my day. The trainer took my sword, slapped me on the shoulder and told me I could spar with him any time—he'd welcome the relief from tedium.

We parted. I fetched my strigil and had another attendant scrape the dirt and sweat I'd raised from my body, the oil taking it easily away.

I drew a crowd during this ritual. Each time the attendant flicked away the accumulated gunk, men would dive for it, scooping it in a cloth or small dish. The oiled sweat of a gladiator could be made into an unguent, which was believed to heal and give strength. The blood of a dying gladiator had even more potency, but I had no intention of giving them any of *that*.

I ended the entertainment by walking to the *tepidarium*, plunging into the pool to wash away what remained of the oil. Then I swam, stretching my limbs. I'd learned to swim as a boy fishing in the Tiber, far upstream of Rome. I remembered little of my childhood, but the cool rushing water under the sunshine came back to me as I floated across the pool.

I refreshed myself with a quick dunk in the cold pool in the next room, then walked to the caldarium and eased myself into the scalding hot water. Many bathers choose to move from cold to tepid to hot, but I preferred to go from freezing directly to heat.

My muscles softened and relaxed as I lolled on a bench in the water. I leaned my head against the tiled wall and let myself doze.

"Did you do it, Leonidas?" A man's voice drifted to me. "Did you kill the money-changer?"

I opened my eyes. I first saw the reds, yellows, and blues of the painted wall, a faux window opening to green trees of a lavish garden.

Next I saw who'd spoken, a youngish man with his short dark hair plastered to his head by the water, his limbs slim but muscled.

I didn't know him, but in a city of a million inhabitants it wasn't surprising. His question meant word had spread. The fact that I hadn't been dragged off to the Tullianum to await trial and execution meant there was doubt.

"No," I said.

He seemed to believe me. "But you were there. You saw him."

"Yes."

The man was undaunted by my clipped answers. "I heard about his sister. Such a pity." He shook his head with the air of one confident such tragedies would never happen to him.

"His sister?" I asked, trying to sound nonchalant. "What has happened to her?"

"It was long time ago. A few years anyway." He leaned closer to me, thrilled to be the one to impart the tale. "She was violated by another money-changer. This Selenius's friend."

He gave me a nod and withdrew, as though allowing me time to digest the information.

Poor woman. To be raped and then have her brother die violently was much to bear. I wondered if someone was out to gain vengeance on Selenius's family. Such things happened. I'd suggest to Cassia that we find out who'd attacked the sister—he might be the murderer.

"They say *you* did it," the man went on. He'd inched imperceptibly nearer to me. "So many saw you wandering about yesterday, but all say you had no blood on you at all. They also saw you with a boy. For enjoyment?" He wiggled his brows up and down.

"No." I snarled the word so fiercely the young man scooted down the bench again.

"Then what were you doing with a boy?"

Did he have nothing to do all day but chatter in the bath about other people? Probably not. If he was a patrician, he was probably an aedile, on the first rung of the ladder to senator. A pampered man's pampered son.

I realized I had to have some explanation for Sergius. I was a man people noticed, and they noticed what I did. "He was lost," I said, my voice retaining its growl. "I took him home."

"Ah." Disappointment coated the word. The young man slid a little closer again. "My father imports the best wine. He gives me as much as I want for my own purposes. Share some with me?"

The hope in his eyes was unmistakable. There was no shame in a man lying in bed with another man as long as he did not do it to excess and kept his liaisons private. I preferred women, who were softer, smelled better, and were far less arrogant.

"No," I said abruptly and rose from the pool.

If I'd been any other freedman, the lad might have had his servants beat me for rudeness, but a hero of the games was given some latitude.

I stepped out, leaving him staring after me. Maybe the sight of my naked body would sate him for a while. I turned around briefly and let him see the rest of it—the least I could do for his information, whatever good it might do me.

He was wise enough not to pursue me, and I returned to the changing room, dried off and donned my clothes.

IF NOTHING ELSE, BEING CLEAN MADE ME FEEL BETTER. Now my stomach growled, reminding me I had missed several meals.

I left the Campus and its many entertainments and returned to the street of shops in the Pallacinae. I found a tavern and squeezed onto a stool at the corner of a table, asking the harried barmaid to bring me lentils and whatever vegetables they had cooking.

She returned before long with a bowl of lentils and limp-looking greens, along with a crackling piece of bread. I dunked the bread into the broth and scooped up the lentils and veg, enjoying every mouthful, though the broth was weak and the vegetables old. The wine was indifferent as well, but I drank it down, thirsty after the hot bath.

I realized, when I was finished, that I had no money to pay. I'd given Marcella and the man who'd applied the strigil my last coins. Cassia hadn't known I was short of funds, or she'd have made certain I had at least the price of a meal.

I confessed my lack of coin to the barmaid. "My slave will be along later with it." Cassia would be vexed, but she believed in paying our debts as quickly as possible.

The barmaid, who had shining black hair and skin tanned from hot summers, cocked her head and assessed me. "No matter." She gestured for me to follow her. "Come with me."

I assumed she'd lead me to the back to wash up or stir pots of beans, but she took me up a flight of stairs to a tiny room dimly lit by a small square window. It had a slab of a bed covered with reeds, much the same as my own.

The barmaid began to undress. I remained in the doorway, not sure how to tell her she'd be disappointed.

I didn't have the chance. The barmaid caught my hand and dragged me to the bed, busily kissing me while she untied my belt and dragged off my tunic.

Then she proceeded to use me thoroughly. I don't think

she noticed that this former gladiator couldn't raise his sword. She had me flat on my back, finding creative ways to take pleasure from me and my body. I'd been with women plenty—I'd been a fixture at a brothel near my ludus—but this woman, as much as she tried, delighted nothing in me.

I thought of Selenius's sister and her defilement. No doubt hers had been far more violent and terrifying, but I had an inkling of what she'd felt. She hadn't been a person to the man who'd taken her, only a body to be used.

But that was what a gladiator was, wasn't it? A fighting body, performing for money? It was why we were *infamis*, and why a barmaid thought I'd be more than happy to pay for my dinner by letting her play with me.

By the time she wore herself out and fell asleep, the afternoon had come, heating the city. I slipped away, sliding on my tunic and moving quietly down the stairs into the street.

I felt unclean, so I stepped into the baths close to home and washed my body all over again. It cost an *as* to enter this complex, but I told the attendants that Cassia would come by to pay later. They knew both of us and acquiesced. No paying my way with my body again today.

I was known and accepted in this bath complex, so I had to talk with men I'd become acquainted with while I soaked. That is, they talked, and I mostly nodded. But I learned why the vigiles had broken off their hunt for me last night and I hadn't been arrested by the cohorts this morning.

Apparently, the *garum* shopkeeper had reported seeing a man come *out* of the *macellum*, but hadn't first seen him going in. The cohorts were now looking for this person, who had been described as dirty, young, and frightened. I had a feeling I knew who they were talking about.

The sky was darkening by the time I left the baths and made my way home. Cassia wasn't there when I arrived.

I stood in the doorway of our little apartment, looking over the room, my bed in the far corner, Cassia's little bunk on the other side of the table. A balcony opened to my right, larger than most as it was poised on the flat roof of the shop below.

I always knew when Cassia was out, and not because our domicile was so small I'd notice at once. I could walk in with my eyes closed and know she wasn't here.

The air was different, empty. Silent. Cassia was often humming or singing softly. Her two long stolae hanging on pegs near her bed and her cloak for cooler weather looked forlorn and waiting, as did her spare pair of sandals tucked neatly against the wall.

The table held her writing tools, tablets and stylus, papyrus and charcoal sticks, lined up exactly even with one another. In the middle of the table was the cup Sergius had dropped, stuck together again, the cracks in the clay almost invisible.

I lifted the cup, examining the crude drawing, running my finger over the letters that meant my name. *Leonidas*. A name that hadn't been my own, but Leonidas was who I became.

When I heard her step behind me, a tightness in me loosened. Cassia began speaking as soon as she saw me, her words flowing around me.

"Nonus Marcianus told me how to mix a paste that would mend it in a trice," she said, motioning to the cup in my hand. "I saw him this afternoon, as I wandered about on all my errands."

I heard her unwind the *palla* that kept her head covered from the sun and mitigated the offense to men who disapproved of a woman running about by herself. Slave women did not have the same restrictions that patrician and equestrian women did—a Roman lady should stay at home and not show herself, unless she traveled in a covered litter or sedan chair with attendants. Cassia's former mistress had insisted Cassia never leave the house unless she was muffled, to keep shame from the household, she'd said.

Cassia went on she set a basket on the table. "When you take it to Sergius, perhaps I could go with you? To see the hills again, breathe air that doesn't have the stench of Rome in it would be ..."

She stepped next to me and inhaled as though trying to find the clear air of Campania in the heart of this city.

The breath cut off. I looked down to see her staring at me, her expression changing from her usual animation to bewilderment. She delicately sniffed again, then turned away, color rising in her cheeks. She blinked rapidly, ducking her head so I would not see.

I realized that though I'd bathed again after the tavern, the scent of the barmaid and her zeal must linger. Cassia would know what it meant.

I opened my mouth to explain, but Cassia bent over the table, her back to me, her chatter resuming. "I went to the tavern while I was out and found us dinner—lovely, fresh endives and some greens, and there's bread left over from this morning. What did you learn at the baths?"

CHAPTER 7

CASSIA LAID OUT OUR DINNER, AS SHE DID EVERY NIGHT—
a meal prepared by the tavern at the end of our street and a
flask of wine from the shop downstairs. She'd instructed the
tavern keeper exactly how to make the food I was used to,
and now he and his wife prepared the dishes and had them
ready as a matter of course.

I watched while Cassia poured two cups of the wine
from a small flask, sweetening it with honey. She talked all
the while, even though she'd asked me what I'd found out,
never letting me speak.

I sat down and chewed through a salad that had been
flavored with lemon, almonds, and a drop of honey, and
endives roasted with a little vinegar and salt. The barley had
been cooked in a rich broth of vegetables—I suspected some
leftover pork ended up in the vegetable broth as well, but I
didn't fuss. The meal was fresh and good, a far cry from the
one at the other tavern.

As I ate, Cassia told me about her afternoon.

"I saw Selenius's sister, Selenia," she said as she neatly

sliced off a bit of endive. "She has much to do preparing for her brother's funeral and helping her son take over the shop. She is shattered, Selenia is, but young Gaius seems capable enough. He's nineteen and has been assisting his uncle for several years, and at least understands the business. Gaius knows all about the forgeries, by the way."

I took advantage of Cassia putting the endive into her mouth to break in. "You asked about the forgeries outright?"

Cassia swallowed and sipped her wine. "I hinted. Young Gaius crumpled at once. He was so ashamed, and begged me to say nothing. His uncle, you see, and another friend, had come up with the idea. Selenius would give out these chits to select friends for nothing, they would hie off to whatever city accepted them, and the shipping agents there would pay out. The friends would then return to Selenius, and they'd divide the lot."

I'd thought of something similar as I dozed in the baths.

"Wouldn't the agents in the other cities catch on after a while?" I asked. "When their money was never replenished?"

"Ah." Cassia smiled, her melancholy fleeing. "That is the beauty of it. Selenius would pay back *one* of them. Then a man would arrive with another false voucher for a smaller amount of money from the same shipping agent. Selenius would then use that money plus more from the take to pay the next agent. Then one of his friends would withdraw funds from *him*, bring it to Selenius, and he'd pay the next one in line. He had all the agents believing they'd been paid back, when in fact, he was floating the same money from one to the other to the other. Astonishing."

Cassia sat back, a little smile on her face. Any clever arrangement involving numbers pleased her. The fact that

Selenius and his friends had committed blatant fraud and theft was beside the point.

"Even so." I lifted my bowl, poured the last drop of broth into my mouth, and set the bowl down with a thump. "Someone would catch on eventually. Maybe they did."

"And were so angry that they killed Selenius?" Cassia finished, nodding. "I think so too. I've asked young Gaius to give me a list of names of these shipping agents who've been skimmed. I promised I'd say nothing—his uncle is dead and can't answer for the crime anymore—and Gaius will find a way to pay back all the money without argument. I'll discover if any of these men were in Rome yesterday, and if so, we'll find them and see if they indeed killed Selenius in a rage. Rest assured, your name will be cleared, Leonidas."

She spoke with great confidence, but I knew better than to relax. If Romans decided they wanted justice, they'd have it, no matter who had to pay. They might think a champion gladiator being torn apart by wild beasts a fitting end to the problem.

I finished my meal in silence. Cassia chattered on, about Selenia, the sister, and her grief. Cassia had pretended to be a slave working for Marcianus to gain admittance to Selenius's house and ask questions—in fact, Marcianus had accompanied her, saying he'd been sent to look at Selenius's body.

"Marcianus confirmed that Selenius was killed midmorning yesterday, as he suspected, which ought to clear you. You were fast asleep."

True. The idea of bed appealed to me, so I rose and set down my wine cup.

"They're looking for a man," I announced. "I heard this in the baths. A shopkeeper said he saw a man come out of the center of the shops but not go in, much earlier than he saw me. I think they're talking about the man I met in the tunnels. He was afraid, and he had blood on him." I'd thought I'd caused the blood on his tunic, but Marcianus had said I'd given his wrist a clean break, so perhaps not. "I'll look for him in the morning."

I mumbled this last as I walked into my bedchamber and kicked off my sandals. My tunic followed them to the floor, and I pulled a blanket around my naked body before stretching out on my pallet and entering the land of Morpheus.

MY OBLIVION LASTED A FEW HOURS AND THEN I WAS awake again. This happened sometimes—either I slept for a night and half a day, or I woke in the small hours, slumber eluding me.

I pulled on my tunic Cassia had hung on its hook and slid on my sandals, which were now lined up in perfect parallel by the wall.

The rest of the apartment was as neat, the supper things long gone, towels folded, Cassia's tablets and papers stacked at exact right angles to the table.

I expected to see Cassia in her bed, curled on her side. In sleep was the only time she allowed herself to be untidy, her limbs askew and her hair tumbling.

Her pallet was empty, however, the blanket smooth. I felt a moment of alarm, then I heard a rustle from the balcony. Releasing a breath, I stepped through the doorway to the flat space that served as our makeshift terrace.

Cassia sat on the one stool that we kept here, a folding tripod she'd found secondhand at a market stall. She leaned back against the wall of our apartment, moonlight glittering on her tear-streaked cheeks.

I paused in perplexity. Cassia scolding, lecturing, teasing, or rolling her eyes at me I understood. Cassia crying, I did not.

She hadn't even wept when she'd discovered she'd been tossed from the lavish villa in which she'd grown up to be slave to a former gladiator, a brute of a man who was the lowest of the low.

My foot crunched on grit as I stepped out to the balcony. Cassia jumped and wiped her eyes.

"Did I wake you?" she asked with an attempt at her usual brightness.

I dropped to sit on the edge and dangle my legs over the wall. We had no railing here, wooden or otherwise, but the space was wide. We didn't worry about thieves climbing up from the street to our apartment because we had nothing to steal.

"No," I answered. "What makes you cry?"

I heard her start, as though she'd expected I would not notice. "Nothing important."

Though I'd lived solely with men all my life, I'd known enough women to realize this was not a true answer. Women said, *It's nothing,* when it was the most serious thing on earth.

I also knew that cajoling her would do no good. If Cassia did not want to tell me a thing, she would keep it firmly to herself.

I faced the street, listening to the rumble of delivery wagons and the shouts of carters in the distance.

We sat in silence for a while. A cooling breeze drifted through the narrow street below, driving away the smells and stuffiness of the June night. I thought of Sergius resting his head trustingly on my shoulder as I carried him the long way to Marcella's farm.

"I like children," I said.

Cassia drew an abrupt breath. "Pardon?"

"I like children," I repeated without turning to her. I mused on this for a moment. "I didn't know."

I heard a rustling and then Cassia was beside me, folding herself to sit and hang her legs next to mine. She stared off into the street as I did. "I think I do too," she said. "Or perhaps I simply like Sergius."

"Maybe."

Again we fell silent, both of us marveling at this new thing we'd discovered about ourselves. The coolness and moonlight transformed Rome into a silver and black mosaic, the harsh lines of the buildings softening, the smell of so many people packed together eased.

"Do you think our benefactor is keeping you from being questioned for the killing?" Cassia asked in a quiet voice.

Our benefactor hadn't showed his hand, or the rest of him, for that matter, in our lives since he'd found me this apartment and sent Cassia to me. As far as I knew, he'd forgotten about us.

"I don't know," I said.

We watched the moonlight for a while, cut by the smoke from the perpetual fires burning to heat the baths. Entire forests had been razed to keep Romans in warm bathwater.

"You are a good man, Leonidas," Cassia said. "I will find out who did this crime and clear you of its taint. I promise you."

I rested my hand over hers and gave it a brief squeeze.

We sat again for a while before she gently withdrew her hand and climbed to her feet. Without a word, I stood and let her lead me back into the house.

I went straight to bed, exhaustion coming over me once more. I removed my sandals and lay down in my tunic this time, pulling the blanket to my chin.

As I drifted off, I felt the blanket be adjusted, a light hand resting briefly on my forehead. Then her voice, softly singing, Cassia's liquid tones easing the noise of my thoughts. Sleep came like a friend this time, and I surrendered into its arms.

DAWN LIGHT TAPPED AT MY EYELIDS. "LEONIDAS!"

The frenzied whisper mixed with the gray light woke me. I raised my head to find Cassia at the end of my bed, dressed, her hair coiffed, her eyes round.

I'd thrown off my blanket in the night, so I sat up, the tunic bunched around my thighs, and rubbed a hand over my face. I gave a wordless grunt for answer.

"He's here," Cassia went on in the same whisper. "The man who attacked you in the tunnels. He's asking for your help. Prostrating himself for it, I should say. Do get up —*please.*"

CHAPTER 8

I SWUNG MY FEET TO THE FLOOR, THE INSIDE OF MY mouth tasting musty. Barefoot, sleep in my eyes, I trod to the outer room, Cassia behind me.

My man from the tunnels was facedown on the floor, a mass of dark skin, bones, rags, and hair. A bandage wrapped around his right wrist, the only clean piece of cloth on him. He lifted his head when he heard me come in, his dark eyes filled with terror.

"Help me," he pleaded. "They're after me."

"Who?" I asked, but I knew. The magistrates needed someone to answer for this crime, and when they couldn't pin it on me, they'd find the next person any witness had seen. Exactly why I'd spirited Sergius out of town.

"I did not kill this money-changer," he said. "I was in the tunnels to hide, not to murder."

"And to rob," I said. "You attacked me."

"I feared you'd come to drag me back."

"Back where?" I demanded.

"The quarries," Cassia said from behind me. "Look at his hands."

Slaves put into the quarries or mines around the empire didn't last long. They were worked from dawn to dusk and beyond, given little to eat and little time to sleep. When one died, he was replaced with another. As there had been so many prisoners taken in battle and captured in vanquished cities throughout Rome's history, the next body wasn't hard to find.

"I come from Espania," the young man went on. "My name is Balbus. My master sold me to the quarries when he brought me to Rome. I ran away. I hid in the tunnels. Now they think I killed the money-changer. I never did."

For a flicker of time, I wished I was back in the ludus. There, I'd never had to think—every hour of my existence was planned. I knew exactly what I had to do every moment of the day. Even when I was out on my own, I knew how long the job I'd been hired to do would take and what time I was expected to return.

Now I had to decide for myself what to do. I could not pass off the responsibility to another person, or shrug and ignore the world.

Too many possibilities presented themselves to me. If I helped Balbus escape, I might be arrested for the murder with him. Even our benefactor might not be able to help me then.

If I did *not* assist Balbus, he'd be rounded up by the cohorts or the vigiles and tried for a crime he might not have committed. They'd condemn him to the games to be torn apart by beasts or throw him right back into the quarry to be worked until he dropped dead.

On the other hand, if I gave up Balbus to the magistrates, the crime would be considered solved, and I'd be left in peace.

But a terrified, desperate, and innocent man would die. I could not be the one who condemned him.

Then again, if I helped a wanted criminal and was caught and executed with him—what would happen to Cassia?

The last question made me pause the longest. If I were taken and condemned, Cassia might suffer a similar fate. When a slave killed a man in a house, all the slaves there could be put to death as an example to others. Cassia's life was not her own. The best I could hope was that our bene-factor would step in and give her to another master, one who wouldn't be cruel to her.

I cursed our benefactor under my breath. A wealthy and powerful man—we assumed—had taken charge of our lives for whatever reason—and we didn't know who he was. When he could be useful and solve this problem, he was a ghost.

"Did anyone see you come here?" I asked Balbus.

"It was dark," he answered, his voice weak. "I don't think so."

I couldn't send him to Marcella. The thought of Xerxes's wife and children, along with Sergius, rounded up and sold into slavery for harboring a fugitive and an escaped slave rippled bile through my stomach.

"I know a place you can hide," I heard myself say.

Cassia remained silent. She not expressing an opinion surprised me, and I glanced at her to see that her expression held relief and approval. In her eyes, I'd made the right choice.

"Stand up," I told Balbus. My voice took on the tones of my toughest trainer. "You're going to be scrubbed and shaved. Then I'll take you to a place. You say nothing from now on. Understand?"

Balbus opened his mouth to answer, then closed it and gave a nod.

Cassia snatched up her palla and wrapped it around her, ducking past me and outside. She lifted the pot we used to fetch water as she went, and I knew she was on her way to the fountain at the end of the street. This would not be seen as unusual, as she moved purposely to and from this fountain every morning.

I had Balbus next to my bed, naked and shivering, by the time she returned, his rags of clothes in a corner ready to be taken out and burned.

Cassia kept her modest self on the balcony while I sluiced water over Balbus and scraped him down with my strigil—we had no oil, so water would have to do. I doused him again when I finished. The water was cold, and he let out a strangled shriek, which he suppressed when I glared at him.

I barbered him myself as well. I stropped a blade while Balbus watched nervously, and then I shaved him clean, face, scalp, and all. I was not trained with a razor, and usually had my whiskers scraped by the barber down the street, but I had a steady hand and only nicked him a few times.

I swept up his fallen hair and put it with his clothes to be incinerated—who knew what vermin was in it?

Any tunic I lent him would fall right off him, but Cassia had already solved the problem. While I debated what to put on him, she came inside, averting her gaze, and thrust a handful of cloth at me.

This turned out to be one of her under-tunics, hastily cut so it would end just above Balbus's knobby knees. There wasn't much difference between a slave woman's garb and a man's, so I soon had him tucked into it, a rope tied around his waist.

Once I was done, Balbus looked a completely different person. Gone was the scraggly hair and beard that had hidden his face, and the dirt that had given him a foul odor. Before us stood a respectable-looking if overly thin slave, his broken wrist rewrapped in a clean bandage. I'd wrapped my own and my fellow gladiators' broken and sprained limbs often enough to become almost as good at it as Marcianus.

Only when I was ready to march the man out did Cassia come to me. "Where is this safe place you will take him?"

I shook my head. "If I don't tell you, you won't have to lie if you're questioned."

Cassia pursed her lips as she thought about this, and then stepped back and let us go.

I put a heavy hand on Balbus's shoulder and steered him out of the apartment and down the stairs. When we reached the street I ordered him to walk one step behind me, and if he valued his life, not to run off. I'd kill him myself if he did, I promised him.

It was the first hour, and Rome was coming alive. Plebeian men and women, freedmen, freedwomen, and slaves rushed about to buy food and drink for the day, and to run errands before the sun climbed too high. Bakers shoveled bread into and out of roaring ovens; fish sellers yelled that their catches were fresh from the coast; fowl clucked and fussed; and vegetable sellers set out mountains of lettuces, cabbages, fresh green stalks of asparagus, and baskets of berries gathered from the nearby fields.

I could not resist pausing to buy a small measure of strawberries, using the coins Cassia had replenished in my pouch. I ate the bright, cool berries as we walked along, sharing a grudging few with Balbus, as a master might do with a slave.

Balbus was starving, I could see that. Where he was going they'd at least give him a meal. Probably a good one.

I took him to the river via the Campus Martius, not wanting to cut through the Forum Romanum at its busiest hour. We crossed the river at the Pons Agrippae and entered the Transtiberim, that growing expanse of Rome on the other side of the Tiber.

When the bored guard at my hiding place saw me, he gave a look of surprise, but unlatched the gate and let us in without question.

The sound of the gate closing after us gave me a moment's qualm, the habitual shiver at being locked in. I forced the qualm to pass, reminding myself that I could walk out again whenever I liked, a free man.

The yard behind the wall was full of activity. The morning coolness was as good for training as it was for the rest of Rome to conduct business and shop.

Men in nothing but loincloths industriously hacked at posts with wooden swords. Others built muscles by lifting lead weights or did various exercises under the tongue-lashing of a trainer, and still others sparred in the middle of the dirt yard.

Balbus looked around and shrank back. "This is ..." he whispered, then remembered his vow not to speak.

"My ludus," I finished. "This is where you will hide."

"Leonidas!" A good-natured bellow filled the yard, causing all training to stop.

The gladiators wiped brows, lifted off leather helmets, looked around. They stared—some in welcome, others in hostility, the *tiros* I didn't know in eager curiosity. A retired *primus palus* visiting the school was something to talk about.

The man who'd shouted had a body full of scars, a left ear half gone, and was missing several fingers on one hand. He was one of the hardest, toughest men I'd met in my life. Under his bullying, I'd become a champion.

At the moment, the man's grin could light the sky. "I knew you'd come back to me!" he shouted.

His voice was thunderous. All of Rome would know I'd come back too.

Aemilianus, or Aemil as he was called, had in his day been the most dangerous gladiator in the empire. He'd always fought to win, no draws. He'd retired ten years ago, bought a handful of gladiators and opened this school. He trained the best, like me and Xerxes, and aediles paid whatever Aemil asked in order to put on the most lavish games.

Aemil had the light brown hair of a Gaul, but what set him apart from other Gauls was that one of his eyes was blue, the other a green-brown color. He'd often fought without a helmet so that his mismatched eyes could unnerve his opponents, which was why he was missing part of an ear.

He had a Gaul's build, large and bulky as opposed to the shorter trimness of a Roman. Aemil had a theory that I was part Gaul too, as I was fairly tall and broad, and that could be true. I had no knowledge of my family. I'd been on the streets alone since my memories began.

"Who's this?" Aemil asked, staring bluntly at Balbus.

I grabbed the young man by the neck, which seemed to be the best way to haul him about, and drew him forward.

"Can you put him to work?" When Aemil hesitated, I added. "I'll pay."

"You bring me a slave, and you'll pay *me*?" Aemil eyed Balbus, who had the sense to keep his mouth shut. "What's wrong with him?"

"Underfoot." I snapped out the word.

"Ah." Aemil nodded sagely. "Your woman doesn't like him. I can always use more help, so yes, leave him. What's his name?"

I shrugged. "Give him one." Aemil had helped me come up with mine, erasing whatever boy I'd been forever. He could erase Balbus too.

"Fine." Aemil turned to Balbus. "We'll call you Hermes, because you'll be fetching and carrying and being a messenger to anyone I say. You're too skinny for heavier work." He looked Balbus up and down again. "Slave to gladiators is the lowest thing you can become. Even lower than *me*." He chortled. "You going to live with that and not try to throw yourself into the river? I'm not feeding you and keeping you if you're going to wallow in despair. Understand?"

Balbus swallowed hard and nodded.

Aemil peered at the bandage on his wrist. "You wrapped that," he said to me.

"I broke it," I answered, offhand. "He irritated me."

Aemil shook his head then flashed me a grin. "So now I have to wait for him to heal before I can use him. No wonder you're offering to pay me." He turned back to Balbus and jabbed his thumb at the barracks. "Go in there and help clean it up. Then come and ask for work. I have plenty."

Balbus flashed me a grateful glance. I remained stoic, as though only ridding myself of an annoying slave, but I silently wished him luck. Emptying the slop buckets of gladiators was far better than being bound to a stake while a lion tore out his entrails, and he knew it.

Aemil watched the man scamper away before he turned to me. I held out my money pouch, but Aemil waved a hand. "Pay me by coming back, Leonidas. Go a few rounds with my new *primus palus* in the next games. The man's an arrogant turd, but good, very good. Not as good as you were though. Teach him some humility and make me money. What do you say?"

I thought of my old life—the days, weeks, months, years of monotonous training followed by the white-hot desperation of a battle for my life. I hadn't felt fear in the amphitheatres, only heat, determination, and the need to survive.

The smell of blood, dead animals, and dead men came to me, along with the odor of packed bodies in the seats above me, the memory of sand burning under my bare feet, the airless weight of the helmet locked around my head, and the grim resolve in the eyes of the man I faced, usually a friend I'd sat next to at the feast the night before.

Aemil had shoved me into every game, sometimes several rounds on the same day, taking more and more money for my appearances, while he coolly negotiated what compensation he'd receive if I were killed.

Aemil called himself the paterfamilias of our gladiator family, but he was a father who sold his sons to the highest bidder. He was a businessman first and foremost. If I died spectacularly at one of these exhibitions he wanted me to do now, he'd earn an enormous sum.

I took his hand and slapped the pouch into it. "I say no."

Aemil's wrong-colored eyes flickered with rage, but I cared nothing for his disappointment. I turned my back on him and walked away.

I MADE MY WAY BACK OVER THE TIBER VIA THE PONS
Aemilius, its six piers stretching across the water just south
of the Insula. The Cloaca Maxima, the great sewer, came
through an opening in the thick embankment wall not far
downstream.

As I pushed through the flow of humanity on the bridge,
the waste of the city pouring into the river not far away, my
thoughts were scattered. Returning to the ludus always did
that to me.

That part of my life was over, and I wanted it to be so,
but what unnerved me was that Aemil's offer had been
briefly tempting. I could slip back into the routine so easily,
where I didn't have to think, but only do. They'd made me
into a machine as mindless as the great mill wheels that
ground the grain for our daily bread.

Whenever I entered the ludus these days, I had to fight
to not take up a wooden sword and join in the training, and
then file to the mess for my barley and fresh vegetables, and
to my cell for a massage and to sleep. Over and over again.

I forced my feet to take me around the cattle market and
through the valley between the Palatine and Capitoline,
letting the stream of people, donkeys, and hand carts sweep
me with them to the Forum Romanum. Columns of temples
to both gods and government rose around me, towering
edifices of stone that we surged, antlike, around.

I continued walking without ceasing, not halting when
people called out to me, ignoring them to turn into the lane
that led to the fountain where Cassia drew water, and
thence home. My new home, where my decisions could
affect the life of not only myself but the woman who'd come
to depend on me, through no fault of her own.

Cassia was there. She'd heaped some bread on a plate and was setting it on the table when I walked in.

I snatched a hunk from the top and began to chew it as Cassia made a note of the time I'd returned. I trusted her notes did not mention Balbus at all.

"Shall you sit down?" she asked me from her stool as she tore off a miniscule piece of bread and bit into it.

"No," I said around my mouthful. "Going back out."

She frowned. "Where? You just got in."

I knew she'd persist if I didn't tell her where I was off to, so I said, "Selenius's shop. I want to ask the other shop-keepers about him. They must have seen *something*. Or someone."

Cassia nodded, her curls dancing. "An excellent idea. I'll come with you."

"No," I began.

"Do not worry, I will stand behind you like a good servant. I imagine the reason you don't want me to go is because your methods of questioning might be less than polite."

I couldn't argue, because she was right. I'd planned to be as brutal as people expected of me if necessary, which I should have done with the baker in the first place. If I'd shaken the sestertii out of Quintus and gone home, I wouldn't be in these current difficulties.

I finished my hunk of bread and washed it down with a cup of the wine merchant's cheapest vintage, while Cassia more carefully downed her piece. I needed to beat what the baker owed us out of him, or we'd be drinking piss and eating seeds fallen from the back of grain wagons before long.

"Come with me then," I growled, clattering my cup to

the table. "But don't talk. You drive a man to distraction when you talk."

Cassia sent me a smile of triumph. "Only because that man does not know how to answer." She fetched her palla and wrapped it around her body like a modest matron, and followed me out.

CHAPTER 9

We walked through Rome at its busiest hour to reach the *macellum.* Cassia kept a few steps behind me, as a slave should, but the streets were so crammed, we wouldn't have been able to travel side by side in any case.

We had to step out of the way several times for litters borne by Gauls, no doubt chosen for their huge musculature. Inside the litter would be a matron or her eldest daughter, perfumed and bejeweled, out to visit a friend, or making a journey to a temple to petition a god or goddess for whatever matrons and daughters petitioned them for.

Lictors—men who accompanied patricians and acted as bodyguards, messengers, and announcers—pushed us aside at one point. The man they protected, who was swathed in a toga with a narrow purple stripe, swaggered by, chatting with another purple-striped man, senators on their way to pretend to govern Rome.

We had an emperor who'd decided he could do what he liked, when he liked, with whom he liked, and the senators could only discuss how to keep themselves and their interests safe from him. They were powerless, and Nero knew it.

That did not take the arrogance out of the men who walked by in their bubble of protection, or from the lictors who shoved us bodily out of the way. They carried bundles of staves, *fasces*, that symbolized the time when these high-born men could have their guards beat anyone they liked. The fact that the reeds were symbolic did not stop the lictors from using them for their original purpose if they felt peevish.

While I noticed the usual stares at me as I moved along, a half head to a head taller than most Roman men, we were not accosted. The streets were so crowded I doubted anyone could get close to me to arrest me for Selenius's murder if they wanted to, and if they did, they might cause a riot.

I led Cassia through the Subura, which was full of humanity—from the dregs who lived in miniscule apartments to wealthy men moving from their villas at the tops of the hills to the Forum Romanum, or to baths, temples, and everything in between. I could understand why Sergius preferred to travel via the tunnels that ran beneath the streets, as unsavory as they were. There, at least, it was quiet and not crowded.

We turned into the *macellum*, which was lively this morning. Vendors sold everything from produce and live chickens to cloth, carpets, lamps, beans, and cheap jewelry. Romans and travelers from all over the empire came to the market, many to use the money-changers who stood by their benches to switch the currency of far-off cities for Roman coin. On the fringes of the shops were cutpurses and thieves, waiting to relieve these foreigners of their gains.

Shopkeepers and their clients were too busy to gawp at a former gladiator striding in, his modest slave behind him with her basket. We moved without hindrance to the interior shops of the *macellum*, the sun shining brightly into its atrium.

Boards were in place over the counter of Selenius's shop, but I spied movement within the open door. I ducked inside, Cassia at my heels, to find a young man bent over a cupboard, a flickering oil lamp lighting the gloom. A male slave, middle-aged with a surly face and gnarled hands, swept the floor.

The young man looked irritably over his shoulder when he heard us enter, then he jerked upright and gaped at me.

Before I could speak, he saw Cassia. "Oh, it's you," he said, losing his worry. "The *medicus's* assistant." He must have assumed she belonged to Marcianus. "What do you want?" he asked as he returned to rifling the cupboard.

Cassia stepped in front of me. She kept her voice quiet and demure, her head bowed, showing the expected deference to the young man I gathered was Selenius's nephew and adopted son. She was good at playing her part.

"This is Leonidas, sir," she said. "He found your uncle."

Gaius Selenius the Younger jerked around again. He had a jutting chin, short, flyaway hair, and small eyes. He looked much like the older Selenius, but with youthful vigor.

"Oh," Gaius said. "The gladiator." He concluded his assessment of me dubiously. "I've never seen you fight. I'm too busy to go to the games."

Most of Rome shut down during games, as they were public spectacles, often held in conjunction with religious celebrations, like Saturnalia. I wondered if his uncle or mother had kept him from going or if young Gaius was squeamish.

"What do you want?" he asked. "My mother is expecting me home. I am here to fetch my uncle's records."

"Leonidas offers his condolences," Cassia extemporized. "It is sad to lose one of the family. Your mother said you were very close?"

Gaius shrugged. "My mother loved him. He was her younger brother. I found him demanding and strict, but he raised me when my father died. He became a father in truth ..."

The lad broke off, mouth twisting, eyes filling with tears. Cassia moved to stand next to him without touching him as she radiated sympathy.

Gaius cleared his throat. "I'm the head of the household now." The thought obviously terrified him. "My uncle shall have a grand funeral. And I will take over his business." More trepidation.

Cassia smiled encouragingly. "I am certain he would be honored."

Gaius didn't look so certain, but he accepted Cassia's polite concern.

The room had been cleaned of blood, though I could see where it had seeped into cracks in the floor. The wall where Selenius had lain had been scrubbed, the patch he'd leaned against now a bit whiter than the painted brick around it.

I studied the door to the tunnels. Cassia, catching my gaze, pointed at it.

"What is there?" she asked Gaius, as though curious.

Gaius glanced at the door but turned away, indifferent. "Don't know. Uncle never opened it."

"Maintenance tunnels to sewers," the slave with the broom volunteered. "Old part of Rome coming up to meet the new."

Gaius wrinkled his nose in distaste. "Have it sealed up."

The slave leaned on his broom, as though happy of the excuse to stop. "Costs. 'Swhy the master never did it."

"Yes, well," Gaius said impatiently. "We'll see the state of his finances, and if there's money, we'll seal it up. I don't want the smell coming in here."

"Deep part's too far down to bring bad air here," the slave went on.

Gaius scowled at him. He obviously wasn't having an easy time convincing his uncle's slaves he was in charge now. Some slaves were freed on their master's deaths, but not all, and some remained as freedmen doing the exact same jobs they had before, suffering the exact same blows when their masters grew irritated with them.

"Come," I said to Cassia, a slave who hadn't obeyed me from the moment I'd met her. "My condolences," I said to Gaius. "May the gods bring you prosperity."

Gaius bobbed his head at my politeness, looking as though all the gods together with Fortuna leading the charge wouldn't do him much good.

Cassia gave Gaius a bow and meekly scurried to me as I turned to leave. She was the very picture of the demure, duteous slave. She would have made a fine actress, though she'd be offended if I told her so.

Once outside the shop and out of earshot of Gaius, she whispered, "We should look inside the tunnels."

I agreed, but there was nothing we could do while Gaius went through his uncle's things and the slave swept up.

We wandered through the shops instead, which were lit by the oculus above the atrium as well as arched openings high in the walls, and asked about Selenius and the day he'd died. That is, Cassia asked, and I frowned at the shop-keepers who tried to dismiss her outright.

No one had seen much of interest or out of the ordinary

the morning of Selenius's death. Selenius had arrived at his normal hour, his nephew in tow. As per usual, young Gaius had left at midmorning to return home, as business was most brisk in the early morning. Several more customers had gone to Selenius and come out without being covered in blood or remarking on finding a dead body. A few described seeing Balbus go in—a hairy slave probably on an errand for his foreign master, they said—but they'd not observed him come out again. And they'd seen me.

They hadn't, to my relief, noticed Sergius. The boy must have traveled back and forth through the tunnels, unnoticed.

The shopkeepers within the *macellum*, even the other money-changers, hadn't thought much of Selenius. He was successful, but less than honorable, happy when a customer didn't thoroughly count his takings.

Cassia, who was good at suggesting things until others opened up with what they knew, pried out from some of the other money-changers that they suspected Selenius of his forgeries, but they didn't know for certain whether he was guilty of them.

What they did know was that Selenius bullied his slaves and was firm with his nephew, though perhaps no harder on him than a master would be to an apprentice.

No one, it seemed, was very sorry Selenius was dead.

Cassia casually mentioned the network of tunnels that ran beneath the area, but none seemed to be aware of them. Rome was an ancient city—buildings fell to ruin and were rebuilt or burned, the ashes leveled and more built on top of it. I, like most Romans, was aware of the most important ancient monuments, like Romulus's hut and the rostra in the Forum, but the day-to-day buildings, even some of the most prominent temples, came and went. It was not so surprising that the shopkeepers didn't know much about the sewers that ran beneath us, only that they worked.

I found the *garum* vendor who'd noted my entrance to the *macellum* that day. The same two Gauls I'd seen lingering before were there again. Most Romans loved the fish sauce made by fermenting fish in salt—Cassia and I were exceptions.

The two slaves were quite tall and had very fair hair, which meant they'd come a long way from their northern homeland. Some of the prisoners brought back from the Claudian campaigns in Britannia had been very tall and pale, others small and dark. The larger ones made good gladiators—they were arrogant and ruthless fighters. The one who'd defeated Xerxes had definitely been merciless. He'd died under my sword in a later bout.

Cassia approached the *garum* seller's counter, producing a coin and asking for the fish sauce she hated. I imagined she'd throw it into the river the first chance she got.

The Gauls ceased their conversation and looked at me. We sized up one another, none of us speaking.

Cassia leaned to the shopkeeper, indicating the Gauls, who'd moved off, still eying me. "Is their master a regular customer?" she asked, as though curious about the odd foreigners.

The shopkeeper nodded, ready to gossip. "Sends them every day. He's fond of taking Gauls for servants. Has a house full of them. Blond giants, every single one of them, even the women." He chuckled.

"They were here the day Selenius was killed," Cassia stated.

The shopkeeper's amusement faded. "They were. I stay open later than most, as people often remember the *garum* at the last minute." He jerked his thumb at me. "I saw *him*. Going in."

"I saw *them* as well," I said, breaking my silence. "And you."

The shopkeeper finally understood that Cassia wasn't simply passing the time of day. He turned a sharp eye on me. "I never left this stall to go murdering Selenius," he snapped. "Anyway, why should I?"

I shrugged. "Why should *I*? I'd never met the man."

"Well." The shopkeeper waved a vague hand at me. "You're a trained killer."

"In a fair fight," I said. "What happened to Selenius was slaughter."

Returning my attention to the Gauls, I could imagine one holding down Selenius while the other cut his throat. They'd be strong enough to overpower him without much trouble, silencing him quickly.

But I'd not noticed any blood on them that day. They'd have been covered with it. However, they might have changed out of their blood-soaked clothes, bundling them into the large baskets they'd carried.

The two men regarded me without expression. I wondered if they were often blamed for whatever had gone wrong on any given day—when in doubt, accuse a slave. The shopkeeper, on the other hand, grew manifestly nervous. His worry might mean he was guilty, or only afraid he'd be accused and arrested, whether he'd committed the crime or not. Such things happened in our fair city.

He shoved the jar of *garum* at Cassia. "Take it and go. Don't come back here again."

Cassia calmly set the jar into her basket. "Cease pointing the blame for this murder on others," she said. "And you won't see us."

She turned and stepped past the giant men who watched her without speaking. She walked by me too, as though she were a great lady and I her bodyguard.

I gave the Gauls and the shopkeeper one more stern look, and followed Cassia out.

THE STREETS WERE QUIET AS WE EXITED THE marketplace, the sun reaching its zenith. We walked with a slower tread, the heat seeping into our bones. Even the beggars and stray dogs began to crawl off into the shade to sleep.

I wanted to start for home, but Cassia tugged my tunic. "Let's visit the baker first," she said. "You need to have another word with him."

She strode purposefully in the direction of Quintus's bakery, and I had to hurry to keep up with her.

CHAPTER 10

As he had been two days ago, Quintus was finishing his business for the day. He handed a round loaf of bread to a dark-skinned woman who loaded it into her basket and departed, giving me a startled glance as she walked away.

Quintus hadn't seen us, and he turned back to his ovens. "A moment ..." He shoveled several loaves out of one oven with his large bread peel and slid them into the tube-shaped holes in his wall to cool. "Now then, what do you—"

He froze when he saw me, his face becoming whiter than his flour-dusted tunic. "Leonidas." He upended the handle of the long bread peel and leaned heavily on it. "I swear to you, I do not have your money. That is why I sent you to Selenius. Now he's dead and can't pay me."

Cassia set her basket on the tiled counter, lifted out a tablet, and made a show of checking the marks within it. "You really ought not to employ the services of others if you cannot pay them, you know." She turned the tablet around and tapped a row of scratches. "Quintus Publius, ten sestertii."

Quintus paid no attention to Cassia or her tablet. He focused on me, his eyes filled with deep fear. "I have told you. Selenius owed me much. He cheated me. That's why I sent you to him. I thought if anyone could shake it out of him, it would be Leonidas the Gladiator ..."

"Or, he was dead already," I cut in. "And you knew. You sent me to be caught for the murder."

I hadn't thought Quintus's face could lose more color, but his countenance became nearly as gray as the dead Selenius's. "I promise you I did not know. I did not know until the boy told me."

I stopped, my heart going cold. "What boy?"

Quintus waved his hands at the air over his counter. "Boy who hangs about the street. Don't know his name. Was following you that day. When I sent you off, he told me Selenius was dead and then ran away."

I carefully did not look at Cassia, who intently studied her basket. "You didn't call after me," I said to Quintus. "When the boy told you, you didn't try to stop me."

Quintus shrugged. "You were gone too fast. And I thought ..." More lip wetting. "I thought that, if Selenius was truly dead—and I only had the boy's word for it, mind you—you'd at least search his shop and bring back the money."

"Then I would be in the Tullianum awaiting execution for stealing," I said. "I'm not a thief."

Quintus peered up at me as though realizing he had badly miscalculated my character. He didn't offend me—I'd given up that particular emotion a long time ago.

Cassia pushed her basket toward Quintus. "Will you put one of those loaves that are cooling in here, please?"

Quintus forced his attention to her, but shook his head. "They're promised to another. I have more inside—"

"No, one of those." Cassia pointed at the round openings that held the loaves he'd just taken from the oven. "You can make more for whatever wealthy man is buying them." She leaned across the counter to the Quintus, who was a head shorter than she was. "You owe Leonidas ten sestertii. He could take you to court for not paying him, and then you'd owe him more. Or he could bring suit against you for trying to make it look as though he'd killed Selenius." She straightened. "Or, you could simply give me a fresh loaf of bread."

Color at last returned to Quintus's cheeks, red blotches of it. He snarled, yanked one of the new loaves from its cooling place, and dropped it into Cassia's basket.

"Excellent," Cassia said. "I'll be back tomorrow for another."

"Another?" Quintus asked, startled.

"The price of a loaf is half a sestertius," Cassia answered serenely. "I will come to your stall for the next nineteen days, and you will give me a fresh loaf of bread made from your finest flour. Then you will have paid the debt." She lifted the basket and covered the bread with the cloth within. "Good day."

An emotion at last broke its way through my numbness as we turned away and left Quintus spluttering. It was mirth.

THAT AFTERNOON, WE DINED ON FRESH BREAD, OIL, fruit, and boiled lentils. We sat on stools at our table, the door to the balcony propped open to allow in whatever breeze might amble down the lane.

We were somber as we ate, however.

"You don't think that little boy killed Selenius, do you?" Cassia asked me after a long silence.

Though I did not want to consider the question, I knew I had to. "It is possible," I said, turning over my thoughts. "When Sergius heard Quintus tell me to go to Selenius, the lad knew Selenius was dead. That means he'd seen Selenius's body."

Sergius had stared at me in shock when I'd arrived in the doorway—I'd thought because of Selenius's dead body. But perhaps he'd been running there ahead of me to cut me off, to try to keep me away, gaping in dismay when I'd found Selenius anyway.

Cassia gave me a morose nod. "Seen Selenius dead only because he plays in the tunnels? Or because he killed the man himself?"

"Why would he?" I tore off a piece of the bread, dunked it in my lentil broth, and stuffed it into my mouth. I chewed, spat the grit that lingered in every loaf into my hand, and swallowed.

"Perhaps Selenius tried to beat him," Cassia said quietly. "Suppose Selenius caught the boy sneaking around the tunnels, dragged him out, and beat him. The other men we spoke to said Selenius could be a brute. His nephew said so as well. Or—Sergius was a brothel boy, and Selenius might have grabbed him for another reason. Sergius could have fought back, grabbed a weapon—knife, even a sharp tile—and struck out." She touched her throat.

I shook my head, searching for any explanation to show Sergius could not possibly have done it. "The blow held strength. And landed in the exact place that would kill Selenius."

"He might have simply swung his weapon, and Fortuna did the rest. Even a small person can harm another when they are desperate enough." Cassia spoke from experience, one she did not like to talk about.

I drank a sip of wine. The vessel I held was copper, dented on one side of the lip, the bottom greenish from corrosion. "I don't want it to have been Sergius," I said in a firm tone.

Cassia gave me an understanding look. "What will you do if…?"

"Nothing." I set down my cup. "The hairy slave who was seen leaving the shops has vanished. Selenius's sister and nephew will have no one to prosecute. They'll hunt through the countryside for the slave for a while, but then give up."

Cassia nodded. "And the matter will die." She let out a long breath. "You know that even if Sergius or Balbus did not kill Selenius, either of them could have seen who did."

"I know."

"Will you ask them?"

I tapped one foot under the table while Cassia watched me, her dark eyes troubled. Her lashes were as black as her hair.

"No," I concluded.

Cassia lifted her spoon, delicately scooping up more of her broth. "Good," she said.

We finished our meal in silent understanding.

IN THE TENTH HOUR, WHEN ROME WAS BATHING, slumbering, or simply waiting for night, I took Cassia to the narrow street near the potters' area of the city, and to the door Sergius had shown me.

I'd wanted to explore alone, but as before, Cassia insisted on joining me.

She'd wrapped herself well against the sun and prying eyes and carried a canvas bag that made an occasional clinking noise. We looked like any freedman and his slave out on an errand, except that everyone knew of me, and everyone we passed watched us then turned to the nearest passerby and pointed me out.

I'd chosen the hour well though, and not many were in the hot streets to remark upon us. The lane in the Figlinae was completely deserted, shutters closed against the sun. Any person on the rare balcony high above us looked across the hills and dreamed of fresh air, paying no attention to the street below.

I found the narrow door that did not look much different from doors that led into shops and apartments. It was locked, but I nudged stones with my foot until I found a sliver of metal similar to what Sergius had used to open the other door. I inserted it into the keyhole and wriggled it about, and soon the lock clicked.

After returning the metal piece to its hiding place, I opened the door. The tunnel beyond was dark and damp, but at least it was cool.

I went in first in case another desperate man lurked, waiting to attack, but the tunnel was quiet and empty. Even the rats had decided to find someplace to sleep.

Cassia closed the door, fitting it carefully into the frame. Only then did she remove from her canvas bag the lamp and bottles of oil she'd brought. By the light from the cracks in the door, she filled the lamp and resealed the bottle, setting the lamp on the floor. My task was to light the wick.

I struck stone against stone until a spark flashed and finally caught on the twist of linen. A tiny flame began, sputtered, and then rose, bathing us in a small, golden light.

Cassia held her bag close when I reached for it, and

waved for me to lead the way. What else she carried, I didn't know—Cassia had only said she'd brought things to help us in the dark.

The first part of the journey was easy, ten steps leading upward and then a straight tunnel diving back into the hill. I heard Cassia whispering behind me, counting, it sounded like.

The light showed me what the darkness had hidden during my last journey here, that the tunnel was lined with brick, with a long, vaulted arch of cement and brick overhead to support the weight of the earth above us. Stones covered the floor, fitted into place with barely a space between them. The floor slanted inward slightly from the walls to carry any water that might accumulate down through grated drains to the sewers.

"Stop!" At Cassia's abrupt tone, I halted and swung back, ready to defend her.

Cassia was rummaging in her bag, and as I reached her, she drew out a small wooden peg and a spool of string. She tied the string to the peg and took out a wooden mallet.

"Drive this into the wall—just there." Cassia held a peg to a crack in the wall and handed me the mallet.

I secured the peg in a few short blows. Cassia unwound the string a bit, nodding at me to move on. She counted out the next twelve paces and stopped me again, holding up another peg for me to tap into the wall.

I grunted as I finished. "At this pace, we will reach Selenius's shop in maybe two days."

"If our lamp fails us and we're in the pitch dark, you'll be happy of the path I'm marking." Cassia hefted the bag over her shoulder and unwound more string. "I do not want to spend my last days lost in the sewers."

I could not argue with her logic. I'd only found my way through the tunnels with the help of Sergius and Balbus.

We went slowly along, Cassia halting me every twelve paces to secure another peg. I had to find handy cracks in the brick wall, so the string zigzagged up and down, but she was right—if we were here in the dark, we could follow the string back out, like Theseus and Ariadne in the minotaur's labyrinth.

We weren't likely to meet ancient beasts back here, only humans, rats, mildew, and filth. Bards would never sing of *our* walk through the sewers of Rome.

When we came to a junction I had to close my eyes and think very hard about how I'd come the other way. I'd been trying not to lose Sergius in the dark, not making notes of my progress.

I remembered hurrying down a slope, hoping I wouldn't have to wade through excrement from the nearest latrine. Ahead of us, one tunnel rose, and the other continued level.

"This one," I said, pointing to the rising tunnel.

Cassia studied both directions as I held up the lamp. "Are you certain?"

"No." I started into the upward sloping tunnel.

Cassia pattered behind me, halting me at the twelfth step. I tapped another peg into the wall. "Did you bring enough of these?" I asked, shouldering the mallet. "And how would you know?"

"I calculated what we need based on the distance between the two points." She gave me a nod. "I brought more than enough. Plenty of string too. We won't get lost. Don't worry."

I turned away and continued, ignoring her whispered counting behind me. She began softly singing the numbers after a time. Cassia liked to turn everything into a song.

We came upon a door, a very ordinary one—vertical panels of wood held in place by horizontal cross pieces. I paused, holding the light to it, and Cassia stopped beside me.

"This can't be Selenius's," she said. "We haven't come far enough."

I gently pushed on the door, finding it locked. I hoped I wasn't waking a family on the other side, one with a stern paterfamilias who kept an ax and a huge guard dog.

"Selenius's door will be locked." I kept my voice quiet. "If his nephew hasn't had it bricked up yet."

"He would not have had time since we left him this morning," Cassia said, ever reasonable. "Even if his slave is taking care of it, they'd have to bring in the supplies and labor. I imagine his mother has young Gaius at home this afternoon. She was so very distressed at her brother's passing. She hasn't been well since … well, she was …" I knew Cassia could not bring herself to say the word.

Selenius's sister had been the only one who'd loved the man, it seemed. His colleagues had thought him a cheat and brute, his nephew a harsh taskmaster. But some men showed those they were fond of a different side.

"The door will still be locked," I finished. I should have brought Sergius's lock pick with me instead of returning it to its place under the stone. But I had no wish to travel back through the tunnels to fetch the piece of metal.

"No matter." Cassia reached into her bag and pulled out an iron bar, which tapered to a flat edge at the end. That explained the clanking. "You'll be able to pry it open."

I pretended to peer into the bag. "Did you bring dinner and a change of clothes as well? Perhaps a sedan chair to carry us home?"

Cassia only gave me a look and returned the pry bar to the bag. "Let us get on, shall we?"

I tramped ahead, stopping when Cassia's singing reached numbers eleven and twelve again.

In this way, we traversed the tunnels under the Esquiline Hill, circling down toward the Clivus Suburanus — I hoped.

The lamp began to sputter before we reached our destiny, and Cassia replenished its oil from the jar. More efficiency. The string was a precaution, but I doubted Cassia had not brought enough oil. She'd have calculated the exact amount needed.

Selenius's door lay at the end of a side passage — I remembered that as we rounded a corner and found a door blocking us.

There was no handle and the thing was, of course, locked, probably bolted or chained on the other side.

Cassia silently handed me the pry bar and took the lamp. I placed the tapered end of the bar in the crack between door and doorframe and pulled.

A board broke off with a loud snap. Cassia stepped back from the sudden draft that poured into the tunnel, holding her hand around the lamp's flame so it would not die.

I kept my body behind the door while I peered through the opening I'd made. The room beyond was dim, light coming through the cracks in boards over the stall window and around the ill-fitting outer door. But I recognized the cube of the room, the mosaic on the counter, the wall against which Selenius had been lolling.

My shoulders slumped in some relief. We'd reached our destination, but on the other hand, we'd found nothing in the tunnel to tell us who else had been there.

Cassia stumbled as she came to me, her bag swinging. I

reached out to steady her, but she regained her feet quickly, peering down at what had made her trip.

"A loose stone," she said.

"Kick it aside," I said, wondering why she sounded so happy.

"No, no—don't you see? A loose stone *in* the floor." Cassia put her feet together and rocked back and forth on a block that moved.

"There must be many loose stones. It's an old tunnel."

"But one just *here*." Cassia waved the lamp dramatically at the floor, splashing oil. "Very convenient."

I understood her excitement, but I did not want to hope. Hope could be deadly. I crouched down and applied the pry bar to the stone.

It came up after only a few tries to reveal a cavity beneath. Cassia dropped to her knees and peered inside with interest, then set down the lamp and started to reach into the hole.

"Wait!" I stopped her—who knew what would crawl out of such a place? I thrust the iron bar into the space and lifted out a bundle of cloth, which clattered when I dropped it to the tunnel floor.

Cassia tore open the knots that held the bundle closed and spread out the cloth.

We stared down at a garment that had been splashed heavily with blood, now dried and brown. A thin-bladed knife rested in the middle of the linen, blackened with the same gore.

CHAPTER 11

NEITHER OF US SPOKE AS WE GAZED AT THE bloodstained clothes and knife.

The man had stood in front of his victim, I decided. The tunic was splashed from neck to hem in a spray that would have come from the throat when it was cut. If the killer had stood behind Selenius, Selenius's body would have blocked most of the blood.

Cassia put her hand to her mouth and made a soft gagging sound.

"Selenius knew his killer," I said calmly. "Trusted him."

"How do you know that?" Cassia asked through her fingers.

"He didn't fight," I said, remembering the body slumped under the counter. "His hands were unmarred." They'd held no bruises or abrasions from Selenius trying to hit his killer.

"You mean he did not expect the person to attack him." Cassia swallowed as she looked back down at the cloth. "This tunic is far too big to fit Sergius." Her words held relief, and the same relief coursed through me.

"But not Balbus." I calculated the garment's dimensions. "This was made for a thin man."

I'd be sorry if Balbus had done this. He hadn't struck me as being evil, in spite of his attack on me. He was desperate and terrified, as any runaway slave would be. If he'd killed Selenius it would have been to save himself.

"Balbus was carrying a knife when he tried to stab you," Cassia reminded me. "The killer discarded this one. And Balbus never wore this tunic." She gingerly lifted an unstained part of the hem. "This is expensive linen, finely woven, the stitches precise and strong. This was made by a good tailor, and not long ago. It's not worn enough to have been bought secondhand, though I grant it might have been stolen."

Tunics and other clothing were stolen from laundries all the time, the thieves then selling the garments for a nice sum.

"The killer brought a change of clothing with him?" I asked doubtfully. "Meaning he knew the murder could get messy?" I shook my head. "No. This wasn't planned. The two men began to argue, one caught up a knife—"

"And already had a change of clothing ready," Cassia said. "Because he comes to this shop often."

We looked at each other. I read sadness in her expression, pity, and regret.

"We don't have to tell anyone," I pointed out. "We can put the tunic and knife back. No one has found it but us—who else would look?"

"But the magistrates will go on hunting Balbus," Cassia returned. "If he's found, he'll be thrown to the lions. Or they'll come for *you*. No, Leonidas, we have to report this. We have laws for a reason."

I tasted bitterness. "Your same law would see Balbus

torn apart, or me sent to the games for a crime I didn't commit. It saw you taken from the home you'd known all your life and sent to serve a gladiator who was supposed to have broken you."

Cassia swallowed. "I know. But ..."

I grabbed the tunic and knife, rolled the cloth into a ball, and stuffed it into the canvas bag Cassia had let slide to the floor. I took up the pry bar and climbed to my feet.

"We'll take these out," I said. "Burn them, throw them into the river, I don't care. Maybe you can talk me around by the time we get out of the tunnels, and I'll take them to a praetor instead—but I don't know."

The fact that Cassia didn't argue with me but only rose, took up the lamp, and followed told me much. She didn't want to cause Selenius's family more tragedy either.

I had to concede she was correct in part—a killer couldn't simply cut down men whenever he was angry with them. If he did it once and got away with it, there was nothing to stop him doing it again.

But I'd have the entire journey through the tunnels to think about it. I would put off the decision until we emerged into the light of day—or dusk, which it must be by now.

My mistake was in letting Cassia walk behind me. Not until she cried out did I understand how foolish I'd been to think us in no danger.

I turned. He held Cassia around the waist, a knife pressed to her throat. The hilt of the knife glittered softly in the light of the dropped lamp flickering at Cassia's feet, her dark curls sliding free of her palla to frame her terrified face.

My numbness fled. Rage like molten iron burned through my blood, clashing with the freezing dread at the image of Cassia falling, her throat slit, my Cassia dead before me.

I dropped the bag but hefted the pry bar, the fighting man in me ready to strike at my enemy.

"I like her," young Gaius Selenius said, tears in his voice. "She was so kind to my mother. I don't want to hurt her."

I wasn't certain whether he meant Cassia or his mother in his last declaration, but it didn't matter.

A few moments ago, I'd been ready to hide the crime and let Gaius go. He'd rid himself of an uncle who'd been a fraud and beaten him whenever he'd liked, and I suspected worse besides.

But if Gaius harmed Cassia I would kill him. He'd die, and then I would. It would be a tragedy worthy of any dramatist.

"Let her go," I snapped. "You can flee Rome—your mother can too. I'll destroy the clothes and knife. We'll let the magistrates think a passing madman killed your uncle."

Gaius shook his head, but the knife didn't waver from Cassia's throat. "I heard you talking. *She* wants to have me arrested." His arm tightened on Cassia's waist.

Cassia spoke rapidly, her voice shaking. "Leonidas is a trained killer, Gaius. You'll never escape him."

"I don't care." Gaius's words were petulant. "I'll fight him—he can kill me. I'll die honorably, in a battle with you as witness."

"No," I said in hard tones. If I killed a man of the merchant class, though he was a murderer himself, I'd likely not be granted the dignity of dying in the games. They might crucify me instead, just to set an example.

But if he didn't let go of Cassia, I'd break his neck and dump his body into the Tiber.

"He must have been awful," Cassia said to Gaius. "We heard that he ill-used you. And if his fraud were discovered, it would go badly for you and your mother."

"I care nothing for that!" Gaius cried, his voice rising again. "I could take his beatings. His dishonesty at least made us money. I killed him because he touched *her*. He is supposed to protect her, and he did the worst thing a man could do to a woman—especially his *sister*. And *still* she loved him."

Cassia's brief intake of breath sounded loud in the stillness. "Oh, Gaius, no. I'm so sorry."

He had a knife to her throat, nothing to keep him from slicing her as he had his uncle, and Cassia felt sorry for him.

Gaius had just confirmed my suspicions that Selenius had been more than simply a brute and a trickster. I remembered how the young man in the baths had told me Selenius's sister had been violated by one of Selenius's friends. That was likely what the rumor had become when the gossip spread from the house. The truth, I realized now, was more terrible than that.

I recalled Cassia's mention of her visit to Gaius and his mother Selenia, how upset Selenia had been at her brother's death. Perhaps not because she'd loved her brother and he'd been murdered, but because she'd realized her son killed him, and she knew why.

Gaius had nearly broken into tears when he'd told us Selenius been a father to him. A father who had done such a horrible thing to his mother.

"He raped her," I said, the blatant word ugly. "You couldn't stop him."

Tears ran down Gaius's face. "He said it was her duty to be with him. He dishonored her and violated her—his own *sister*. She wouldn't let me accuse him, wouldn't let me make him pay for what he'd done. Wouldn't let me bring shame on the family." Gaius hiccupped air. "That day … that morning … I was doing his bidding as usual. He and my mother had argued before we'd come, and he'd beaten her to the floor. While we were here, he began to taunt me. Said he'd had whores far better than my mother, that she was weak and stupid and had born a weak and stupid son. He'd laid his knife on the counter. No one was outside. I grabbed it—I don't know what I meant to do. But then I was swinging it at his throat. It went right through." Gaius gulped and the knife came too close to nicking Cassia's skin. "I had to do it. I had to avenge her."

"I know," I said, feeling sick. "I would have done the same. But Cassia has not harmed you. Let her go, or you will die. Painfully. I won't let you fight back, and so you'll have no honor, and I'll throw away your body. Your mother will always wonder what happened to you."

Cassia's alarm grew, not for herself but for me. But I couldn't halt my tongue. If young Gaius hurt Cassia, I'd pull off his arms and roll his torso along to an opening of the sewers, flushing him away with the rest of Rome's refuse.

Gaius sobbed now, clinging to Cassia as though loath to release her. His eyes closed tightly with his tears, and he turned his head.

Two steps took me to him. One squeeze of my fist broke the hand that held the knife. Gaius screamed, trying to fight, but too late.

I had him on the ground, his arm twisted behind him, my foot on his skinny thighs. I held the iron pry bar to his throat.

"A gladiator stabs, he doesn't slice," I said in a harsh voice. "More likely to make a hit, and death is quicker."

Gaius continued to wail and sob. Cassia picked up the knife, holding it loosely in one hand, as I'd taught her, but she had to brace herself on the wall with the other, her breath ragged.

I lifted the pry bar, drew back my foot, and kicked Gaius in the head. He went limp, and mercifully, the sounds pouring from his mouth ceased.

I waited in Selenius's closed shop, Gaius slumped under the counter where his uncle had died, while Cassia went to fetch his mother.

At Cassia's insistence, I relinquished the bloody clothes and knife to her. What she'd do with them, I didn't know, and I did not ask.

I knew she was canny enough not to walk into Selenia's house and announce we'd captured her son, so I did not worry about her going by herself on her errand. She'd persuade Gaius's mother to come, and come alone.

I sat on the floor, though a perfectly good stool reposed near the cupboard. I leaned my head against the wall and closed my eyes, trying to let the silence of the place calm me.

Gaius was tied with strips torn from his bloody tunic — even if he woke, he'd not be attacking me. We'd searched him for more weapons, but he'd had none.

He'd likely been returning at this quiet hour, as we had, to retrieve the tunic and knife from under the stone. Yesterday, this shop had been alive with cohorts, the other shopkeepers, and gawpers. Today would have been his first chance to return unnoticed. We'd been right to search the tunnels as soon as we could.

Gaius had likely kept a change of clothing here, in the cupboard perhaps, in case his uncle had him work through the night, or perhaps he simply didn't like wearing anything dirty.

I didn't know what would become of Gaius and his mother, and I was no longer interested. I could prove now that I didn't kill Selenius, and that Balbus hadn't either, but that wasn't what relieved me.

I'd been imagining, awake and asleep, the child Sergius, having been frightened by Selenius, slashing out with the knife and killing the man. Or creeping up on him and doing the same.

Sergius was the small, innocent boy I'd been before life had made me otherwise. I'd later been labeled a killer, and sent to the games where I could murder for other people's entertainment.

No more killing, I'd vowed the day I'd gained my freedom and the *rudis*, the wooden sword that symbolized it. And yet, murder followed me.

I couldn't keep myself from death. But I could save Sergius from it, and Cassia.

Cassia arrived with Selenia in tow. Only Cassia and Selenia entered the shop, so Cassia must have persuaded her to leave the litter bearers and maids outside in the street. She couldn't have stopped Selenia from bringing servants altogether—a Roman matron did not hurry through the streets on foot and alone.

I kept my eyes closed and the cold wall behind me as Selenia cried out upon seeing her son. Cassia explained to Selenia what had happened, and Selenia broke down, Cassia comforting her.

They could leave Rome, Cassia said. "No one will question that you wanted to go far from the place of your brother's death," she went on, her voice soothing. "Take your son and go. We will say nothing."

"He didn't mean to be cruel," Selenia replied brokenly. I wondered whether she meant her son or her brother. "Yes, I'll take Gaius far away." She drew a sobbing breath. "I have your word?"

"You have our word," Cassia reassured her.

The word of a slave and a gladiator should count for nothing. We weren't people to most. I was marginally a person now that I'd been freed, but only just.

But Cassia had a way with her. I opened my eyes a crack to see the matron swathed in her silks from the East hugging Cassia and crying.

I rose at long last, lifted the unconscious Gaius over my shoulder, and trudged through the deserted shops to the dark street. I loaded him into Selenia's litter then helped her in behind him. It was Cassia who gave the order for the litter bearers to start down the street, the maids trotting along after it.

I took Cassia's hand and led her home.

Two days later, we left Rome and went along the Via Appia to the Via Latina. Cassia was perched on a donkey, Sergius's precious cup wrapped in a bundle before her.

I led the donkey—the beast had been my idea, although Cassia had insisted she'd be able to walk the five miles to Marcella's farm. I knew she couldn't and pointed out that she'd pay for her pride by having to travel the last part of the distance slung over my shoulder. That argument had convinced Cassia to pay the few coins for the donkey.

We shared a loaf of Quintus's bread as we went along,

Cassia chattering to me. She could find enough to talk about to fill a five-mile journey and have plenty left over.

She told me that Selenia and Gaius had left the city early this morning, heading for a house Selenia had inherited in the north, near Tuscana. Cassia had heard this from servants of Selenia's household—the family would sell the business and turn to growing wine or some such thing.

Cassia hadn't left our apartment since we'd returned from sending Gaius and Selenia home, but Cassia, through the vast number of acquaintances she'd made since coming to me, could discover what happened at the far end of town without stirring a step.

Cassia had found out—through these same connections—how I'd had to pay for my dinner at the tavern in the Pallacinae. She'd not said so directly, but she'd made a show of putting extra coins in my purse, saying I'd not be caught without them again. Other than that, she never mentioned the matter.

Now Cassia turned her face to the sun, what bit of it she let show from behind her draped wrap. "How lovely to be in the open air again." She let out a happy breath. "There's no place more beautiful than Campania, Leonidas. We'll go there sometime."

I only made a neutral noise. Traveling cost money, and who knew how far our benefactor would let us out of his sight?

For now, it was enough that we could breathe air that held none of the smoke and stenches of the city, that the sun shone warm and the breeze was cool. The men in Rome would hunt a foreign slave for a murder and then give up when they couldn't find Balbus, safe in his disguise in the ludus. Selenius's shop would be taken over by another money-changer, and the man's death would be forgotten.

We'd give Sergius back his cup with my name on it, eat Marcella's hearty food, and curl up for the night in the warmth of her barn. Then back to Rome to exist a while longer.

"You'll have to take another job when we return," Cassia said around a bite of bread. "A loaf a day is all very well, but that will end in time, and our coffers are fearsomely low."

"They always are," I muttered.

Cassia pretended not to hear me. "Perhaps you could guard someone all the way to Neapolis," she said. "It's lovely there, across the bay from Herculaneum. Beauty you've never seen, Leonidas."

"I *have* seen it," I answered. "I was hired out for games there, years ago."

"Oh." She sounded a bit disappointed, then brightened. "Then you would see it again, but this time we could wander the streets and eat in the best taverns, and climb the hills for the view. Delightful."

"Delightful," I repeated. "When I look for this job, I'll make sure the employer knows it must be delightful."

"You are making fun of me, Leonidas."

"Yes." I kept my face straight. "Or we can return to Rome, and I can sleep." I was already tired, longing to reach Marcella's where I could lie on straw and close my eyes. Cassia and Marcella would talk—and talk—and I'd lie back and let their voices drift over me.

"You are always sleeping, Leonidas," Cassia said without rancor. "One day, you will have to wake up."

"One day, I will," I said.

"I have your word?"

"You do." I might be *infamis*, but I honored my promises, and Cassia knew it.

"That's all right then." Cassia turned her face to the road.

Before long, she started to hum, a clear tune she liked. In another few yards, she was softly singing.

The words flowed around me to be caught by the breeze and rise into the clear blue sky.

AUTHOR'S NOTE

THANK YOU FOR READING! I HOPE YOU ENJOYED THIS glimpse of the new Leonidas the Gladiator Mysteries.

As you might guess, while this is the first offering in the series, it will not be Book One. The first novel will introduce Leonidas and Cassia and show how they came to know and depend on each other. I'll go into more detail about the characters' backgrounds, the mysterious benefactor, and how Leonidas begins to solve crimes.

I don't know at the moment when that book will be finished—please check my website: www.gardnermysteries.com or sign up for my newsletter at http://eepurl.com/5n7rz to be notified when it is ready for pre-order and released.

If a vegetarian gladiator surprises you, archaeologists have discovered, by studying the bones of gladiators and other athletes, that their diet consisted mostly of vegetables, with a little starch, like barley and beans, to supplement it. Gladiators were fed the best foods available, as the more robust a man was, the better he performed and the more money could be made from him. Gladiators also had regular massages after their training and the best physicians to look after them.

I will explore more about the gladiators' world and more of Rome in the time of Nero in the novels.

When picturing the Rome of Nero, we have to erase from the city much of what we think of as "Roman" (e.g., the Coliseum, Trajan's column, the Pantheon as we see it today, and more)—these were great building projects of the later first and early second centuries AD (Hadrian rebuilt Agrippa's Pantheon, though he left Agrippa's name on the portico). We must imagine Rome before the fire of AD 64, when warrens of streets were wrapped with wooden and stone buildings.

Among my research materials for this era, I found mapping projects of early first-century Rome, which helped me follow Leonidas about the streets, and a fascinating digital reconstruction of Nero's Domus Aurea (Golden House), which did not exist at the time of this story, but will come into future novels.

Again, I hope you enjoyed a look into Leonidas's world. More to come!

All my best,

Ashley Gardner

THE NECKLACE AFFAIR

Captain Lacey Regency Mysteries by Ashley
Gardner

CHAPTER 1

ON AN EVENING IN LATE MARCH 1817, I CLIMBED TO THE third floor of Lucius Grenville's Grosvenor Street house in search of peace, and found a lady weeping instead.

In the rooms below me, Grenville's latest revelry tinkled and grated, Grenville celebrating recovery from a near-fatal injury. The entire *haut ton* had turned up tonight, Lucius Grenville being the darling of society, the dandy all other dandies aspired to be. The famous Brummell had fled to the Continent, Alvanley grew stout, but Grenville reigned supreme. He was an epicure who knew how to avoid excess, a sensualist who could resist the temptations of sloth and lechery.

I'd enjoyed speaking to a few of my friends below, but the transparent way Grenville's sycophants tried to exploit my acquaintance with him soon grated on my patience. I decided to sit in Grenville's private room and read until the festivities died down.

I used my walking stick and the balustrade, hand-carved by an Italian cabinetmaker, to leverage myself up the stairs.

My leg injury, given to me by French soldiers during the Peninsular War, did not affect me so much tonight as did the near gallon of port I had drunk. I could never afford what Grenville had in his cellars, so when he invited me to partake, I took enough to last.

Therefore, I was well past foxed when I at last emerged onto the third floor and sought the peace of Grenville's sitting room.

I found the lady in it, weeping.

She sat squarely under the scarlet tent that hung in the corner of the room, a souvenir from Grenville's travels in the east. The entire room was a monument to his journeys — ivory animals from the Indies reposed next to golden masks from Egypt, rocks bearing the imprint of ancient American animals held pride of place near hieroglyphic tablets from Persia.

The lady might have been pretty once, but too many years of rich food, late mornings, and childbirth had etched their memories onto her face and body. Her large bosom, stuffed into a satin bodice and reinforced with bands of lace, quivered with her misery.

I took two steps into the room, checked myself, and turned to go.

"Captain Lacey?"

I halted, bowed, and admitted to be he. I had no memory of who she was.

The woman swiped at her wet cheeks with a handkerchief so tiny she might as well not have bothered. "May I make so bold as to speak to you? Mr. Grenville said you might assist me."

Had he, indeed? Grenville was apt to volunteer my services, as I'd been of some use in solving problems that ran from innocuous misunderstandings all the way to violent murders.

I ought to have walked away then and there and not let myself be drawn into the whole sordid business. I was tired and quite drunk and had no reason to believe that I could help this sorrowful lady.

But her red-rimmed eyes were so pleading, her wretchedness so true, that I found myself giving her another bow and telling her to proceed.

"It is my maid, you see."

I braced myself for an outpouring of domestic troubles. My head started to pound, and I sank into the nearest comfortable chair.

"She is going to be hanged," the lady announced.

CHAPTER 2

HER BLUNT STATEMENT SWEPT THE FOG FROM MY BRAIN. I sat up straight as several facts clicked into place.

"You are Lady Clifford," I said.

She nodded, dejected.

"I read of it in the newspaper this morning," I said. "Your maid has been accused of stealing a diamond necklace worth several thousand pounds." The maid was even now awaiting examination by the Bow Street magistrate.

Lady Clifford sat forward and clasped her doughy hands. "She did not take it, Captain. That horrible Bow Street Runner said so, but I know Waters would never have done such a thing. She's been with me for years. Why should she?"

I could think of a number of reasons why Waters should. Perhaps she saw the necklace as her means of escaping a life of servitude. Perhaps she had a lover who'd convinced her to steal the necklace for him. Perhaps she bore a secret hatred for her employer and had at last found a way to exact revenge.

I said none of these things to Lady Clifford.

"You see, Captain, I know quite well who stole my diamonds." Lady Clifford applied the tiny handkerchief once more. "It was that viper I nursed at my bosom. *She* took them."

I knew from gossip which viper she meant. Annabelle Dale, a gently born widow, had once been Lady Clifford's companion and dearest friend. Now the woman was Earl Clifford's mistress. Mrs. Dale still lived in the Clifford home and, from all accounts, continued to refer to Lady Clifford as her "adored Marguerite."

But all of London knew that Lord Clifford spent nights in Mrs. Dale's bed. They formed a curious ménage, with Mrs. Dale professing fierce attachment to her old friend Lady Clifford, and Lord Clifford paying duty to both mistress and wife.

"Do you have evidence that Mrs. Dale took it?" I asked.

"The Runner asked just the same. *He* could produce no evidence that Waters stole the necklace, yet he arrested her."

The arresting Runner had been my former sergeant, Milton Pomeroy, who had returned from Waterloo and managed to work his way into the elite body of investigators who answered to the Bow Street magistrate.

Pomeroy was far more interested in arresting a culprit than in slow investigation. He was reasonably careful, because he'd not reap a reward for the arrest if he obtained no conviction. But getting someone to trial could be enough. Juries tended to believe that the person in the dock was guilty, and a maid stealing from an employer would make the gentlemen of the jury righteously angry.

However, I conceded that Lady Clifford would know a

maid she'd lived with for years better than would Milton Pomeroy. Interest stirred beneath my port-laden state.

"As I understand the story," I said, "your maid was upstairs in your rooms the afternoon the necklace disappeared. Before you and your husband and Mrs. Dale went out for the day, the necklace was in place. Gone when you, Lady Clifford, returned home."

Her lip curled. "Likely Mrs. Dale was nowhere near Egyptian House as she claims. She could have come back and stolen it."

My injured leg gave a throb. I rose and paced toward the windows to loosen it, stopping in front of one of Grenville's curio shelves. According to the newspaper, the other Clifford servants had sworn that Mrs. Dale and Lord Clifford hadn't returned to the house all afternoon. "You want very much for Mrs. Dale to have stolen your necklace."

"Perhaps I do. What of it?"

I touched a piece of jade carved into the shape of a baboon. "You must know that however much you want Mrs. Dale to have taken it, someone else entirely might be guilty."

"Well, Waters is not."

I studied the jade. Thousands of years old, Grenville had told me. The carving was intricate and detailed, done with remarkable workmanship. I rested the delicate thing on my palm. "You might be wrong," I said. "Are you prepared to be?"

"Mr. Grenville promised you would help me," Lady Clifford said, tears in her voice. "Waters is a good girl. She doesn't deserve to be in a gaol cell with common criminals. Oh, I cannot bear to think what she is suffering."

She broke into another flood of weeping. Some ladies

could cry daintily, even prettily, but not Lady Clifford. Her large body heaved, her sobs choked her, and she blew her nose with a snorting sound.

I set the miniature beast back on its shelf. Lady Clifford might be wrong that the solution was simple, but she was in genuine distress. The fact that some of this distress was pity for her poor maid made up my mind.

Lady Clifford sniffled again into the abused handkerchief. "Mr. Grenville said I could rely on you *utterly*."

The little baboon smiled at me, knowing I was caught. "Very well, my lady," I said. "I will see what I can do."

"I DID NOT EXACTLY SAY THAT," GRENVILLE PROTESTED.

I eyed him from the opposite seat in his splendid carriage. I had awakened with the very devil of a headache, but I felt slightly better this afternoon, thanks to the concoction that my landlady, Mrs. Beltan, had stirred for me upon seeing my state. Grenville had arrived at my rooms not long later, and now we rolled across London in pursuit of the truth.

In his suit of finest cashmere and expensive kid gloves, Grenville's slim form was a tailor's delight. I bought my clothes secondhand, though I had a coat from Grenville's tailor that he'd insisted on gifting to me when my best coat had been ruined on one of our adventures.

I said, "Lady Clifford strikes me as a woman who so much wishes a thing to be true, that it is true. To her. But this does not mean she is mistaken. If the maid did not steal the necklace, I have no wish to see her hang."

"Nor do I," Grenville said. "Her predicament played on my sympathy. Lady Clifford might have exploited that, but I sensed she genuinely cares for poor Waters." He gazed out at the tall houses of Piccadilly then back at me, a sparkle in his eyes I'd not seen since before he'd been injured. "So, my friend, we are off on another adventure. Where do we begin?"

"I should speak to Pomeroy," I said.

I imagined my old sergeant's dismay when I turned up to muck about in what he'd believed a straightforward arrest. "And I'd like to speak to the maid Waters if I can. And we can try to discover what became of the necklace—whether anyone purchased it, and from where, and trace backward from there, perhaps to the culprit."

Grenville grimaced and glanced again at the city rolling by outside. "A needle in a haystack I would say."

"Not necessarily." I had pondered this all night, at least, as far as my inebriation would let me. "A master thief would try to get the necklace to the Continent, to be reset and sold. In that case the necklace is gone forever, and the maid obviously did not escape with it. At most, she was an accomplice. As highly as Lady Clifford speaks of her, we cannot rule out the possibility that Waters was coerced by a lover to steal the jewels. A petty thief, on the other hand, might try to dispose of the necklace quickly, close to home, which means London. If I were the thief, I'd find a pawnbroker not much worried about where the merchandise came from, one who knew he could reset and sell the thing with no one being the wiser."

"Your knowledge of the criminal mind is astonishing," Grenville said.

I gave him a half smile. "Sergeant Pomeroy likes to tell me about it over a pint now and again. And Sir Gideon Derwent has worked to reform criminals most of his life. He's told me many interesting tales."

"Very well, then, a petty thief who seized an opportunity might sell it to a shady London pawnbroker. But what if you were Mrs. Dale? A gently born lady, who likely has no knowledge of unsavory pawnbrokers?"

I shrugged. "If she is the evil viper Lady Clifford paints her, she either passed it to a confederate to dispose of it for her, or she is hiding it to pin the blame on the maid and upset Lady Clifford."

"A dangerous proposition. Would Mrs. Dale risk hanging to gloat over her rival?"

"I have no idea," I said. "The ways of lady rivals are unknown to me. But if the maid or other servants stole the necklace, we will find it at a pawnbroker's."

"Yes, but which one?"

"We check them all," I said.

Grenville gave me a look of dismay. I had always wondered how Grenville would respond when my adventures turned into dogged work, but to his credit, he did not try to wriggle out of his offer to help. "It will take less time if we recruit Bartholomew and Matthias and divide the search."

"Some areas are more likely than others," I assured him. "Not every corner in London sports an unsavory pawnbroker. And the theft will be talked about. We might be able to pry loose some information, at the very least."

Grenville squared his shoulders, wincing a little because the wound he'd received during our last investigation still pained him. "Very well. I will change my boots and soldier on."

The carriage listed around the corner, and I braced my walking stick against the floor to steady myself. The handle was shaped like a the head of a goose and bore the inscription, *Captain G. Lacey, 1817.* A gift, and a fine one, and it gave me an idea.

"I know someone who does understand the ways of lady rivals," I said.

Grenville knew exactly whom I meant. He shot me a grin. "Ah, but will she help?"

"Who can say? She will either be interested or show me the door." Lady Breckenridge was nothing if not unpredictable.

"Her observations are usually directly on the mark," Grenville said. "I saw her last week at a garden party, where she told me that if I'd hurt myself during the Sudbury affair, it was my own fault for not taking proper care when it came to you. Any friend of Captain Lacey, she said, was bound to come to some kind of danger, and that I was a fool to take what you did lightly."

My fingers twitched on the walking stick. "Considering I almost got the poor woman roasted alive, that remark was almost kind."

"And probably true, with regard to me. I tend to believe myself untouchable."

I still hadn't quite recovered my guilt over the incident, though Grenville had cheerfully taken the entire blame himself.

"I will write to her," I said. "And discover whether she will condescend to see me. If she does not think it too dangerous to associate with me."

"She would be an excellent person to ask for the lady's point of view."

"I hesitate to mention it," I said. "But so would Marianne. She's been an actress for some time, so she'd have seen female rivalry, as well as, I'm sorry to say, petty theft."

Grenville's expression went still, even blank, which I'd

come to learn was his way of stemming his anger. Marianne Simmons, who had lived upstairs from me before Grenville had spirited her away to a fine house in Clarges Street, was a bit of a sore point between us.

Marianne, as poor as she was, did not like cages, no matter how luxurious, and she'd flown from Grenville's almost at once. I knew why, and the reason was a good one, but I suspected she'd not yet told Grenville. She'd softened toward him when he'd been injured, but I hadn't spoken to her since his recovery.

"I am afraid I've not seen much of Miss Simmons of late," Grenville said in a cold voice. "But please, do ask her advice if you think it would be helpful."

"I've not seen her either. I wondered if you had."

"Not since shortly after our return from Sudbury." His frown held frustration, anger, and concern.

"I would not worry about her. Marianne is resilient and will turn up when she feels it necessary."

"Indeed."

Grenville glanced out the window again, and though he'd never admit it, even under torture, I knew he was struggling to regain his composure. The closest we'd come to a permanent falling out had been over Marianne. He knew that I knew her secret, and that I had given her my word not to tell him. Grenville and I had made an agreement not to speak of the matter, but I knew it grated on him.

Grenville at last turned back to me, his lips tight but his equanimity restored. "I will obtain a map and ask Gautier about pawnbrokers," he said. "If we divide the task between us and Matthias and Bartholomew, we can make short work of the search. And while they put lists together, you and I shall take a repast. Anton is experimenting again, and I need someone to help me eat his creations. If he continues on this bent, I shall grow too stout for my clothes, and my reputation will be at an end."

The troubles of the very rich, I thought dryly. Not that I would refuse a lavish meal prepared by Anton, Grenville's French chef. My pride ran only so deep.

CHAPTER 3

ANTON DID NOT LIKE US TO TALK ABOUT BUSINESS WHILE we dined, especially when he was in a creative mood, so I endured the lobster brioche, asparagus soup, squabs stuffed with mushrooms, and a large and tender sole drowning in butter to please him. After each dish, the chef hovered at Grenville's elbow to wait for his precise opinion and hear what might be improved.

To me it was all ambrosia, but Grenville thoughtfully tasted each dish then critiqued its texture, flavor, piquancy, and presentation. I simply ate, while Bartholomew and Matthias, Grenville's two large, Teutonic-looking footman, kept our glasses topped with finest hock. Being Grenville's friend had decided advantages.

Once the final dish—a chocolate soup—had been taken away, Grenville bade Matthias bring out the map of London. Mathias laid out the leaves of it on the table, and the four of us bent over it. I was always fascinated by maps and resisted tracing the route to my own street, Grimpen Lane, off Russel Street near Covent Garden.

I tapped the area that showed Bond Street, Hanover Square, Oxford Street, and north and east up into Marylebone. The necklace had been stolen from the Clifford house in Mayfair. The areas I'd indicated could be reached fairly quickly from there and were rife with small shops and pawnbrokers, though those in Bond Street were less likely to purchase a strand of diamonds tossed at them by a serving maid or known thief. But one never knew. A Bond Street merchant had only last year been arrested for selling stolen goods brought over from France and Italy.

Bartholomew and Matthias turned eager eyes to me as they received their assignments. The brothers enjoyed helping investigate these little problems, and I often envied them their exuberance. Bartholomew had become my valet-cum-errand runner in order to train himself to be a gentleman's gentleman, but while he now held himself above other footmen, including his own brother, he'd never forgo the chance to help on one of my inquiries.

Grenville provided the shillings for hackneys to each of us, and we went our separate ways, agreeing to meet at a coffee house in Pall Mall that evening.

Grenville had been given the Bond Street area, because the proprietors there knew him well. Grenville was a Bond Street shop owner's greatest treasure. Not only did he have exquisite taste, but he paid his bills.

Matthias and Bartholomew hastened north toward Marylebone, and I turned to Conduit Street and Hanover Square.

I found that pawnbrokers were less willing to speak to me unless I made the pretense of wanting to purchase something. Questions were not welcome, and clients kept in confidence.

I let them infer that I shopped for a gift for a friend and

had difficulty choosing. The proprietors thawed a bit as I looked over bracelets that had once adorned the wrists of debutants and earrings pawned by wealthy matrons. That the jewelry now lay in trays for me to pick over meant that they'd been sold to pay off the ladies' gaming debts. In a world in which highborn women had little to do but gamble and gossip, ruin lay very close to the surface.

I found earrings encrusted with tiny diamonds, emerald brooches, and strands of sleek pearls. One shop carried a comb made of ebony with a sprinkling of sapphires that made me imagine it against Lady Breckenridge's dark hair. I eyed it regretfully and longed to be deeper in pocket than I was.

Nowhere did I spy a strand of diamonds that matched the description Lady Clifford had given me.

North of St. George's, just off Hanover Square, I found a possible candidate in a dark and dusty little shop. When I professed to the short, gray-haired proprietor with a protruding belly that I was looking for just the right string of diamonds for my lady, he admitted to recently having purchased such a thing. I tried not to hope too much as he fetched it from the back room and laid it out for me on the counter that it was the necklace I sought.

The diamonds lay against a black velvet cloth like stars against the night. The necklace winked even in the dim light, brilliance in the drab shop.

"Beautiful," I said.

"At a fair price. Fifty guineas."

Too dear for me, but far too low for Lady Clifford's diamonds. Her husband had valued them at three thousand guineas, Lady Clifford had told me. Even if the proprietor suspected the necklace to be stolen, he'd likely try for a higher price than fifty.

"Who would part with such a lovely thing?" I asked him.

"A lady down on her luck. What lady, I did not ask. A servant brought it, a respectable-looking lady's maid. Sad, she was. It was a wrench for her mistress to let the necklace go, she said, but she had debts to pay. It happens, sir. The way of the world."

My heart beat faster. "An unhappy tale," I said.

The pawnbroker nodded. "Pretty little thing, the maid. Probably worried she'd lose her place if the mistress had pockets to let. Felt sorry for her. Gave her more than I should have by rights."

I decided to approach the thing head on. I looked the proprietor in the eye. "You must have heard that Countess Clifford had a diamond necklace stolen. Her lady's maid was arrested for the deed. Can you be certain that the lady's maid who brought this in was not the thief in question?"

The man did not blink. "I read the newspaper account, of course. But these are not Lady Clifford's diamonds, sir. I saw her ladyship's necklace once, and I'd not forget a piece like that. The Clifford necklace was set in Paris and is much larger, the diamonds more numerous. And see here." He lifted the strand and pointed to one of the stones. "Cut is not quite exact, is it?"

I peered at it. The diamond, as beautiful as it was, had been cut slightly askew, the facets not straight.

"Lady Clifford's would be of higher quality, that is a fact," the proprietor said. "This bauble was intended for lesser gentry; possibly a country squire had it made for his wife. This would never be fobbed off on Earl Clifford. And I assure you, sir, were someone to bring me Lady Clifford's necklace, I would send word to a magistrate at once."

He said this with a virtuous air. I could not be certain whether he truly would send for a magistrate, but I saw no guilt in his eyes, no nervousness of a man who had stolen goods hidden behind his counter. If he were a very good criminal, of course, he would have mastered hiding his complicity, but short of forcing him at sword point to prove he did not have the necklace, there was not much I could do.

I thanked the man and left his shop, which was the last on my list. I took a hackney to Pall Mall, rather short of information.

I found Grenville already there. He bade the host bring us both a cup of rich, almost chocolaty, coffee while we waited for the footmen.

Grenville had found out little himself. The Bond Street proprietors had opened up to him, had readily talked of Lady Clifford's necklace, which was beautiful, they said, but they had no idea what had become of it.

"The task is a bit more difficult than I expected," Grenville said glumly. "The thing might already be cut up and in Paris."

I had to agree. When Bartholomew and Matthias arrived, however, the blond, blue-eyed brothers were pink-faced and grinning.

"Matthias has got it, sir," Bartholomew said. He dragged a straight-backed chair from another table and straddled it back to front. "Clear as day. In a pawnbroker's near Manchester Square. One large diamond necklace, brought in not three afternoons ago."

Grenville leaned forward, excited, but I tried to keep my skepticism in place. Though I hoped we'd found an easy end to the problem, I had learned from experience that solutions did not come so readily.

We had to wait until the publican had thunked down two glasses of good, dark ale for the brothers and retreated.

Matthias and Bartholomew both drank deeply, thirsty from their search, then Matthias began.

"'Twas not much of a shop," he said, wiping his mouth. "It's in a little turning full of horse dung and trash. I told the proprietor that my master was looking for something nice for his lady and sent me to scout, but I didn't mention who my master was, of course. Would have swooned if I'd told him, wouldn't he? That someone like Mr. Grenville would even think to soil his boots in such a place would have him so agitated he wouldn't be able to speak. So I kept quiet, and he came over quite chatty."

"Good thinking," I said, as Matthias paused to drink.

"What he had in the front was mostly cheap," Matthias continued. "The sort of thing I'd expect him to show gentlemen of not much means. I said that my master was looking for something better, because he'd just become flush in cash and wanted to please his lady. Well, as soon as I said that, the proprietor came over all secretive. He shut the door of the shop and drew the curtain, and told me he had something special. Something he was keeping for customers who were obviously up in the world."

"And did he show it to you?" Grenville asked.

"That he did, sir. He brought out a necklace. My eyes nearly popped when I saw it. Lots of stones all sparkling. Much nicer than anything in that shop. Out of place, like. I professed my doubts, saying my master wouldn't have truck with anything stolen. Proprietor grew angry, said he'd never buy from thieves. If a highborn lady wanted to bring her necklace to a pawnbroker's, why should he mind? He paid her a sum which near ruined him, he said, and would be glad to get it off his hands."

I exchanged a look with Grenville. "A highborn lady," I said. "Not her maid?"

"Highborn lady," Matthias repeated. "I couldn't ask him for a description, because he was already getting suspicious of me. So I thought I'd nip off and tell you."

Grenville snatched up his gloves. "Well, if this pawn-broker is anxious to have it taken off his hands, we will oblige him. You've done well, Matthias. Lacey, come with me?"

I went out with him to his sumptuous carriage, and the two footmen pushed aside their ales and followed, not about to let us finish the problem without them.

When we reached Manchester Square, Grenville was set to leap down and charge into the shop, but I persuaded him to let me have a look at the necklace myself. Matthias was correct—if the grand Grenville walked into a down-at-heel pawnbroker's, the news would fly around London and be picked up by every newspaper in the land. I, on the other hand, in my worn breeches and square-toed boots, could enter any shop I pleased without all of society falling into a swoon.

Grenville was disappointed, but he conceded that we needed to go carefully, and said he'd wait in the carriage around the corner.

I had little difficulty persuading the proprietor to show me the necklace. It was much as Lady Clifford described it —a large stone with three smaller diamonds on either side of it, all linked by a gold chain. When I'd asked Lady Clifford for more particulars, she'd looked blank, as though she could not remember anything else about it. I wondered what it must be like to have so many expensive baubles that the details of them blurred in the memory.

I played my part as an ingenuous husband, recently come into some money, wishing to ingratiate myself with my wife. The proprietor volunteered that these were the goods, from a lady, in fact. A true lady, well-spoken and well dressed, not a lackey or a tart. I suppose Matthias had made him nervous with his questions, because the proprietor was happy to tell me all.

Grenville had supplied the money with which to purchase the necklace if necessary. I paid it over and returned to the carriage with the diamonds in my pocket, the pawnbroker happy to see the necklace go.

Satisfied that we'd found it, Grenville was ready to call on Clifford and confront Annabelle Dale on the moment. I persuaded him to fix an appointment for the next day, saying I wanted to be certain of a thing or two before then.

Grenville chafed with impatience, but he'd come to trust my judgment. I gave him the necklace to lock up in his house for the night, and we parted ways.

Once Grenville was gone, Matthias with him, I told Bartholomew to fetch us a hackney, then I returned to the shop near Hanover Square. There, I talked the proprietor down to a price I could afford and took the smaller necklace home with me. Bartholomew was full of questions, but I could only tell him that I did not know the answer to them myself.

The next morning, I received a note from Grenville that fixed a visit to the Clifford house in South Audley Street for three o'clock that afternoon. Lady Breckenridge, to whom I'd written the previous day, sent me a short and formal reply, as well, also giving me leave to call on her near three.

I had Bartholomew clean and brush my coat, and I left my rooms in plenty of time to hire a hackney to Mayfair.

As I walked toward Russel Street, however, a large carriage rolled up to block the entrance to tiny Grimpen Lane, where my rooms above the bake shop lay. Grimpen

Lane was a cul-de-sac, no other way out. I halted in annoyance.

I knew to whom the coach belonged, which annoyed me further. I did not at the moment want to speak to him, but I was unable to do anything but wait to see what he wanted.

A giant of a man stepped off his perch on the back of the coach and opened the door for me. He assisted me in, slamming the door as I dropped into a seat, leaving me alone to face James Denis.

Denis was a man who had his hand in most criminal pies in England, who obtained precious artworks—the ownership of which was hazy—from half-wrecked Europe, and bought and sold favors of the highest of the high. He owned MPs outright, and with a flick of his well-manicured fingers, had them manipulate the laws of England to suit him. London magistrates, with only two exceptions that I knew of, answered to him. Denis had the power to ruin many without a drop of that ruin touching him.

I thoroughly disliked what Denis was and what he did, but I was not certain how I felt about the man himself. I'd never, in the year I'd known him, gotten past his façade. He was so thoroughly cold and revealed so little of himself that anyone could reside behind that slim, rather long face and dark blue eyes. Denis was only in his thirties, and I had to wonder what on earth had happened to him in his short life that had made him what he was.

The carriage remained squarely in front of the entrance to Grimpen Lane, and I knew it would remain there until Denis had gotten from me what he wanted.

"The Clifford necklace," he said without greeting me. "You've undertaken to find it."

He did not ask a question. That he already knew about my involvement did not surprise me. He paid people in my neighborhood to watch me and report to him everything I did.

I saw no benefit in lying. "I have. What is your interest?"

"Let us say I have had my eye on the piece. I would very much like to be informed when you have found it."

"Why?" I asked, curious in spite of myself. "It is a Mayfair lady's necklace. Expensive, yes, but hardly in your league."

His expression did not change. "Nevertheless, report to me when you have found it. Better still, bring it to me."

I regarded him as coolly as he regarded me. "I know you find this repeated declaration tedious, but I do not work for you. Nor do I ever intend to work for you. Lady Clifford asked me to discover what has become of her necklace, and that is what I will do."

Denis did not like the answer *no*. He'd been known to punish—thoroughly and finally—those who told him no too often. But I could not say anything else. I had pledged myself to Lady Clifford, and that was that.

"I did not say I would not allow you to return the diamonds to Lady Clifford," Denis said. "I want to examine the necklace myself first, is all."

"Why?"

"That, Captain, is my business."

Meaning I'd never drag the reason out of him, no matter how much I tried. "What is special about this necklace?" I asked instead. "You betray yourself with too much interest."

Denis tapped his walking stick on the roof and almost instantly, the pugilist footman wrenched open the door. "That I can determine only when I hold it in my hands. Good day, Captain."

The footman helped me climb to the ground. Denis

turned to look out the opposite window as the footman closed the door again, finished with me.

I was happy to go, but he'd started me wondering. Denis did not involve himself in anything that did not bring him great profit. A missing lady's necklace should be, as I'd told him, far below his notice. I would have to find out.

The carriage rolled on, unblocking the lane, and I continued on my way to the hackney stand.

Once I reached Grenville's house in Grosvenor Street, we rode in his carriage to our appointment with Lord Clifford.

Lord Clifford's study, where he received us, was crammed with books up to its high ceiling, the tall windows letting in light. I saw no dust anywhere, but the place smelled musty, as though damp had gotten into the books.

Lord Clifford was a tall man with a bull-like neck and small eyes. He wore clothes that rivaled Grenville's for elegance, but he looked more like a farmer in his landlord's clothes than a gentleman of Mayfair.

"Lot of nonsense," Clifford said to us after Grenville introduced me and told him our purpose. "Waters never took the blasted necklace. I told the magistrate so, and he released her. She is home, safe and sound, back below stairs, where she belongs."

CHAPTER 4

GRENVILLE AND I STARED AT HIM, DUMBFOUNDED.

"You made your inquiries for nothing, gentlemen," Lord Clifford said. "All I had to do was have words with the magistrate. If my wife hadn't gone ranting to all and sundry that the necklace had been stolen, her maid would not have been arrested at all. Serves her right for not leaving me to deal with it. Some housebreaker took it, must have done. The Runner had it all wrong."

"I would not say our inquiries were for nothing," I began.

Clifford gave me a look that told me I should not speak before my betters. "Of course they were. I told you. The bloody thing's probably on the Continent by now. Long gone."

"What the captain means is that we may have found your necklace," Grenville said. He removed a box from his pocket and opened it to reveal the necklace Matthias had run to ground yesterday.

The earl stared at it. "Who the devil gave you this?"

"I purchased it from a pawnbroker near Manchester Square," Grenville answered.

Clifford studied the diamonds a moment, then he snorted. "Well, he played you false, then. This is not my wife's necklace."

Grenville blinked, but for some reason, I felt no surprise.

"Are you certain?" Grenville asked.

"Of course I am certain. I gave her the damned thing, didn't I? My diamonds were of much finer quality and more numerous, the smaller stones surrounded by even smaller ones. I've never seen this necklace before."

I dipped into my pocket and removed the strand I'd persuaded the proprietor off Hanover Square to sell me last evening. "What about this one?"

Grenville shot me a look as Lord Clifford examined the stones. "Yes, this belongs to my wife. But it is not the necklace that was stolen. She's had this since before we married. Bit of trash." He tossed the necklace onto a satinwood table and did not ask me where I'd obtained it. "Someone has played you for a fool, Grenville. Probably my wife. She is eaten up with jealousy. Her maid never stole the necklace, and neither did Mrs. Dale, as much as she's putting that story about."

"Can you be certain about Mrs. Dale?" I asked.

"Mrs. Dale was with me at the time the necklace disappeared." Lord Clifford touched the side of his nose. "You gentlemen understand what I mean."

Grenville looked pained. "Quite."

"So," I said, "not at Egyptian House, as she told the Runner."

"Well, of course not, but she could hardly confess where she truly was, could she?" Lord Clifford jerked his thumb at the necklace in Grenville's hand. "Enjoy the bauble, gentlemen. You bought it for nothing. Teach you to go mucking about in a man's affairs. Should be ashamed of yourself, Grenville."

He made no such admonishment to me—whether because he expected someone like me to not know any better or because he caught the angry look in my eye, I didn't know. Grenville, his sangfroid in place, bade Clifford a cool good afternoon, and we took our leave.

The sangfroid slipped, however, as the carriage pulled away from Lord Clifford's door. "Boor," Grenville said between his teeth. "I've never liked him." He transferred his annoyed stare to me. "Where did you find that other necklace? Why did you not tell me about it?"

"Because I was not certain," I said. "It was a pure guess, and I could have been entirely off the mark."

"Bloody hell, Lacey, you do play your cards close to your chest. What is this all about?"

"I am not sure, truth to tell. Lady Clifford sells one necklace and has the other stolen, or so she claims. Too much coincidence."

Grenville heaved a sigh. "At least the maid has been cleared. Perhaps Lady Clifford only harangued about the necklace being stolen to push the blame onto Mrs. Dale. For vengeance. Then feels remorse when her beloved maid was accused instead and turned to you to unravel the tangle."

"I do not think it is quite so simple." I thought of Lord Clifford throwing aside the necklace I'd bought, proclaiming it a "bit of trash." He'd not even asked where I'd found it or why I'd had it. "But I am happy the maid was allowed home."

"And what has the second necklace to do with anything?"

"I am not certain. I need to think on it."

Grenville put the pouch containing the wrong necklace we'd bought into his pocket. "I suppose I can find a use for this," he said.

I doubted he meant to give it to Marianne. He'd buy her something new, something another woman hadn't already worn. Marianne might not appreciate it, but Grenville treated her better than she deserved.

"Can you ask your coachman to let me out here?" I asked, glancing out the window. "Lady Breckenridge answered my request to call on her, and her house is only a few doors down."

I knew Grenville was irritated with me, but he agreed. As I descended at Lady Breckenridge's door, Grenville gave me a pointed look. "We will speak later."

Which meant I would have to confess everything. I tipped my hat to him, he muttered a goodbye, and the carriage rolled away.

LADY BRECKENRIDGE, COOL IN A GRAY SO LIGHT IT WAS silver, her dark hair threaded with a wide bandeau, regarded me from beside the fireplace in her very modern drawing room.

I'd sat in this drawing room amongst the highest of the high a few weeks ago, when the double doors between this chamber and the next had been pulled open, the room filled with chairs and people. We'd listened to a tenor make his London debut, and while I'd not thought much of the young man as a person, his voice had filled me with joy.

The drawing room had been restored to its former arrangement of sofas and chairs, footstools and side tables, grouped together under a chandelier dripping with crystals.

The chandelier was dark today, the room illuminated by sunlight streaming through the two front windows.

Lady Breckenridge did not sit down, so I remained standing.

"Business, your letter indicated," she said.

"Indeed," I said. "I thank you for agreeing to admit me."

She lifted one dark brow. "Gracious, Lacey, your conversation has become as stilted as your letters. I had half a mind to ignore your request on that transgression alone."

The note I'd dashed off to her yesterday afternoon, written on a scrap of paper I'd torn from a letter she'd sent me during my sojourn in Sudbury, had requested a half hour of her time and said nothing more. I suppose it had been a bit abrupt.

"Forgive me," I said, giving her a half bow. "I ran away to the army before I was able to complete my upbringing and learn the gentlemanly art of entertaining letters. I was in a hurry."

Lady Breckenridge did not smile. "It was not so much the form of the letter, you know, as the request within it. If you wish to see me only in a matter of business, I hire gentlemen to take care of that for me. I can give you their direction."

I'd offended her, I realized. Not long ago, in this very drawing room, I'd told her that I counted her among my circle of close friends, of which I had few. I realized that my hasty missive yesterday must have seemed brusque, demanding, and nothing to do with friendship.

"I beg your pardon," I said, giving her another bow. "Grenville admonishes me in much the same way. I get the bit between my teeth, and I forget that I am easily rude. I said 'business' because I hate to take advantage of friendship, and I find myself needing your help."

Her dark blue eyes remained cool. "Ah, you thought yourself softening the blow. I must say, you do not read your fellow creatures well."

"I never pretended to."

Lady Breckenridge regarded me a moment longer, then she uncrossed her arms, moved to a settee near the fireplace, and reposed gracefully on it. She sat in the middle, so if I tried to join her, I'd either crush against her or force her to move.

I chose a chair instead, one near enough to her to be conversational but not so close as to impose myself.

Lady Breckenridge was not a woman who flirted or was coy, and she did not like coyness in return. She asked for honesty and was somewhat brutally honest herself. Her marriage had been unhappy, her husband a bully. I suppose she had taught herself to trust cautiously.

"Well, then, what is this business?" Lady Breckenridge asked. "If it is entertaining enough, I might consider forgiving you both the letter and the presumption."

"It's to do with Lady Clifford's stolen necklace."

Lady Breckenridge stopped short of rolling her eyes. "Good God, I am bloody tired of hearing about Lady Clifford and her bloody necklace. The woman has a flair for the dramatic, always making heavy weather of something—her husband, her daughter's marriage, the hated Mrs. Dale, her losses at cards, her stolen necklace. If you ask me, she sold the damned thing to pay her creditors and professed it stolen so that her husband would not discover she is up to her ears in debt."

"I wondered if she might game deeply," I said.

"She has a mania for it. Sometimes she wins, mostly she loses. Lord Clifford has come to her rescue before, but I gather he has made it clear that she is to cease. Not that she has."

I thought about the smaller necklace Lord Clifford had sneered over, declaring it one his wife had owned before their marriage. The pawnbroker had told me that a lady's maid had brought it in for her mistress who was "down on her luck." Lady Clifford selling her own jewelry to get out of debt explained the transaction, but Lady Clifford hadn't claimed *that* necklace to be stolen.

"Grenville and I and our footmen searched every jeweler's and pawnbroker's up and down the center of London," I said. "If Lady Clifford had sold the necklace, surely we would have found it, or at least heard word of it." As I had with the smaller necklace.

"My dear Lacey, if I wanted to sell my diamonds and pretend them stolen from me, I wouldn't rush to flog it to a pawnbroker. I'd be much more discreet. There are gentlemen who do that sort of thing for you."

"What sort of men?" I asked. I'd not heard this, but then I was not much of a card player. I preferred more active games of skill—billiards, boxing, horseracing.

"Oh, one can find them if one knows where to go," Lady Breckenridge said, looking wise. "Who, for a percentage, are willing to smuggle bits and pieces out of the country while you go on a tear about having them stolen. You pay off your creditors, your husband or wife or father never knows, and embarrassment is saved all around."

"She might have done such a thing, true. But why then loudly point at Mrs. Dale? Lord Clifford tells me that Mrs. Dale was—shall we say, entertaining him—at the time the necklace went missing. Mrs. Dale would have to reveal that alibi to save herself, possibly in a public courtroom. The world knows that Lord Clifford is carrying on with his wife's companion, but would Lady Clifford wish to publicly acknowledge it?"

"Lady Clifford rather enjoys playing the wronged woman, I think," Lady Breckenridge said. "Much sympathy flows her way, though much disgust as well, I am afraid. The way of the world is such that when a man is unfaithful to his wife, it of course must be because the wife has not done enough to keep him at her side."

I heard the bitterness in her voice. Lady Breckenridge's late husband had been notorious for straying. While Lady Breckenridge had professed she'd been rather grateful for his habit, because it kept the boorish man away from her, I imagined that she'd faced blame the likes of which she'd just related. Hardly her fault that her husband had been cruel and uncaring.

"I am sorry," I said.

"I did not say such a thing to stir your sympathy, Captain. It is only the truth."

I knew that when my wife had left me, no one had blamed me harder than I had myself. I'd blamed Carlotta as well, yes, in my rage and heartbreak. I could have behaved better toward her, but she ought to have told me how unhappy she'd been. And I'd never forgiven her for taking away my child. My girl would be quite grown now. I hadn't seen her in fifteen years.

The last thought hurt, and for a moment, there in Lady Breckenridge's sitting room, the pain of it squeezed me hard. I studied the head of my walking stick, the one Lady Breckenridge had given me, as I fought to regain my composure.

"Captain?" she asked. "Are you well?"

Her voice was like cool water in the darkness. I looked up to find Lady Breckenridge watching me, her arms stretched across the back of the settee now, which made her more graceful and lovely than ever. The pose was practiced, probably trained into her by a ream of governesses and her aristocratic mother.

"I beg your pardon," I said.

Any other lady might express curiosity about my thoughts and why I'd let my attention stray from her, but not Lady Breckenridge.

"You have not told me precisely why you need my help," she said.

I did not know quite how to begin. This was the first investigation in which I'd found a place I could not go, people I could not question. I was generally accepted among Grenville's circle if not embraced, because my pedigree measured up even to the most snobbish. Additionally, because I took rooms over a bake shop in a genteelly poor section of town, I was able to speak to the denizens of Covent Garden and beyond without awkwardness. But an aristocratic lady's private rooms were beyond my sphere, and I doubted Lord Clifford would invite me to return his house, in any case.

"Say it all at once, and I shall respond," Lady Breckenridge said. She sounded in no hurry.

"Lady Clifford's maid was released, absolved of the crime," I said. "But I know Pomeroy. He will harass the household until he finds another culprit to take to trial—a footman, another maid, even Mrs. Dale. I'd like to find the true culprit, and the necklace, before that happens. To do so, I will better need to know the layout of the Clifford house and what happened on the day of the theft. Unfortunately, Lord Clifford has made it clear that I am unwelcome, and I have no idea when I will be able to speak to Lady Clifford again."

"I see," she said after a thoughtful moment. "And so you thought to ask me to speak to her for you."

I could not tell whether she were pleased at the prospect or dismayed. Her tone was neutral, her look direct.

"Discreetly," I said.

"By all means, discreetly. It would have to be. Lady Clifford and I don't exactly see eye to eye. Not a pleasant task you thought to set me."

"You see now why I did not want to presume upon our friendship," I said.

"Indeed. You do this sort of thing often, do you not, speaking to people whose conversations you would never dream to seek in ordinary circumstance. Such as when you played billiards with me at Astley Close while you looked into the Westin affair."

I gave her a smile. "Touché."

"You did not like me, but you wanted information. I thought you a vacant-headed toady of Grenville's, and I sought to teach you a lesson, but I failed in that regard. You intrigued me mightily, you know."

"I am honored."

"Cease the Spanish coin, Captain. I will help you, because you are never interested in a thing unless it is worth the interest." Her eyes took on a mischievous sparkle. "But if I am to do you this favor, Captain, you must do me one in return."

"Of course," I said at once. "Tell me what it is, and I am your servant."

"I highly doubt that. I will ask you when I am finished interrogating Lady Clifford."

I had to wonder what she had in mind, but I was happy that she was willing to help. "I will be obliged to you," I said.

"Goodness, you must truly be fascinated by the Clifford problem if you rashly promise that. But do not worry. I will discover what I can—discreetly—and report to you. Lady Clifford loves to talk about herself, in any case. I do not imagine I will have much difficulty."

"Could you contrive to speak to Mrs. Dale, as well? I very much would like to talk to her, but I've never met the woman."

"I will manage it." Lady Breckenridge spoke with firm self-confidence. "I believe she is an opium eater."

I stared. "Mrs. Dale?"

"Very likely in the form of laudanum. She has the look—red-rimmed eyes, rather pasty complexion, trembles a bit but strives to hide it. Such things happen."

Indeed, some people took laudanum for legitimate ailments, as I did when the pain in my leg proved too great, but then they could not leave off when they felt better. Poets apparently produced works of genius in this state. Grenville had an aversion to laudanum, even a fear.

"Tell me, Lacey," Lady Breckenridge said. She straightened up and sat neutrally, no artifice. "Why are you so interested in this theft? Aside from making certain your galumphing Runner does not arrest and hang the wrong person, that is. The solution is simple. Lady Clifford sold the necklace to pay her debts, she tried to push the blame on her rival, and her maid inadvertently was arrested instead. The problem is ended."

"Perhaps," I said. I rubbed my thumb over my engraved name on the walking stick. "But there seems to be more to it. And truth to tell, when I found Lady Clifford in such misery, I wanted to help her. Doubly after I met her husband."

"Yes, Clifford is ghastly. You are quite the romantic, Captain Lacey, ever one to assist a lady in distress."

"Sometimes there is no one else to care," I said. "If that is romantic, then so be it."

Lady Breckenridge rose, came to me as I got to my feet, and put her hand over my much larger one. "It is one of the reasons I have decided to call you friend." She rose on her tiptoes and pressed a light kiss to my cheek. "Now, do go away. I must dress if I am to pay a sympathy call on Lady Clifford."

AS I LEFT LADY BRECKENRIDGE'S HOUSE AND WALKED down the street to find a hackney, I felt anew her kiss on my cheek. It reminded me of other kisses she'd given me, on the lips, as well as the few precious times her head had rested on my shoulder. My mood, soured by the encounter with James Denis and the dressing down Lord Clifford had given us, lightened considerably.

I had the hackney driver let me out at Southampton Street, and I ducked into the Rearing Pony for a restorative measure of good, bitter ale before walking home.

The city was darkening, clouds rolling in to spoil the sunshine and drench us in more rain. The last shoppers were purchasing supper in Covent Garden as I made my way through, and I paused to be entertained by a troupe of acrobats near one corner.

I continued the short way down Russel Street and turned in at Grimpen Lane, and made for the outside door next to the bake shop that led upstairs to my rooms. Mrs. Beltan, my landlady, who owned the shop, stood at her doorstep to watch me approach, looking impatient.

"There you are, Captain," she called. "I wasn't certain what to do. A gentleman has called on you, and I didn't want to let him up in your rooms without you here." She stepped close to me as I neared her and lowered her voice to a furtive whisper. "He is *French*."

CHAPTER 5

I LOOKED PAST MRS. BELTAN INTO THE SHOP AND THE gentleman there. The man was on the small side, with gray hair cropped close against a fine-boned face. He wore respectable clothing, nothing very costly. I did not know him, but he looked harmless.

"Sir," I nodded at him as I entered the shop. "We can talk in my rooms above and let this good lady retire."

The man bowed back to me. "Thank you, monsieur."

His accent was quite thick, as though he spoke English only when he could not avoid doing so. I stood back to let him pass and tipped my hat to the anxious-looking Mrs. Beltan.

"Do not worry," I murmured. "The war is over. I doubt we'll reenact Vitoria in my sitting room."

Mrs. Beltan gave me a displeased look, but she shrugged her plump shoulders and retreated. I took the unknown Frenchman upstairs and unlocked the door to my rooms.

Bartholomew had already stoked the fire, though the lad was nowhere in sight. The Frenchman moved to the fire and held his hands out to it. The coming rain had turned the evening cold.

"How can I help you, sir?" I asked.

He turned and regarded me with a cool gray stare. Though he was, as I'd observed, a small-boned man, he held himself with dignity, almost arrogance. "I have heard that you are a man to be trusted, Captain Lacey. A man of honor."

"I make that attempt, yes."

I closed the door behind me but didn't lock it then moved to the cupboard for brandy and two glasses. I had no worries about offering my brandy to a haughty Frenchman, because Grenville had given the stuff to me, so it was the best France could supply.

The man stood silently as I poured out and brought him a glass. He passed the goblet I handed him under his nose, then his expression changed to that of a man who'd unexpectedly come upon paradise.

He closed his eyes as he poured a little brandy into his mouth, then he pressed his lips together and rocked his head back in pure delight.

When he opened his eyes, I saw tears in them. "Thank you, sir. This is exquisite. I have not tasted such . . . in many years." He spoke heavily and slowly, pausing to make a low "hmm" noise in his throat.

"My friend Mr. Grenville has impeccable taste," I said. "You are an émigré?"

He had the bearing of wealth and breeding, but his cheap clothes, his heavy accent, and the fact that he was in London at all told me he'd fled France long ago, when Madame Guillotine had been searching for victims.

"I am. I was. . . hmm . . . once the Comte de Mercier du

Lac de la Fontaine. A long time ago now. Now the English call me Monsieur Fontaine."

An aristocrat, which explained the bearing. Likely the master of a vast estate, with hundreds of peasants toiling to keep him in silk stockings and the best brandy. All gone in the blink of an eye. I wagered that Fontaine's estate was now in the hands of a nouveau riche banker from Paris.

My wife lived somewhere in France, in a small village with her French officer lover. I doubted that this man knew her—I was willing to believe he'd fled France when the first danger had flared in Paris, before England and France went to war.

"What may I do for you, Monsieur le Comte?" I asked.

"My daughter, she is . . . hmm . . . married to an Englishman of some respectability. He is a member of White's club and quite proud of the fact." De la Fontaine gave me the ghost of a smile. I envisioned a pompous young Englishman pleased with himself that he'd landed the daughter of a French count.

"Do I know him?" I asked.

"It is possible you have met him, but he holds himself above all but the . . .hmm . . . top of society. He is acquainted with your friend, Mr. Grenville."

Which meant that Grenville at least tolerated the man. If Grenville had disapproved of this son-in-law, he would have found himself eventually pushed out of his precious White's.

"I can't speak for Grenville," I said. "If you wish me to ask him something on your behalf, I can't promise to. I suggest that you write to him yourself."

Monsieur de la Fontaine's smile vanished, and the cold aristocrat returned. In spite of his cheaply made suit, he had the bearing of a leader, one whose ancestors had held their corner of France in an iron grip.

"No, indeed, Captain," he said stiffly. "I have come to speak to *you*. About this affair of the stolen diamonds."

"Lady Clifford's necklace?" I asked in surprise.

"Not . . . hmm . . . Lady Clifford's, Captain. Mine. The diamonds that this English comtesse wishes you to find belong to me."

THINKING IT THROUGH, I DECIDED I SHOULD NOT BE VERY astonished. At the end of the last century, French émigrés had sold what they could in order to flee France, sometimes giving ship captains everything they had in return for being smuggled across the channel. The necklace had been made in Paris, the pawnbroker I'd spoken to had told me. Everything fit together.

"Captain, may we sit?" de la Fontaine asked.

I noticed his hands trembling. He might once have been a proud aristocrat, but now he was an elderly man, his bones aching with the rain.

"Of course." I gestured him to the wing chair, the most comfortable in the room and closest to the fire. I refilled his brandy while I dragged my desk chair over to his and sat.

Another sip of brandy restored the comte's stern but dignified stare. "Do you believe me?" he asked.

"I do," I said. "The necklace came from your family?"

The count tapped the arm of the chair with his brandy glass. He was angry, and holding the anger in. "The diamonds entered the de la Fontaine family during the time of Richelieu. They were . . . hmm . . . handed down through the generations. Cut, re-cut, set, and reset. They reached their present form in the middle of the last century, when my grandfather was the trusted confidant of the king's official mistress. She had them set into the necklace as a gift to him. My grandfather gave them to my father, who gave them to my mother on their marriage. When my mother passed, they came to me, and I determined to give them to my own daughter when she married. My only son was killed fighting Napoleon for the English, and my daughter is all that is left of the de la Fontaines."

He caught my sympathy and my amazed interest. A necklace created by the mistress of Louis XV would be worth far more than the several thousand pounds Lady Clifford had claimed the necklace cost. James Denis's interest also became clear. Denis would not concern himself with a simple lady's necklace, but he'd consider one with such a history well worth his notice.

"Why the devil does Earl Clifford have it, then?" I asked. "Did you sell him the necklace to pay your way out of France?"

The anger built in de la Fontaine's eyes. "I never sold it, Captain. Everything else, yes. Hmm. Everything. To save my daughter, it was worth it. But I kept the necklace. It was her legacy. Then it was stolen from me. I had it before I crossed the Channel—when I arrived on this shore, it was gone."

"The ship's captain? Or crew?"

He shrugged. "In France, I had met an Englishman— Lord Clifford—who'd agreed, for a very large sum, to arrange passage for me and my daughter and son. My wife had succumbed to illness the year before, and my children were all I had left. I feared for their lives, and so we went. The voyage was fairly easy, and the captain seemed sympathetic. But when we disembarked, I discovered the meager belongings I'd managed to carry were all gone, and we had nothing but the clothes on our backs. When I reached

London, I applied to Clifford for help, but was turned away at his front door. I was too proud to beg at his scullery for scraps, so I walked away. But the necklace was gone—I assumed stolen by the captain or one of his men. Lost forever. It . . . hmm . . . broke my heart. But at least I was alive and safe and so were my children."

"I am very sorry for your circumstance," I said.

I too, had lost much at the hands of others, and he had my sympathy. My estimation of Lord Clifford, not high in the first place, took a decided plunge.

Fontaine leaned forward. "And then, one evening last summer, my daughter and her husband took me with them to Vauxhall." He chuckled, still with the humming sound. "Taking the old man out to entertain him. As we supped in the pavilion, Captain, I saw the necklace. The jewels belonging to my family were hanging boldly around the neck of Countess Clifford, wife of the Englishman who'd helped me and my children fly from France."

"You are certain it was the same?" Even as I asked it, I knew he had been.

"Very certain. My wife handed the necklace back to me the day she died, telling me she wished she could have seen our daughter wearing it. I walked up to Lady Clifford and introduced myself. She pretended to remember me as an émigré her husband had helped, but I knew she had no idea who I was. She never once blushed that she wore my daughter's inheritance, as you say, under my nose."

"It is likely she did not know," I said. "I've met Lord Clifford."

"Then you know what sort of man he is. I'd not have taken his assistance at all had I not been desperate. That night, he knew that I knew, but he looked at me and . . . hmm . . . dared me to say a word."

"You did not go to a magistrate? Report the theft?"

"I am French, I am in exile. You have just finished a long war with France, and even the fact that my son lost his life fighting Napoleon for the English has not made me beloved here. What am I to tell a magistrate? I have only my word. Any paper about it, any proof I have that the necklace belongs to the de la Fontaines is long gone. Earl Clifford, he has money and influence. I have . . ." He opened his hand. "Nothing."

He was correct. De la Fontaine knew he could not prove the diamonds had belonged to him, and even I had to decide whether to believe him. He could be luring me into finding the necklace and giving it to him, whereupon he'd be several thousand pounds richer, and I'd be in the dock.

But I did not think he lied. De la Fontaine did not have the bearing and manner of a liar, and I could verify the story by browbeating Lord Clifford—a task I'd cheerfully perform.

"And what do you wish me to do?" I asked.

De la Fontaine finished his brandy, set down the glass, and rested his hands on his knees. "What I would wish is for you to find and return the necklace to me, and tell the earl that you have failed in your quest."

"And the moment your daughter wears the necklace to a soiree with your respectable English son-in-law? She or he will be accused of stealing it. Or at least of purchasing stolen goods."

He closed his eyes. "I know. I have no solution. I considered having the stones reset, but given its provenance . . ."

The fact that Madame de Pompadour had commissioned the necklace would be worth as much as the diamonds themselves. I appreciated his dilemma.

"Then I do not understand why you believe I can help," I said.

De la Fontaine opened his eyes. He had deep blue eyes, and now they looked old and tired. "I want someone to know the truth. I want you to find the diamonds and make certain they are safe. If they must reside with Lady Clifford forever, then so be it."

His resignation decided the question for me. Remembering Clifford snarling at Grenville that he ought to be ashamed to interest himself in the affair, and then watching this aged, exiled man slump in defeat, angered me not a little.

"You may leave things in my hands," I said. "I might be able to find you some justice."

De la Fontaine shook his head, his ghost of a smile returning. "Do not make promises, Captain. I have grown used to losing."

I rose, made my way to the brandy decanter, and poured him another glass. We'd finish all the brandy quickly at this rate, but Grenville would be happy to know it had been drunk by two men who appreciated it.

"Why do you not return to France?" I asked as the liquid trickled into his glass. "The king is restored, the emperor dead. There is peace now."

Fontaine saluted me with his goblet before he drank. "All I had in France is gone. My daughter is here, married to her fussy Englishman, and I have grandchildren who are growing rapidly. This has been my life for nearly thirty years. I have no reason to return."

I nodded, understanding. I was much like him—except for the fact of his ancestors ruling France and having diamonds set for them by Louis XV's beautiful mistress. My ancestors had been wealthy landholders, but their little estate in Norfolk was as nothing compared to the vast acreage this man must have commanded.

Now we both had nothing, reduced to wearing second-hand clothes and enjoying brandy gifted to us by a wealthy acquaintance. Out of place, wondering how this came to be, and not knowing what to do with ourselves.

We did finish the brandy. De la Fontaine seemed to want to linger, and I let him. He asked me how I came by my injury, and winced in sympathy when I described how I'd been beaten to a bloody pulp by a band of French soldiers then strung up by the ankles. One of the more sympathetic men had cut me down after a time, but when English and Prussian soldiers had attacked the French deserters' camp, killing them to the last man, they hadn't noticed me among the dead.

De la Fontaine shook his head at my story and told me how his son had been in the infantry, dying at Badajoz. I hadn't met the young man — I'd been cavalry in the Thirty-Fifth Light Dragoons, and we'd been fairly snobbish about the infantry.

"Bad fighting there," I said. "Brave lad."

"*Oui*. So I have heard."

We finished the decanter in silence. When de la Fontaine made to depart, I gave him a box of finely blended snuff — another gift from Grenville. I rarely took snuff, preferring a pipe the rare times I took tobacco, but de la Fontaine thanked me profusely.

I led him back down the stairs, and we took leave of each other. De la Fontaine shook my hand in the English way, lips twitching when he saw me bracing myself for a farewell in the French way.

Still smiling, he walked down Grimpen Lane, a bit unsteadily, through the rain. I leaned on the doorframe and

ASHLEY GARDNER & JENNIFER ASHLEY

watched him, wondering how the devil I was going to find
the blasted necklace for him.

✸

THREE DAYS PASSED. I TOLD GRENVILLE ABOUT DE LA
Fontaine's visit and his assertion that the necklace was his.
Grenville professed to be amazed, and his anger and disgust
at Lord Clifford escalated to match my own.

Grenville and I continued searching for the necklace,
taking into account Lady Breckenridge's intelligence that a
lady wishing to sell her jewels to pay her creditors would
find someone very discreet to make the transaction for her.
Her man of business, perhaps, if she could hide such a
dealing from her husband.

However, when Grenville and I visited Lady Clifford's
man of business, we found a dry, very exact man who
seemed to march in step with Lord Clifford regarding
household affairs. Ladies were fools and ought to do nothing
without the approval of their husbands. In his opinion, Lady
Clifford had carelessly lost the necklace and tried to pretend
it stolen to shift the blame from herself.

This left us no further forward.

I could see that Grenville was losing interest in the problem. Lord Clifford's grumbles about Grenville poking his
nose into other gentlemen's business were beginning to
circulate through the *ton*. While Grenville refused to bow to
public opinion—any indication that he cared about such a
thing could spell his downfall—he also did not believe there
was much more to be done. Though Grenville agreed that
de la Fontaine's story was creditable, he also suspected that
the necklace would never see the light of day.

I saw that I would be soldiering on alone. I had not yet

heard from Lady Breckenridge, but I did hear again from Denis, whose carriage pulled in behind me when I left Grenville's on a wet evening three days after de la Fontaine's visit.

The rain that had begun the afternoon I'd met de la Fontaine had continued with little abatement. The downpour was not as freezing as a winter rain, but still as drenching. When the carriage halted next to me and the door opened, I could not help but yearn for the warmth of its plush interior, in spite of the coldness of the man inside.

"De la Fontaine," Denis began as soon as I was sitting opposite him, the carriage moving on its way to Covent Garden. "One of the wealthiest men in France before the terror. Now living in a back bedroom in his proper English son-in-law's house, treated like a poor relation." Denis shook his head, but no emotion crossed his face. "Not a happy tale."

CHAPTER 6

I DO NOT REMEMBER MENTIONING DE LA FONTAINE TO you," I said. Not that I was amazed that Denis knew all about de la Fontaine's visit to my rooms. He kept himself well informed.

"He is quite right about the necklace's provenance," Denis said, ignoring my statement. "A heavy blow to him that he lost it."

"Am I correct in guessing that you did not know that Lord Clifford had de la Fontaine's famous necklace?" Unusual for Denis, who hired people to roam Europe looking for such things for him, the rightful ownership of which was, to Denis, a trivial matter.

"I confess that I did not." Denis's brows drew together the slightest bit, a sign that the man behind the cold eyes was angry. "Hence why I wish to examine the piece myself. I knew the de la Fontaine necklace had disappeared many years ago, but not until Lady Clifford made a fuss about hers being stolen and involved Bow Street did it come to my attention that the two were one and the same. I had not thought Clifford resourceful enough to steal such a thing, but perhaps he seized an opportunity. Or perhaps the ship's captain stole it and sold it to Clifford, neither man appreciating what it was." Again the small frown. "Clifford owes me much money and has been reluctant to pay. He might have reported the necklace stolen to prevent himself from having to sell it to pay me, or in case I took it in lieu."

"Lord Clifford owes you money," I said. "I might have known."

"Many gentlemen owe me. Including you."

I let the remark pass. It was an old argument.

"If Clifford were to sell the necklace," I asked, "or his wife were to, how would they go about such a thing? Beyond common pawnbrokers and jewelers I mean. Who would they contact?"

Denis gave me a touch of a smile. "Me. I know of no other who could discreetly dispose of so obvious a piece."

"But if they did not realize what it was?"

"They might try the usual avenues, of course, but as soon as it came onto the market, jewelers in the know would put two and two together. Most likely the jewelers or pawnbrokers would offer the necklace to me, or at least ask for my help in shifting it."

"And you have not heard of it coming up for sale?"

"No. Not yet."

I twisted my walking stick under my hand. "If you do hear of it, will you tell me?"

"As I said, I want a look at it first."

"I am aware of that. But I've pledged myself to find it. Will you tell me?"

Denis regarded me in silence while I kept twisting the stick. There was a sword inside the cane, a fact he well knew.

ASHLEY GARDNER & JENNIFER ASHLEY

When he spoke, Denis's voice held a careful note. "You have done me good turns in the past, Captain, and you are fair-minded. But I like to keep the balance clean, or at least bending slightly in my favor. If I do keep you in the know regarding this necklace, I will expect a like intelligence in return."

I hadn't the faintest idea what I could know that would interest him, but I was certain he'd come up with something devious. Denis liked things all his own way.

"It is a simple matter," I said. "I want to be informed if the necklace comes up for sale or when you lay your hands on it."

"Certainly. I will allow you to be in on the bidding."

"Bidding?" I clenched the walking stick, which stopped its twirl.

"If the necklace proves to be the de la Fontaine diamonds, I will assuredly wish to sell it," Denis said. "I am not in the business of assisting impoverished French émigrés or feckless English aristocrats. Clifford owes me money, and whatever price I can obtain for the necklace will more than suffice to pay his debt. He will not fight me for it."

"The necklace is de la Fontaine's," I said angrily.

"De la Fontaine's family stole the original diamonds themselves, you might be interested to learn, during some continental war long ago. And who knows from whence it was originally looted? Such famous pieces often have murky histories."

"You are splitting hairs. The necklace belongs to de la Fontaine, and I intend to give it back to him."

Another twitch of lips. "Of course you do. I will inform you if I come into possession of it, to that I will agree."

I sat still and looked at him, the impeccably dressed young man, kid-gloved hands folded on his walking stick.

I wondered, as I always did, how he'd come to be like this. Who was James Denis? What of his family? What sort of child had he been that he'd become a man who bought and sold precious objects, people, secrets? Had he loved and lost? Raised himself from nothing? Or been defeated and climbed out of the ashes?

If I asked, he'd never tell me, so I did not ask.

Denis looked at me as though guessing my thoughts. He knew by now exactly where I'd come from, who my people were, and what I'd done for the last forty years of my life. Denis was that thorough. I would have to be just as thorough about him.

One of his brows twitched upward. "Did you truly think I would tell you exactly where to find the necklace, Captain?" he asked. "It is worth far more than Lord Clifford understands. De la Fontaine understands. Perhaps it will ease your conscience if I tell you how many peasants de la Fontaine and his family worked to death in France during the height of their power. They lived quite well on the backs of many."

I knew that if de la Fontaine had come from landed wealth, then yes, he'd worked it out of others. But I couldn't help thinking of the broken man whose only joy these days was the chance sampling of Grenville's brandy and the occasional treat outing with his daughter and her stuffy husband.

"Have you become a republican?" I asked Denis.

He gave me a small shrug. "I must believe in every man being allowed to do what is best for himself, or I would be out of business."

He fell silent to look out the window at the rain, the conversation finished. We didn't speak until Covent Garden, where Denis had his coachman halt, and he bade me good night.

❦

Now four people wanted the necklace: Lady Clifford, Lord Clifford, de la Fontaine, and Denis. Five people. Me.

I'd find the damn thing, and to hell with the lot of them. I would check de la Fontaine's story, and if he hadn't told me false, he would win the diamonds. I'd do something to placate Lord Clifford to keep him from turning his wrath on Lady Clifford. Clifford was the sort of man to blame his wife for his troubles. I cared nothing for what Denis thought of the matter. He'd find some other piece of art or jewelry on which to turn his attention soon enough.

When I entered my rooms in Grimpen Lane, Bartholomew was there, my fire roaring, my coffee hot. There were compensations for allowing him to practice valeting on me.

"Post's come," he said, pointing to a small pile of letters on my writing table. "I say, Captain, Mr. Grenville is asking for my help tonight. I've got your dinner in. Can you manage on your own?"

"It will be a struggle," I said, sitting down at the writing table. Bartholomew had left a plate of beef in juice sitting perilously close to my post.

Bartholomew grinned. "Aye, sir. I'll be back before morning."

"Stay at Grenville's and return tomorrow. No need for you to be rushing across town in the middle of the night in the rain. I can manage to hobble downstairs for a bit of bread on my own for breakfast."

"Are you certain, sir?" Bartholomew liked to believe I'd be hopelessly lost without him. "I can tell Mr. Grenville you can't spare me if you like."

"Mr. Grenville pays your wages, not me. What entertainment is he having tonight? I'm not expected, am I?"

"No, sir. It's his circle of art fanciers. They have supper and talk about Constable and Dah-veed and that French chap with the name like the sound of your throat closing up."

"Ingre?" I asked.

"That's the sausage. Sorry, sir, Mr. Grenville didn't tell me to tell you to come."

"Thank God for that. I'm hardly in the mood to talk about the intricacies of David and his pupils. David was a radical revolutionary, did you know that? Probably ran Comte de la Fontaine out of his home personally, thereby allowing de la Fontaine to be preyed upon by an Englishman looking to line his coffers. Possibly best I do not bring this up at Grenville's supper with his art critics."

"No, sir." Bartholomew gave me a dubious glance. He never knew what to do with me when I started waxing philosophical.

"Never mind. Go on, then."

Bartholomew poured me more coffee then made ready to depart with a look of relief.

I was glad to see him go, because I'd recognized the handwriting on the top letter of the pile as that of Lady Breckenridge, and I wanted to read her missive in private. I shoveled in beef and bread while Bartholomew scrambled upstairs to gather a few things to take home with him.

As soon as Bartholomew had trundled down the stairs and out—slamming the door hard behind him—I wiped my hands, broke the seal on the letter, and opened it.

My dear Lacey, Lady Breckenridge wrote. *I think that I shall never forgive you for persuading me to undertake this decidedly dreadful task. I must invent many more favors for you to do in return.*

I smiled, but with a touch of uneasiness, and read on.

I have been seeing much of Lady Clifford of late, and I cannot express what a relief it is to return to my quiet home in the evenings. Barnstable brings me thick coffee, which he liberally laces with brandy, bless him. Though I believe an entire decanter of the stuff would not be enough to rid myself of the taste of the Clifford household. Heaven help you, Lacey.

But I will cease complaining and come to the heart of the matter. It was easy enough to worm myself into Lady Clifford's household. I approached Lady Clifford on the pretext of asking her to assist me with one of my musicales—there is a soprano who sings like an angel—I believe you will agree when you hear her.

Who knows why Lady Clifford so readily believed I sought her help. Her taste in music is appalling—or, I should say, nonexistent. But I soldiered on, and she professed delight.

The poor woman has not much more to do in her life but play cards and gossip. Even her companion, Mrs. Dale, does all the embroidery for her, while Lady Clifford sits and pretends to conduct interesting conversation. She does knit on occasion, for the poor, though so badly that I suspect the poor simply unravel the yarn and use it for some more practical purpose.

These drawbacks are not entirely her fault. Her husband, I have now observed firsthand, tells Lady Clifford outright that anything she endeavors is foolish, and so she gives up before she begins. Lord Clifford tried to include me in one of these rants but, as you can imagine, he had no success in that regard.

Lady Clifford is much too easily cowed by him. Bullies are encouraged by meekness, as I have come to know.

Mrs. Dale, the companion, is not as easily cowed, but her

strength lies in her silences. She is able to remain perfectly still, eyes on her sewing, no matter what storms rage on around her. She is not quiet like a serene pool—more like a stubborn rock that refuses to be worn down. Because of this, she hasn't much to say for herself, although I note that, when we ladies are alone, some rather sarcastic humor comes out of her mouth. Not often, but it is there.

Mrs. Dale does indeed take laudanum, as I suspected. Her excuse is headache, which, she says, is why she likes to sit so quietly, but that is all fabrication. When anything unnerving happens in that household, it's a quick nip from the laudanum bottle. And believe me Lacey, unnerving things occur all the time.

For instance, Mrs. Dale mislaid Lady Clifford's knitting basket (on purpose, I suspect). Instead of simply telling a servant to find the blasted thing, Lady Clifford went into hysterics. She screeched at Mrs. Dale about her every fault, until Lord Clifford, who was home, had to come to see what was the matter.

I stepped to the next room, pretending the need to refresh myself —and indeed, I was developing a headache as fierce as Mrs. Dale's supposed ones. I heard Lord Clifford quite clearly tell his wife that the loss of the knitting basket was her own fault, that she could not keep account of any damned thing, and there was a reason he'd begun to favor Mrs. Dale over her.

I am not certain he'd have said such a thing had he known I was listening, but then again, Lord Clifford hasn't the best of manners. But really, what a thing to tell your wife! Lady Clifford cried all the more, Mrs. Dale joined her when Lord Clifford stormed out, and I returned to two weeping women.

But interestingly, I found them trying to console each other. Dear, dear Annabelle wasn't to blame, said Lady Clifford, and Mrs. Dale cried that dear, dear Marguerite was brave to suffer so much.

They continued weeping and embracing even after I sat down and pointedly started going through the guest list for the musicale. I gather that the two were the dearest of friends before Lord Clifford decided he wanted both his meat and his sauce in his own house. Saves him the bother of going out for it, I suppose. The two ladies are putting up with it as best they can.

The truce did not last long, however. Before another hour was out, Mrs. Dale was once more a hard-hearted, ungrateful bitch, and Lady Clifford a slow-witted fool.

I took Mrs. Dale aside and asked her why she stuck it here. I do not for one moment believe that she has fallen in love with Lord Clifford. From all evidence, she rather despises him.

Mrs. Dale blinked red-lined eyes at me and bleated that she stayed because she had nowhere else to go. This I can well credit. Her husband hadn't a penny left to his name when he died, and Mrs. Dale immediately went to live with her girlhood friend, Lady Clifford. She's been in the house ever since. Mrs. Dale did not say this, but I also had the feeling that she does not want to leave Lady Clifford to face Lord Clifford on her own.

Both ladies are well under Lord Clifford's thumb, and I strongly suspect that his interest in Mrs. Dale is more a game of power over his wife than any sort of sentimental feeling.

This was confirmed by my maid who spent the time in the kitchens while I was there (and by the bye, she is not very forgiving of you, either). Lord Clifford apparently satisfies some of his baser needs with maids below stairs, including the very maid arrested for stealing the necklace.

Of the necklace itself, I haven't a dratted clue. I have run very tame in Lady Clifford's house but have been unable to find a trace of it. I began with the most obvious place, Lady Clifford's own bedchamber and dressing room. The woman has many baubles — Lord Clifford does not stint on hanging finery on her. He must be of the ilk that believes a jewel-encrusted wife reflects well on him. However, the necklace in question was nowhere in Lady Clifford's chambers that I could see.

Next was Mrs. Dale's meager chamber, but again, I had no luck.

What I discovered there was that Mrs. Dale wears Lady Clifford's castoff gowns, modified to fit her rather narrower figure. Her jewelry is quite modest. Again, I suspect, gifts from her dear Lady Clifford before their falling out.

Lord Clifford might favor Mrs. Dale in his bed these days, but he certainly hasn't rewarded her with anything costly. Or, if he has, she neither displays these gifts nor keeps them in her bedchamber. I assure you, I was quite thorough.

Other rooms revealed nothing. I could not do much searching in the main sitting room, because Lady Clifford and Mrs. Dale were sitting in it. Constantly. I took a quick look at the dining room, but I had little time, and it's likely anything hidden there would be found by a servant.

Not that the staff of Lady Clifford's house is anything like efficient. I would sack the lot of them, and I told the housekeeper so. The housekeeper is an exhausted stick, not pretty enough for Lord Clifford, I gather, and he does run rather hard on her when he bothers to notice her at all. Were it my lot in life to be a housekeeper, I'd certainly try to find a better place.

Nonetheless, the servants at least attempt to keep the large house clean, and anything hidden in the public rooms would come to light eventually. That leaves the kitchens, the chambers of the servants themselves, and Lord Clifford's private study and bedchamber.

A servant might hide the necklace for her employer out of loyalty, but I do not think so in this case. I have not seen here the sort of affection some servants have for their employers. Barnstable looks after me as though he still regards me as the naïve young wretch who first married Breckenridge, ages ago it seems now. The staff in the Clifford household simply do their jobs, and from what my maid tells me, the family is not much respected below stairs.

As I say, that leaves Lord Clifford's private study and bedchamber. If I can contrive to enter them, I will, but apparently, there is but one reason a lady enters Lord Clifford's bedchamber, and forgive me,

Lacey, but there is a limit to my interest in this little problem. Lord Clifford's chamber might have to go unsearched.

I am afraid this letter will not help you much. In conclusion, if the stolen necklace is still in the house, it is well hidden. And if it secretly has been sold, I cannot tell either, because no one here ever discusses the necklace at all. A forbidden topic, I gather.

The atmosphere is strained and full of anger, and Lady Clifford, Mrs. Dale, and Lord Clifford make a strange threesome. There is no love lost between them, and much misery exists.

Now, then, Lacey, in return for my prying, I will ask one of my favors right away—and that is for you to attend said musicale tonight. I have observed that you dislike crowded gatherings, but you must put a brave face on it and come. If nothing else, your presence will give me a chance to speak more to you about this problem.

Wear your grand uniform and stand about looking imposing, as you do, so that my guests will have something to talk about. They grow bored and need a good whisper about the captain friend of Grenville's who turns up at Lady Breckenridge's gatherings now and again.

Besides, in truth, you will quite enjoy the soprano. Unlike Lady Clifford, I do have fine musical taste, and I shall have Barnstable look out for you.

Ever yours in friendship,
Donata Breckenridge

CHAPTER 7

BARTHOLOMEW WOULD NOT RETURN TONIGHT, SO I HAD to dress myself for the musicale. Bartholomew was convinced I could no longer do this on my own, but he kept my clothes so clean that they always looked fine, no matter how clumsy I might be at buttoning my own coat.

I peered into the small square mirror in my bedroom as I brushed my thick hair and fastened the braid across my chest. The regimentals of the Thirty-Fifth Light consisted of a dark blue coat with silver braid and dark cavalry breeches with knee-high boots. I wore the regimentals for social occasions, this being the finest suit I owned.

Imposing, Lady Breckenridge had written. I glanced into the aging glass again. She either flattered me or poked fun at me.

I took a hackney across London to South Audley Street and entered Lady Breckenridge's house with a few moments to spare.

Lady Breckenridge prided herself on her musicales and soirees, styling herself as one of the tastemakers of London.

Therefore, her sitting room was filled to overflowing, and I sidled through the crowd as politely as I could.

Sir Gideon Derwent was there, his kind face breaking into a smile when he saw me. Next to him was his son Leland, a slimmer, younger version of the father, and a pace behind them, Leland's great friend, Gareth Travers. The Derwents were a family of innocents who invited me to dine with them at their house in Grosvenor Square once a fortnight. There, they'd beg me to entertain them with stories of my army life. Travers had a bit more cynicism, but he seemed to enjoy the unworldly companionship of the Derwents as much as I did.

We took seats for the performance. Lady Breckenridge, dressed in a russet gown that bared her shoulders, introduced the lady as Mrs. Eisenhauf, a young Austrian who was just beginning her career. A pianist played a few strains on her instrument, and the soprano launched into her aria.

I found myself floating on a cushion of music, sound that filled my entire body. The woman's voice soared, loud and full, then dropped to the tiniest whisper, never losing its strength and quality.

Those around me were enchanted as well, but after a time, I stopped noticing anyone else. I heard only the music, observed only the curve of Lady Breckenridge's cheek, her face soft with enjoyment. Lady Breckenridge might once have been the naïve young wretch she described, but she'd left that girl far behind.

For a moment, I forgot about necklaces, weeping ladies, de la Fontaine's unhappiness, and the cold rain outside. There was only this bliss of warmth and music, and Lady Breckenridge's smile.

The aria ended, not in a crescendo, but in a few low notes of pure sweetness. As soon as the lady closed her mouth, the room erupted in applause and shouts of *Brava! Brava!*

They surged forward to meet her, swamping Lady Breckenridge, who stood next to her protégé. I wondered why Lady Breckenridge had brought me to this crush if she wished to speak to me privately as her letter had stated. I'd never get near her.

I spied Lady Clifford, dressed in a blue velvet gown too tight for her figure, her high feathered headdress bobbing as she moved among her acquaintance. Hearing snatches of her conversation, I learned that she took much of the credit for arranging the gathering and persuading the soprano to sing.

Lady Clifford spied me watching her. She made her way to me, clamped her hand around my arm, and drew me into a corner.

"Have you found the thief, Captain?" she asked, a bit too loudly for my taste.

"I am afraid I've turned up nothing, yet," I had to say.

"I wanted to tell you, I believe my husband was right that I made a mistake asking for your help." She smiled at me, but the smile was strained. "You have no more need to bestir yourself. Waters came home, and so that is all right. The real thief will be found by the Runners, eventually. Nothing more for you to do."

I hid my surprise at her request, but perhaps Lord Clifford had bullied her into dismissing me. "You at first believed Mrs. Dale had taken the necklace," I said. "You told me so."

Lady Clifford flushed a blotchy red. "As to that—I again made a mistake. Annabelle has many faults, but she would not be so foolish as to steal something so valuable as the necklace. I did not realize . . ."

She trailed off, not telling me what she hadn't realized.

"Did your husband tell you that I found your other necklace, Lady Clifford?" I asked.

"Other necklace? What other necklace?"

"The one you took to a pawnbroker near Hanover Square. Your husband identified it as a yours. Said it was a necklace you'd owned before your marriage."

Her flush deepened but I saw relief in her eyes. "Captain, really, you should not have interfered there. It was mine to sell as I pleased."

"You sent Waters to sell it for you, did you not? The proprietor described her."

"Yes, well I could not go myself, could I? Not to a pawnbroker's." She nodded so vigorously that her feathers bent and swayed as though she stood in a heavy wind. "I see what you are thinking, Captain. That I sold the larger diamond necklace as well, for my own reasons. Well, I did not. I certainly did not."

"I believe you," I said.

Her agitation dissolved into surprise. "Do you?"

"I do. Would you like me to continue to find the answer? And the necklace?"

"No," she said quickly. "I think it doesn't matter anymore." She paused then shook her head, feathers dancing. "No, it does not. But I thank you, Captain. Thank you for believing me."

She clutched my arm again, fingers crushing, then at last released me and flowed back into the crowd.

I still could come nowhere near Lady Breckenridge, so I enjoyed myself sipping brandy and speaking to the Derwents and Gareth Travers. I asked Sir Gideon his opinion of Lord Clifford, and he gave me a surprising answer.

"Not a good-humored man, certainly. And his household is not a happy one, from what I hear. No, his benevolence lies elsewhere. He has given much money to help the London poor and is a staunch supporter of many of my reform efforts. He's made speeches in the House of Lords on my behalf."

I contrasted this picture to the snarling, unpleasant man I'd met, and Sir Gideon chuckled.

"You are amazed, Captain. Yes, it comes as a bit of a shock to those who have made his acquaintance. I offer no excuse for his demeanor. Some men are born surly, I suppose. But he was able to convince the magistrates to release his wife's maid. He speaks loudly to the right people about the appalling conditions of prisons and of corruption among magistrates. He was able to bring her home and have the charges dismissed."

"To think, I imagined this would be a simple matter," I said.

"Nothing is simple where Lord Clifford is concerned. He is a cipher, Captain, even to me."

I thanked Sir Gideon for his opinion, and we turned the conversation to other matters.

Guests seemed determined to stay until breakfast, but once the soprano said her farewells and departed, they began to migrate toward the doors. Lady Breckenridge edged me away from the lingerers, until we ended up relatively alone at the fireplace.

She put her hands to her cheeks. "My face hurts from all this bloody smiling. The things I suffer for my artists."

"But you enjoyed the performance," I said. "The pleasure I saw in you was real."

A hint of the earlier smile returned. "Yes," she said. "But cease the compliments and listen, before someone decides to drag me off into an inane conversation. I have something to tell you that was not in my letter. Which, I trust, you read carefully."

"Every word," I said. "It was quite intriguing."

"I am certain it was. However, when my maid was dressing me this evening, she imparted intelligence from Lady Clifford's kitchens. Waters, the maid, was enjoying telling her harrowing tale of Bow Street gaol and being up before the magistrate. Reprieved at the last moment by testimony from Lord Clifford."

"Sir Gideon has been telling me that Lord Clifford is a bit of a reformer who worries the magistrates."

"Gracious, there is more to the story than that. According to those below stairs, Lord Clifford was persuaded to intervene on the behalf of young Waters by Annabelle Dale. Begged him tearfully, said an upstairs maid, who overheard the conversation. Apparently, Mrs. Dale asked Lord Clifford to help for 'poor, dear Marguerite's sake. We must all do what we can to spare Marguerite.' Extremely interesting, do you not think?"

Exceedingly. *Spare Marguerite.* Spare her from what?

"Life in the Clifford household must certainly be interesting," I said with feeling.

"I agree." Lady Breckenridge glanced across the room at Lady Clifford, and her mouth tightened with impatience. "I believe I will be more careful of the favors I do you in future."

"Investigating crime is not always a pleasant thing."

"I never thought it was. Certainly nothing for a gentleman or a lady who knows better. But that is why you interest me, Lacey. You never do what you ought."

"Nor do you."

The look she gave me was measuring. "But I am an aristocrat and have the excuse of being removed from my fellow beings. You must strive to be utterly respectable, and yet, you do not always bother. I believe that is why I like you."

"I am obliged to you for that liking."

She regarded me for one more moment, her expression unreadable. "I can never decide, Lacey, whether you are complimenting me or mocking me, but it is no matter. I see that Lady Clifford has cornered an admiral. I am afraid I must rescue him. Good night, Captain."

I bowed. "My lady."

She sashayed away, throwing that sincere smile over her shoulder, and I stood for a moment, enjoying watching her go.

As I left the Breckenridge house, settling my hat against the rain, I wondered. Had Mrs. Dale actually taken the bloody necklace as Lady Clifford had first suspected? Just as she'd hidden Lady Clifford's knitting basket and caused a scene? Perhaps guilt had made her beg Lord Clifford to bring home the maid. Or perhaps Mrs. Dale had shown benevolence toward the maid to land herself in Lady Clifford's good graces again.

Whatever the answer was, I was growing thoroughly tired of this problem. It was late, the cold rain made my injured leg throb, and after the beauty of the soprano's voice and Lady Breckenridge's smiles, all else seemed drab, dull, and not worth bothering about.

I would lie in bed all the next day, have Bartholomew fetch me coffee, read the newspapers, and tell my blasted curiosity to go away. I was cold and sore, and I deserved a rest. Earl Clifford and his odd household could worry someone else.

I became so enamored of this idea that I thought of little else as the hackney bumped me back to Covent Garden. Therefore, my dismay was great when I walked into my bedchamber and found a woman lying fast asleep between my sheets.

CHAPTER 8

I WOKE THE WOMAN WITHOUT HESITATION. "MARIANNE, what the devil are you doing?"

Marianne Simmons, actress from a Drury Lane company, once my upstairs neighbor, and now, in theory at least, Grenville's mistress, sat up and blinked china-blue eyes at me.

"Blast you, Lacey. Your voice is loud, and my head aches something awful. You weren't using your bed, so I saw no harm in borrowing it."

"I remember locking my door before I went out," I said.

"I stole your key months ago and had my own cut."

She could easily have done. I'd grown used to having Bartholomew here to let me in, plus I'd spent most of the last month out of London. Marianne could have stolen the key from my drawer at any time, me none the wiser.

"I am too tired to argue with you," I said. "Make use of the bed if you must, and I'll adjourn to Bartholomew's attic. Tomorrow you can tell me why you aren't sleeping in the house Grenville keeps so nicely for you."

"*That* is none of your affair. And good heavens, the attics must be freezing. This is a large bed, and there's a good fire. Plenty of room for both of us."

I was exhausted and aching, that was true. "I imagine myself explaining to Grenville why I was in a bed with you. He'll call me out for it, and then I'll have to let him shoot me, because I have no desire to kill him. My death will be on your head."

"Do not be ridiculous, Lacey. First, *he* is far more interested in supping with his art friends tonight than in calling on me. Second, you look all in. I'm certain a climb to the top of the house to a freezing room will kill you. When I was in a traveling company, we slept seven or eight to a bed such as this, too tired to do anything but snore." She scooted to the far right of the bed and patted the mattress beside her. "I promise not to touch you."

I believed her. Marianne, as far as I could tell, had very little interest in men apart from how much money they could give her. The exception was Grenville. She'd professed genuine confusion and not a little dismay that he'd not yet asked of her what most gentlemen asked of her.

I knew Marianne had no amorous designs on me—she regarded me as a person from whom she could borrow candles, coal, food, drink, snuff, and now, my bed. I use the word "borrow," but in truth Marianne never repaid what she took, whether in cash or in kind. I'd not stopped her, knowing that without what she took from me, she'd have gone hungry and cold many a night.

She was right that it was a long way to the top of the house, and Bartholomew relied only on the heat from the chimney. Fine for a robust youth, bad for a man twice his age whose stiff limb was hurting him very much tonight.

I smothered a sigh, went out to the front room, and

stripped down to my shirt and drawers, and returned. I did not don the nightshirt that Bartholomew had left on the bed to warm, because Marianne had helped herself to that too.

The bedchamber was dark enough for modesty, and I slipped under the covers without having to blush. I admitted that the bed was nice and warm from Marianne's body, and true to her word, she kept herself on the far edge.

I lay back, tiredness and hurt overriding my common sense. "Be gone before Bartholomew returns in the morning," I said. "I might not be able to awaken you in time."

"Not to worry, Lacey. I am adept at covertly leaving a gentleman's bed."

"And never say such a thing to Grenville."

"Thank you, but I know how to manage *him*."

"Is being here part of your efforts to manage him?" I asked, closing my eyes.

"No, this is my effort at seeking a bit of quiet. You are the only person on this earth who does not plague me to tears."

"I am pleased to hear it."

I searched for the oblivion of slumber, but though I had nearly nodded off in the hackney, my mind, treacherously, was now wide awake. My body wanted to sink into the dubious comfort of my mattress, but my thoughts could not rest, and I fidgeted.

The bed shifted, and I guessed without looking that Marianne had propped herself on one elbow. "Perhaps you should talk about it," she said. "Let loose what is in your head so that you can sleep."

So she might say to one of her paramours. I knew gentlemen who professed that what they most enjoyed about their mistresses was that the ladies actually listened to their troubles.

At this moment, talking was exactly what I needed. I found myself telling her everything, from the moment I'd met Lady Clifford in Grenville's private sitting room to my evening at Lady Breckenridge's musicale. I did not know how much of this Marianne already knew, but she listened with interest to my tale.

When I finished, I did indeed feel better. Quieter in mind, ready to let it all go for now and seek sleep.

"Lady Clifford and Mrs. Dale," Marianne said thoughtfully. "At each other's throats one minute, oozing affection for each other the next, then back to baleful glares? Do I have the right of it?"

"So Lady Breckenridge tells me. And now Lady Clifford has entirely changed her mind about accusing her rival and wanting me to investigate the matter. Damn the woman."

"Her rival," Marianne repeated. She went silent as she settled down and arranged the covers over her. "I've been an actress for a while, you know. I've worked in several companies, both meager and great. When you are thrown side by side with men and women for long stretches at a time, where modesty and politeness go hang, you learn much about people."

"Seven or eight in a bed helps with that, presumably."

"Exactly. Men *and* women stuffed together. No privacy at all—for anything. Privacy is for the wealthy. What you describe of Lady Clifford and Mrs. Dale I've observed before, several times. Lowly actresses or highborn ladies, there really is not much difference, despite what people say."

"A love triangle is a triangle, no matter where it is placed, you mean?" I agreed with her. In the army, I had been thrown into close contact with men and women of all walks of life. Though rigorous care might be taken to separate the ranks, we all bathed, ate, loved, and died together.

"I mean that you are viewing the love triangle, if there is one, the wrong way around," Marianne said. "Not Lord and Lady Clifford broken apart by Mrs. Dale. I mean Lady Clifford and Mrs. Dale, broken apart by the maid, Waters."

My eyes opened. "Lady Clifford and Mrs. Dale?"

Marianne laughed. "Gentlemen are so shocked when they learn that women do not prefer them. It grates on their pride, I believe. But it happens more often than you like to think, and can you blame them? Men like Lord Clifford can be quite awful."

I lay still, thinking of the tangle in light of Marianne's speculations. "Lady Breckenridge never put forth this idea."

"Because Lady Breckenridge has no use for other women, and so she does not watch them particularly closely. As horrible as her own husband was, she would never turn to ladies for consolation. And so, she might not recognize the need in others."

I turned my head to look at Marianne, unashamedly stretched out beside me, her head on my pillow. "And you?"

She shrugged. "I too, have little use for women, but I've been thrown among them far more than has your Lady Breckenridge. Lady Clifford and Mrs. Dale sound like lovers who had a falling out over something. Or someone. This Waters, is she pretty? And I imagine that Mrs. Dale has no choice but to comply when Lord Clifford makes advances to her. He could turn her out of his house, after all, if she resists."

And Mrs. Dale had professed to have nowhere else to go.

I let out a breath. "Good God."

"Think of it that way, and I'm certain it will help. Good night."

So saying, Marianne turned over, dragged the quilts over her, and fell fast asleep. Or at least, she pretended to.

Marianne had given me much to think about. Most people would believe, as I had, that Mrs. Dale and Lady Clifford were enraged at each other because of Lord Clifford's amorousness. Two women fighting to possess the same man.

But thinking on what Lady Breckenridge had told me, both women thoroughly disliked the bullying Lord Clifford. A romance between the ladies, on the other hand, especially if they'd quarreled over Lady Clifford's affection for her maid Waters, might explain Lady Clifford's spiteful accusation that Mrs. Dale had taken the necklace. It would explain her about-face on the matter as well.

Perhaps it hadn't been brought home to Lady Clifford what could happen to Mrs. Dale—Newgate, ignominy, hanging—until the maid, Waters, had returned to describe her harrowing ordeal.

It also threw into new light Lady Breckenridge's observation of the two women crying and hugging over the missing knitting basket. They'd been comforting each other after Lord Clifford's harangue—lovers who cared more about each other than for the brutal man who bullied them both.

Mrs. Dale had begged Lord Clifford to help bring Waters home. Because she felt sorry for her "dear Marguerite" and wanted to spare her more pain? Or to try to restore peace between herself and Lady Clifford? Both, possibly.

"Hell, Marianne," I said.

Marianne only snored.

TRUE TO HER WORD, MARIANNE WAS GONE BEFORE I woke. The window showed sunshine, the rain finished for now, the bed beside me empty. I heard Bartholomew in my front room, and a moment later, he strode into my bedchamber with his usual energy, coffee balanced on a tray.

"Did you not see your nightshirt?" he asked when he saw me in my underclothes. The garment lay across the bed again as though it had never been worn.

"I didn't bother to make a light," I said, extemporizing. "I was exhausted."

I felt a bit better this morning, although by the light outside the window, the day was already moving on to afternoon. Talking things over with Marianne, followed by a good night's sleep, had restored my vigor.

Bartholomew left the coffee and lifted the nightshirt. As I sat up and reached for the coffee, Bartholomew frowned at the nightshirt, then he delicately sniffed its collar. He raised his brows at me.

I took a nonchalant sip of coffee, telling myself he would not recognize Marianne's perfume. Bartholomew had started working for me before Grenville had taken up with Marianne, and the lad did not accompany Grenville on his visits to her in Clarges Street. Grenville had a different staff for that house, in any case.

"Not a word," I said.

Bartholomew drew himself up. "A gentleman's gentleman is discreet, sir."

"I know you are, Bartholomew. A bath, I think."

"Sir." Bartholomew went away, carrying the nightshirt over his arm.

As I bathed and let Bartholomew shave me, I again considered Marianne's revelation about Lady Clifford and Mrs. Dale.

I'd met two hermaphrodites, as people had called them, in the village where I'd grown up. They'd been elderly ladies, styling themselves as a lady and her companion. Everyone knew, but of course did not mention in public, that they were lovers, or at least had been.

I didn't remember much about them except that one was kind to me, and I couldn't remember to this day which had been the lady and which had been the companion. They'd passed away within months of each other when I'd been about nine years old. No one had bothered them, but then, they'd been two spinster ladies who'd lived quietly, well past the age of anyone's interest.

Lady Clifford, on the other hand, was a married lady prominent in society. And Mrs. Dale was a poor widow, dependent on others for her bed and board. Dangerous for any gossip about her to circulate. They would have to be secretive.

Last night I had thought about letting the investigation go, leaving the Clifford family to sort out their own troubles. But then, there was de la Fontaine. His tale had tugged at me. I knew that I sympathized with him because I felt he was like me—a long way from his old life, unsure of his place in the world, dependent on others when he did not want to be.

The necklace belonged to de la Fontaine. He should have it back.

To find it, I needed to speak to Lady Clifford again. After breakfasting, I penned a letter to Lady Breckenridge asking her to fix an appointment for me with Lady Clifford. I could imagine Lady Breckenridge's exasperation when she received the note, and I would be in her debt again, but I also knew that she'd arrange the meeting.

I decided to leave it at that and make my way to Hyde Park and the stables for a little exercise. At one time, I'd given riding lessons to a lad I'd met while investigating the Hanover Square problem. The lad's father stabled his beasts in Hyde Park and generously allowed me to ride one of his geldings whenever I liked, even now that the boy had returned to school. His father had told me he recognized a man who could handle horses right enough.

It was nearly two when I rode out, I having slept longer than usual. The fashionable hour wouldn't begin until five, but plenty of riders and drivers already moved about the park, enjoying the respite from the rain.

I walked and trotted the well-trained gelding, letting him canter a bit down an empty stretch of the Row. I turned down a lesser path to keep riding and spied Grenville astride his bay ahead of me, his tall hat shining in the sunshine.

I nudged my horse into a faster trot to catch up, but as I neared Grenville, another man on horseback swung out of an intersecting path. I recognized Lord Clifford, who began bellowing as he rode at Grenville.

"What do you mean by it, Grenville? Hounding a man's womenfolk until they're ill with it? My wife's life hung by a hair's breadth, all because of you and your interfering captain."

As I spurred my horse forward, Lord Clifford leaned down and tried to drag Grenville from the saddle.

CHAPTER 9

My horse leapt forward in a burst of speed. Grenville's mount was already dancing sideways, Lord Clifford's doing the same. My long cavalry experience let me steer my gelding between them and wedge the two horses apart.

"What the devil?" Grenville said, out of temper. "Have a care, Clifford."

Lord Clifford was red-faced, spittle flecking his mouth. "What will you do, Grenville, have me thrown out of the Jockey Club? Doesn't matter. I refuse to be a member when fellows like you hold sway. You nearly killed my wife."

Clifford tried to ride around me and at Grenville again, but I remained firmly between Grenville's horse and Clifford's. I rode better than either of them, and Clifford would not get through me.

"Explain yourself," I said to him. "What happened?"

"My wife swallowed a large dose of laudanum last night, that is what happened. Only the care of her ladies brought her back to life. She cited some nonsense about guilt and misery, and how she never ought to have spoken to either of you. You gentlemen have turned my house into Bedlam, and I will not have it."

"Is Lady Clifford well?" I asked quickly.

"She will recover. Likely she only took it for the attention, but this was your doing, Grenville. Stay the hell out of my private affairs."

With that, he turned his horse and spurred it cruelly. The horse leapt away, ears back, gravel flying from his hooves.

Grenville was breathing hard. "Damn the man. He is an ogre. He doesn't care that Lady Clifford might have died, only that her troubles have disrupted him." He removed a handkerchief from his black coat, brushed away the dust Clifford's horse had kicked up, and carefully folded the handkerchief again. "I will have to do something about him, I think."

"He is not wrong," I said. "Our interference, especially mine, did lead to her distress of mind, but something does not quite ring true. I spoke to Lady Clifford last evening. She told me she'd changed her mind about Mrs. Dale being the culprit, and that she no longer wanted me to pursue the matter. She was agitated about it, but hardly in a state to go home and take too much laudanum."

"Unless she did not administer it herself," Grenville said. "You did say that Lady Breckenridge believed Mrs. Dale drinks laudanum for pleasure. She'd have a bottle close at hand."

"Possibly, but why she'd want to kill Lady Clifford is unclear to me." I told Grenville the theory about Lady Clifford and Mrs. Dale being lovers, or at least former lovers, without implying that the idea had come from anywhere but my own head. Any mention of Marianne would likely turn this conversation in an uncomfortable direction.

"You might be right," Grenville said. "It's a very insular household, and something like that would be kept quiet. But does it have any bearing on the lost necklace?"

"I have no idea," I said. "I hoped to speak to Lady Clifford today, but . . ." I broke off. "I will try to find out."

"I, for one, will be pleased to be quit of Clifford and his family. They are devilish melodramatic."

While Grenville, I realized, disliked personal drama of any kind. No wonder Marianne drove him distracted.

"My boyhood home could be as melodramatic," I said. "Histrionics seemed to be the sought-after state, in my father, the housekeeper, the staff—anyone he controlled. My father was a bit like Lord Clifford, in fact."

Grenville straightened his hat, his face still red, but he regained his composure as I watched. "Well, I am pleased you turned out as well as you did, my dear fellow. My boyhood home was devoid of emotion at all. We were calm and careful from sunrise to sunset, sunset to sunrise. My father tolerated no dramatics of any kind. I'm not certain which is more devilish uncomfortable—too many emotions or none at all."

"Perhaps that is why you and I rub along well," I said. "I find your coolness restful, you find my volatility interesting."

Grenville raised his brows. "I do hope our friendship has progressed beyond that. Shall we ride on, Lacey? It is a fine afternoon, the park is not yet crowded, and I dislike to waste the opportunity simply because Clifford put me off."

He turned his horse and guided it onward, and I followed.

I admired Grenville's ability to brush aside bad encounters and continue serenely with his day, as though no one could possibly upset him. Perhaps he was practiced because he'd been raised to it, but I'd never learned the art of it, and doubted I ever would.

I RECEIVED WORD FROM LADY BRECKENRIDGE THE NEXT morning that I could call on her, but when I arrived at her house in South Audley Street, the lady she had in her front sitting room was Mrs. Dale.

Annabelle Dale was much as Lady Breckenridge had described—red-rimmed eyes, past her first youth, thin and pale. She regarded me calmly, though her fingers twitched in her lap.

I was introduced, Lady Breckenridge and I sat down, and Barnstable brought coffee with cakes—an innocuous gathering. When Barnstable departed, Mrs. Dale set aside her cup and lifted her gaze to mine.

"Well, Captain Lacey. What did you wish to ask me?"

"I wanted to express my regret for the harm this incident has done," I said, "and to ask after Lady Clifford. Is she well?"

"She will recover. She has done this before, unfortunately. Living with his lordship is a great trial to her. He does everything to set us against each other." She smiled, and I could see that once, Annabelle Dale had been quite pretty. "It piques him that he cannot, not forever."

"But you and Lady Clifford must have had a bad quarrel," I said. "She was willing to accuse you of stealing her necklace."

"It is nothing we have not weathered before. I've known Marguerite since we were girls. She feels things too deeply and can become so easily jealous. She sought to punish me for . . . well, let us just say it was jealousy. And hurt. She sought to punish her husband, as well. Two in one blow."

"Then she felt remorse when Waters was arrested," I said. "But she was still angry at you, which is why she accused you to me. I think she hoped that I, with my reputation for running down criminals, could find an outside party on which to pin the crime. A known housebreaker or jewel thief. That person would be arrested, and you and Waters would be cleared."

Mrs. Dale pulled a handkerchief from her pocket, but she only clutched it between her fingers. "You have the right of it. Marguerite can be a fool sometimes. When you spoke to her at the musicale, she realized that you were unraveling her lies, and she panicked. She drank enough laudanum to make her dangerously ill, and of course Lord Clifford went to shout at Mr. Grenville. Mr. Grenville would tell you to leave it alone, and all would be finished."

Lady Breckenridge, who sat with her elegant legs crossed, her cup held daintily, broke in. "Lady Clifford does not understand the captain, then. He is like a bulldog — does not let go once he sinks his teeth in. He will have the answer to the problem, no matter who does not wish him to find it."

I winced a little at her assessment, and she raised her brows at me over her cup.

"I realized that," Mrs. Dale said. "And so I felt you deserved the truth. Please understand, and leave Marguerite be, Captain. She was silly to approach Mr. Grenville in the first place, and now she is paying for her foolishness."

"I understand," I said. "Lady Clifford is a most unhappy woman, and she is lucky she has you to look after her." I leaned forward, resting my arms on my knees. "The necklace was never stolen, was it?"

Mrs. Dale glanced quickly at Lady Breckenridge. "I can hardly answer that."

"I have no interest in telling Lord Clifford," I said. "Neither, I am certain, has Lady Breckenridge. Yesterday, Clifford went so far as to try to assault Mr. Grenville in the park. My loyalty was never to him. It was Lady Clifford who asked for my help, and to Lady Clifford that I answer."

"And I am most discreet," Lady Breckenridge said. "You may tell Lady Clifford that she will remain on my guest list, no matter what happens. Clifford is a brute and a bully, and she deserves more than being her husband's creature." Which was one of the most generous things I'd ever heard Lady Breckenridge say about another woman.

"I am right, am I not?" I asked. "If the necklace truly has been stolen, then I will find it and the culprit. If not, I will leave it alone. But no search of your house, not by you and your servants or by Pomeroy and his patrollers has turned up the necklace. What became of it, Mrs. Dale?"

Mrs. Dale pulled a bit more on the handkerchief, and her face burned red. "I threw it into the Thames."

I stared at her. Lady Breckenridge quickly set down her porcelain cup. "Dear heavens," she said. "Why?"

"Marguerite asked me to. She hated the thing. She loves the little strand of diamonds her mother left her, but Lord Clifford has forbidden her to wear them, saying they are not prominent enough. Marguerite decided that if she pretended the large necklace had been stolen, she'd never have to see the bloody thing again. She had no way of knowing things would escalate into such a mess, that her husband would be goaded into hiring a Runner who would arrest poor Waters. Marguerite gave the necklace to me, and asked me to drop it into the river. So I did."

"Good Lord." Lady Breckenridge lifted her cup and took a large swallow of tea.

De la Fontaine's legacy, swimming in mud at the bottom of the Thames. "Mrs. Dale, you do know those diamonds were worth thousands of guineas, do you not?"

Annabelle Dale shrugged. "What is that compared to peace, Captain Lacey? Thousands of guineas well spent, I think."

Her voice was calm, her hands quiet around her handkerchief. Mrs. Dale, stuck in the Clifford household, too poor to live on her own and subject to Lord Clifford's unwanted attentions, could have hidden the necklace, planning to use it to fund her way to freedom. But watching her, I didn't think she had. I saw understanding for Lady Clifford in her eyes, and fierce devotion.

This, in other words, was a gesture of love from Mrs. Dale and one of defiance by Lady Clifford. A gesture they could reveal to no one but themselves. The necklace had become a symbol of victory of two women over the man who held them in thrall.

"And then you quarreled," I said gently. "And in her burst of anger, she accused you of stealing the necklace. No proof, of course. Lady Clifford must not have truly believed you would be arrested, or at least did not think about it too much. Waters would not have been taken either, except that Pomeroy likes to arrest people. You then asked Lord Clifford to use his influence to save Waters."

Mrs. Dale nodded. "Marguerite was so fond of her, was so heartbroken, and of course Waters was entirely innocent. I have some little power with Lord Clifford, and so I used it."

"It was kind of you."

She met my gaze again. "Please leave it alone, Captain. Let her be at peace."

I nodded. How I would explain to de la Fontaine that his beloved family heirloom was at the bottom of the Thames, I did not know. Some waterman would find the necklace in the mud, years hence, and consider himself lucky. He'd either turn it in for a reward or try to keep it.

A strange ending to a strange problem.

"Thank you, Mrs. Dale, for being so candid," I said. "You may assure Lady Clifford that I understand and will cease with the matter altogether."

Mrs. Dale folded back into her seat and pressed her handkerchief to her mouth. "Thank you," she whispered. "Thank you."

When Barnstable had seen Mrs. Dale out, Lady Breckenridge rose and plucked a cigarillo from a box on the mantelpiece. She lit it with a spill from the fireplace and blew out a gray plume of smoke.

"You do like to keep your friends in the dark, Lacey. I had the wrong solution all this time. Why would Mrs. Dale do such an odd thing? She hasn't two coins to rub together —why not tuck the necklace under her cloak and run off with it? Gracious, I would have."

"I would have been tempted to do the same," I said. "But Mrs. Dale is devoted to Lady Clifford. Very much so. She'd never have left her alone to face Lord Clifford."

Lady Breckenridge drew again on the cigarillo, and her brows rose as she released the smoke. "It is like that, is it? I know now why Grenville grows so frustrated with you. You like to keep the most interesting tidbits to yourself."

"If I must."

She gave me a steady look. "Well, I will decide whether to grow offended or to admire your integrity. But in the meantime I will call in another favor for my assistance on this problem. And no, I will not tell you what it is until time."

I saluted her with my teacup. "I will wait with anticipation."

"I highly doubt that." Lady Breckenridge smiled. "I will write when you are to call on me again, and then the balance might be paid. Now I must bid you good afternoon. So many things to do."

I had not thought to leave so soon, but I conceded that a dowager viscountess would have a full schedule during the high season. She softened the dismissal by kissing me again, this time pressing her lips to my mouth.

AND THAT, I THOUGHT, WAS THE END OF IT.

Lord Clifford still hung out a reward for the return of the necklace but made clear he wanted no one else in his household accused. Pomeroy continued to try to hunt down a thief, but because he could turn up no evidence of anyone else having taken the necklace, he soon moved to other, potentially more lucrative cases. I hadn't yet told de la Fontaine that his daughter's legacy had been tossed into the river, trying to decide how to impart this without betraying Lady Clifford.

Not half a week later, James Denis sent me a letter — brief and to the point — instructing me to pay him a visit. He'd send a carriage for me to avoid my excuses of not having enough shillings to pay my way across town.

I disliked obeying commands from Denis, but this time, I was interested in what he had to say. Denis's sumptuous coach carried me to Curzon Street, and once inside the house, I was ushered into his uncluttered study.

Denis waited, his hands folded on the blank surface of his desk while one of his pugilist footmen gestured me to an armchair and poured a glass of brandy for me. As soon as he and a second footmen took up their places — one at the door, one by the window — Denis spoke.

"I have found the diamond necklace belonging to de la Fontaine," he said.

My brows shot up. "Found it? Muddy, was it?"

Denis's eyes flickered, and for the first time since I'd met him, I sensed that I'd puzzled him.

"I located the necklace in France," he said.

"France?" My turn to be puzzled.

"In the possession of a minor aristocrat in the court of Louis XVIII. A minor aristocrat willing to give up the necklace for a fraction of its worth, because he was too ignorant to understand its value. According to his story, he bought the necklace from an Englishman in London three years ago and carried it back to France with him when the Bourbon king was restored to power."

My mind swam as I struggled to rearrange facts. "What Englishman? Clifford? Three years ago? He was certain?" But what then had Mrs. Dale thrown into the Thames?

"I had the necklace examined by a jeweler," Denis continued. "One of mine. He is the best in the business and quite reliable, I promise you. He proclaimed the diamonds real and the necklace de la Fontaine's. That means, Captain, that the stolen necklace you and Mr. Grenville have been chasing all over London is a copy, a paste replica. You have been led down the garden path."

"By whom? Clifford?"

"Assuredly, since he is the man who sold it to the Frenchman."

Bloody hell. No wonder Clifford had been so furious with Grenville and me for trying to find the necklace. Lady Clifford had made a fuss and gained the attention of Bow Street, but then Lord Clifford had done everything in his power to stop the investigation and deter Pomeroy. I wagered that Clifford didn't care two figs for how much we'd disturbed his household; he was only worried that we might reveal he'd been forced to sell his wife's jewels and humiliate him. Damn the man.

Denis opened a drawer, drew out the necklace, and laid it on a velvet cloth on top of his desk.

The diamonds glittered against the dark cloth, facets white and sharp blue in the candlelight. The center stone was the size of a robin's egg, perfectly cut from what I could see. The surrounding pieces, large diamonds encircled by smaller ones, were just as fine. I was no expert in jewels, but even the slowest person could see that this necklace was remarkable.

"It could be yours, Captain, if you wish it."

I lifted my eyes from it, entranced. "What on earth would I do with such a thing?"

"Sell it, give it to your lady, restore it to de la Fontaine . . . Whatever you like."

I sat back, my enchantment with the jewels gone. "For what price?"

"You are a resourceful man, Captain. I could use you, as I've told you before. Pledge yourself to me, and the necklace is yours." His voice held nothing, no emotion, his face, even less.

"You'd never believe I would agree to that, would you?" I asked.

"Not really." He nearly smiled, as close to amused as I'd ever seen him. "But I thought it worth a try." Denis closed the cloth over the magnificent diamonds and slid them back inside the drawer.

"That belongs to de la Fontaine," I said.

"De la Fontaine does not have the resources to buy the necklace back from me, nor does he have much to offer me in kind. He has cut off all ties to anyone who might be useful to me, preferring to live quietly in middleclass London with his daughter and grandchildren. He at least has found contentment with his family."

"Which is why you should return the necklace to him," I said in a hard voice. "He wishes to give it to his daughter."

Denis pressed his palms flat on his desk. "You have a strong sense of fairness, Captain, which is why I continually attempt to recruit you. I have not said I would not give the necklace to de la Fontaine. His son-in-law has a political bent. He hopes to win a seat in the House of Commons as soon as he can. Perhaps I can help him with such a thing."

Which meant that Denis would control that seat in Commons, and de la Fontaine's son-in-law would back any bill Denis wanted him to, vote the way Denis wanted him to —jump up and touch the ceiling whenever Denis wanted him to.

"For once, could you not do something out of benevolence?" I asked. "Imagine what such a gesture would do for your credibility."

Denis signaled to the pugilist at the door, who came forward. The interview was at an end. "I told you about the necklace as a courtesy, Captain. What I do with it is for me to decide. I imagine de la Fontaine will have it in the end."

"Leave him alone," I said with heat. "He has lost everything. Let him die in peace."

Denis's brows rose the slightest bit. "The Comte de la Fontaine used to be a great tyrant. He is one of the reasons the revolution in France began at all. He fled as soon as the tide began to turn, because he would have been among the first to the guillotine. The cry for his arrest had already gone out."

"He lost his only son, in our war."

"Fighting the republican bastards who drove him from his home," Denis said smoothly.

"Perhaps." I stood up, finding myself next to the pugilist who'd halted beside my chair. "But he's had to live thirty years in poverty in the damp of London, and is now a poor relation to his rather thick English son-in-law. That is enough of a punishment for any man, do you not think?"

Again, the look of near amusement. "As you say, Captain. I will keep you informed. Good day."

I knew Denis wanted me to be grateful to him for bothering to tell me about the necklace at all. He also wanted to rub my face in the fact that he'd used everything I'd done in my investigation to further his own wealth and power.

He might be right that de la Fontaine had possessed the same kind of arrogant ruthlessness that Denis himself had now. But the world turned, and it changed, and eventually all tyrants fell to become dust.

I wrote to de la Fontaine, telling him that Denis had the necklace, and suggested he apply to a magistrate I knew who was not in Denis's network. I then wrote to the magistrate in question, informing Sir Montague Harris of all that had happened, though I kept silent on the roles Mrs. Dale and Lady Clifford had played in the necklace's loss. After all, they'd only disposed of an inexpensive copy.

I had no way of knowing whether de la Fontaine would act against Denis or end up bargaining with him. Or perhaps drop the matter altogether.

I somehow did not think he'd choose the last recourse, and I was correct. Several days later, Sir Montague replied to me, saying that he'd spoken to de la Fontaine, but that de la Fontaine had not wanted to prosecute either Denis or Lord Clifford.

I received a letter from de la Fontaine himself soon after that. In it he thanked me for my assistance, told me that the necklace had been returned to him, and made a vague suggestion that perhaps we might share fine brandy again one day. Nothing more. Not until months later did I see his son-in-law stand for Parliament and be elected by a land-slide. James Denis had won again.

For now, I was finished with the business. I tied the last two threads of the affair the day after I received de la Fontaine's letter. The first came in the form of a note from Lady Breckenridge, calling in her favor and bidding me to attend her at her home.

CHAPTER 10

SUCH A DELIGHT," LADY BRECKENRIDGE SAID. "CAPTAIN
Lacey answers a summons. I hear from Grenville that you
do not always comply."

She'd received me in her sitting room, she wearing a
deep blue afternoon dress, its décolletage trimmed with light
blue ribbon woven through the darker cloth. The ribbon
matched the bandeau in her hair and brought out the blue of
her eyes.

She did not invite me to sit down. We stood near the
fireplace, the heat from the coals soaking into my bones. I
leaned on the walking stick she'd given me, its handle warm
under my palm.

"I can be abominably rude at times," I said.

Lady Breckenridge shrugged, her shrugs as smooth and
practiced as Denis's own. "You do not rush to obey those
who seek to command you. Your independence makes
people puzzle over you."

I gave her a wry smile. "They puzzle over why a poor
nobody does not hasten to snatch from every hand."

"Your behavior does give others something to talk about, Lacey."

"Including you, my lady."

Her gaze went cool. "I admit to the curiosity, but I choose very carefully to whom I speak about what."

I believed her. "I beg your pardon," I said. "I was teasing and meant no censure. You have invited me here to call in your favor. Perhaps you should tell me what it is."

She smiled. "Have done with it, you mean? I can imagine you wondering like mad what I would ask of you as you rode over from Covent Garden. But you may cease worrying. The task is very simple. I wish for you to meet my son."

I blinked in surprise. I'd never met Lady Breckenridge's son, who would be about five by now. The young Viscount Breckenridge stayed with his grandmother in the country much of the time, so I had been told, tucked away with nannies and tutors and other caretakers.

Lady Breckenridge seldom spoke of the boy, but observing her now, I realized that her silence was not because she had no affection for him. I saw in her the same thing I'd seen in Marianne during the Sudbury School problem—a woman who loved desperately and protected fiercely.

I gave her another half bow. "I would be honored, my lady."

"Very well, then." She turned from me in a brush of faint perfume and tugged on a bell pull. When the ever-efficient Barnstable glided in, she said, "Tell Nanny to bring Peter downstairs."

"You mean you wish me to meet him now?" I asked. "He is here?"

Barnstable had already disappeared to carry out his

lady's wishes. "Before you can change your mind," she said. "Shall we?"

She slid her hand into the crook of my arm and more or less forced me to guide her out of the room.

The staircase hall of Lady Breckenridge's house was plastered in pale colors, with niches holding vases of hothouse flowers. Paintings from centuries past hung on the walls—originals, not copies. Wide stairs with a polished railing ran up into the dim recesses of the house.

I heard a door shut high above us. In a few moments, two people came down the stairs: a tall, slender woman in neat black, and a small lad for whom the black-clad nanny slowed her steps.

The boy's suit was a miniature of what Grenville would wear, down to the pantaloons and well-shined pumps. However, Viscount Breckenridge would never attain Grenville's taut slimness. He had a sturdiness that spoke of developing muscle, and in a dozen or so years, he would attain the large, powerful build of his father.

The lad stopped a few stairs above me and stared with undisguised curiosity. I was in my regimentals, my braid neatly fastened, my unruly hair somewhat tamed, my boots as polished as Bartholomew could make them. I saw the lad take note of my height, the breadth of my shoulders, my bearing, my uniform.

"This is Peter," Lady Breckenridge said, a note of pride in her voice. "Peter, this is Captain Lacey, my friend I have mentioned."

Peter was inclined to do nothing but stare, but at a surreptitious nudge from his nanny, he bowed correctly. "How do you do?" he asked.

He was far too polite for a lad of five. He ought to be tearing up and down the stairs and shouting at the top of his voice. But perhaps he'd been persuaded to be on his best behavior for me—either that or I'd stunned the lad.

I made a formal bow. "How do you do, Your Lordship."

I'd never been one to seek the company of children, except for my daughter, but I decided that a brief smile was called for. Young Viscount Breckenridge grinned back at me then quickly hid it.

A pang bit my heart. My daughter and I had exchanged such covert smiles when we were supposed to be formal and serious, knowing we'd both be scolded if caught. I missed her with an ache that had never subsided.

"Do you ride?" I found myself asking the boy.

"Yes, sir." The small voice held a scoff, as though I were an idiot for asking. He was a lordship after all, born to horse and hound.

"Perhaps your mother will allow you to ride with me in the park sometime. I have some modest skill."

"Will you show me how to ride like a cavalryman?" The scorn vanished, and Peter sounded like a normal, eager boy.

I glanced at Lady Breckenridge, but she looked in no way dismayed. She went to Peter and took his hands. "If you are good, darling. Now give me a kiss good night."

Peter obeyed, and I was pleased to see that he kissed his mother with affection. There was no strain between Lady Breckenridge and her son.

Introductions over, Peter was taken his slow way back upstairs with nanny. He glanced back down at me over the banisters but did nothing so undignified as wave. I gave him another friendly nod, and he continued climbing, seeking his nursery once more.

I turned to Lady Breckenridge. "Have I fulfilled my obligation?"

The smile she gave me eased some of the hurt in my

heart, enough to make me believe that the pain could be assuaged a bit were I often enough in her presence.

"Excellently well, Captain," Lady Breckenridge said. She touched my arm again, her fingers warm.

I dared lift her hand to my lips. "I am pleased to hear it, my lady," I said.

THE LAST THREAD OF THE NECKLACE AFFAIR WAS TIED when I accepted Grenville's invitation to dine at Watier's that night. Watier's, famous for food provided by chefs of the Prince Regent, offered the deepest gaming in London. Games of macao and whist relieved gentlemen of their fortunes in one room, while the dining room provided excellent cuisine with which to ease the sting.

Grenville was in full dress that evening, which meant that he wore a suit so tailored to his figure that he might have been poured into it. Pantaloons that emphasized his muscular calves were buttoned at the ankle above fine leather pumps. His quizzing glass hung on a fine gold chain, ever ready for scrutinizing the gauche.

After we'd finished our excellent meal and looked in on the games room, I was dismayed to see Lord Clifford making so bold as to approach us. A few of the dandies looked up with interest when Clifford walked to Grenville and put a hand on his shoulder.

Grenville glanced disdainfully at the large hand on his immaculate frock coat, but Clifford did not notice the censure. He let go only after he'd turned Grenville away from the crowd.

"I want to thank you, Grenville," Lord Clifford said.

"Do you?" Grenville's voice was icy. "Whatever for?"

"For agreeing to stay out of my business. Decent of you."

I suppressed my sudden urge to punch the man, but this time it was Grenville who took retribution. He stepped back one pace, lifted his quizzing glass, and studied Clifford through it.

"Let me see," Grenville said. "You stole an extremely valuable necklace from a wretched French émigré who was trying to remove his family from the dangers of France. A necklace you later sold—probably for a fraction of its worth—to cover your debts, whatever they were, giving your wife a copy so she wouldn't guess what you'd done. Then, when the false necklace goes missing and Lady Clifford seeks our help, you harass and browbeat her so much that she attempts to take her own life. All the while betraying her with her closest friend and companion, the only comfort she has. I'd say there was not much decent in the entire business."

Clifford flushed. "I told you, Grenville, what goes on in a man's household has nothing to do with you."

"Oh, but it has. Your wife reached out to me and Captain Lacey, because she had nowhere else to turn. And you may be correct that your household is your business, but the fact remains that you stole the diamonds from de la Fontaine in the first place. Not very sporting of you. In fact, one might call that a crime."

"Fontaine was hated among the French," Clifford said. "They'd applaud me."

"Ah, you are a latter-day Robin Hood, stealing from the corrupt rich to give to the . . . well, to yourself. And then to sell them and drape your wife in paste diamonds. Dear me." Grenville shook his head.

We had the attention of much of the room. Though we

spoke in low voices, Grenville's attitude of derision spoke volumes.

"I had to sell them," Clifford said. "I'd promised Derwent a large sum for his damned reforms and then had some bad luck at games. I sold the necklace to pay my debts and not leave Derwent standing. Would have made me a laughingstock. Nothing else to be done."

"You might have explained to your wife," I said. "You ought to have trusted her with the truth."

"Damn it, Lacey, you've met my wife. You know what she is. She would never be able to keep her damn fool mouth shut. She'd blab all to her blasted companion, upon whom she's much too dependent. A wife should know who is master, after all."

So, he'd taken Mrs. Dale to his bed to keep Lady Clifford under his thumb. A man who ruled his household by manipulation, lies, and fear. How was he better than a French aristocrat who'd made a hundred peasants labor for him?

He wasn't. De la Fontaine had risked all and given up everything to take his children out of danger. Even after it had been safe for him to return home, de la Fontaine had stayed in his reduced circumstances to be with his one remaining child and his grandchildren.

Grenville's look turned to one of unfeigned disgust. He sniffed, lowered his quizzing glass, adjusted his gloves, and said, "I believe, Lord Clifford, that I will have to disapprove of you."

"What the devil does that mean? Why should I care whether you approve or disapprove of anything I do?"

Lord Clifford did not realize his danger, but I knew quite well what Grenville meant. Clifford might be an earl, but such was the power of Lucius Grenville in the fashionable world that if he wanted a man to be cut, that man would be cut. *One can be an earl,* I could imagine Lady Breckenridge saying in her clear, acerbic tones, *and still be invited nowhere.*

Grenville did not wait. There, in the very crowded gaming rooms of Watier's, with one movement of his slim shoulders, with one spin on his immaculate heels, Grenville turned his back on Lord Clifford, and ruined him.

End

AUTHOR'S NOTE

I hope you enjoyed *The Necklace Affair*, a shorter adventure in Captain Lacey's saga. This novella started off as a short story, written to keep myself entertained (and sane) while I waited eight hours in a jury room to see whether I'd be called (I was not). The story remained unpublished, forgotten in a file on my computers for years. When I began republishing the Captain Lacey series, I found it, rewrote it as a longer novella, and fit it between *The Sudbury School Murders* and *A Body in Berkeley Square.*

If you are new to Captain Lacey, it's best to start with Book 1, *The Hanover Square Affair*, as the Captain's story progresses with the series. The E-book of *Hanover Square Affair* is free at all vendors.

Visit my website www.gardnermysteries.com for links to the Hanover Square Affair and for more information on the series.

Thank you again!

Best wishes,

Ashley Gardner

A Disappearance in Drury Lane

Murder in Grosvenor Square

The Thames River Murders

The Alexandria Affair

A Mystery at Carlton House

Murder in St. Giles

The Gentleman's Walking Stick

(short stories: in print in

The Necklace Affair and Other Stories)

Captain Lacey Regency Mysteries, Vol 1

Includes

The Hanover Square Affair

A Regimental Murder

The Glass House

The Gentleman's Walking Stick

(short story collection)

Captain Lacey Regency Mysteries, Vol 2

Includes

The Sudbury School Murders

The Necklace Affair

A Body in Berkeley Square

A Covent Garden Mystery

Captain Lacey Regency Mysteries, Vol 3

Includes

A Death in Norfolk

A Disappearance in Drury Lane

Murder in Grosvenor Square

Anthologies

Murder Most Historical

Past Crimes

ABOUT THE AUTHOR

Award-winning Ashley Gardner is a pseudonym for *New York Times* bestselling author Jennifer Ashley. Under both names—and a third, Allyson James—Ashley has written more than 85 published novels and novellas in mystery and romance. Her books have won several *RT BookReviews* Reviewers Choice awards (including Best Historical Mystery for *The Sudbury School Murders*), and Romance Writers of America's RITA (given for the best romance novels and novellas of the year). Ashley's books have been translated into more than a dozen different languages and have earned starred reviews in *Booklist*. When she isn't writing, she indulges her love for history by researching and building miniature houses and furniture from many periods.

More about Ashley Gardner's mysteries can be found at the website: www.gardnermysteries.com. Stay up to date on new releases by joining her email alerts here: http://eepurl.-com/5n7rz

CPSIA information can be obtained
at www.ICGtesting.com
Printed in the USA
LVHW08s1625270718
585141LV00004B/187/P